MATERIAL GIRL

Louise Kean is a top consultant for the film industry and the author of three other novels, including *The Perfect 10*, rights to which have been sold in the United States. *The Perfect 10* was inspired by Louise's real-life experience of losing half her body weight – going from size 24 to size 12 in a year. As a result of the huge publicity the book received, Louise is now in great demand as a freelance writer and pundit on the modern woman's experience. She is 31 and lives in Richmond and isn't 'taken' – for now at least.

Visit www.AuthorTracker.co.uk for exclusive updates on Louise Kean.

D1076102

F/2064024

By the same author

Toasting Eros
Boyfriend in a Dress
The Perfect 10

LOUISE KEAN

Material Girl

HARPER

Harper
An imprint of HarperCollins*Publishers*
77–85 Fulham Palace Road,
Hammersmith, London W6 8JB

www.harpercollins.co.uk

A Paperback Original 2006
1

A catalogue record for this book
is available from the British Library

ISBN-13 978 0 00 719893 1
ISBN-10 0 00 719893 0

Typeset in Sabon by Palimpsest Book Production Limited,
Polmont, Stirlingshire

Printed and bound in Great Britain by
Clays Ltd, St Ives plc

Acknowledgements

In the process of writing this book about a woman in search of some strength and a little courage, and who finds inspiration in the women around her, I realised how lucky I am to be surrounded by a band of such incredible women. They are my inspiration in business and in pleasure. Their strength in the face of the rubbish that life sometimes dishes out never fails to amaze me.

So, in no particular order, I'd like to let them know that I deeply value their strength and support: Maxine Hitchcock, Helen Johnstone, Ali Gunn, Julia Bennett, Amanda Koster, Nicola Mumford, Natalie Whitehead, Naomi Conway, Alice Weston, Rachel Kennedy, Karen Sheard, Clare Bradshaw, Amy Kean, Laura Kean and Eileen Kean.

'Beauty is the hardest drug of all.'
Bob Colacello

'Death is one moment and life is so many of them.'
Tennessee Williams,
The Milk Train Doesn't Stop Here Anymore

ACT I

Late One Night at Gerry's . . .

Scene I: Passion

I see the sign at the top of the first flight of steps. It's waiting for me. In big red letters it says,

'Don't waste time.'

My heart stands still.

It's an advert for planning your tube route before you leave home, picking up a map – available at all stations – and deducing that it's far quicker to use the Piccadilly line, wherever humanly possible, than the District line, which is a geriatrically slow, joyless and painful push-pull to Earls Court, during which time any fresh and evil grey hairs on an otherwise sandy-blonde head will multiply ten-fold, and you'll age five years. At least.

But of course it means more than that.

Monday. If it's before ten a.m., and you take the left-hand exit at Green Park tube station, and it's not raining – that central London rain that pesters rather than soaks – and you don't have to thrust your umbrella up clumsily and fast in those strange seconds when you are outside but seemingly not getting wet, then run up the steps as quickly as you can, and you'll burst onto Piccadilly like a deep-sea pearl diver coming up for gasped air.

Some people who are unaccustomed to the city are scared of its barking noise and its whippet speed and the sheer bulk of it – like a giant bellowing fat man on roller skates! – but London has never scared me. Even on my first visits as a child, squashed onto the coach from Norwich, taking huge bites out of my pre-packed ham and tomato sandwiches as soon as the back wheels of the coach were off the slip road and on to the motorway, and chewing on the straw I'd plugged into my carton of Five Alive, I was never scared because my mum was always with me. It was just the two of us taking our daytrip to London one Saturday every six months. As the coach finally pulled up and collapsed at Kings Cross we'd edge our way along the narrow aisle, bumping limbs on arm rests, shuffling towards the huffs and petrol-smelling puffs coming from the open coach door. Initially Mum would inch along behind me, but then twirl in front in one graceful manoeuvre like a Pans People dancer as she thanked the coach driver and jumped down to the street. She'd look up at me as I stood on the edge of the bus step, ready to throw myself off, and she'd say,

'Now hold my hand, Scarlet.'

She'd reach out and take my sticky Five Alive hand as I jumped, and not let go again until we were climbing back onto the coach at the end of the day, grubby and happy and swinging a carrier bag each. Once Mum and I stopped coming I didn't visit London again until I was eighteen and studying at a college in Brighton. Richard, my little brother by three years, is six foot three inches tall – mum says he 'dangles from clouds' and 'accidentally head butts low flying birds' – and yet the first time he had to take the tube on his own, aged seventeen, he was afraid.

'Afraid of what?' I asked, perplexed, and he said, 'Getting

in the way,' as tuts and groans and exhausted coughs pushed past him at speed. But still London has never threatened me. It just makes promises that it sometimes fails to keep.

Turn right towards Piccadilly Circus. It's a neon big-top of flashing traffic lights that always seem to be on amber: I never know whether to stay or go. Large red and blue delivery lorries toot their clowns' horns; cars edging backwards, forwards, backwards, forwards. Advertising boards flicker, sizzling with the streams of electricity that crackle way above our heads, like horizontal streaks of lightning, accidents waiting to happen, claims waiting to be filed, damages waiting to be spent, while pop music sprays out from the open doors of Megastores, and French and German and Japanese students, with cameras constantly clicking, idle lazily on the steps of an Eros streaked by the dropped bombs of pigeons fat on Starbucks muffin wrappers.

McDonalds and Gap and Body Shop and Virgin. The four corners of the Circus, tomorrow the world . . .

I've lived here for eight years now, and if I was tripping down memory lane as well as Piccadilly I could nod a moment of acknowledgement to most corners of Soho, and Covent Garden, and Bloomsbury, and Marylebone, and Hyde Park, and Knightsbridge. I fell face first onto the pavement on that corner once, at three a.m. with one shoe on and one shoe off, drunkenly unbalanced and confused by the sudden three-inch difference in my leg lengths. And I stood on that corner for half an hour once, trying drunkenly to convince a doorman that he should let me and my rowdy group of actors and ad execs into a lap-dancing club, and that no, I wasn't drunk, and wasn't this a meritocracy? I was more impressed with the use of that word than he was, given that it didn't actually make any sense at the time. London has conspired with me in fun too many nights for me to recall, and it has let

5

me dream, perhaps a little too much. It has never offered me stability, or routine – the trains don't even run on time and a London crazy can hijack your day by performing a striptease in Leicester Square, and your favourite café can serve you coffee and toast one morning and be an urban jewellery boutique two days later. It's like a wonderful and exciting but slightly shallow old friend. Some days you feel like you mean everything to it, like it's protecting you and loving you back, offering up surprises at every turn for your own personal entertainment. Other days you don't even seem to exist and you get barged off the bus and you lose a heel in a hole in the street, and you can't get cash from the machine, or a cab in the rain. You just can't let it disappoint you, you have to see it for what it is. Some days it is simply off finding its fun elsewhere.

As you stare down Piccadilly, Green Park is to your right, the grass occasionally planted with a man in a suit, slumped in a deckchair that you can rent, ten pounds for two hours – who are these men that sit in the park at nine forty on a Monday morning? Why aren't they walking crazy quickly, breaking a sweat on their freshly shaved upper lips, late for work? There must be something wrong with them, to just be sitting there at this strange working time of day, dressed up to litigate or administrate. Their wife must have left them in the middle of the night. Or they got to work only to be fired for sending too many personal emails, most of which could be classed as pornographic by any HR department worth its salt. Suits look out of place in the park, sitting on the grass, or in their ten-pound deckchairs that slope down the hill, pointing everybody's feet towards the horses and carriages parked side by side in the Queen's driveway.

Walk ten paces towards the Circus on Piccadilly and you are sucked into the shade of the Ritz walkway. It's really a time tunnel. Occasionally, the day after a full moon, plump accountants have been known to enter at one end but never come out of the other. But it's only ever plump accountants . . . There are five steps between each column, and on the left two men in peaked hats and expensive overcoats offer to open big gold-plated doors for you, that lead into the most famous hotel in the world. Most days I want to go in, but I never do. I could drown in wealth for a day, or a lifetime. I could live in a lift or a laundry cart. They wouldn't let you be uncomfortable at the Ritz; it has diamonds for sale in the window that are as big as apples.

Glance around you as you walk diagonally across Albermarle Street. You'll begin to notice that most faces are bored. Some are as blank as a freshly wiped blackboard. But that's any city on the way to work. It's the architecture that makes it magical, and the buildings that breathe. Don't be confused, that isn't smog: it's just Fortnum & Mason letting off some steam. All cities are a mirror of bored faces. The trouble starts when you try to ignore it, or shrug your shoulders and think that it's okay. If you do, if you accept it, and try to overlook the palpable everything in the air, then somewhere your name gets rubbed off a list. A small part of you doesn't exist any more, and that's just the start. Soon you won't register anything, and they'll get you, the zombies, the bored, blank faces – that's what happened to them. They noticed everybody else was bored, and they shrugged and tried to ignore it, and it got them. That night they rolled over in their sleep, and breathed in, part-breath, part-snore, a strange sleeping gasp. And those gasps mean that you have just inhaled something bad. They breathed in boredom that night, and woke up the next day with a blank look on their face. Blank as they poured their coffee, blank as they showered, blank as they locked the door, blank on the train. If I wasn't so scared of suffocating I'd sleep with tape over my mouth. Ben sleeps with his mouth wide open.

Last Friday Ben offered to cook dinner for us both, if I could get home from work before ten o'clock. He bought two microwave meals. Three years, and that's what we are – one stringy chicken chow mein, one runny lasagne. Ben has never told me he loves me. He says it doesn't mean that he won't.

We live together in Ealing, in a little flat above a shop that sells organic moisturiser, wooden rocking horses and chilli oil. It's called 'Plump and Feather'. There are always five people in there, and one of them is always talking animatedly with the lady who runs it, who wears long linen things and has a lazy salt and pepper plait in her hair, and a beatific smile that implies she has just finished teaching a yoga class and she might actually be God herself. And there is always a child. Just one. Not always the same one. I don't know whose they are.

There is a door at the side of the shop with a worn-out-looking bell. If you press it Ben will answer because he always seems to be in and I always seem to be out. He gets in from work at a quarter to six. He is the manager of an electrical store in the precinct in Ealing. I get in around three a.m. if the shoot I'm working on has run late into the night, or if the actors have insisted I stay until the very end to remove their make-up for them, and not just leave them a bottle of quality cleanser and a stack of cotton wool. Or if we've finished on time and then gone for drinks. Mostly shoots don't finish more than an hour late because they have to pay the crew overtime. Mostly it's the going for drinks that makes me late home. It hasn't always been that way. Gradually, like a tap dripping into a bath that will overflow soon, my nights have got longer. I'm not always working, but recently the idea of going home to that flat turns my stomach, like discovering something small and white in a chip-shop sausage.

Only half the bed and a bowl in the kitchen seem like

8

mine, the bowl that I eat my cereal out of, either when I get up at eleven a.m. or when I roll in late at night. Ben does a weekly shop, and buys tins and things – I see them in the cupboards next to my muesli. And he always buys me two more boxes of Alpen. He buys long-life UHT milk. Nothing fresh seems to last more than a day in that flat. I bought some roses from Tesco not long after we'd moved in. I bought a vase as well, and filled it with tepid water and a little sugar like my nanny used to do, and I bashed the stems the way she did, and dropped my orange roses in. They had already wilted the following afternoon, their heads hanging heavily on their stems like starving foreign children without the energy to support their necks. The next morning they were dead. My mother swears by Tesco's roses, 'At least two weeks, sometimes more!' I'm not suspicious, but . . .

I started an argument with Ben about domestic stuff that night, screaming at him that he had left a ring of filth around the bath. He looked bewildered as I shouted, oblivious to the argument that really raged in my head where I yelled, 'My flowers died! It's a sign! No good will come of this!' I'd thought that Ben might buy me flowers or do some-thing significant on the day that we moved into our flat. Nothing. We didn't even have sex because he was too tired from lifting boxes. And we didn't have sex the following morning because his stomach felt bad from the 'moving in' curry we'd eaten the night before.

I'm afraid that I have left it too late, made a bad deci-sion, and now I might not find somebody else. I hadn't said 'I love you' for nine years when I said it to Ben. Of course I'd said it to my mum and dad, and Richard and his boys, my nephews, I say it all the time to them. But my recent relationship past was more ships in the night than dropped anchors. Three months here, six months there, nobody that lasted long or went any deeper than dating does. That's what caught me off-guard with Ben – the need to spend time together was violently instant. I didn't think we were playing games, although admittedly he was married, but he told me straight away that he was unhappy, and that emotionally it was over, and we only discussed her once. We were sitting in a pub behind Green Park, and we'd just played three games of drunken pool, and he'd won all three. We slumped down into the snug with dopey smiles and he said, 'She doesn't even like me any more, Scarlet', and I said, 'I won't be a shoulder to cry on. We have something, Ben, you and I. We have a strange and certain chemistry. This is new to me. I have never felt like I've found a new best friend before. So I'm not just a cushion for you to fall onto when you snap your marriage apart and you're thrown back by the blast. This already means more than that. I wouldn't be doing it if it didn't.'

It wasn't until later that she seemed to consume us both – like she'd slipped into the room silently and was a constant third person in the corner looking on.

I'm getting older, I'm thirty-one. My breasts have fallen an inch in the last year. I have stretch-marks around my bottom, and even a couple on my stomach. I have lines, plural, around my eyes. Last night I traced the lines with my middle fingers. These tiny red routes that map all my days spent in the sun, all the late nights that I didn't moisturise, that I drunkenly swiped at my eyes and rubbed hard, too hard, to remove thick black kohl and mascara, with every swipe breaking every rule in my make-up artist's manual. I pulled gently at the skin on my cheekbones, watching as it lazed back into place. The spring has sprung, my bounce isn't what it was, my ball has deflated. It's a fresh fear that has crept up on me, maybe it lives in the creases of laughter lines or crows' feet, and it makes you scared to leave. Then you hate yourself for being a coward and staying without affection, and the lines get deeper, and the fear moves in permanently and brings all its bags with it. Soon you don't even recognise yourself – who is that girl constantly on the brink of tears? Do I even know her? And who is that desperate exhausted girl picking apart every little thing that her boyfriend says, nagging and needy, clawing for some much needed sign that he cares? Oh Christ, it's me. So then you convince yourself it would be crazy to leave, and that you expect too much and want what you shouldn't. You convince yourself you're crazy because it's easier that way. You don't know what else to do, when you don't even know yourself anymore.

After four months of our affair, Ben left his wife for me. They had been married for a year, but together for ten. I'm obsessed with her now, significantly more than I am obsessed with him. I haven't met her, but I've seen pictures. She's all limbs. She played hockey for her school. She is elegant, and her smile seems to carry on around her cheeks to her ears, and she's got a dimple in her chin. She doesn't wear much make-up, and she wears cream round-neck T-shirts and black trousers to work, and low black court shoes. She is sensible and she smiles. Ben forgot to take the photo of them on honeymoon out of his wallet, or at least that's what he told me when I found it and cried. They were standing on Etna smiling at the camera with their arms around each other, the volcano smoking in the background. It erupts every year, Ben said when I found the photo, and as if that was so interesting it might startle away my tears. And the eruptions occur along the same plate in the earth, so a series of sooty mouths smoke in a black ashen line. Sometimes the tour guides that work on Etna only get a couple of hours' notice, he said, before their livelihood disintegrates again for that year; nodding his head, imparting the tidbit that he picked up in Sicily with his brand-new wife. I don't know where he has put that photo but I have a horrible feeling that I will find it some day, by accident, stuffed into one of his computer books. I wouldn't believe him if he told me he had thrown it away. I know that he loved her.

The night that Ben and I first kissed, we inched towards each other with smiles. We sat on stools at the bar facing each other. We were a human mirror, both with our hands propped on our stools between our legs. With another inch forwards our knees touched. Then I leant across and put my hands on Ben's knees to support myself. Then he kissed me, grabbing a handful of the hair on the back of my head. We kissed for a minute, but then he pulled away and said, 'But I love Katie', and it's the only time I have ever heard him use that word about another living person. Then he kissed me again.

I'm obsessed with what she does, what she likes, this woman I feel Ben and I have wronged together. I have a victim, and I want to know what makes her smile. I want to make her laugh, to know that she's happy. I don't suppose I needed Ben but I took him anyway, because I fell in love, and it was like nothing I had ever known. At the time it was full of promise. Now I realise that there is a bridge between us that we'll never cross, and that maybe nobody ever does. He wants a tattoo on his thigh but it can't just be a rose or an anchor or a Chinese symbol, it has to mean something. It has to represent something of significance to him. He's been thinking about it for the last six months and nothing has occurred to him yet . . .

Keep walking along Piccadilly and you'll pass the Royal Academy of Art on the left. You can only glimpse it from the road but it has a large courtyard with a fountain in the middle. In the summer you can sit out in that courtyard late into the evening – they have a bar and a jazz band, and you can see the sun set, sipping on a cold beer, surrounded by banners for exhibitions that aren't ever as appealing as just sitting late into the night, drinking a beer or a cocktail or a glass of wine. Or sometimes all three . . .

Helen calls as I trip across Old Bond Street.

'It's definitely true,' she says, sounding shell-shocked and numb, somehow absent from herself.

'How do you know?' I ask.

'I checked his phone. He has texts.'

'Who from?'

'Her name is Nikki – with an "i".'

'How awful.'

'I know. I suppose he could have spelt it wrong . . . or it might be abbreviated . . . not that it matters . . .'

Helen falls silent and I know what she is thinking – that the 'i' in Nikki means she is younger than we are. It's the first time, really, that they can be younger than we are. I don't think it should mean anything, while knowing that it does.

'What are you going to do?'

'I don't know.'

'What do they say?'

'Sex stuff. She calls his cock a dick. Apparently she likes licking it like a lollipop.'

'How awful.'

'I know.'

'What about the babysitter?'

'I drove him home last night when I dropped Deborah off.'

'Does your sister know you're having sex with her babysitter?'

'Hmmm? No . . . I don't think so.'

'Did you do it again?'

'In the back of my car.'

'Okay.'

'I have to go. I have a squash match in an hour, I need warm-up time.'

'Helen, why don't you sleep with somebody from squash, if you want something . . .'

'I don't want something, particularly. I have to go. I'll speak to you later.'

Helen's husband Steven is having an affair with somebody called Nikki, with an 'i'. Speak of infidelity begets infidelity. I feel like I started it. I clearly remember the night I sat them both down and guiltily told them I'd been seeing a married man. Steven said, 'But most people find most people attractive, don't they? Just pick somebody single instead, Scarlet, because somebody else always comes along.' Helen hadn't even blinked. That didn't seem like the right thing to say in front of your wife. Or ever.

So now Helen is having an affair, or sex at least, with the seventeen-year-old kid who baby-sits her eight-year-old niece. He is a beautiful young blond boy, with skinny muscles that all seem to curve towards his groin. A curtain of long hair hangs across one of his eyes, and his pout squashes through. He has just moved down from Liverpool with his family, and when he speaks it's with a soft Scouse accent, to ask for fat coke and a pepperoni pizza for dinner, or a blowjob. Helen describes him as pretty. 'My beautiful boy,' she says. She was only seventeen when she started seeing Steven, and she's been with him ever since. 'Steven was just never that pretty,' she says, 'whereas Jamie is the best-looking boy in his class. Do you remember Paul Vickery?' she asked me. Of course I did. He was the best-looking boy in our class. He had black hair and cheeky eyes and the makings of a teenage six-pack.

'He was shagging an older woman too, wasn't he, at the time? I could never have got Paul Vickery,' she smiled, shaking her head.

'You've kind of got him in the end, Helen,' I say, and she nods, because it hasn't escaped her either.

Take the last chance to turn left just before the Circus, and walk up Air Street. It's short and dark with narrow pavements, banked by a cramped dry-cleaner's and a cramped café. But you're through it in moments, and you'll explode onto Regent Street. Don't overestimate the speed of the buses, don't wait for the pedestrian crossing or the traffic lights, just run across the road, it will take them forever to catch you. Walk straight up part two of Air Street. Cheers, the themed pub full of American summer students and interns, is on the right. At nighttime it gets packed with young English guys, all hoping to get lucky with a sorority girl giddy and drunk on dreams of Prince William.

China White is on this street. It's no more than a hole in the wall, an unassuming door and some Chinese letters by the side of a tiny box window that has fairy lights in it against a white background. You can't actually see in, but I think they can probably see out. Trendy eyes dancing at the window, searching for the next victim of an undisclosed door policy. You're at the bottom of Soho.

At school, Helen and I and a group of boys in our class threw stones at a girl called Jenny with buckteeth and big ears and a lazy eye. One lunchtime we threw stones at her in the playground. I held on to mine for ages, rolling it around in my ten-year-old hand, desperate to drop it on the ground and just run away, but then somebody saw me hesitating, so I threw it low and fast and it hit her on the knee. I saw a trickle of blood squirt down her leg onto a dirty sock that sat lazily around her calf because the elastic had gone. She didn't cry, just stood in the corner covering the one side of her glasses that wasn't protected by plasters to gee up her lazy eye. She wasn't allowed to get the good glass

15

scratched, those glasses were expensive I'd heard her mother shout at her when she picked her up from school most days. Jenny's mum wore a fur coat and Jenny wore socks that didn't stay up. Jenny's mum would half talk, half shout – 'Did you scratch that glass? It's expensive!' – and Jenny would say 'no, no, no' really quickly, three times like that in succession, as she ran to keep up with her mother's old fur. She did the same in class, when Mrs Campbell asked if it was Jenny who had knocked pink paint all over the aprons. It wasn't her at all: it was Adam Moody. Mrs Campbell didn't punish her or anything, she just assumed that she had been close by, and she was clumsy, and I suppose a little ugly and easy to blame. The day we threw stones I heard Jenny muttering 'no, no, no' as she covered the good glass . . .

Helen and I haven't spoken about it again. But I'm racking them up, all these bad deeds that make me hate myself. I threw a stone at Jenny, and then I took Ben from his wife.

Walk through Golden Square. Cut through one gate on the south side, and exit at the gate on the east side. There are already a couple of men sitting on different benches, swigging from cans of lager. One of them looks unwashed and tired and drunk and old. He has bare feet and long dirty toenails that you glimpse by accident but you will never be able to forget. He looks like he is cultivating those nails to enable him to scamper up trees, forage for berries. They could lever him into bark, half man, half cat. The other guy looks ordinary, in jeans and a T-shirt. But he has a can of special brew too.

The night that I met Ben, in a bar on Old Compton Street, he stared at me for twenty-five minutes. At first I thought he might be having some kind of seizure or fit. He just stared. His friends were talking around him, but he wasn't engaging with the conversation. I thought it suggested passion, which is rare these days. It was quite something to feel the heat of his undiluted attention. Something about me meant that he couldn't look away. I was unnerved but amazed. It felt terribly wonderful.

I went over to Ben and introduced myself. We realised within twenty minutes that both our dads are called Patrick, and that they both wear a glass eye. Those things aren't that common. I'm not superstitious, but . . . The difference is that my dad lost one of his real eyes playing national league badminton, and if he has three beers at family parties he pops the phony one out to scare the kids. Ben's dad lost his eye in an accident at the printing factory, but refuses to admit that he has a glass one. I don't know how that works exactly, but I hope he cleans it . . .

Ben snores so loudly I have tried to convince myself it's not even him. It's such a huge noise that some nights it is impossible to sleep through. I make-believe that it is a large and loud wind pushing through an autumn forest, or a gentle wave thudding onto a Thai beach as I rock in a hammock between two palm trees. I keep thinking it might help soothe me back to sleep. It hasn't worked once.

Everything that I thought I knew has changed. Men say they like a challenge, when really they don't. They want an easy life. They think somebody promised it to them. Women think that somebody promised them a white wedding and a baby, and happiness as well. Secretly we feel cheated without them. If only the dress and the baby were all it took.

Walk past the flower stall at the top of Berwick Street market, through to Wardour Street. Cut through St Anne's Court, past the tour guide telling a group of German tourists that the Beatles recorded some of their biggest hits here, except he can't remember which ones exactly, at this very studio. Cross over Dean Street, and through Soho Square. They have

17

shut the little house in the middle of the square, because of drugs and booze and cottaging. They closed down half of Soho Square's smiles at the same time. But people still lie on the grass in all weathers with cardboard coffees next to them at nine-fifty in the morning. Walk through and towards Charing Cross Road. Turn right. You're out of Soho.

I consider darting into Grey's. It's the large bookshop on Charing Cross Road. It's been there for just over a century, getting bigger and bigger, gradually stocking more and more cookery and diet books. And other books, all the other kinds. I was in Grey's twice last week. Isabella works behind the counter, mostly on the till. She's a reason to buy, a need to delve into my purse, a depository for my loose change. I met her first by accident three weeks ago. I tripped over a woven mat at the front of the store as I nipped in to buy a poetry book for grand borrowed words for Ben's third anniversary card – we don't count the affair; we go from after that, from when he left – so I didn't have to think of my own. I copied into his card:

> A long time back
> When we were first in love
> Our bodies were always as one
> Later you became
> My dearest
> And I became your dearest
> Alas
> And now beloved lord
> Our hearts must be
> As hard as the middle of thunder
> Now what have I to live for?

I was wearing impractical grey court shoes that day, with three-inch heels and purple soles. Some days I feel like I'm balancing on the top of the world in stilettos, and everybody is watching as I try to keep my balance and still look good, in heels. My purple soled shoes point violently before me with every step that I take, leading me on. It was one of these points that caught under the mat as I ran in, and I almost collapsed, tripping forwards, halfway between running and falling, not sure how it would end. I stopped myself by diving into a table of books by an author whose repackaged backlist was hot property now he'd had a bestseller. A few copies of his second book fell to the floor but I didn't bother to pick them up, knowing they'd be sold in twenty minutes anyway. I straightened and checked myself, muttering 'shit' under my breath, and looked around to see if anybody had noticed. I saw her then, oblivious to what was happening with me, leaning forwards on the counter with her elbows beneath her, flicking through *Vogue*.

Her hair is unkempt as if she's been out the back sleeping or shagging in a storeroom, and her long, dirty-blonde tresses have been mussed up. She has these huge breasts. They jut out like balloons about to burst. Her eyes are always smudged with black kohl, and her lips are glossed with a cheap little stick that she keeps under the counter. Her voice is deep and her words are rounded and moneyed. Grey's know there is a reason to put her on that desk, front of store, like a poster, but the living breathing kind, the most attractive thing about the purchase you'll make, even if it's Shakespeare or Keats or Byron.

I found myself flirting with her on that very first day. I felt my own smile, the blood rushing to flush my cheeks into pink cushions. I felt my freckles, and my figure, and I found it hard to look Isabella in the eye. She flirts with everybody, I can tell. I felt a charge of electricity in me that day, hot wiring my senses, an urge to reach out and touch her, to

19

grasp her, to kiss the cheap gloss off her lips and grab her head by her long, dirty-blonde hair.

She has wild hair, like mine. Her chest, like a shelf for a thousand second glances, is shockingly apparent, like mine. Ben always says, when I plead with him to say something nice, 'good rack', and he laughs like it's the funniest joke anybody has ever told, and not just really stupid, and slightly offensive. He never says anything that might make me feel good about myself. When I plead with him sometimes he just gets annoyed and says, 'I don't do it to order, Scarlet, my mind has gone blank now!' and I scream, but silently. It makes me hate him a little, even if it passes. I never say anything at the time, but bring it up later when the arguments begin. Then I say, 'You say you don't do it to order, Ben, but you never bloody do it! Who is going to say something nice to me if not you, my boyfriend?' Generally he squirms, but still says nothing. I saw his eyes glaze over halfway through reading the poem in his anniversary card, and he pecked me a kiss at the end, with his eyes closed. His card to me read:

> Dear Scarlet,
>   Still gorgeous!
>   Luv 'n' hugs
>   Ben

He won't even spell it properly. I assume he doesn't want me getting any ideas.

I've been into Grey's three times since the fall, for poetry. I think she must recognise me by now. I check my hair, my own lips, my own smudged and more expensively glossed smile courtesy of the freebies I get sent in the hope that I'll slick them all over somebody famous, and not just keep

20

them for myself. I've bought *Orlando*, and *The Bell Jar*, and *On the Road*, all to impress Isabella. I feel a madness grip me when I see her, scared that my tongue will loosen and suddenly say something huge and strange and unfamiliar to another woman. I feel like I want to ask her out, to touch her hair and her hand, run my fingers across her lips, and trace the smooth round lines of her face. She is twenty-three maybe.

She's me. A younger me, if I focus on her hair and her breasts and the gloss on her lips. Her eyes aren't as deep as mine: hers are darker, and the wrong shape. I would like to kiss her. A younger me. I mention my age in so many conversations these days, it's like it's dripping out of me, like a shaving cut on my ankle that won't stop bleeding. I'm thirty-one! I've said it first! Then I pause, and I wait for the pay-off – *Oh my God! You don't look it!* If a younger man smiles at me on the tube, or if he winks at me in a bar, if he tries to chat me up, I end up blurting out, 'I've got bras older than you.' I guess I'm admitting that I want to fuck a younger me, with my young tight skin and smooth thighs, but the contents of my young head as well. Back then I was front of store too. Back then I was good enough for anybody, and I felt like I could get anybody I wanted, if I put my mind to it. Because I know how Isabella feels – the rapt attention, the spotlight. I've felt it too. I want to keep feeling it, but now the spotlight is shifting.

When I was twelve, and my teeth stuck out angrily at the front, my mum marched me to the dentist to get braces. I was forced to wear a head brace at bedtime that looked like a motorcycle helmet with elastic bands that dug into my cheeks and left marks in my skin until breaktime the following morning. I had a perm that my brace flattened every night, and I was too scared to wash my hair in the mornings in case the curls fell out as my eighteen-year-old hairdresser said

they might, so I tried to coax the flat bits of my hair up with backcombing and hairspray.

Mum and I went together to get my brace one weekend. We got my first bra the weekend before, and my perm the weekend before that. She showed me how to shave my legs and told me to wear sanitary towels and not tampons for the first year of my periods. She called me every night at ten p.m. to say goodnight. Sometimes Richard would deliberately run a bath so he didn't have to say goodnight to her, and I'd make up a story like he had a stomach ache or something, so Mum didn't feel bad. Mum put me on a diet for six months when I was fourteen. No boys had been interested in me up until that point. She said, 'You might not believe this but I'm just trying to make it easier. You should have every choice there is, Scarlet, I want you to hold all the cards.' I'd told her that I'd been called a few names on the way home from school by a ratty older girl who was known as the local thug and the local bully. She shouted 'thunder thighs' at me as I hurried home on my own one day, and the same thing the following week. Kids will always remind you what bit of you it is that stands out.

Then one night I had my first brush with magic. A year after the diet and the braces and the perm and two days before my sixteenth birthday, I went to bed. I woke up the following morning and something had changed. I went to bed a slightly goofy teenager with puppy fat and frizzy hair, and I woke up kind of pretty. Straight-toothed. Slim. Sleek-haired. No more spiteful red elastic-band marks in my cheeks. No more thunder thighs. That day I walked to school with Helen as usual, and three boys from the local comp rode past us on their bikes but then rode back and did wheelies in front of us. One shouted out, 'Oi blondie! I want to snog you.' I told my mum that weekend and I thought she'd be pleased. But she sighed heavily and said, 'Believe me, Scarlet, when I say that I did it for the right reasons.'

I'll wash my hair later this week and go in and see Isabella then. I wonder if this makes me gay, but I've always thought that there is something not quite right about lesbians, who, like vegetarians, seem to spend their entire lives trying to replace meat. I've often thought that they are just too scared to admit that they actually quite like the meat, because they've spent so long thinking they shouldn't. It's really far more judgemental than fucking a man. Or eating a bucket of KFC. Would the sex equivalent of a vegetarian tucking into a guilty KFC be a lesbian having a one-night stand with a fireman? And a really well-cooked juicy steak would be the equivalent of a ten-year relationship with a six-foot chiselled paediatrician called Doug? I don't think I could ever give up meat completely.

Turn left off Charing Cross Road, and cut down through that little road with antique book shops and framers, and a dance shop at the end that sells tutus and taffeta and beautiful ballet pumps for children – ivory satin with ribbons that trail across the window. It leads you out onto St Martin's Lane. Yes, you could have just walked a straight line down Piccadilly, and through Leicester Square, but who cares? It's more fun this way. And now Starbucks is calling.

There is a sign resting on the counter, above the muffins and chocolate cake. It tells me that my barista's name is Henri and he is single. Then, in what I think might be his own handwriting, it says, 'He is nice guy, give him a try.'

This is the reason I am scared of being on my own. My barista is so desperate he is advertising himself with the croissants. I always believed relationships were supposed to be more than that: equal parts attraction, chemistry, fireworks, which make a life-changing love. These are the things I have always dreamt of, that I dream of still – it's more than selling yourself on the cheap and anybody who wants to make an offer is in with a chance. Henri isn't looking for much, but he has resorted to advertising himself with the muffins. The void between the fairytales in my head and the life I am living widens daily.

I deliberately don't walk through Chinatown anymore. There is a small door there. I haven't seen it but somebody told me about it a couple of months ago, late one night, in Gerry's. It was a stocky Russian film extra who smelt like pepperoni. He said that one day he and his friend had gone into Chinatown to sleep with a prostitute, up the stairs behind one of these little doors that has a broken neon sign outside saying 'young model'. The Russian pepperoni guy had gone upstairs while his friend waited downstairs. Ten minutes later the Russian came back down with a cheap fading smile, and found his friend ashen, blabbering and crazy. There were tears in his eyes. He said that he had been leaning on the frame of the door, whistling to himself, thinking about his turn upstairs with the young model. Suddenly he'd felt a suction like a giant Hoover pulling him back through the adjacent doorway. He grabbed hold of the wooden frame around the door but his fingers slipped away. He grabbed instead for the broken neon sign that said 'young model' but had been dragged backwards, sucked into the doorway, screaming. Nobody had even noticed.

'But what was in there? How did you get out?' the Russian asked him.

With that his friend had collapsed. He awoke eight hours later, shouting 'Sylvia!' and he hadn't spoken since. The pepperoni Russian thinks it is a time portal. He said that his friend loved a girl, Sylvia, when they were children, but he hadn't seen her for twenty years. So I don't walk through

Chinatown now. I can't run the risk of being sucked thirty years into the future, finding myself staring with alarm at old-aged Ben and I as we shout the same spiteful lines at each other only with bent backs and brittle bones. Plus the cobbles in Chinatown play havoc with my heels.

Walk up Long Acre. My agency said that The Majestic Theatre is on the right-hand side, because I can't tell one theatre from another. I stop at the front entrance and consider the posters that already hang in the glass boxes at the top of some small stone steps, adjacent to big crimson doors. '*Dolly Russell returns to the West End*' says one, and underneath is a picture of an actress, in Forties furs and a pencil skirt, with a cigarette-holder in one hand, backlit on a sparse stage. It is obviously an old shot – she must be well on the way to seventy now. I've brought the thick concealer in case I need it, and two different types of base to smooth out lines. Her face bears an arrogance that you don't see these days. She looks like a woman who made men chase her, in a time when women were far more compliant. Maybe that's the last time love existed, back when we were all a little more selfless. I moaned to my mother on the phone last week, almost crying because I am so emotionally exhausted all the time, and of course confused. She said, 'Jesus, Scarlet, will you stop whining? Don't tell me about this awful modern female experience you girls are having. I wasn't allowed to do A-Levels, for Christ's sake.'

She is generally more sympathetic than that; she must have been having a bad day.

When Mum left I always knew it wasn't my fault, and I never dreamt I could get her to come back. My life changed, but it wasn't that bad. My weekends with Mum were now packed full of fun and adventure and talking. She seemed happy and the way that she put it everything was exciting. Dad was never a great talker, and now Mum and I could witter on all day about nothing and not hear him sighing dramatically in the background because he couldn't hear the football on the TV. Sometimes on a Friday night I even went so far as pouring salt in Richard's baked beans as they sat simmering on the hob, crossing my fingers that he would get stomach cramps in the night. Then he wouldn't be able to come and see Mum that weekend, and it would just be the two of us instead.

She moved out to a house on the other side of Norwich and she painted it herself. She let me help, and we both put on oversized shirts that she bought at Oxfam and tied our hair up in scarves so we looked like 1940s war widows working in munitions. We painted her living room orange! Dad would come and pick me up on Sunday nights and they'd look at each other on the doorstep with confusion, trying to remember who the other was. They were like chalk and cheese, they were never even meant to be a part of each other's lives. My mum would smile at least, and ask Dad how he was. My dad would look embarrassed and batten down the hatches of his emotions as always, particularly now that my mother had become a whirlwind on her own. He would give nothing away.

A year ago I asked Mum if Dad ever told her he loved her. 'Yes,' she said, nodding earnestly, 'but only when I asked of course. The thing is, Scarlet, with your father, he was raised differently. You never knew his parents but they were both very strict. Whereas you know Grandma and Grandpa, they can't stop giving you hugs! I was so lucky, Scarlet, and so loved, that I found it easy to show it to your father. I hope that's how I make you feel now, I don't ever want you to guess about my feelings for you, and neither should Richard. Of course, Richard is so kind, so good-natured, he has nothing but love in him, and he was lucky when he met Hannah so young, but they are so right for each other, and she is such a lovely girl, with such a lot of love to give too.'

She looked at me out of the corner of her eye, with concern.

'I love you and Richard utterly. When I left people didn't think that was possible, but in a way I left because I loved you. I always thought you knew that. Katharine Hepburn said "loved people are loving people", and I believe that. Your dad didn't have that sense of being loved, and he didn't know how to show it to me.'

'Is that why you left?'

'Scarlet, things are rarely that black and white. I loved him, it was very hard. But you know that your father loves you, don't you, Scarlet?'

'Of course, he's just not . . . demonstrative.' Dad has never hugged me with abandon, he chooses his words carefully, and trips over sentiment clumsily. He can't express himself, I know that. He can laugh, and does. But he can't cry.

'You've noticed that, Scarlet, and yet . . .'

'And yet?' I asked, waiting for her to go on.

'Be careful, Scarlet. There isn't just one type of man for you.'

Mum lives by the sea now, in a little village called Rottingdean, a couple of miles outside of Brighton, on her own. She prefers it that way. She takes long walks on the beach and reads a lot, and sees films with the man who lives next door.

Standing outside the Majestic Theatre I read the poster in the opposite frame: 'Tennessee Williams's The Milk Train Doesn't Stop Here Anymore: previews start Monday 20th!'

There is a guy selling the Evening Standard a little further up the road. I check my watch and skip up towards him, rummaging for forty pence in my bag. It is always too late to get a paper by the time I get out in the evening, and it's

27

my only source of news. If half the world goes up in smoke I'll read it in the *Standard*. Otherwise I might never know. Plus I like to leave it for Ben so he can do the sudoku. It's a little thing I do, a point of contact, the *Evening Standard* left on the kitchen table. I hope he smiles when he sees it in the mornings, before I am even out of bed. I hope he thinks of me when he picks it up. I think of him when I leave it there at night.

I hold my hand out with my forty pence.

Behind the stand the old guy is wearing a flat cap and an overcoat. His glasses are thick and slightly smeared with grease. He smiles at me and I notice he only has his front four teeth, top and bottom, the rest are missing. I wonder if he can still whistle.

'Have you got it?' he asks.

'Is it forty pence?' I reply.

I look down at the two twenty-pence pieces in my outstretched palm, confused.

'Or have you lost it?' he asks, lisping the words through his four teeth.

'Sorry? I don't understand.' I offer him my forty pence again, but he doesn't take it. He smiles. Perhaps he is an idiot.

'Your passion for life,' he says. 'You had it . . .'

I stare at him. He smiles and takes the forty pence from my hand, and replaces it with an *Evening Standard*, folded in half. A man walks over and offers him forty pence, which he takes as he passes him a paper and says, 'Thank you, sir.' An older woman nudges me out of the way as she offers him her change, and he passes her a paper and says, 'Thank you, dear.'

I turn and walk back towards the theatre. I feel a buzzing in my bag, and reach in for my phone. I am standing outside The Majestic's back door when I answer. 'Hello?'

28

'It's me,' Ben says. 'I popped back to get the post, in case they'd delivered my Xbox game. They hadn't, but you have a letter . . . from some clinic.'

'I'll open it when I get home.'

'Why have you gone to a clinic?'

'Women's stuff.'

'Okay. I'll see you later then.'

'Ben – we have passion, right?'

'Sorry?'

'We have passion . . . in our lives . . .'

I sense him squirming at the end of the phone.

'I don't understand what you mean, I'm working . . .'

'I have to go,' I say, and hang up.

I stare at the cobbles beneath my feet. Snapping myself out of my trance I reach forwards for the handle of the theatre's back door, but as I do I notice a piece of paper, a leaflet, is stuck to the bottom of my shoe where my heel has pierced it. I have been walking with it pinned to me all this time, like a cheap joke. I lean against the wall, trying to keep my balance as I lift my foot in the air, and snatch the leaflet off. It's an underground map.

On the front, in big red letters, it says,

'Don't waste time.'

Scene II: Politics

You know those days just before Christmas when there are lights everywhere, in Highgate village or anywhere in London? I don't mean the orange and red neon glory lights of Oxford Street or Regent Street, with their torrents of swarming shoppers below who fill every spare inch of pavement, as those lights, unlike puppies, are just for Christmas, and not for life. I am talking about the branches of white lights that string across the high streets of villages, dusting the everyday with Christmas sparkle, enough to remind you that it's supposed to be the most wonderful time of the year. Some of those dotted lights even shine out from people's windows, the optimistic ones. I think they should leave those lights up forever, for every day of the year. I'd like a life like that. Those strings of cheap diamonds are like a shared and hopeful smile. They punctuate the functional with magic, and increasingly that's what I feel slipping away. My magic reserves are depleted, like dwindling natural resources, and they need a little topping up. I need a world with a little more magic.

Rain spits at the tips of my shoes sticking out in to the alley, as I loiter inside the backdoor of The Majestic, leaning against a grubby wall. I could call Ben back. My phone sits in my hand like a grenade. I always call him back. Ben can leave cross words for hours, for days. It's like he wears blinkers or has tunnel vision. I know that men and women think differently but Ben is like a computer.

The Ben that I recognise now is his reflection in a monitor, on his PC screen: he is mostly otherwise engaged with technology. I check his phone constantly. I hate myself for doing it – I know it makes me a cliché. The act of rifling surreptitiously through his texts when he isn't in the room, while nervously listening for the sound of his feet padding down the hallway to signal his return, epitomises the change from 'old confident me' to 'fresh and pathetic me' like an exclamation mark. But I have found texts from her. They always end with a kiss. I sat outside her office for an hour once, crying. She organises events for banks. Ben never fails to remind me, subtly or otherwise, that it was he and Katie that were hurt by their break-up, as if they are an exclusive club with a restricted membership of two.

Katie. I have to whisper it, like a swear word in a nursery. Apparently my feelings at the time paled in comparison to how badly they both felt, even given his constant emotional yo-yoing back and forth, from me to her to me to her. Ben doesn't think it was painful for me, as I tried desperately to begin a proper and exclusive relationship with him, this man that I had fallen in love with, as he sat and cried for somebody else, and I hugged him to try to make it better. They are friends again now, but I'll never be Katie's 'favourite person' apparently. Ben finds it easier to blame me for the breakdown of his relationship rather than the two people who were actually in it, and in a way I let him. I do feel guilty about her. I feel like being obsessed with her gives me a reason to stay with Ben. Leaving him now would be like kicking her in the teeth again, this woman I've never met.

A part of me believes that Ben would like me to leave, so that he can go back to her and settle back into his old-man chair in his old-man relationship and just call me a 'phase'. He can pretend that he didn't want anything else, just for a little while.

Ben 'catches up' with Katie once a month, either on the phone or in person. When I tried to say that I thought that once a month might be a little excessive, he told me I couldn't tell him what to do. I tried to explain that I wasn't telling him what to do, but rather letting him know how his actions made me feel, and he told me, with irritation in his voice and a hateful exhausted look on his face, that I had to get used to it because it was going to happen whether I liked it or not.

I think that Ben would prefer life to escape him rather than acknowledge that he is terrified of getting in touch with his emotions, but I don't want that. Happiness isn't fear. Fear leads to hate, and hate leads to the dark side . . . I know because Ben and his mate Iggy watch *Star Wars* constantly – the DVD Special Edition, the Director's Cut Four Disc DVD, the Special Director's Cut Ten Disc Super Edition. Cue Darth Vader heavy breathing. But I'm not ready for the dark side. I can still feel the force, even if Ben can't. And I've always been afraid of the dark . . .

I suppose I should acknowledge that Ben thinks he's just fine. 'Men don't talk,' he says, like that's reason enough for us not to sort things out, not to be happy.

I throw my phone into my bag in despair. My head is hot but the rain cools the air around me as I feel my face crack and crumble like an earthquake in a desert, my make-up disintegrating as I start to cry.

I startle myself with a short sharp laugh of surprise.

Then I cry again.

The prospect of leaving Ben makes me shake. I cannot

contemplate being without him, of how scared I am of being alone no matter how cowardly it makes me feel . . . I desperately grab in my bag for my phone again, as if I am suddenly on a ten-second deadline and if I don't speak to him before the timer runs out our relationship will explode. I find it and claw it open, and hit his number.

I just need to hear his voice. I need us to say important things that cement our feelings for each other somehow, so that I can get through the day. Ben and I don't discuss marriage or kids, because I don't want to put too much pressure on him. But, then, I am thirty-one now and I want those things, and maybe he does too. Lots of other people do, so why not us, and why am I so scared to say it? I don't have to goad him into loving me and then, and only when he tells me he is ready, will we be allowed to admit that we want babies. I am not going to be scared to say that I want to have children anymore! Maybe if I just say it then he will too . . .

It rings five times before he answers and I immediately say, 'Ben, it's me.'

'I'm working . . .'

'I want to have children.'

'Sorry?'

'I want you to know that I want to have children.'

'Right . . .'

'And?'

'And what? I'm working . . .'

'I am telling you that I want to have children.'

'Well, yes, I suppose you do . . .'

'Well what do you think?'

'About what?'

'About having children?'

'I think I want to have them too . . .'

He sounds like he is searching desperately for the right

answer on some quiz show, like *Blockbusters*: 'I'll have whatever will make her stop talking please, Bob?'

'Soon?' I ask. 'Do you want to have them soon?'

'I . . . I don't know. Maybe. I don't know. I haven't really thought about it.'

'Well . . . what do you think about?'

'What? I'm working.'

'Yes, but I'm thirty-one.'

'Right . . .'

'I think about things . . . about marriage . . . and stuff . . .'

'Right . . .'

'What do you think about those things?'

'I . . . I don't know . . . Scarlet, I'm working . . .'

'Oh, okay, do you want to talk about it later?'

'I . . . I don't know . . . maybe . . . another time . . .'

I want to cry. Again. I realise we haven't even had a conversation. Ben has just deflected me. I kick my words at him like weak volleys to his chest. He doesn't even have to move off his spot. He doesn't even have to stretch. He just stands there and bats me away with 'maybes' and 'I don't knows' and I don't even challenge him for anything more. A stronger woman would punch that ball back out of his hands, make him stand three feet from the penalty spot, then fire it at his testes. But I am not that woman . . . I thought that I was, but then I met Ben. If one person shuts down eventually the other one does too. I kick like a girl now.

'Okay, I'll see you later then,' he says, finishing the conversation off.

'You can't wait to get off the phone, can you?'

'No, it's not that, but I'm working.'

I can hear his mates in the store laughing in the background. I can hear that they are watching *Dude, Where's My Car?* again.

'But . . . but what about . . . I just . . . Okay, fine. I'll see you later.'

The phone line goes dead.

I don't know who is more scared, me or Ben? It's like Halloween round at our flat. But it's the prospect of staying with him as our relationship rots beneath us that scares me the most.

And what if there is nobody else out there for me? Helen always tells me not to be ridiculous when I say that, but I worry that Ben and I just don't try anymore, and what will make that any easier with somebody else? Maybe I am just creating problems, but I have a head full of questions. Maybe he's having an affair? Maybe he doesn't like sex? Or intimacy? Or anything that means you have to be close to another person? This is the man I want to marry, a man who won't even give me a hug unless I ask for it and sometimes not even then. Will we even kiss at the altar?

Of course, the thought that constantly lingers is: Why did you leave your wife if you don't love me? Did you start loving me and then stop? Are you seeing her again? I know they didn't do 'public displays of affection', or 'pda's' as Ben once described them. I thought expressions like that were the reserve of eight-year-old girls. At the time I wasn't even talking about a passionate kiss, I was asking him for a peck on the lips on a half-full Virgin train. But Ben won't do public displays of affection, not on a train, not now. The obvious question is of course, why?

But Ben won't ask the 'why' questions either. He says 'this is who I am', even if he knows it won't make him happy. As long as he can't get upset, then he need never ask 'Why?'

I don't want that life. I want a deliberate passionate honest time.

It's my mother's fault for calling me Scarlet.

You can't give a child that name and not expect her to live . . .

There is a loud cough – somebody is lurking awkwardly at the end of the corridor and has probably heard my entire conversation with Ben, and has certainly seen me standing here crying like some pathetic soap-opera wife.

He's large, he looks fleshy and heavy like a saturated sponge.

I swipe at my tears.

'Can I help?' he asks.

'I don't know, maybe – do you think anybody has a relationship where the man comes up behind the woman while she is, say, washing up, and puts his arms around her waist, and whispers in her ear, "You look gorgeous even when you are washing up"? Does anybody have that? Even after three years? Or ever? Or is that just in films? Is that too much to ask? Because that's what I want. Do I want too much? And also, to have somebody who says nice things to me, like, "You look really pretty tonight", or "You really make me laugh", or just something sometime that is spontaneous, you know? That makes me feel wanted, or valued at least. Do men do that, anywhere? Or is that just in romantic comedies? Also, I'd like to be hugged in the middle of the night, and sometimes even woken up to have sex. Does that sound strange to you? Because I know some men who just aren't interested, at all. I know one man in particular who has explicitly been told that it is very much okay to wake me up in the middle of the night to have sex, and I won't be annoyed, or tired, in fact I'd love it! I would love to have sex with him in the middle of the night! I have actually told him that he can do that. But he never wakes up! Not only that, he never even rolls over and hugs me! We sleep in the same bed, and he never even hugs me . . .'

'Do you hug him? Do you wake him up?' the saturated sponge asks me directly.

36

'I used to. I gave up. It felt like I was in the persuading business. And who wants to feel like they are persuading somebody to hug them? It's degrading . . .'

'Does this man, is this, your husband?'

'Boyfriend,' I whisper, ashamed and mildly appalled to be having this conversation with somebody that I assume is a new colleague. But then Helen always says, 'Scarlet, you'd ask advice from the speaking clock if it would answer you back.' I suppose I am hoping that soon somebody, anybody, might tell me what I want to hear. Until then I'll simply add to the weight of various strangers' experiences that I am amassing in my head.

'I think that . . .' I see his thoughts flash across his wide face like a red line that signifies a heartbeat across a monitor. I see him actually thinking about what I've said in an effort to answer it, and not just recoiling at the emotion of it all. He and Ben would not be friends. Ben would probably accuse him of being gay. Of course he might be gay, but he seems too big . . . He starts to speak, then stops, then starts again.

'I think that if I was in bed each night with a woman that I loved, I would want to hug her, and kiss her, and . . . certainly wake her up if she was offering what . . . has apparently . . . been offered. I would certainly do that. And if I loved her, of course I would want to hold her. Who else do you get to hold like that? Not your mum, or your friends. Who else can hug you like that? I mean, not all night, a man needs sleep, but certainly I would want to, and would hug her . . . Oh Christ . . .'

I am crying again.

'What's your name?' I ask, regaining control and sweeping a finger beneath each of my eyes to mop up my tears.

'Why?'

'What do you mean why? I'm not undercover police . . .'

'Gavin,' he says, with a degree of suspicion.

'Okay, Gavin, who maybe has drugs in his pocket or some outstanding parking tickets? Do you think I should break up with him and go speed-dating? Except my best friend Helen said her cousin went and she said the whole process made her feel like she was a human iPod. You just keep skipping past really good songs, thinking the next one might be better . . .'

Gavin looks a little bewildered. His cheeks are flushed, as if he has just climbed three flights of stairs, or necked two glasses of red wine in quick succession.

'I'm the stage manager,' Gavin says.

'Okay . . . does that mean you aren't allowed to answer questions about speed-dating?'

'I don't mean to upset you again . . . or more . . . but you can't be in here if you are nothing to do with the theatre and . . . I'd rather take it up the arse from a seven-foot convict with the nickname Big Greased Shirley than go speed-dating.'

'My God! You'd hate it that much? Do you think that's a masculinity issue? That you don't want to be judged by women? I mean, it could be okay . . . some people say it's fun . . . speed-dating . . . not taking it up the arse . . . but some people say that's fun too . . . I've never . . . I mean, I've thought about it, but . . . I'm not that kind of girl . . . except what is that kind of girl, really? A girl who likes sex? That's fine, isn't it, today? In this century? Like when men describe a woman as "dirty" but in a good way, I always thought that meant taking it up the . . . you know . . . but then I found out it just means that she'll smile during sex . . . or not kick you off. But also, I am allowed to be in here. At least I think I am. Like I'd just be standing here crying if not? Of course I could be just watching the rain and crying over my rubbish relationship . . . except of course it's not rubbish . . . that's unfair . . . and I'm not that pathetic. At least I'm trying not to be . . . or maybe I am . . . but I'm Scarlet White, I'm Dolly Russell's new make-up artist.'

I offer Gavin my hand to shake, thrusting my *Evening Standard* back under my other arm.

'Scarlet White? In the dining room with the lead piping?' Gavin shakes but doesn't seem in any way stirred.

'Hmmm, just the half a mile short of funny,' I say, eyeing him with suspicion at the cheap and quick jibe.

'Okay, well Dolly won't be in for a couple of hours yet – she's a late starter, the first wave of pills and gin don't break on her beach until noon – but that's good if you want to have a look around, and I can introduce you to some people, the rest of the crew – the director's downstairs freaking out about the karma of the curtain . . . it's too heavy apparently – he says it could bring us all down . . .'

Gavin's delivery is so dry it's as if he's reading his lines from a sheet of paper. I wonder if I'll ever know when he's joking. I don't know whether to laugh or not now. He must be my age. He is twice my weight and height. He has that slightly ginger but just brown hair that suggests Scottish ancestry to me, although that's unfounded as I don't know anybody Scottish and never have. Still, Gavin looks like he could wear a kilt and toss cabers on BBC1 on Sunday afternoons.

He ducks expertly as we weave our way along a maze of thin grey corridors, and somehow he manages not to bang his over-large head on a thousand dirty pipes hanging from the ceiling above us. The pipes are so close together that if he wasn't ducking so swiftly he'd actually be banging out a tune. Part of me wishes he'd stop ducking because I want to know how it sounds, although Gavin would end up with concussion. I skip to keep up in my heels, my purple skirt swishing silk at my knees, my legs in fishnets flashing beneath. We are moving at speed, Gavin's stride is long, and I start to feel a little sticky in my black cashmere cardigan that crosses directly over my heart. Neither Gavin nor I speak for what must be a whole minute; it's a long, strange silence like the ones observed on the radio on VE Day or September 11th. I feel us trapped in a moving, uncomfortable bubble, thinking desperately of something to say while trying to catch my breath. A very short man appears around the corner in front of us. I mean, he is clinically short. Gavin acknowledges him with a nod of his head, and as I hug the wall to let him pass I glance down and see that he is completely bald on top.

'Goodness, I didn't even realise! I should have read the play beforehand, I know, but it was such a last-minute booking . . . normally I work on film sets, TV commercials . . . I haven't done that much theatre, or any, really . . .'

'Didn't realise what?' Gavin asks as we turn the corner.

'That there were dwarves in the play. Is it a fantasy? Or science fiction? I didn't realise Tennessee Williams wrote that sort of thing as well.'

Gavin stops abruptly and looks at me, and I screech to a halt a couple of steps later and turn to face him.

'What?' I ask.

'He's an electrician . . .'

'Oh . . .'

I see Gavin shaking his head as he starts walking again and I run a little to keep up, my heels clicking on the cold concrete of the floor, my back sweaty under my cashmere, my top lip prickling under my make-up, my hairspray starting to scratch at my head. I don't think I have ever been this mortified. Gavin isn't talking to me. Maybe he and the dwarf are really good friends, although they'd look ridiculous walking down the street together. In my mind I can only picture the smaller guy sitting on one of Gavin's massive shoulders, perhaps in a jaunty hat and eating an apple . . . but I know that's wrong. I decide to break the silence with a change of subject, terrified of how Gavin might choose to introduce me to the rest of the crew, especially if there are any more . . . electricians.

'So Gavin, pretend you have a girlfriend . . .'

He stops and glares at me again.

'What?' I ask.

'I do have a girlfriend,' he says.

'Oh. I didn't mean anything by it, Gavin . . . Okay, well, moving on, what if you and your girlfriend were just sitting on the sofa one night, watching the TV, and she said to you, "Say something nice to me"?'

'Why?' he says, and I can't decide if he is just irritated, or if he already hates me like Greenpeace hate Shell. Either way I carry on regardless – I can't make it any worse.

'Because she's just had a miserable day, her feet really hurt because she's been breaking in new sandals, she's had a row with her dad about the importance of correctly filling out cheque-book stubs, and she needs somebody to say something wonderful. She needs to feel special . . .'

'I mean,' Gavin says, pushing a door open then turning back to address me, 'why haven't I said something nice anyway?'

'Oh . . .' That's floored me.

He steps back to allow me to walk through the door before he does.

'Exactly,' I say. Exactly. I think my voice might have just broken.

The stage is in front of us, and all of the house lights are up. It is smaller than I anticipated, and apologetic without a spotlight.

'I'm not having this conversation if you are going to cry again.' Gavin talks over his shoulder at me as we stride along the aisle. 'Plus, do you talk about anything else? Have you tried cracking a few jokes? Or is it just constant relationship angst over a mound of self-help books and copies

41

of *Cosmopolitan*? Because if that's the case I don't think I blame this guy . . .'

I blink twice in quick succession. I am startled and affronted. I can talk about other things; I talk about other things all the time!

'I can talk about other things . . .' I say, sneering at him.

'Well thank God for that,' Gavin says, and stops walking abruptly behind a short Indian man who stands with his back to us while gesticulating wildly, his hands conducting an imaginary opera. Nobody appears to be paying him much attention, and a clove cigarette flashes wildly between the stubby fingers of his left hand, sprinkling ash and sparks onto his chocolate-brown suede loafers. He wears a dark grey suit and a black polo-neck, and has very thick and very high dark hair that seems to have been set in one of those old-lady hairdresser's, an hour under the machine with a *Woman's Weekly* and a word search, sucking on a boiled sweet, all clicking teeth and concentration.

Young people in jeans and Sergeant Pepper and Mr Brightside T-shirts mill around in front of him paying him no mind, while every couple of seconds somebody completely new appears and carries a large plank of wood precariously from one side of the stage to the other. Everything that could possibly be covered in material has been – a dark-red brushed velvet with a grey and brown pattern of twisted leaves. The stage needs sweeping. It is insulated with a thin layer of dust, broken up by discarded McDonald's wrappers. I count at least five Starbucks cups that have toppled onto their sides like the drunks on Tottenham Court Road.

Gavin says, 'Tristan', but the little man in front of us doesn't turn around. He is shouting in a low, thick theatrical voice that he has shoplifted from the men's floor of a 1950s department store.

'But fucking love! I can't fucking make it work! It's

42

obviously too dark! It's too heavy and shameful and dirty and depressed – it's an old velvet whore hanging from its whore's bed – it's been used, it's on the cheap, it's dragging all of us down with it to its old rotten-toothed whore old age . . .' His shoulders droop, and the clove cigarette burns close to his fingers. He takes a violent last drag and stubs it out on the aisle. I hear him whisper, 'Now I'm depressed.'

When nobody says anything, he takes a huge breath and demands of the room, 'Has anybody got any uppers?'

'Tristan?' Gavin repeats, but louder this time.

Tristan spins around to face us. He is wearing oversized black plastic sunglasses reminiscent of Jackie Onassis, although they are clearly very cheap. His suit is well cut but still appears to be a size too big for him. So this is Tristan Mitra. He tilts his head down to look at us above his plastic glasses and something devilish twinkles in his eyes as he flashes me a huge wide charming smile. I've read about him in the *Standard*. It was the opening night of his debut play as a director, an all-male version of *The Sound of Music* at the Brixton Art House, and the press were trying to track him down for a quote because of its rave reviews. They found him in the Charing Cross police station on Agar Road. He'd been arrested for being drunk in charge of a wheelchair on Old Compton Street. He'd run over the feet of twelve sets of tourists, but unlucky thirteen had been a policeman. They found the owner of the wheelchair in a pub at the bottom of Wardour Street with a bottle of vodka and a beef pie. He said that Tristan had offered him two hundred quid for the chair, plus the vodka, and he had just really fancied a drink. But now he couldn't get home.

Tristan has appeared in the gossip columns as well – he's rumoured to be having an affair with Phillipe Ellender, the set designer, and I read a thing last week that said he might be having a thing with Dolly Russell herself, which seems utterly bizarre. When they asked him for a quote he said, 'Loving somebody and not telling them can hurt more than being rejected by them. It's like rejecting yourself.' And even though he has a reputation for being able to drink all night, he recently came home so appallingly trashed that he flew into a jealous rage directed at his mother's chinchilla, Charlton, and tried to microwave it . . . The RSPCA got involved at some point, that's why it was in the paper.

'Gavin! Love! Mountain of a man! Giant Gavin! Ho, ho, ho, green giant!' he sings and does a strange little dance, 'Giant Gavin! Love! . . . Are you on any prescription medication? You're not on codeine, are you?'

'No,' Gavin replies flatly, and Tristan stares at him still, but his smile begins to fade.

'I had morphine once,' I say, to try and cheer up this strange little man, this large-voiced wide-eyed director of the stage, who is no more than five foot five.

His face explodes into a huge smile again and I can't help but smile too.

'Morphine! I'd fucking kill for some morphine now!'

He has the most English voice I have ever heard, a cross between James Bond and the Queen, it's made of silk. When he says 'morphine' he exclaims it, like his own personal Eureka!

'Gavin, love, giant, man mountain, bouncy castle, can we get any morphine? Is there a hospital nearby? Better yet, St John's Ambulance Headquarters? They are easily fooled those St John's guys, they don't get that much action you see.' He lowers his glasses and winks at me and I feel myself blushing. He notices it, stops, smiles and winks again. 'So they'll chuck anything at you given the chance. Last year I was at the Streatham fete with my mother – she was selling chutney –

and frankly I was bored stupid, and I saw the St John's Ambulance there and couldn't believe my luck! I wandered over and just casually mentioned that I'd twisted my arm unpacking two boxes of Mum's finest, and asked them to improvise me a splint and they bloody did it in seconds out of a bloody *Daily Telegraph*! It was fucking marvellous! It was splint poetry! Broken-bone poetry! It's dark in here, isn't it? I think it's the bloody curtain . . .'

Tristan spins around to face the stage and it feels like the light has gone out. Next to me, Gavin sighs quietly.

'Could it be the glasses?' I ask.

'No, love, no . . .' Tristan turns back to face us, but doesn't take them off. 'I wear them all the time now. I got them free from some fucking teenage magazine –' He lights another clove cigarette without offering either Gavin or I the pack, and inhales deeply. Blowing out a large smoke ring, he points through its centre at nothing with his finger. '– *Jackie* or *Shirley* or *Tarty* or something like that, some teenage slutty magazine. And it was one pound fifty at the newsagent's! And these were stuck to the front of this magazine, like a bloody godsend! My eyes had been so red that month anyway, and above them it said something like, "How to know if the time is really right to let him touch you" . . . or "Give him your cherry but keep the box that it comes in" . . . or "Don't let him lick you" . . . or something.' He stops and counts something on his fingers and mutters quickly.

Gavin and I exchange a glance. Tristan is like a walking spotlight. I don't want him to spin around again. I don't think Gavin likes him as much as I do, but maybe he's just too high up. I am five foot five, five foot eight in my heels today, and Tristan is at least three inches shorter than me. If we stood back to back in bare feet we'd probably be the same height, except his hair is really high.

'And I just thought perfect!' Tristan is talking again. 'They ground me, but let me be me. They steal the me from me. They remind me that everything is filtered, through experience. You know not one person that comes to see this shit-shambles of a play will see it the same? We all see it through our life filters – who we've loved, who we've screwed, who's screwed us. If they were the fucking *one*, or they just wanted to get their leg over and then they did it with your best mate one Wednesday night after football practice.'

Tristan stops talking and lowers his glasses again, fixing me with a stare. His pupils are almost black. I feel the colour rushing to my cheeks. I am caught in his tractor beam.

'By the time you reach twenty you are emotionally shot to shit, and I'm thirty-six! That's fucking awful, isn't it? How the hell did that happen? But that's the world. That's life. That's London. *Non, regrette rien.* We are all a little damaged –' he pushes his sunglasses back up to cover his eyes, '– shop soiled with the juices of lovers old, just not broken, not quite broken. Do you have any uppers?'

'No, sorry.' I shake my head and feel really bad. I would love to be able to give him an upper right now – not that I think he needs it, but he just really seems to want one. We stand in a temporary silence, which I decide to smash.

'Sometimes I say to Ben, that's my boyfriend, I say, "Say something nice", and he says, "I don't do it to order", and I say, "Okay, Ben, but you never fucking do it!"'

I hear Gavin sigh but I ignore it because I have Tristan's full attention, as long as his eyes are open under his sunglasses.

'"You never do it, Ben!"' I carry on. 'And I just think that if you are going to be with somebody it might be nice if they said nice things, to cheer you up, and let you know why they are with you – that it's not just killing time, because they don't love you and they don't initiate sex so really there isn't much point, but they aren't ending it so . . .'

Tristan whips off his sunglasses and stares at me in alarm.

'I want you to know that I haven't taken these off for four days and that includes sleeping and a court appearance,' he says, nodding his head at me to make his point, so I completely understand the gravity of his action. The whites of his eyes are riddled with red veins like worms inching around his massively dilated pupils.

'Fucking hell,' he says, shaking his head now. 'Are you in an actual relationship? Do people still do that? We should definitely talk about that – I'm interested. Just not right now. But let's definitely talk later. Who are you?' He asks me with the accent on 'are', as if I may be an imposter, or an alien, or it might actually be important to somebody.

Gavin answers before I can. 'New Make-up for Dolly.'

And I don't sound that important after all. I'm not even the original. I'm a replacement, sloppy seconds – again.

'Right, right, right, right.' Tristan nods with each word, with complete understanding. 'What happened to Old Make-up?' he asks Gavin seriously.

'She quit.'

'But why?' Tristan asks.

'Dolly spiked her drink.'

Tristan's eyebrows rise simultaneously and a smile tweaks the corners of his mouth.

'With what?'

'The doctor said it was probably speed.'

'Lucky bitch,' Tristan whispers and gazes off to one side, as if remembering some long-forgotten afternoon with a long-forgotten lover in a long-forgotten field, somewhere long forgotten. He turns back to Gavin.

'Who's Dolly's dealer?' he asks seriously.

'I don't know, Tristan,' Gavin replies, with no more expression in his voice than if he were reading the Ikea instructions for a self-assembly three-drawer chest, but Tristan doesn't seem to mind.

47

'Right. Right. Right.' He nods his head again, computing the information.

'Make-up,' he turns to me.

'Yes?'

'Who's your dealer?'

'I don't . . . I don't really have one . . .'

'Right. Okay. Two things. Number one – watch your drinks. If you think she's spiked it bring it to me and I'll test it . . . Let's go to Gerry's later and we can talk properly then. You do go to Gerry's, right? Next door to the Subway at the bottom of Dean Street? Fucking Subway, how did they get to be everywhere all of a sudden? But I do love their meat!'

Gerry's is a bar in Soho that is open all night for people like me, and Tristan, and anybody really. People who need to carry on drinking for a little while after the curtain goes down.

'Yep.'

'Good.' He nods and turns to leave.

'What was the second thing?' I ask before he goes.

He pivots on his heel and fixes me with another smile, sucking on the arm of his plastic glasses.

'Are the pillows real?' His eyes jump down to my chest and he moves his glance from one to the other as if a tennis match is being conducted across my cleavage.

'They're all mine,' I say with a smile.

'Good for you. Lady luck. No jogging, though, Make-up, it could be carnage. Gerry's then. Gavin! I'll be back in ten, I need to do a thing.'

He pushes on his glasses and walks towards the front of house, disappearing quickly through a set of swing doors.

Gavin and I stand in silence and watch him go. I feel exhausted. Something crashes loudly on the stage behind us.

'Maybe he doesn't want to hurt your feelings,' Gavin says while still staring at the swing doors.

'Tristan?' The pillow talk could have offended less of a girl than me. I'm used to it, however, from Ben.

'No, your bloke. This Ben.'

'And just drifting on without any kind of emotional investment isn't hurting my feelings?' I ask, still staring at the swing doors myself.

'I don't see a gun to your head . . .' Gavin turns to me as if breaking out of a trance. I snap myself out of it as well. I wonder whether Tristan has opium sewn into his suit. He has left us both dazed and a little cloudy.

'But . . .' I shake my head to clear it, 'but I love him, Gavin . . . it's so hard . . .'

'Nothing is that hard really . . . look at the facts . . .' He turns and walks towards the stage. I follow.

'Okay,' I count on my fingers, 'he doesn't say he loves me. He doesn't want to have sex with me. He doesn't say nice things to me, even when I ask him to . . .'

'Has he ever said anything nice to you?'

'He said I was "electrifying" once . . .'

'Electrifying? What does that mean?' Gavin looks nonplussed.

'I know. Pretty much nothing. It made me sound like a waltzer at a fun fair . . .'

'Or a broken hair-dryer,' Gavin offers as we walk through a small door at the side of the stage.

'Thanks, Gavin, thanks very much.'

'Is he seventy-five? Or a miner?' he asks.

'No . . . He's thirty-three and he runs a branch of Dixons . . . Are there any miners left? You know, after Thatcher?'

'Not really. You should leave him.' He says this with some certainty, and I wonder how he can be so sure.

'But why doesn't he leave me, Gavin, if he wants to? I love him! If he doesn't want to be with me, why is he still with me?'

We reach a small door backstage that has been freshly painted lilac. A sign that reads 'Do NOT disturb' swings from the doorknob, as well as what looks like a lavender sachet, the type they sell at school fetes, that somebody's granny made at her club. Gavin turns the knob as he says, 'Because he's weak.'

I feel hugely disloyal. I hate that Gavin has just said that. He doesn't even know Ben. I have painted this picture, and it is obviously an awful one.

'I don't know, Gavin, I don't think that's fair. He's come from a really hard place, he left his wife for me, and . . .'

I start to defend him, but Gavin fixes me with a stare, from way up high. Maybe that *is* it – he's weak. I hadn't thought of that.

'Scarlet. He's weak. Most men are.'

'But I thought that men were supposed to be the strong ones?' I say, quietly confused.

'They are . . . This is it.' Gavin shrugs at the little room and it feels like the room shrugs back.

'We might need you to make-up some of the other leads. Our Cast Make-up, Greta, is about eighty. She's always got a hipflask full of Drambuie on the go. We can't let her do eyeliner. We haven't got enough insurance.'

'Fine.' I dump my make-up box on a table covered in flowers and cards, in front of a long, thin, badly lit mirror. 'As long as Dolly's okay with me doing it I'm happy to.'

'It's cool, you could get here at midday every day and still have time to do the two other principals before she turns up.'

'Anybody I know?' I unclip the three locks on my carrier. It's like a portable Fort Knox, but the prospect of it falling open on the tube and thousands of pounds' worth of make-up tumbling out to be crushed under loafers and court shoes is unthinkable.

Gavin passes me a polystyrene cup of instant coffee that has appeared like magic. 'Arabella Jones and Tom Harvey-Saint,' he says as I take a sip.

I spit it back out all over Gavin's huge trainers.

'Didn't realise he was in it, did you?' Gavin smirks at me.

'No . . . I didn't realise he was in it.' The blood rushes from my legs to my head and I lean back against the table urgently.

'Fancy him, do you?' Gavin asks, but as if he is reading court notes back to a jury.

I gulp but don't answer.

'Watch out Ben,' he whistles, and edges towards the door.

The side of the room that isn't the table and mirror and flowers and cards is cushions and more flowers, a large gold chair with deep red velvet backing, and a tall lamp with a fuchsia scarf thrown over it to soften the light. It's a tiny space crammed with decoration, an old room dressed up to the nines.

A noisy fan blows hot air out in the corner, but it seems fairly warm anyway.

'Do we really need that?' I ask Gavin, nodding at the heater.

'Yep. The pipes are rubbish and she likes it to be twenty-four degrees.'

'The lighting in here is terrible,' I say, spinning around, trying to find another plug socket.

'She won't have it any brighter either, and when you meet her you'll see why,' he says. 'Do you need anything before I go?'

'Where's the kitchen?'

'Down the hall, second turn on the left.'

'Where's the bathroom?'

'Hers is opposite, you can use that if you're discreet. Anything else?'

51

I rack my brain, trying to stumble across the gaps in my knowledge, all the necessary pieces of information that could be missing. Theatre is new to me, it's not my thing. I do shoots. I do hanging around all day eating crap from a van and dabbing sweat off actors or singers with a puff pad. I do wine at lunch on set and pretty much all afternoon. I do big airy warehouse spaces, not strange little rooms with scarves thrown over lamps and bad heating.

'Is Tristan crazy?' I ask finally, as it seems to be the most pertinent question I can ask. 'I mean, previews are supposed to start next week, aren't they? That's why they got me in and didn't wait for someone with theatre experience, my agency said. But it kind of . . . doesn't seem ready?'

Gavin smiles and the room feels warmer. He coughs, looks away, and then back at me. It is a theatrical move. Maybe you can't help it if you work in this environment, maybe these strange dramatic pauses and looks and asides are contagious? Maybe *everybody* here is crazy.

'Is Tristan crazy?' he repeats. 'No more than any of the rest of them. He likes the sound of his own voice. And he can be very charming, for a short bloke from Streatham with a pill habit. But you'll get used to it. He calls everybody "love" so he doesn't have to remember names. It's actually quite clever. But you're okay, you'll be Make-up.'

'Isn't it funny, I mean funny strange – maybe funny tragic for me – that one man can be so easy with it, and another so mean?' I sip my coffee and lean back on the counter.

'With what?' he asks, half of him out of the door, but still loads of him in the room.

'The L word. Love. Ben won't say it. Tristan can't stop. So is he gay?'

Gavin takes a step back into the room and pushes the door ajar behind him. 'No, not gay. I'm sure he'll tell you. He told me three days after I met him and it took him a while to warm to me, he said because of the height thing. It's . . . Tristan is a non-libidinist. That's his phrase, not mine. It means he doesn't think about sex. Or care about sex. He doesn't want sex.' Gavin's eyes widen like spaceships in his face, illuminated and strange and high up in the sky.

I stop myself taking another sip of coffee, and angle my neck to look up at him and make sure he isn't joking. But he nods his head and doesn't even smirk.

'He doesn't care about sex?' I ask.

'Nope.'

'And he doesn't think about sex?'

'Nope.'

'But men are supposed to think about sex every seven seconds or seven minutes or something, aren't they?'

Gavin coughs, embarrassed. We've spent at least half an hour together this morning . . . reckoning on those figures Gavin has felt fruity and not admitted it a few times already.

'Christ, that's the statistic that keeps me awake at night when Ben doesn't want to . . . you know . . . But Tristan doesn't even think about it? How does that work? How do you stop yourself? That would be fantastic!'

'You think? Christ, I think it would be awful.'

'But Gavin, I mean, if it didn't even bother you, if you didn't even think about it, life would be so much easier. If I didn't miss sex so much there would be far fewer problems in my relationship.'

'It's not fantastic, it's weird. And so is your bloke by the sounds of it, so don't go thinking that not thinking about sex is an answer to anything. Sex is the thing that keeps most of us going!'

'Shouldn't that be love, Gavin?'

'I'll take sex over love most days. It doesn't hurt half as much, under normal circumstances at least!'

53

I grimace at Gavin, but he just winks and I blush. It's not him, I blush if anybody winks at me. I find it intimate and peculiar and sexual. I'd blush if my own grandmother winked at me, and then of course I'd throw up.

'So Tristan doesn't have sex, ever?'

'Oh no, that's not true, I think he has it quite a bit. It's just not about him. He doesn't care if he gets it or not. I think he does it for other people . . .'

'But – I'm sorry, Gavin, for all these questions – but how does he get . . . you know . . . aroused? If he doesn't want it, or care about it?'

'My guess is Viagra. Any more questions?' Gavin pulls the door open again with one of his huge hands. He could be a one-man circus, with a few lights around his torso, offering rides on his palms for fifty pence or a pound. I'm sure I could sit in one of those hands.

'Gavin, what's your girlfriend like?'

'What's she like?'

'Is she freakishly tall too?' I smile at him and I see a smile form in his eyes in return. The big Gavin smiles must be rationed, like chocolate in the war.

'Not freakishly tall, but not short like you either.'

'I am not short, I am five foot five, which is two inches above average. Is she pretty?'

'Why all the questions about my girlfriend?'

'I'm just interested, Gavin. Other people's relationships interest me. I just wonder what you go for, what your type is. Everybody has a type. Some men just go for baubles, decoration. The only thing more attractive to a man than a beautiful woman is an easy life. And I just wondered what your type is. Beautiful or easy?'

Gavin looks at me with an element of serious concern. I don't think he likes this line of questioning. But he answers anyway.

'Arabella? She is very beautiful. And not at all easy. So there's your answer I guess.'

'Arabella from the play? But Gavin, she's stunning!'

'And?' he asks me, like a dry old maths teacher waiting for an answer from a stupid young pupil.

'And nothing, nothing at all. That wasn't surprise, I just meant . . . good for you!'

Gavin lowers his head and inspects the coffee I spat out onto his trainers, which is drying into a dirty stain that looks a bit like the birthmark on Gorbachev's forehead.

'We'll see,' he says, half out of the door now. 'She *is* gorgeous. But she's definitely not easy, and it can wear you down.'

'Not easy is the best kind!' I say, as he is almost gone, but I hear him mutter 'Tell that to your boyfriend,' just as the walkie-talkie on his belt starts spewing white noise and static, and I hear a muffled voice say,

'Dolly's at the back door.'

My door opens again and Gavin pokes his head back in. 'Dolly's arrived,' he says, and turns to leave.

'Should I wait here?' I shout, a hint of panic in my voice.

'Depends on her mood. She might throw you out, she might want to meet you straight away. You may as well stay, I suppose. I'll try and gauge how she is before she gets down here.'

'Should I be scared?' I ask him.

'I don't know, are you scared of most things?'

'It's starting to feel that way.'

'Well if you are she'll sense it, like an attack dog, so try and keep it under control. And don't worry, with any luck she'll be hammered.'

Gavin shuts the door.

I unpack and inspect my brushes to see if any of them need replacing, and open up a couple of samples that a new make-up company have sent me. I check my own hair in the mirror and mess it up a little, and re-gloss. The trouble with talking is that it wears your gloss away. I think about sitting, but I don't know where Dolly will want to sit, and I don't want her to burst in and chuck me straight back out again for nabbing her favourite spot. I try to lean back nonchalantly, cross my arms, uncross them, strike a relaxed non-fearful pose that doesn't just look ill at ease and terrified.

I spot a press pack sitting on the desk, and a picture of Tristan sticks out. Somebody has childishly drawn long eyelashes on him, and a pencil-thin moustache. Below the picture the text reads:

Directed by Tristan Mitra, Tennessee Williams's The Milk Train Doesn't Stop Here Anymore *has been staged at The Majestic once before, starring Hollywood screen idol Joanna Till. The play marks Tristan's debut in the West End, fresh from the success of his all-male adaptation of* The Sound of Music *at the Brixton Art House. He previously worked for the DSS for thirteen years, but was fired, which he believes intrinsic to his direction of the play.*

I pick up another page and see a heavily air-brushed close-up of Dolly. You can tell it's air-brushed because no matter how good the make-up there would still be the suggestion of lines around her eyes and lips, but her face is like a porcelain mask instead. I skim-read text. It mentions Laurence Olivier and David Niven, but then nothing of note for two decades, until recently when it seems she's been in some TV movies, playing '*the popular grandmother detective Mrs Mounting for the Hallmark Channel series* Mrs Mounting Investigates.' From David Niven to the Hallmark Channel then. I toss the pack back onto the counter, sit on my hands to stop them from shaking, and wait for Dolly Russell to make her grand entrance.

Scene III: History

After twenty minutes and a series of fearful moments and with still no sign or news of Dolly, I wonder if there has been some kind of problem; if she has thrown a tantrum on learning of my lack of theatre experience, or is upstairs leading a drunken conga across the stage, or has Gavin pinned to a wall somewhere, teaching him her version of living. Just then somebody begins knocking a tune on the door – tap tap, tap tap tap tap, tap tap tap tap . . . pause . . . tap tap . . . I recognise it as the Tapioca song from *Thoroughly Modern Millie*. I love musicals. Everybody in a musical is so in love with life itself that they keep bursting into song.

When I was very little and Mum had housework to do on rainy afternoons, she used to sit me and Richard in front of BBC2 to watch the likes of *Calamity Jane*, or *Seven Brides for Seven Brothers*, or *Hello Dolly*, or *Thoroughly Modern Millie*. She said she thought them far less harmful than violent cartoons starring He-Man and the Masters of the Universe that were showing on the other channel. Richard would be bored within minutes and sit in the corner scribbling with crayons or banging things. I'd get annoyed at the interruption, but not enough to turn off the TV. After about twenty minutes Mum would wander in with a bottle of polish in her hand and say, 'Oh I'll just watch this bit for five minutes' as the seven brothers high-kicked at a barn dance, or Julie Andrews sang 'Babyface', then she'd settle down on the sofa. After a couple of minutes, when I was certain she was staying put, I'd get up and go and sit next to mum, curling up on the sofa beside her. She'd tuck me under her arm and stroke my hair as she hummed along to the songs and the rain poured down outside, flooding the holes in the driveway, and Richard scribbled joyously on his paper – and then the walls – in the corner.

I shout 'Come in' but the tapping continues, so I trip to the door and throw it open. Tristan Mitra practically falls through.

'Tristan?'

'Make-up!' he exclaims with a beam. I smile back at him. 'Why were you tapping the Tapioca song on my door?' I ask.

'What better song to tap?' he asks, and because I don't have an answer we stand in what could be an uncomfortable silence, before it is mercifully shattered by Tristan exploding with laughter, a false falsetto laugh that catches us both off-guard.

'Are you looking for Dolly?' I ask him, straightening my skirt, ruffling up my hair.

'Not at all, not one bit. I was looking for you! Looking at you. You really are quite gorgeous, but then you know that. Of course you know that, what beautiful woman isn't aware of the effect she has on the people around her, but is it a curse as well, I wonder? Does it leave you slightly bewildered, Make-up, when somebody isn't quite as impressed with you as you think they should be? So much so that it has you reaching for the lipstick and the diet books?'

'I'm sorry, Tristan, I don't think I remember the question . . .'

He waves his hand, it isn't important.

'I thought you might want me to fill you in on the theatre, and Dolly herself, before the old monster descends.'

He turns his hands into claws, makes his teeth into fangs, and pretends to walk down some stairs. He looks like he is attempting the *Thriller* dance. I don't know how to react and he laughs again, hard and loud like a punch in the air.

I think he must have found those uppers.

'That would be helpful, Tristan, if you wouldn't mind, if you have time. I really don't know much about this theatre stuff at all, or Dolly, and I feel that I should . . .'

Tristan moves into the little room and suddenly it feels crowded and claustrophobic, what with the lilies and the velvet and the cards, and Tristan as well, who seems to be everywhere all at once. He is half the size of Gavin, but twice the presence. I tuck myself away in the corner by my make-up box, but he wanders over and stands in front of the brushes laid out on the table, appraising them seriously.

'Smoke and mirrors, smoke . . . and . . . mirrors . . .' He selects a cheekbone brush of fine hair and, with closed eyes, sweeps it down the length of his nose.

Opening his eyes slowly he turns to face me.

'So, The Majestic Theatre.' He gestures around him with a sweeping motion of his arms. 'Well. I always say that if you're going to fill a gap you should fill it completely. Let's start at the beginning.' He taps the end of my nose with the brush delicately, and then steps back to appraise his work.

'The Majestic Theatre on Long Acre, Covent Garden, was commissioned in 1880. Queen Victoria instructed that somebody build a "beautiful building to fill an ugly space, and quick!"' he says, doing a fair impression of the Queen's low, moneyed voice, while simultaneously his eyebrows tango and his chin tucks into his neck to signify an old lady's multiple chins. 'But it was twelve spiteful years in the making. The first of those years was spent attempting to evict the tramps and drunks and whores who lived on the intended site, a sprawling old hat factory, wrenched from the family Hobson – hat makers for three centuries – after William Hobson the ninth dabbled with opium to ease the pain from his arthritis and became joyfully addicted. Lucky bastard.' Tristan smiles and circles the make-up brush on my cheek softly and slowly as if to aid concentration.

'Of course, the family didn't realise before it was too late that their profits and their business were going up in smoke – ha! So, ignored by the bank, which had more pressing concerns in India and America, Hobson's hat factory became three floors of filth and sin. But the drunks and the tramps and the whores are the most resilient of us all, Make-up, clutching on to life, so far down that there are no rules, getting by because not getting by is the graveyard. Hobson's hat factory was their home, and there's no place like home. They kept coming back. And who can blame them?'

Bored with the cheekbone brush, Tristan replaces it on the side and addresses the counter as he searches for a new and exciting tool.

'Each night they were herded up and horded out with horns and whistles and truncheons and punches, to allow the necessary preparations for the following night's demolition. But by midday they were grubbily sneaking past the hired security, or getting them drunk on cheap vodka, or laid, or high! Wonderful, wonderful, ingenious! And so the process would begin again that night, with whistles and bells and punches, a mini war, before the place could be blown. But by the following midday they were back again . . .'

'Tristan?' I interrupt, as he flicks the back of his hand with an eyebrow brush, 'how do you know all of this?'

'Research, Make-up.'

'Oh,' I say. 'It must have taken you ages!'

'Not really. I could tell you the same about most of the theatres. I have to know the history of a theatre before I work there. It would be like you applying a new eye-shadow, say, to a client, and not knowing where it came from or what was in it . . .' he says with a smile.

'Oh. Right. Exactly,' I say, desperately trying to remember any of the eye shadow science I learnt at college. Nope, mostly forgotten.

'Where was I?' he asks.

'Drunks and whores who wouldn't leave,' I say.

'Right. Well. One black January London night when the construction unit had taken all that they could, soaked in swearing and spitting and the vomit and faeces being thrown at them in buckets, and the urine being sprayed on them from third-floor windows like vile spurts from peculiar water pistols, they took action. Forty-seven drunks and tramps and whores vanished the night they blew up the old hat factory, at one a.m.'

Tristan widens his eyes.

'Hell!' I say, appalled.

'The explosion woke the bits of the city that were sleeping, but nobody cared. And by nine a.m. all the rubble had been cleared.'

'My God, they just blew up all those people?' I ask, confused.

Tristan nods his head theatrically.

'Yes, Make-up, they did. Business is business, and they had plans in place, people were already on the payroll. The architect of The Majestic, Henry Lee, was the brother of the renowned architect Charles Lee, who had just remodelled Her Majesty's Theatre into an Opera House to gushing critical acclaim. *The Times* said, "*Charles Lee uses line with a conventional splendour.*" Henry was twelve years younger than Charles, but two inches taller and with size twelve feet. Their mother had been startled by the pregnancy that was Henry, believing that at thirty-four she was well past child-bearing age. Henry had always felt like a mistake, poor bastard. His mother looked bemused when she saw him. His father, the civil servant Charles Lee Senior, met Henry's adoring stares with a mixture of irritation and anger. When Henry's mother died of a blood disease at forty-four, Charles Lee Senior took a ten-year-old Henry to one side at her burial and whispered, "It was you. You were too much for her."'

Tristan says it in a thick, comical Irish accent.

'Tristan, are you making this up?' I ask, irritated that he has taken me for a fool.

'No! Absolutely not! Make-up, what would make you say such a thing?'

'Well, you didn't say they were Irish for a start.'

'That was just for colour, Make-up – do you want this to be interesting or not?'

'Can't you just tell me about Dolly now?' I ask, fidgeting.

'Soon, Make-up. Patience is a virtue. Cleanliness is next to Godliness and patience is the hobby of angels.'

I sigh. He gives me a reproachful look and carries on.

'The Majestic was Henry's first commission, and a fateful one. He dreamt of six tiers to seat two thousand people, but was plagued by doubts and insecurities, violently ripping up new plans, sometimes throwing them on the fire and beginning again. Then there would be nine tiers, then twelve, then twenty! At the age of thirty-three he had been drinking heavily for eight years, to soften London's hard edges, even though he knew that softening hard edges was not necessarily an advantage for an architect. Henry had recently fallen savagely and obsessively in love with a Spanish prostitute named Vanessa who had long, thick dark hair like a mare's, and which had never been cut. It was overrun with lice like wood mice in a forest but Henry didn't care. She had large pendulous breasts that sat heavily on her chest, ravaged by little stretch marks where the pendulums began to swing. This was Henry's favorite spot – he would lay his head on those tears after six or seven minutes of furious drunken lovemaking that inevitably ended shamefully limp. He would weep quietly as she tickled his cheek with strands of her long, black, infested hair.'

'Yuk,' I whisper, grimacing.

'Close your eyes and have some humanity,' he says to me, as he sweeps a brush across my eyelids. 'All of the money from The Majestic's commission was quickly slipping away, spent on cheap sloe gin and night after night with Vanessa, who had got wise to the drunken architect's feelings and upped her prices. But that's women for you. And poor Henry was in love, helpless in the face of her inflation. When his pockets were finally empty he began stalking her late into the night, jumping clumsily out from the shadows, tripping over his drunken size twelve feet only to blow her a kiss and run away. Vanessa carried on whoring, Henry carried on behaving erratically, and The Majestic's construction faltered as more plans were thrown on the fire. Finally, the foreman, frustrated by Henry's absence from the site for five straight days, called his brother, Charles Lee, to report Henry missing. Henry was found three days later on the floor of an old boarding house in Hoxton, with a bottle of whiskey in one hand, a gun in the other, and the original set of plans laying face up on his chest, dusted with blood. A single gunshot to his head had finished him off, or maybe it was Vanessa, or maybe it was The Majestic.'

'Oh no, how terrible!' I say, instinctively covering my mouth with my hand.

Tristan removes it and places it on my lap.

'Wait, it gets worse. Charles Lee wiped the blood from the plans, accepted the commission to finish The Majestic for five times the fee that had already been paid to his dead brother, and reworked them. A strangely sober three-tier theatre was completed on Long Acre in 1892. It still had the curved lines of Henry's original plan, shaped like a sympathetic woman, but the softer edges had been hardened, to ensure it stayed up when horses trotted past.

'Unfortunately for the theatre's investors the shows that had been scheduled to appear at The Majestic had long since found alternate sites, some of them enjoying splendid runs that had already come to an end! The theatre, although completed, stood empty for fifteen months. Then in 1893 Dickie Black and Leonard White of the Black and White Circus enquired whether the large, vacant, sad and lonely building on Long Acre with a flaking painted sign hanging over its curved entrance still had its entertainment licence, and whether it was for sale. The investors had just that week taken the expensive decision to have it demolished and the land sold on, but instead took a very reasonable price, and had none of the trouble of getting rid of the sad old girl.

'Black and White immediately posted a huge red and gold sign below The Majestic that read, "*Coming Soon! Black & White's Freaks Circus of Passion, Politics, Fairytale and Violence.*" Six weeks later they replaced the '*Coming Soon!*' with a '*Now Open!*'. It became an instant hit with local workers, soldiers in from the docks, drunks and whores and commoners and thieves. Bearded ladies and midgets galloped around the stage nightly, drinking their way through every show, spraying their audience with whiskey and ignoring the fights and the flatulence, laughing and shouting and swearing at the audience and each other. The performances became more and more debauched, full nudity was de rigueur by the time the police moved in one sticky summer night in 1899, closing the act and the theatre down for breaching public decency laws and open acts of pornography.

'Black and White hotfooted it to Venice rather than face the pornography rap, plus a second and more sinister charge of attempting to breed freaks by mating them. The Majestic stood cold and lonely again through two punishing winters.'

'No, Tristan,' I put my hand up. 'Stop it now. You are making it up. Nobody breeds freaks,' I say, shaking my finger at him reproachfully.

'Oh, Make-up, so naïve. They still do it to this day in some of the southern states of America.' Tristan nods his head at me convincingly.

'Shut up, no they don't, you are being ridiculous.' I stand up but Tristan pushes me back down onto my stool.

'Make-up, I'm not finished. And who has done the research, you or me? And who wants to look like a fool in front of Dolly Russell, perhaps the last true Hollywood starlet, when she asks you what you know about theatre?'

'I can just say some stuff about plays and things. I've read some . . . Arthur Miller,' I say, thankful that I could remember the name of an American playwright.

'And the cartoon section in the *Sunday Times* as well, Make-up? Come on now, sit down, you need to know this.'

Tristan is obviously enjoying himself.

'But don't you have stuff to do?' I ask, exhausted.

'Yes. This. Now, in March 1901, looking for a venue to stage his dancing act The Sabines, Pierre Christophe Magrine, a French businessman who had made a name for himself as a slick mover amongst his contemporaries, and the chorus girls if you get my gist, bought The Majestic as a venue for his style of evening entertainment. On the day the renovators removed the boards from the entrance, triumphantly kicking the door down, an evil stench seeped out. Covering their mouths with handkerchiefs, swiping at their watering eyes, they weaved their way to the back of the stage, following the smell as it became increasingly passionate, leading them finally to a small locked cupboard, big enough for a chair and a mirror and a shelf. Evil curiosity made them break that door down too, and a dozen well-fed screaming rats hurtled out across their feet. The workmen found the bearded lady decomposed in her dressing room. She still sat stiffly on a small chair in front of a mirror that had been smashed. By the streaks of blood on the glass it was fair to say that punching her reflection had been the dying act of a circus freak. The floor of the theatre was littered in rat droppings, and the walls were stained sticky and brown with cigarette tar, but The Majestic was cleaned up again.'

'She killed herself because she was ugly?' I ask, appalled.

'Not just ugly, Make-up, a freak.'

'But lots of women have hair on their faces, most girls wax, or laser, or whatever . . .'

'Not back then, Make-up. Back then it made you a freak, and freaks don't get married and have kids and get loved back.'

'Yes they do, that's an awful thing to say! You don't just love somebody because of the way they look . . .' I admonish him, slapping away the brush he's been running up and down my nose.

'Hush, Make-up. No lies in here please, let me finish my story. The Sabines – feathered, sequinned and high-kicking – remained at the theatre for nine years before Magrine set sail for Hollywood and the moving pictures. By this time The Majestic had established itself as a popular venue for light entertainment. Magrine sold the theatre on to a fresh set of investors, and a new management board was established. A series of light comedies played throughout 1910 and 1911, decadent and fun and attended mostly by lower middle-class workers, but disaster struck in 1912 when a discarded cigarette in a props cupboard sparked a blaze that had, by the time the firemen arrived, gutted the entire front and back of stage. All sets were destroyed, as was the curtain and the boxes. The roof had substantial fire damage, as the heat had crept quickly up the walls, and the building was judged to be unsound unless the top tier was pulled out. One unusually mild September night in 1913, The Majestic went from holding a spectacular one thousand seats to a mere six hundred and forty-three. Some of the bigger bitches of the time suggested that "The Majestic" was far too grand a name for a two-tiered theatre, and that it should be changed . . . But after an extensive renovation that lasted five years and employed the art deco style so popular in Paris at the time, although in clumsy contrast to the front of house, The Majestic, still known as The Majestic, reopened in 1918.'

'Ta da!' I say. 'And then they showed some plays, and then it was Dolly Russell's turn, and then . . . '

'Stop it. I've nearly finished.' Tristan glares at me.

'Do you promise? I feel like I'm back in my history A-level,' I say.

'But weren't they good times?' he asks.

I think about history class, sitting next to Helen, flirting with Simon Howells across the room over textbooks filled with black and white pictures of war.

'Yes, actually,' I admit with a shrug.

'Good. Then learn something new. The Majestic became known for its musical theatre, staging 267 performances of *No, No, Nanette* before it transferred to The Palace Theatre at Cambridge Circus. And although The Majestic fared well in the Twenties with numerous Noël Coward productions, nothing ever seemed to really take off. The Majestic just couldn't get a hit. It became known amongst actors and crew as a "warm up" theatre, with shows that sold reasonably but

rarely sold out. It was then that The Majestic earned its nickname, in theatre circles, as The Bridesmaid. For example . . .'
He takes a step back and strikes an affected pose.

'Fur and feathers and lipstick: "*What's next for you, darling?*"'

He jumps a foot and turns to face the space he has vacated.

'Cravat, purple shirt and slacks: "*I'm starting rehearsals next month for Noël Coward at The Bridesmaid, darling.*"'

A jump. 'Fur and feathers and lipstick: "*Where were you hoping for, darling?*"'

Jump. 'Cravat, purple shirt and slacks: "*The Apollo. Damned shame. Maybe next year. Drink, darling?*"'

He stands still and straightens his now-crooked glasses.

'A faulty oil lamp started the blaze that ravaged the old girl again, in 1931. It swept through The Bridesmaid like fleas in a halfway house, killing two tramps who slept under the sympathetic curves of the front entrance each night. The theatre was left for dead for two years, occasionally sighing and groaning to let Londoners know it was still there. She was past her best, charred and black with soot, damp from fire hoses, with rotting carpets and rats, the terrible rats, infesting her again, chewing at her insides. A sad and lonely old Bridesmaid, hoping for a little luck and love.'

'Why are you looking at me like that, I have luck and . . .' My words trail off.

'Make-up, don't be so sensitive. The Majestic was spectacularly reopened on the third of September 1939! Ta da! Of course, the timing was a little unfortunate, and her big night was dampened spitefully by the speech made by Neville Chamberlain at eleven fifteen that morning –

"*This country is at war with Germany . . . now may God bless you all, and may he defend the right. For it is evil things that we shall be fighting against . . .*" Still, the old girl was up and running again just in time: some nights they acted by candlelight, some nights they acted in the dark, which was more than could be said for other prettier theatres who dropped their curtain at the first sound of a siren.

'Ivor Novello musicals trilled though the Forties and Fifties, with their beguiling talk of kingdoms of love and beauty and starlight, stepping lightly aside for the more sombre, stern faces of *The Postman Always Knocks Twice* and *A Streetcar Named Desire* as the Sixties drew in. *The Milk Train Doesn't Stop Here Anymore* first opened in 1968.'

'With Joanna Till?' I ask, feeling, finally, like I can contribute – I read that name in the press pack.

'That's right. Well done. Gold star. Initially it was a far from controversial or even noteworthy opening. Lacking the public pulling power of *Cat on a Hot Tin Roof*, or *Streetcar*, the critics called it a *"strange little play for the strangest little theatre in the West End, and surely only being staged as a vanity project for Joanna Till."* '

'Joanna Till had been one of the first studio stars in her youth, an international beauty with platinum curls that framed a pale complexion and a perfect cupid's bow permanently painted on her delicate lips throughout the 1920s. By the time she came to play Mrs Goforth, the dying monster at the heart of the play – who has seen off numerous husbands and is now a recluse in an Italian villa dictating her memoirs to her young and beleaguered assistant – Joanna was an alcoholic who ate barely one meal a day, and whom few saw out of make-up. But an old beauty still sang in her eyes, reminding those close enough that she was once the greatest prize to be won, the cup on the table, the lady in the booth at the front of the mile-long "dime for a kiss" queue. The memory of what she had been haunted all of her movements. Her fingers danced and flickered nervously about her face, trying to cover every line simultaneously, attempting to distract any audience from the age that had set in and which now clung to her once-beautiful features like an evil moss to smooth pebbles in a lake.

'One of the only members of the company that she allowed close was her young co-star Edward "Teddy" Hampden, who played the impertinent but handsome visitor Chris, and who, at thirty-five, was twenty-eight years Joanna's junior.'

'Good for her!' I mutter, but Tristan ignores me.

'Joanna could be heard giggling from behind her dressing-room door in the afternoons, after matinee and before evening. She rarely spent any time alone, aside from "the half" – the half an hour before each performance when she would shoo away her young admirer and compose herself. But even then, occasionally, he was allowed back in. The controversy murmured in every nook of The Bridesmaid. Teddy shot Joanna through the heart, six hours after she finished their affair over a cajun salmon lunch at the Savoy.'

I gasp. Tristan nods his head seriously.

'Although they had been involved for barely three months they were being too indiscreet, and news had reached her husband, the world-famous director Sir Terence Till. Sir Terence placed an outraged and irate long-distance call from a set in Egypt telling Joanna to behave. Teddy at least had the decency to turn the gun on himself afterwards, aiming straight through his heart as well. So the strange little play's curtain failed to rise the following night, as both the leads' hearts were streaked across a dressing-room wall.'

I look around urgently – 'Not this room, Tristan? Not these walls?' – feeling a cold chill run down my spine, the kind you get when you are a kid and somebody pokes out the game 'Does-this-make-your-blood-run-cold?', finishing with a grab on the back of your neck. I shudder.

'It's possible,' he says, seriously, 'it's very possible. Anyway, controversy courted The Majestic again six years later, in

November 1974, when a performance of *Hair* so shocked a four-hundred-pound Presbyterian Texan banker that he suffered a massive heart attack in the second row. The banker died, and so did the show, after two months and below-average ticket sales, even for The Bridesmaid.'

'We should move to another venue,' I say earnestly, nodding my head, ready to pack up my things and dust off the bad luck I can feel settling in on me and Tristan as we sit for too long in one place in this cursed theatre.

'Too late, the tickets have been sold, Make-up. Then, in 1981, as a protest against the Falklands war, some of the younger members of the cast of *The Iceman Cometh* – the ones blessed with better bodies and less inhibition – seized the opportunity to host a naked sit-in on the stage of The Majestic. It quickly descended into a televised orgy that had to be disbanded by policemen in plastic gloves. It was the sight of the gloves that my mum, actually, remembered from the six o'clock news that evening. She hadn't spotted the blink-and-you-missed-it glimpse of an erect penis on television, the first to officially appear on UK terrestrial TV, according to *The Guinness Book of Records*. But she saw the gloves. Typical mum, ha!' he says, shaking his head affectionately.

'So then The Majestic closed, again, for refurbishment in 1989, looking sad and tired, and in desperate need of a facelift, Botox, any and all kinds of surgery that might be on offer. It reopened in 1995, polished and tightened, but some say lacking some of its old character.'

'I wish you hadn't told me the shooting bit,' I say, looking around me feeling creepy, 'I'm going to have trouble going to the kitchen on my own now.'

'Stop it, Make-up, you're a grown woman. So! That brings us up-to-date. *The Milk Train Doesn't Stop Here Anymore*, starring Dolly Russell, and directed by me, Tristan Mitra, will mark her return to the London stage for the first time in eighteen years!' Tristan swirls on the spot and claps his hands like he's just finished conducting a big band.

'And, so, what about Dolly?' I ask, exasperated.

'Oh yes, of course, Dolly. What can I tell you about Dolly Russell? Other than that she drugged the last Make-up? Ha! Don't be put off by that! It just shows guile. Well,' he hushes his voice to a low murmur, to a purr, 'I don't know how old she is . . . maybe seventy-two, maybe sixty-eight, it's hard to say. But she hasn't been on stage for over fifteen years. I've barely had her up there yet, without some screaming match or tantrum or silent seething fit. And that's just me. Ha.'

He picks up my large powder brush. Its bristles still sparkle silver from my last job on Friday, glistening up dancers for the cover of a disco album – two emaciated eighteen-year-old girls who ate half a bag of crisps each on a twelve-hour shoot. Tristan dusts his face with it lightly, breathing in while he does. He leans towards me and, with serious intent, dusts my cheeks with it too. I step back a little, against the counter. He stares at me. I realise that I am his new Girls World. I just hope he doesn't try to cut my hair with nail scissors.

'The light in here is really bad,' I say, embarrassed, 'it's far too dark.'

'Shush,' he says, and moves my arms that I have crossed against my chest back down to my sides, like a shop mannequin.

'She didn't get her Oscar until she was thirty-three, for *The Queen Wants a King*. Have you seen it?'

'I don't think so.'

He picks up another brush, flicks it against his palm, and puts it down again. I want to tell him to stop now but I don't.

'It's very good. It's the only role I've seen her in with no vanity. Isn't that ironic? They demand she be painted and pretty at all times but they give her an Oscar for being plain, as if being ugly were such an impossible task for her that they had to reward it . . . Do you think it's harder to be beautiful or plain, Make-up? I mean, in the mornings, how long does it take you? Because you're a beauty, but I can tell it needs a little work now. A little more effort than it was five years ago, right?'

'Maybe a little,' I say, cringing at the thought of the price of my night cream, and my day cream, and my paraffin cleanser.

'And a little more moisturiser than before? A little more time spent slicking away at those laughter lines?' He picks up a tub of thick cream, and scoops a dessert spoonful onto the back of his hand. He sticks a deliberate finger into it and draws it out slowly, so that a dollop sits clumsily on its end. Reaching out, he takes my arm, and absent-mindedly smears the cream up and down my skin, rubbing it in smoothly as he traces the veins from my wrist to my elbow with his finger. He holds my arm firmly at the wrist with his other hand. I don't pull away but I feel that if I did he would grip it a little tighter, a little firmer, and resist. I am being seduced by a man with no interest in sex. I am certain he knows the effect that he has.

'But it's still worth it of course, all the effort, isn't it? It's still worth the lingering looks on the tube, and the glances that you notice as you walk down the street, the smiles and the winks. The men who can't turn away, who will picture you later, picture you tonight, think of you instead of their dowdy other halves. These men who think you're out of their league, who would love to have a piece of you, an afternoon slice of you with their tea. It's worth that extra twenty minutes in the morning, isn't it, for the approval, isn't it, Make-up?'

73

Tristan dips his little finger into a pot of thick sticky silver glitter. It's not mine, I don't know what it is used for. *Starlight Express* maybe? When he removes his finger the glitter is dripping off it like honey fresh from the pot trickling off Pooh's paws. Nearby, maybe two or three rooms away, a woman is singing 'Somewhere over the Rainbow' soft and high. It feels like midnight.

'Absolutely,' I whisper. He leans towards me again. With one hand on my shoulder for balance, he raises himself up onto his toes so that we are face to face as he smudges the glitter across my lower lip with his little finger. I find it impossible to believe that he has no libido. Maybe it's a rumour that he has spread himself as a cunning plan, like the men who tell women they are gay so that they will let them fondle their breasts. Or was it just me that fell for that, late one night in Gerry's? (When should I start to worry that the extent of my experience is 'late one night in Gerry's'?) And I've done far worse than that.

'She's been married four times,' Tristan says, still staring at me but rubbing his hands together to get rid of the last drops of cream and glitter, 'and has one daughter, whom she never sees – I think she might live in upstate New York near her dad, Dolly's third husband, I believe, the actor Peter Deakin. He did a lot horror stuff, he was the wolf man for a while. I think the daughter's name is Chloe, but she'll tell you if she wants to. And when you meet her, when you meet Dolly, you'll realise she must have been quite something, way back when.'

He reaches for a tissue and wipes his hands, before tossing it casually on the floor, and I lean down to pick it up and throw it in the bin.

Tristan smiles and says 'control, I see' when I do this. I shrug and smile an apology.

He looks at himself in the mirror, touching his hair lightly, straightening his jacket, flicking a speck of white something off his collar.

'Your bloke,' he says, still looking at himself. 'A bit of a monster, is he? A bit of a hound?'

'Not at all, not a monster. Just . . . disinterested . . . not as enthusiastic as I'd like him to be.'

'Ah, but is he disinterested in life as well?'

'No. There are things that he likes, that he loves – PlayStation games, and childish films and things . . .'

'Do you think he's being cruel to you?'

'No, I don't think so.' I thrust my hands into my hair and deliberately mess it up. It's supposed to be messed up, that's the look that I want. Not too polished. Black eyes and gloss and messy hair. I like the drama of it – it counteracts my reality.

'So it's not deliberate, this disinterest, it's not controlling?'

'No, I just think . . . he's gone off me, maybe . . . or . . .'

'You think about it a lot, don't you? You talk about it a lot. I've only just met you, this is the second conversation we've had, and we're talking about it again . . . does that seem a little strange, a little self-involved, if you stop and think about it?'

I don't know how to explain to Tristan that it is what we do these days: figure out ways to be perfect. Isn't that the point? Talk about it and thrash it out and pull your life apart, tear it into pieces to find the bits that don't work and try and toss them out and put it back together. Every TV show that we watch and get hooked on and cry in front of and that exposes all our faults has made pop psychologists out of all of us, hasn't it? That's what we do now! Rip ourselves apart to find the flaws. I don't know who I am supposed to be obsessed with, if not myself? And if I'm not obsessed with anybody, or anything, then what will I do with all that thinking time on the tube or the bus, or staring off into space while I stir my Alpen? I hear talk of people who 'let things go', who say 'fuck it' to diets and their hair and their relationships and love. But that's just propaganda, surely? I don't know anybody who actually lives like that. Nobody really feels like enough any more, do they? Not here at least. And now Tristan is saying I am obsessed with my love life, but who else is there to be obsessed with it, if not me? Certainly not Ben!

'Well, it's a big deal when you're going through it, maybe the biggest thing. And anyway, you brought it up this time, Tristan.'

'Yes I did, didn't I? I wonder if you are just trying to muster up the courage? To say goodbye? If you are slowly putting yourself back onto the market, before it's too late. It's not too late yet, Make-up, they'll still fall at those pointed heels of yours.'

'I don't know about that, I . . . God, I don't know, I don't want to think about it like that, I just want to work it out with Ben.'

'But clearly he doesn't love you, or he loves somebody else, somebody new, perhaps? Or somebody still?' He looks at me in the mirror, and sees my mouth fall open.

I wonder if it is Tristan who is being cruel. He has stumbled over my darkest fears almost straight away, but it feels like he is toying with me. There is a camp menace to him, like Hannibal Lecter playing with make-up brushes. I sit back a little further in my seat in case he decides to take a quick and sudden bite out of my nose.

'I guess I'm just trying to work it all out, in my own head,' I say.

'Do you have any proof?' he asks, matter-of-factly.

'Of what?'

'Of infidelity, adultery – that your man is ripping at the flesh of another?'

'Yes. I think so, anyway. I found a text from his ex, saying that she couldn't meet him as arranged 'later that night', with a kiss. And he told me that was the night he was going out with his mate. But when I confronted him he wasn't even angry that I had checked his phone, he just seemed relieved that I believed him when he said it was a mistake. She meant to send it to somebody else, he said. It didn't actually have his name in it, so I believed him. But I shook and cried for fifteen minutes.'

'So you don't trust him at all?'

Tristan watches himself as he thrusts out his Adam's apple, and his crotch as well, as he talks. He juts out those parts of him that make him a man, but then counters it with a strange swish of his hand, or lightness of touch. It all seems very deliberate, experimental. He is trying to find the moves that work.

'I would trust him, if he could just articulate how he felt, sometimes, about me, but he never does. I feel terrible for not trusting him sometimes. I don't know what goes on in his head.'

'Nor he yours, I'm guessing. And don't feel terrible yet, you might be right! But he told you once? I mean, you fell for him once?'

'He started, but then he stopped. He kind of drew me in, then closed the door. But it's as if I'm halfway through . . .'

'Your leg is caught in his door?'

'Something like that, I suppose.' I laugh sharply.

'Ha! And you don't know whether it will hurt more to try and push the door open, or tear your leg back out!' Tristan folds and unfolds the cuffs on his polo-neck jumper.

'Well . . .' He takes a deep breath and finally looks away from the mirror,

'I need to think about this one some more. The only thing I can offer, from my twisted perspective, love, is that what makes a woman of forty more attractive than a girl of eighteen is not her body but her confidence. Don't fold, Make-up. Don't dither. Toughen up. Let's have some fun.'

'I'm thirty-one. I'm not forty,' I say, as I feel stupid tears rush to my eyes.

'I didn't say that you were, Make-up. Now, how do you feel about nudity?'

'I'm sorry?'

'Nudity, how do you feel about it, and in particular cast session nudity?'

'Uncomfortable pretty much sums it up.'

'But what if it were just me? You see, I've been body-brushing with a toothbrush recently, rather than following any traditional bathing ritual, and I wonder if it doesn't give me a shine that I'd like to share. I've been reading a lot about Major General Charles Orde Wingate, heard of him?'

'Well, Tristan, I can't say that I have . . .' The tears recede and I can't help but smile.

'Churchill described him as a man of genius, who might have become a man of destiny. But he died, in a burning crash of a plane, in Burma. 1944.'

'Okay . . . and he used to conduct sessions in the nude?'

'Hmm? Yes, yes, he did. Of course his were with soldiers, but I think there might be something in it. Strip away our pretensions, make us real, cut to the chase. Beauty is truth after all. If we were all a little nude, once a day, the world would be a much less violent place. I know it's a fucking cliché but I believe it. Of course there is always the danger that somebody is going to become unspeakably aroused, but that doesn't really affect me . . . Do you know he inflicted some terrible defeats on his enemies, on the invincible Japanese! And he believed the best way to survive tropical heat was a diet of raw onions.'

'Have you tried that as well?'

'Yes, I tried. It gets tropical in Streatham in August. But it gave me terrible flatulence. I was like a human wind machine, and the stench! It is impossible to function when you are terrified to be in small spaces, afraid of what your own body might inflict upon those around you . . . I couldn't be in here, right now, with you, if I were still doing it. Of course sometimes it was wonderfully amusing, it depended on the company. In lifts, hilarious! Inevitably it was my mother that made me stop. She's a wonderful woman but with little tolerance for anything other than her own peculiar rituals. It's nothing to do with her legs, she's just that way.'

'Her legs?' I ask.

'They barely work any more,' he replies, nodding.

I remember reading in the *Standard* that he lives with his mother in Streatham, and that she is disabled, but I can't remember how it happened.

'Why don't they work?' I ask, trying my best to seem sincere and not just nosey.

'She has a tumour, Make-up, that is pressing down on her spinal cord, and is hard for them to reach without risking complete paralysis. She says that she is lucky, of course, that it has only affected the lower half of her body, but that's bullshit. She's a religious woman, and I thank God that she is, even though of course I don't believe in it at all.'

I want to say, 'But you've just thanked God', but decide that now isn't the time.

'So she fell over one day and never got up. Dad's dead, so that's that. She's going nowhere, and she cooks a wonderful lamb curry, and . . .' He nods his head quietly, and squeezes his eyes shut.

I don't know what else to say, so I change the subject.

'Do you think Dolly might be here soon, Tristan?'

He presses the balls of his palms into the sockets of his eyes. 'I fucking hope so, love, otherwise we'll never open!'

he shouts, and whips away his hands to clap loudly, spinning in a full circle and biting his lower lip with his teeth, thrusting his groin back and forth like a 1970s porn star, like some second-rate Russ Meyer gyrating horror.

'Are you okay then?' he asks me.

'Yes, but I think I need biscuits.'

'Kitchen's down the hall, didn't bouncy Gavin show you?'

'He told me, I'll find it, it's fine.'

'Lovely Gavin, I have to remind myself that he's not, you know, slow . . . simple, retarded, him being so big. But he's sharp as a tack really. Acid-tongued. I like it. It keeps me on my toes.'

'Okay, well I'm going to go and find those biscuits I think.'

'Good for you, but just the one, mind! Keep your chin up, Make-up. Stop thinking about your bloke if you can. We aren't worth it!' He throws me a huge grin – he doesn't believe that for a second.

'I'll try,' I say, and edge past him to leave. He trots off in the other direction, singing what sounds like 'Anything Goes' segued into 'Let's Get It On'.

I edge down a grey hallway, in and out of the patches of dirty light cast by infrequent and dim bulbs, speeding up through the strange shadowy spots that make me nervous with Tristan's talk of shootings and blood-spattered walls. My heels clicking on the hard cold floor announce me to any potential murderers or psychopaths or evil spirits lurking behind dark doorways: they'll hear me coming and be fully prepared to leap out and grab me, pull me into the darkness with them, smother my face and paw me to near death. I am convinced that's what will happen. I make this daily exhibition of myself, in my heels and my skirts and my gloss, and I put myself on show even though I know that it is dangerous. I don't go unnoticed, and it's a cracked-up world.

Soho is full of loners and losers, producers and pirates, prostitutes and pimps, directors and producers and more producers. Everybody claiming to produce something, so where is it all? I click my way into everybody's view, and it's a perilous route to take. Two roads diverged in a wood, and I – I took the one with the biggest audience, and that has made all the difference. My heels tap out 'look at me, look at me, look at me', and by the way please note that I won't be able to run that fast in three and a half inch stilettos. It is as if I have accepted my fate. I'll be strangled with my own sparkly scarf, a victim of my own need to be appreciated in a world full of crazies.

In a badly lit 1970s kitchen that is dusted in crumbs I hunt through grubby cupboards for some Digestives or Rich Tea.

'Can I help?'

Someone is lurking in the doorway behind me and I freeze, one arm in the cupboard, precariously reaching out on tiptoes back to the furthest corners, looking for the good biscuits that have been scrupulously hidden.

What if I just don't turn around?

'Can I help you?' he says again, but louder this time, and yet I sense he doesn't move an inch, he doesn't come and reach for the biscuits for me. He doesn't really mean to help. What he means is 'turn around and let me see you'.

I rest my weight back onto my heels and drop my arms in exhaustion. I recognise his voice. I don't want to turn around.

'I was just trying to find some biscuits.' I address the Cortina-beige wall in front of me.

There is a dramatic pause, so dramatic it would be noted in a script and the audience might be fooled into holding their breath. I hold mine . . .

'I know you,' he says, quietly, evenly, 'have we worked together before?'

My heart sinks like Leo at the end of *Titanic*.

'Only at Gerry's,' I say.

And still I don't turn around.

It was spring. It was the first week after the clocks had changed, when you feel that extra hour of daylight every evening enriches your life. Every year, that first week after the clocks change, the light takes us all by surprise, and I feel enlivened and hopeful for a summer of love and laughter and finally fulfilled dreams. That first week after the clocks change is the most magical week of the year.

I was working a nothing job that day, which paid only average money. A reality-TV star was filming his exercise video. We were in a studio located off a newly sanitised Carnaby Street. It's all flagship sports stores now, surf brands and trendy trainers. More thought goes into the image on the front of the plastic bags than it does to war or peace or revolution or anarchy or any of those things, that don't seem relevant any more to girls who like to shop and boys who like to watch football. Apathy and the end of conscription go hand in hand, at least that's what my grandfather used to say. The only people that care are extremists. Protesting at anything these days seems at best disruptive, at worst showing off. Just shop instead. I don't even protest at the interest rates on my store cards. Walk through central London on a Saturday waving a placard with a group of gypsies with dogs on bits of string? For what? The spirit of Carnaby, of fashion or punk or change, has become nothing more than a *Daily Mail* headline, a national ticking-off at the odd drug habit. Nothing is persuasive enough to sweep us up, up and away any more. The only counter-culture I'm interested in is the Benefit counter in Selfridges. That's just the way it is. Some things change. Unless I want to picket Chanel to use fatter, shorter models because this impossibly young and impossibly skinny ideal is starting to hurt me, at thirty-one and one hundred and forty pounds. But then I just look unattractive because I can't keep up, because I'm not pretty enough or skinny enough any more. Better to just take a little longer in front of the mirror, spend a little more on powder and paint, and pray that nobody notices.

I had been propositioned three times already that day by the reality star, but each time he failed to realise that he had already met me, and only half an hour earlier had asked me if I'd like to do a line of coke and give him a quick hand-job in the ladies' toilets. I politely declined both. He was a charmless farmer from Devon called Roger, devoid of all charisma, but who had been the least offensive of the fools shut away in a house for the winter. Roger won seventy grand and a couple of months' worth of notoriety, but the car-crash kind. He was loved and hated simultaneously by the same people. His aftershave was so strong, he actually smelt like desperation.

So it had been a depressing day. When we finished at about seven thirty the sun was not long down, and the dark was still light. Somebody suggested noodles so we all ploughed down to Busaba Eathai on Wardour, and crowded around a table. Some of the guys were high already, but I was off everything but the booze, trying to clear up my act and my head. Ben had started leaving me disapproving notes about the little clingfilm bags he was finding in my jeans when he did the washing, and although the coke was rarely mine – I just always seemed to end up with the bag because I've never been a snorter, just a dabber on my gums, and you only need the bag for that – I didn't want another argument. I didn't want another spotlight thrown on the distance between us, and the different directions we were moving in.

We made our way through five or six or ten bottles of South African wine – the cheap good stuff. We crammed noodles into our mouths and felt early spring warmth in the chilled night air. I started to think about wearing open-toed shoes. I sat with the assistant producer, a tiny girl with dark hair and eyes who was up for anything as long as it involved laughter, and the public schoolboy A&R, obviously trying too hard to be 'street' in oversized jeans and a Led Zeppelin T-shirt, but fun nonetheless. He referred to everything and everybody as adding value or not adding value. Thankfully I was informed that I added value, and I was almost tragically grateful.

Three German tourists sat on the corner of our table, laughing loudly at their own jokes – they too added value! It's a strange phenomenon, this sharing of tables. It's peculiarly un-London, to throw open your space and your conversation to any Tom, Dick or Harry who has money to pay and noodles to eat. It's become remarkably popular, I think, because of its possibilities. Lunch is more fun when the opportunity to meet the love of your life is tossed into the pot as well.

The Germans had strong noses and red cheeks that looked like they'd blister in the sun. They were having a wonderful time too. We tried to engage them in conversation, but if their English was broken our German was destroyed – the public schoolboy could ask 'How fast is your woman?' but that was the extent of our European union. They left eventually, to be replaced by two Italian homosexuals who kissed in the corner. They were both very dark and fragile and beautiful and the assistant producer and I were hypnotised as they gently brushed each other's lips. It was the easiest kiss I'd ever seen a man give, and it was to another man. In the end they asked me to stop staring at them. I tried to explain it was because I thought them beautiful, but they didn't care for the reason.

We drank lots and ate little, and the night started to melt away. Then somebody mumbled, 'Gerry's?'

We stumbled across Soho to the bottom of Dean Street, and through the familiar little doorway. It was dark in there, it always is. You lose everybody you know as soon as you get in, they all drift away to talk to strangers. Perhaps that's the appeal of the place – the promise of anonymity. I ordered something large and red and the man leaning next to me at the bar offered to pay for it. I said,

'Uh oh, that's trouble. I shouldn't be accepting drinks from strange men.'

'Then why have you?' he asked.

'Because I'm poor and drunk,' I replied. 'But then you already knew that.'

'I guessed the drunk bit, I would never have known about the poor.'

'How charming.' My eyes focused. 'You're incredibly hand-some,' I said.

'I'm an actor.' He pinched his lower lip between his thumb and forefinger, as if appraising a painting in the Portrait Gallery, or a piece of broken china in a boot sale.

'That makes sense. You may as well play to your strengths.'

'Are you a model?' he asked.

'I am quite clearly five foot five. We both know that I am not a model.'

'You could be a different kind of model, it doesn't have to be catwalk.'

'If you are asking me if I am a hand model, I find that offensive.'

'Not at all. You could be a model of the more glamorous variety.' He reached out and moved a strand of hair away from my eyes. I blinked him away.

'You're hoping I take my top off for a living?'

'Maybe.'

'I'm sorry to disappoint, but these puppies stay caged most days. I'm Make-up.'

'Why don't I ever get a Make-up like you? All mine are married with three kids.'

'Your wife probably hires them,' I said, without a smile.

'I'm not married. Are you?'

'Not yet. I have a "Ben".'

'And where is your "Ben" this evening?'

'Playing Championship Manager with a warehouse assistant from Ealing Dixons.'

'He sounds like fun.'

'Yeah, well, you don't know him. He has other qualities.'

'Like what?'

'You don't care, so I'm not going to answer. Thanks for the drink.'

I walked off, proud of myself. The guy was on the make, I was obviously too drunk, and it showed but I still resisted. I didn't want to meet anybody that night. It had become too frequent, too easy lately. A peck on the lips before home-time turning into a full-blown kiss, and I didn't know who I was kissing and if I would ever see them again. It made me feel wretched. The first time that I kissed somebody else I didn't realise it was happening until my lips were merged with his, and once I'd started, like eating a chocolate digestive at eleven a.m. on the first day of a new diet, it seemed pointless to stop. I'd start my fidelity again tomorrow. And the 'being unfaithful' part, in itself, was so unexceptional and run of the mill and ordinary that it just didn't seem like that big a deal. He was an ad exec and we were drunk at eight p.m. on a shoot for the Carphone Warehouse, and we had stumbled into the wardrobe cupboard to find funny hats to wear. As I said, we were drunk. He kissed me, and I kissed him back, and the passion felt so unfamiliar it was akin to riding the rapids at Center Parcs, or jumping up and down on a bouncy castle – it didn't seem bad, because I didn't love him or care about him. It just seemed like a fun thing to do at the time, and nothing at all to do with Ben. It was three hours later that I experienced delayed shock, like whiplash, and I burst violently into tears.

That was it, I had cheated. I had spent all this time terrified that Ben would be unfaithful, and I had just let a cocky guy from Kent called Dave cop a feel of me through my blouse, and tell me that he loved it when I scratched my nails across his stomach under his shirt. It felt awful then, and awful the next time, four months later at three a.m. in the corner of a bar called Push on Dean Street, with a stuntman I'd met half an hour earlier. He had deliberately set himself alight only two hours previously.

That was just a kiss. Eight months later I went home with a guy called Jonathan who was the post-production supervisor on a short film I'd been working on. I consoled myself that at least I'd known him for three days when it happened. I'd called Ben the next day and told him I'd crashed at my brother's because it was closer, and he hadn't seemed bothered, he certainly hadn't questioned me as I would have questioned him if he had stayed out all night. In a way I wish he had, and I'd been forced to admit it there and then. The lack of suitable grilling the next day just compounded the reasoning in my head for doing it: Ben didn't care.

That night at Gerry's, walking away from another possible indiscretion, I collapsed in a corner and chatted to an old bloke in a checked suit with a red nose and three strips of hair that sat on his crown like rashers of bacon. He was hammered on whiskey, but he managed to tell me that I bore a sharp resemblance to his first and favourite wife, only that I was fatter.

I noticed the handsome sleaze staring at me from the bar, trying to catch my eye. I ignored it, but eventually he was by my side again, putting another glass of red into my hand.

'I can't shrug you off tonight, can I?'

'I'm Tom Harvey-Saint. And you are?'

'Scarlet.'

'That's a very evocative name. Do you have a giant "A" on your chest?'

'Not yet, no, but I'm working on it.'

'You seem sad, Scarlet, and I'd like to help.'

'I bet you would. Help me out of these wet clothes perhaps?'

'Well that's a very depressing way of looking at things. What could be so bad? Look at us, here, tonight, drunk in a glorious city full of beautiful people. What could be so wrong?'

'That's not enough for me. I need more than that. Five years ago that was enough, but not now. I need more than wine and London.'

'Darling, don't say you're tired of London, you know what that means.'

'Maybe I am, maybe I am tired of life. Of my life at least.'

'Maybe you're just drunk, darling, and feeling a little dramatic. Let's not be pompous, it does nothing for you.'

'I'm not being pompous . . . I just feel blue.'

'But Scarlet can't be blue! What can I do?' He was stroking my thigh, running his fingers up and down my leg, his digits creeping towards places they shouldn't. I wanted to shrug him off like a dirty shirt, but at the same time hug him like a five-day-old puppy.

'Christ, I just want something beautiful to happen! And I want it to happen to me! Have I made that many wrong decisions? Are my expectations so disjointed from reality? Have I been that hateful that I don't deserve to be happy?'

'Fuck all that, darling, just live. Wake up. Just have fun. It's every man for himself.'

'No it's not. It can't be.'

'Well what do you think the answer is?'

'I think the answer is to find somebody who wants what

you want. And who wants to be honest. And realises that's a valuable commodity, if you find it. I need somebody to be my refuge . . .'

'I completely agree. My name is Tom and I'll be your air-raid shelter tonight.'

'Oh you'll agree with anything I say right now.'

'Damn right. You have beautiful eyes.'

Tom Harvey-Saint took me by the hand and led me outside Gerry's, into an alley between a pub and a walk-in health centre.

Tom Harvey-Saint had pecs like paving slabs. I had sex with him in that alley, by accident, in that I let him, I was drunk enough to allow lust to take over. It was violent sex, awful, savage; he thrust into me like a kitchen knife.

I crawled home to Ben that night in a cab, but slept on the sofa, in case he could sense it somehow, smell infidelity on my skin. I wish I had told him then, or that I could tell him now. Lies are so depressing.

'Gerry's? Are you a barmaid?' he asks now.

I turn around. Tom Harvey-Saint leans in the doorway, ready for his close-up. He is as handsome as the last time I saw him. He is tall enough to dominate any room, and dark enough to catch any woman's eye. He has wide grey eyes and a full bottom lip that looks like it's just been bitten – it probably has been, for effect. His chest is like a barrel, and his stomach flattens under his belt like a snowboard. He is wearing a dark green short-sleeved polo shirt tucked into khakis. Both of his forearms rest on the doorframe on either side of his head. It looks like a casual pose, but I still can't get out.

'No, I'm not a barmaid. I've just seen you in Gerry's.'

'Good old Gerry's. That must be it then. What are you doing here?'

'Make-up. For Dolly. And you and Arabella as well apparently.'

'Fantastic. I've never had a Make-up that looks as good as you. Mine are always married with three kids.'

'So you've said.' I nod my head at him, but he ignores it.

'I do feel like I know you though . . .' He stares at me and smiles.

I shrug, grit my teeth and hope he'll leave.

'Maybe I'll see you later, then, at Gerry's?' he asks. He can't use my name because of course he doesn't know it.

'Maybe.'

'I'm Tom Harvey-Saint by the way,' he adds, stretching out his hand to be shaken, knowing full well that I would recognise him from his appearances as Rob McKenzie on *Death Watch* – if I didn't recognise him already, that is.

'Scarlet.' I rush out my answer, hoping he'll forget it as quickly, and offer him my hand sharply. Instead of shaking it he grabs it, turns it over and kisses my palm, looking thoughtful for a second, flickers of recognition sparking behind his eyes. When I yank my hand back he seems alarmed.

'Sorry, but I've just bleached my brushes and I don't want you to inhale,' I say.

I dart past him, making sure not to catch his eye, but the hairs on my arms silently stand up and scream as they graze the hairs on his. His neurons and my neurons or his atoms or my protons or something are diametrically apposed or aligned or whatever the science is that means my body lurches towards him dangerously. There is a dark pocket of something wild that hides deep inside of me that threatens my sanity when I am near a man like Tom Harvey-Saint. I practically run back to Dolly's room. Shutting the door behind me I catch my breath. I hold my hands out in front of me and see what I already know, that they are shaking. I feel like he preyed on me, and yet I was compliant at the time.

I think he realised that night that I was past the point of right and wrong or conscious decision-making, and that it was apparent that I didn't know what I was doing, or who with. I just try not to think about it. The only person I have told is Helen. She called him all sorts of names, but I wondered, even then, if I was just making excuses for myself, for my actions. I did it. That's that.

My stomach rumbles, and with still no sign of Dolly I grab my phone out of my bag. I don't have a single bar of reception, so I think fuck it and I take it upstairs. I sit on the warm front steps of the theatre, tucking my skirt in between my legs for modesty, as tourists and runners and couriers stream past. Feeling like I've been submerged in some twisted underworld I gasp in the air. I call Helen.

'Guess who I'm working with?' I ask before she can even say hello.

'George Clooney?'

'I need you to know that if that day ever comes I won't be taking time out to call you, Helen.'

'Will we ever tire of him, do you think?' she asks. She's asked this many a time and I always give the same reply. It's hard to move on from a George moment. He's our thing, our one, at the top of all our 'top three' lists, the one that nobody will ever push off a cliff. It's not his stomach, it's his eyes.

'We will never tire of George,' I reply, 'especially not now he's turned to the body politic. It just makes him more beautiful. He's handsome, and he thinks, and maybe even cares a little.'

'But not about women. He won't marry again,' Helen says with a sigh.

'Yes, but maybe he's hit on the answer? I know he's not sitting in Italy wasting his time thinking, "Where's my white dress? Where's my 'one'?"'

I wonder what life revelation George has hit upon, other than the futility of it all, which I refuse to acknowledge even in my darker moments. I wonder what he's learnt about life that I haven't yet, and if he'd be prepared to share his theory with me, perhaps over a plate of basil and mozzarella in his big Italian villa on Lake Como? In return I'd promise to thrash out the prospect of an all-female US Presidential Race, over amaretto and ice cream, as lights twinkled around Laglio with the sun setting behind us. Perhaps he'd lend me his sweater? Perhaps dreams are the only romance there is left.

'So not George Clooney,' I say. 'Guess again.'

'I don't know,' Helen says.

'Tom Harvey-Saint.'

'Shit,' Helen says flatly. 'Shit. How did that happen? Scarlet, how did you not know that he was going to be there? I mean, that's just rubbish luck.'

'I know. He didn't recognise me at least. It's horrible. This whole job is weird and I'm probably going to be here for months. I don't know if I'll last the day at this rate. The director is this crazy guy who rubbed glitter on my lips, and . . .'

'Which lips?'

'Don't be foul, Helen.'

'Okay.'

We pause for a second. I glance up the road to see if the *Evening Standard* seller is still there. He is, I didn't dream him.

'Did you win your squash match?' I ask her. Helen likes it when I pay attention to the details of her life, and so I should. Shortly after she and Steven got engaged they went out one night for dinner, in Woking, with Steven's best friend Peter and his wife Amanda. Helen told me the following day that they didn't ask her a single question about herself all night. It was a perfectly pleasant evening, but not one question about her. Helen kept asking Amanda where she was from, about the holiday she knew that she and Peter had just taken in Argentina, and wasn't it amazing that there was a glacier at the bottom of Argentina, and how strange that she didn't know that! And what was their house like? What was their village like? And their neighbours, and their goddamn local pub! Question after question. And every time there was a pause in the conversation she waited for them to ask her something about herself. Anything. Not even a big question. 'How is your chicken?' would have done. But nothing came. If the conversation paused the couple filled it by making little remarks to each other instead.

'Did I win?' Helen asks. 'God no, I got completely thrashed. It was a walkover. She killed me.'

Helen sounds flat, her voice smooth like a pebble, when speak of defeat normally results in spits and spikes.

'What's wrong, Hel? You don't seem bothered, normally you'd be destroyed at losing by that much.'

'Steven just texted me. He's going to be late tonight. Work drinks, he says.'

'Oh, Helen, I'm so sorry.' I hang my head in my hands. It's all so tiring, these clouds of lies everywhere.

'No, it's fine. It's good. I'm going to see.'

'What do you mean, you're going to see?' A guy walks past me in a T-shirt that says 'Don't ask if you're ugly'. I hate him instantly.

'For myself, I'm going to see what she looks like.'

'No, Helen, you can't! What difference does it make anyway?'

As I am talking I grab at an old piece of newspaper lying next to me on the steps, scrunch it up into a ball, and throw it at 'Don't ask's' back. He glances around and brushes his arm where it hits him, but I act naturally and I don't think he suspects me. It's a busy-enough street for him not to know.

'Scarlet, what are you talking about? Look how obsessed you were with seeing Katie! Of course it matters. What if she's older? What if she's fat? What if she's eighteen and skinny and stupid? What if her hair is stripy like Tony the Tiger, or she wears orange foundation, or has fake boobs, or long legs, or a mountain of cleavage and a zip on her top that just about holds them in?'

'And what if she is younger, Helen? What if she's really pretty? That's the worst-case scenario, isn't it? But it still won't mean anything. It won't change things. It's not her, it's him!'

I hear Helen fight back a sob at the end of the line. I am surprised. She is stronger than I am.

'I just want to see for myself,' she says, and I know that she will do it no matter what I say.

'Do you want me to come with you, Hel? I could try and get out early?'

'No. No. I just want to do it on my own. Stay away from that sleaze, though, Scarlet. He's a sod.'

'We were both drunk, Helen, I'm sure I was just as bad.'

'I'm sure you bloody weren't.'

'*Don't ask if you're ugly*' is walking back towards me, and I keep my head down. Maybe he *has* realised it was me . . .

'Helen, don't you think we are just a little too used to seeing the best in each other? You know the way that you never think any man is good enough for one of your friends? We think we're wonderful! It's just, nobody else seems to think so . . .'

'That's what friends are for. Is Ben still being . . . Ben?'

'I guess. It's my fault. I need to take action.'

'He needs to take some goddamn action, Scarlet, that's what needs to happen. He needs to get up off his arse and do something!'

'Well I think he might be already. I think he might be doing Katie again.'

'Excuse me?' The T-shirt guy is standing in front of me, with Diesel jeans and a scarf wrapped three times around his neck, designer sunglasses and spiky black hair. And he looks like he's wearing fake tan.

'Hold on, Helen,' I say, and look up. 'Yes?'

He smiles a really broad smile, and asks, 'Do you know where Paul Smith is?'

'No. Sorry.'

'You've got great legs,' he says, and I smile.

'Your T-shirt,' I say, pointing at his chest.

He looks down and smiles cockily. 'Oh, it's just a joke,' he replies and winks at me.

'I don't think it's funny,' I tell him, and smile.

'You're all right, it doesn't apply to you,' he says, with a bigger smile, a more pronounced wink.

'Oh fuck off,' I reply, and turn back to my phone.

'What was all that about?' Helen asks.

'Just some loser in a bad T-shirt,' I say.

'Is he still there?' Helen asks.

'Is there something else?' I ask him, as he stands gawping at me.

'You're just a pair of tits,' he practically spits at me.

'And you're charming. That T-shirt should read, "Don't ask, I'm a prick!"'

'What's your fucking problem?' he starts shouting, at which point I hear the door open behind me, and Gavin's voice saying,

'Are you all right, Scarlet?'

I turn to face the T-shirt. 'I'm fine, Gavin.' I look at the T-shirt guy, who looks at Gavin and slouches off.

'I'll be back in, in a minute,' I say to Gavin and smile. 'Sorry, Helen, what were we saying?'

'Who was the hero?' she asks, and I sense her smiling.

'Just some new guy I'm working with – he's massive' I say, as explanation.

'Oh really? Sounds interesting . . .'

'What were we saying?' I ask to stop her going down that path.

'About Ben being back with Katie? I'm sure that's not true Scarlet. She wouldn't have him anyway, would she?'

'Oh Christ, I don't know. But please don't go tonight, Helen, I don't want you to get hurt.'

'I'm not going to be carrying a gun, Scarlet, it's not a proper stakeout.'

'No, I mean emotionally, I don't want you to get upset.'

'What's done is done.'

'But it's not done yet.'

'Yes it is. I'll speak to you later.'

We hang up.

I am obsessed with what Katie looks like. I could look at photos of her all day and it wouldn't be enough. The volcano-holiday snap was the only one I've seen of them together. Every other photo is of either Ben or Katie alone, smiling absently at the camera, bored even, but smiling. They both wear suitably glazed-over expressions with mountains or the sea as a backdrop. Or they are seated in a restaurant, and Ben has flung an arm loosely around her shoulder, absent of affection. It's not as if I could have known somehow, or guessed that this might be the way it would turn out for me too. I wasn't privy to the photo collection before he left.

Still, Katie is all limbs in these photos, and sensible shoes, and smiles. I've put on nearly a stone since the day Ben and I first met. I feel like it shouldn't make a difference. I don't know if it does. If he loved me it wouldn't matter, I haven't exploded, I'm not vast. Maybe now I'm more of a big twelve than a small ten. Of course the 'if he loved me' bit is crucial. If he doesn't, then that extra stone might mean the world. I have no way of knowing. Even if I asked him, he wouldn't answer.

I stand up and brush myself down, checking for snags in my skirt. Sometimes the sun casts a shadow that's bigger than you are. I don't know how or why, but if it's late in the day and the angle is right, or whatever the science, it casts a fatter, darker shadow than it should.

I wander back inside, push through the swing doors and amble up the aisle as my eyes adjust to the darkness. A series of teenagers are still moving things around at the sides of the stage, but Tom and Arabella are up there now, rehearsing their lines. I recognise her from some BBC Jane Austen or the like. There is no mistaking that she is very beautiful. She is naturally haughty, her bones delicate and fine and serious. Her eyes are dark and intense, almost black. Her jaw-line is perfectly smooth and heart-shaped. She could make any man fall in love with her. I think Gavin must love her. She will need little work from me.

I sit and watch them for a while as they move about the stage, rehearsing their lines, playing out what seems to be an uneasy relationship. Tom acts tired, worn out, nervous. He seems convincing. They adjust their tones, somehow always facing forwards, never turning their backs on me, as they try out different poses, different gestures, varying strengths of voice. I spot Tristan sitting cross-legged at the front of the stage, studying them intently, his hands in prayer, his fingers by his chin, deep in concentration. He sips on a Frappacino now and then, placing it carefully next to him between thoughts.

Tom moves elegantly to the front of the stage, and asks Arabella, '*How long is it till morning?*'

Tristan says, 'A bell tolls.'

Arabella take a couple of paces forwards and looks at her empty wrist.

'*Oh, my – watch has stopped. I'm a watch-winding person but I forgot to wind it.*'

I shiver, sitting three rows back with nobody in front or behind me. It is peculiar to watch them like this, in jeans and T-shirts, without a watch, or the bells, or the props they should need but somehow don't.

I realise Gavin is standing at the end of my row.

'Still no Dolly?' I ask, alarmed that I have forgotten all about her.

'No, she's not coming in. Not today. She wouldn't get out of the car.'

'Why not?'

Gavin slumps down a seat away from me. His knees bang the chair in front of him. He needs at least two seats to himself.

'We don't really know. She pulled up at the back, I opened the door like every other day, but she wouldn't come in. Wouldn't even get out of the car.'

'It's not me, is it?'

'God, no. Scarlet, it's got nothing to do with you. It's her. She's a mad old drunk. They'll never actually get her on the stage.'

Gavin watches Arabella as he talks. His eyes follow hers, even though she is addressing Tristan or Tom or somebody off-stage. I turn to watch her too, and she laughs lightly at some joke that Tristan has made. Gavin smiles.

'Seriously? Do you think she'll pull out?' I ask.

'I just can't see her getting up there, when there is an audience. Tristan needs to talk to her properly. They need to find a decent replacement if she's going to bail. She's the only reason we've sold so many tickets. The first two months are sold out. That doesn't happen too often to us.'

'But people know Tom and Arabella too . . .' I glance back at them on the stage. They are beautiful together, and there is something hypnotic about the couple they make. There are no flaws. It's not quite real, but, as Flash says to Dale after she's been caught in Ming's trance and danced in front of the Hawk Men and Prince Baron: It's pretty sensational. *Flash Gordon* is another one of Ben and Iggy's favourites. I like *Flash Gordon* too – it makes me laugh at least – although I don't like the fact that I know the names of all the characters, and the script word for word.

'They know them, but barely. Tom's got quite a following now, after that serial-killer thing, but Arabella is still small parts. She definitely couldn't open it, even with Tom.'

Their bodies are angled towards us but their faces are turned to a screen at the back of the stage that is being removed by a man dressed in shorts and a 'Kids from *Fame*' T-shirt. It reveals a grand four-poster, plump with bedding. In it sits the little electrician from earlier. You can just about see him in between all the cushions. I cough with embarrassment. I have never thought of myself as 'size-ist' before, and Gavin gives me a reproachful look.

'So what do we do now?' I ask brightly, checking my watch, changing our focus. 'I don't know what to do at midday on a Monday if I'm not in bed or working.'

'Well you may as well go shopping. There's no point making up Tom or Bella now, they are mid-rehearsal. But we're all going to Gerry's later if you fancy it, it's Tristan's assistant's birthday.'

'Do I need to get a card?'

'I don't even know his name. We're just going to Gerry's. I'll see you later.'

Gavin moves off to address a group of guys who stand at the side of the stage talking heatedly about lighting. Tristan glares over at them a couple of times, but they don't notice.

I think I'll go to Selfridges.

Tristan gets up and walks over to the side of the stage as I stand to leave.

'Loves, sorry, can you shut the fuck up? This is hard enough without your girly whisperings.'

They quieten down but I hear one of them mutter, 'dog boiler'.

Tristan spots me heading for the door. 'Make-up, no Dolly! Where are you headed?'

'I was going to go and stock up at Selfridges, I can take a good guess at her base. I'll keep the receipts if I find anything.'

'Great. But you'll come to Gerry's later, right? It's my assistant's birthday, we're all going.'

'Okay.' I beckon him over, and he strides forwards with a smile. He is wearing those sunglasses again, but also now a set of plastic pink beads that swing beneath his suit jacket.

'Yep?' he asks me, tugging off his glasses, wide-eyed and intrigued.

'Should I get him a card?'

'Who?'

'Your assistant?'

'What a lovely idea. Can I sign it?'

I laugh. 'If you want to. What's his name?'

Tristan's eyes are still wide, and he stares at me for a while. His mouth moves but nothing comes out.

'I won't bother with the card then,' I say.

'Just buy him a drink and let him look at you for a while, he's only young, it'll be a treat!'

Tristan moves back to Tom and Arabella.

I'm to be somebody's birthday treat. So why do I feel like all my candles have already been blown out?

I only smile again when I think of Selfridges.

Scene IV: Romance

I trip northwards along Charing Cross Road, back the way that I came, but I turn right at Soho Square and slip onto Oxford Street practically unnoticed. My destination: Selfridges beauty hall. It has been, perhaps, the real love of my life so far. It's a constant, and I think, if it's possible, it loves me back. Whenever I walk through the front doors a plump gust of wind catches my skirts and blows away any London smog. It's Selfridges' way of saying hello. I always nod and say hello back of course. We're old friends.

So I skip down Oxford Street on my weekly crusade, my pilgrimage in the absence of any meaningful religion. I'm no Lionheart, but I know what I believe. I'm Make-up, it's what I do. I make the world a little prettier. And I get a discount.

Unfortunately Oxford Street is now little more than a straight line of shops that's no big jape without credit cards. It's a flood of tourists lapping at your toes, swelling at bus-stop bottlenecks by Poland Street and Oxford Circus tube, but receding again the further you go, as long as you stay on the left-hand side of the street as you head towards Marble Arch. The pavement is cracked and uneven on both sides, so watch your footing. There are dips and crumbles everywhere you walk, where a thousand million billion steps have been made before you. Imagine if every footprint was even a millionth of a millimetre thick, and every step that was taken was built on top of another. The Great Wall of China would run along Oxford Street building up and up with every step of every shopper throughout Christmas, and then the assorted tourist flip-flops of summer, and they'd have to come in and bulldoze it down every autumn, ready for the crowds again come Advent.

Selfridges is on the right, its red flags waving in the wind and beckoning a thousand dainty bulls, like me, to stampede through its halls. My mother was the first person to take me to Selfridges, when I was young, on one of our day trips. It was different in 1980, and so was my mother. It was a couple of years before she left, but I at least already knew that it was imminent. What I didn't know is whether she would take me with her. When she hugged me late at night before I went to bed, as I pleaded to be allowed to stay up to watch the TV shows with the enticing theme tunes – *Hill Street Blues* or *Mash* – increasingly her squeeze was a little too hard. She'd kiss me forcefully on the head as well, to make sure that I felt it, and that I knew it. In this way her torment surfaced nearly every night. Like an alarming burst of flame on a hob that won't seem to catch, it surprised and scared me every time.

She wasn't happy. She was actually unhappy. When the time came for my mum to kiss me goodnight my dad was generally still out at the pub with his friends. Richard and I heard the arguments in the evenings, after teatime but before seven, during news hour:

'But why don't we get a babysitter, you could come too?'

'I don't want to come too, and sit in that shitty pub full of old morose men who have nothing to talk about but darts or football or beer!'

'I know what you think of them, I know what you think of me!'

'It wasn't you when I met you, it wasn't the man that I married, but it is now! They are ancient, you are not!'

'I feel comfortable with them, at least they don't nag me!'

'Because they don't want anything out of life, that's why!'

'So you'd rather stay here and watch the television every night with peanuts and a bottle of wine, than come and be social with your husband and his friends?'

'Without a doubt, Patrick, I would rather do that!'

My dad would leave for the pub defeated, but he would still leave. Maybe he should have stayed one night and sat with my mother instead, but he never did. I loved him but he did what he wanted to do, and yet didn't seem to understand it when she left. I saw the signs, and I wasn't even ten.

My mother was very beautiful, and we went to Selfridges as a treat sometimes on our day trips to London, to buy her face cream and wander around the beauty hall, rubbing lotions on the back of our hands, and then holding them just under our noses to smell our own skin. She told me that every cream, every perfume, smelt differently on each person's skin. It would smell differently on hers than it would on mine, she said, but only a little. The difference would be much more profound on somebody else who didn't have the same blood, but because we were related, to an extent we shared the same skin. But I had my daddy's skin too, so it would still be a little different. She would rub some cream into her hand first, and then my hand as well, and then we'd compare smells. I always hoped the back of my hand would smell exactly like my mother's, and sometimes she conceded that it did, and we'd both grin.

All the women behind the counters paid her lots of attention because she was so beautiful. Her hair was already grey. It had been a tumble of long, dark curls in her wedding photos, but had turned quickly to silver in her first years of marriage, like an adverse reaction to my father or the institution itself, and by the age of thirty-one, my age, her hair was like platinum wool, piled up dramatically, high on her head like the most expensive yarn in the shop. She had huge bright blue eyes, lively and Irish, and a square jaw, and a strong nose. All the women tried to spray her with perfume as we walked past but she just ignored them, and said, 'No thank you, no thank you.' I think she could only afford the face cream.

My father didn't trap her, my mother trapped herself. I think that's what made her sad. He simply settled into the life that they had chosen. My mum chose it too, then quickly found that she hated it, but couldn't break free, not with me and my brother as well. So when she really couldn't take any more, and she finally left, she left without us.

Everybody tells me I look a lot like her. At family parties my grandmother always says it, 'Ahh, it's like looking at Catherine again!' And my mother says it herself sometimes when I see her, which is at least once a month because she comes up to town. She has only met Ben a couple of times, though, he doesn't seem to make it for the dinners that we plan, and I am happy to have her to myself anyway. But I could tell what she was thinking when she met him because her smile gave her away: it's the same one that I give when I am not quite sure about somebody and there are thoughts mashing in my mind that I shouldn't share. She is always polite, and she always smiles, asks questions, and kisses him hello and goodbye. I try to get down to the house in Sussex, she tells me to come and take walks on the beach to clear my head, but it's so hard to find the time. I should go more often . . .

That was the other thing that Ben and I discovered within half an hour of meeting each other. Both our mothers left when we were little. My mum called my brother and me the evening of the day that she left, and the next day, and the day after that. She kept calling us, even if we hadn't done anything and had nothing to say, and arranged to take us for days out to museums and zoos and stately homes. We all knew that she would never come back for good. Ben's mum did come back, after five years away and not a card for contact. One day she walked out and he stopped having a mummy, then five years later she reappeared, when Ben was thirteen, as if nothing had happened, and Ben's dad took her back without question or hesitation.

Ben's an only child. You can always tell them from a mile away. They don't understand that you can argue and make-up within minutes. They don't understand that you can argue with somebody your own age and know it will be okay. They don't understand divided attention. I think there should be posters in clinics and doctors' surgeries and also petrol stations that read:

'*Whatever you do, have more than one child! Make it at least two or nothing!*

'*Warning: Only children are monsters! Crime rates would be cut by ninety per cent if everybody had a brother or sister!*'
I think that Ben might be different if he'd had a brother or sister. It might have made it easier when his mum left, or even when she came back. It would have stopped him feeling so alone. It's like the world shut him out then and now he refuses to come back in.

When I reach Selfridges and push open the heavy doors, allowing a stream of ladies to leave before I enter, I feel the familiar breath of Selfridges' air rush to kiss me hello. I nod hello back. Today I am in search of creams and potions to paint over the cracks before that crucial point when the cracks become too damn obvious, and no paint will do.

I don't know the promise in all of their creams, the dreams they threaten to deliver and whether they ever come true. I don't know how much of the science is real. I don't know whether having a laboratory in France makes me believe their claims any more or less, but I believe that there is a power to positivism that can keep some of those lines at bay. Thinking that you are taking care of yourself, even if those creams are nothing but mayonnaise, is an advantage. You might smile more at least, and smile like you mean it.

I stop in front of the MAC counter: it's a carnival, a riot, an underwater reef, vibrant and unexpected. My eyes swim across whole banks of colour, all things bright and beautiful: nail polish and eye-shadow, eye cream and eyeliner, mascara and brow brushes and brow colour and brow tint, lip tint, lip-gloss, lipstick, lip-liner, lip plump, blusher, highlighter, foundation, concealer, light coverage, medium coverage, matt or gloss.

Matt or gloss seems to be the ultimate decision at every make-up counter and in every life. Do I want my relationship matt or gloss? Reliable and dependable and staying put all day? Or shiny and eye-catching but likely to disappear with half a bag of chips or a large glass of red wine? What about my kisses, my nights out, my walks to work, my boyfriend – matt or gloss? For me there is no contest.

Gloss is our sticky sparkly signature streak. Even a decade ago nobody was glossing. Who started this wet revolution that means our hair will always stick to our lips in the slightest gust of wind? Suddenly, as if they were obligatory like flu jabs for OAPs, we all owned three Juicy Tubes. More than just gloss, it is balms and salves and stains. If you sit on the bus or the tube, somebody will be rubbing something into their lips, diving into their bags for their little pot of almost nothing to smear over their mouths, only to kiss it, talk it, eat it off in moments, and have to reapply again. If the secret to giving up smoking is to replace one habit with another, buy a new lip-gloss, tinted-brown nicotine flavour, and streak it on every time you feel stabs of withdrawal.

When did our mouths become so defenceless? Suddenly they demand such attention. I can't sort out my savings because I have to think about my lips; I can't go and see my mother because I need to think about balm. Ben actually doesn't like the gloss. When we first started seeing each other, during those early affair days that were never quite real, I would always gloss before meeting him. He'd turn up, consistently on time, and he'd lean in to kiss me, and I would be forced to retract slightly. 'Just glossed?' he'd ask, and I'd say yes. 'The expensive one?' he'd ask, and I'd say yes.

Then we wouldn't be able to kiss properly for about twenty minutes, so that I got my money's worth out of my expensive application. The irony, of course, is that I was wearing it so he'd want to kiss me. The thought only occurs to me now that when Ben and I first met, in those strange early days when we were doing what we shouldn't, we kissed freely in public. We rolled around in Green Park on a picnic blanket for Christ's sake, gulping down miniature bottles of vodka, practically dry-riding each other, attracting uncertain looks from the park police who weren't sure whether to film us or intervene. Another night, another clandestine date, and I sat with my legs wrapped around Ben on a bench under a tree, on the South Bank outside the NFT, as an orchestra of student film critics clicked a symphony of wine glasses behind us, and a warm night grew colder as we grew hotter. I thought that he wanted the affection that he and Katie had lost, and I thought I was his answer or his release. And yet now, three years down the line, he refuses to peck me on the lips on an empty train. Something has definitely happened, but I can't think about it now, or again. I'm tired, and it's too hard, and this is Selfridges beauty hall. I'm not going to ruin it. I'm not going to think about the theory that glossed lips spell sexual readiness to the opposite sex, and that Ben doesn't want me to spell it out for him any more.

I spend four hours in Selfridges, wandering all the floors, stopping for a glass of pink fizz in the champagne bar where you can sit and play the 'How many people are wearing sunglasses indoors?' game. Light-headed, I make my way to the designer floors, slipping into two thousand-pound dresses and sandals, dancing in front of gleaming mirrors like Cinderella, before throwing my own clothes back on, clothes that now seem like rags, and reluctantly returning my princess clothes to their rail-thin hangers and the rail-thin assistants who can only manage to hold two items at a time because they haven't been on solids since Lent. Eventually I buy a pot of face soufflé, and one new lip-gloss in 'Fucked-Up-&-Over-Pink'. I don't know what it means, but it sounds about right.

My stomach grumbles that I haven't had lunch, reminding me that I was thwarted in my biscuit hunt and it has now thoroughly worked its way through today's only offering of champagne that I threw down a couple of hours ago, so I grab a slice of pizza from a hole in the wall by Bond Street tube, and idle down South Molton Street, to make my way back to Soho off the tourist track.

I check my watch and it's only just gone five o'clock. I can't get to Gerry's until eleven. For a moment I consider abandoning Gerry's for tonight and going home early, surprising Ben, cooking us both dinner, collapsing in front of the TV, or something. Doing whatever it is that couples do, the kind who spend their evenings together. But the thought fills me with discomfort, I feel full on it, like I've eaten too much pasta and now I can't move, my belly swollen and full of air. If I choose to spend the night at home with Ben it could easily be the end. A few hours is all I'll need to turn our lives upside down, if I suddenly get reckless and brave, and I'm not ready yet.

I take my last bite of pizza and dance past Fenwicks window, stopping briefly to look at scarves.

As I make my way through Hanover Square I feel something lightly dust my face. Somebody must be leaning out of an office window, sprinkling fairy dust, or maybe coke, or maybe anthrax, on Hanover Square. It's lightly powdering us all. For a moment I am in a snow-globe and I turn as I walk, mimicking a mechanical ballerina with her arms outstretched, my palms and face angled upwards, letting whatever it is fall on me. Maybe it will scar. Maybe it will heal everything. I stop in the middle of the square and watch it settle on the pavement. A man in a suit and a boy with a rucksack have stopped as well, in front of me, and are studying the flakes as they fall.

'It looks like snow?' I say after a beat.

'I know,' agrees the boy with the rucksack.

'But it's September,' I say, confused.

'And it's sunny,' adds the boy.

The man with the suit sticks out his hand and catches a flake. 'It's a snowstorm,' he says, as the flake melts in his palm.

'But it's warm,' I say.

'Stranger things have happened,' he replies, and walks off.

The boy shrugs and smiles at me and walks off too.

The flakes have stopped falling. It was a minute-long snow-storm, in central London at the end of an Indian summer. I look down at the pavement, and though it looks a little damp it is already drying in patches.

I cross Regent Street and follow Beak Street back into Soho, then down and along Old Compton Street to the junction of Charing Cross Road and Shaftesbury Avenue.

I am in two minds. I check my watch – it's still not six – and I pivot on the spot. A young guy walks past me, whistles, and says 'nice', but I ignore him.

I fluff up my hair, straighten my skirt, and head for Grey's.

I don't see Isabella for twenty minutes. Just as disappointment starts to bubble in my stomach, I glimpse a mess of long blonde hair and black roots sauntering up from the film section, carrying a couple of books that look like props. She is wearing a cheap silky grey dress that is higher at the front than the back, and falls just above her knees, with a dark red cardigan knotted over her chest. Each breast resembles an empty upturned fruit bowl beneath it. She's chewing gum, but then she is always chewing gum. She wears scuffed black ballet slippers, and she doesn't bother picking her feet up off the ground as she walks. She kicks along the carpet, carelessly creating static with each step.

She makes her way to the till and appears impervious to the stares of schoolboys and salesmen and financial directors and journalists and busmen around her. She doesn't have the time to acknowledge each one, she'd be exhausted, she'd never get anywhere, she'd be here all night. She drops the books she's been carrying lazily behind the till, and bends over to retrieve a sheet of price stickers. I feel the sharp intake of breath from the men around me suck the air out of the room, as her dress falls forwards at the front with her cardigan and the sharp indent of her cleavage is revealed, like a lonely, thin ravine between two ominous mountains, like a parting of two waves. The juices of desire spewing out from all the men around me almost slide me off my feet. Lust can tear a house down, or fire rockets into space. It's the last untapped natural resource, we'll get to it eventually, when the oil runs out and the smoking stench blocks out the sun and the sky turns black. The sparks in Grey's could light Sydney Harbour at New Year, from the static in Isabella's shoes shifting along the carpet to the tiny blue flickers of light dancing around this herd of groins. I am almost scared to trip into their eye-lines, afraid of what might happen if I block their view, afraid they might move to see her and not me, just afraid, really, that I'll be no more than a nuisance and somebody will come along and pick me up and dump me on the street with a thud so I don't spoil their time with her alone.

I don't know what to buy today that won't look like my own pathetic prop, an excuse to give her my money and two minutes of my time. Glancing at the shelves quickly I grab *Don Quixote*. Heading towards the till I see that somebody else is serving too, a bespectacled guy in an ill-fitting jumper. He puts the grey in Grey's. Isabella has just started serving two awe-struck schoolboys in uniform, but Mr Grey is nearly finished with his pissed-off suit whose glance flickers sporadically to the chewing-gum beauty to his right. If I get in line now I'll miss her. I dart to the magazine stand and watch the pissed-off suit try and throw a smile at Isabella before he leaves, but she doesn't catch it. Mr Grey stands at the till for a moment, but when nobody else appears he hits a few buttons to presumably lock his till, picks up a stack of books and heads off towards science fiction. I grab *Vogue* as the schoolboys finish paying, and move quickly to the till.

'Hi,' she says, and smiles.

'Hi,' I reply, and pass her my Cervantes and my *Vogue*.

She runs the codes under the plastic thing that bleeps.

'This one's heavy!' she says, flipping *Don Quixote* over and widening her eyes. 'It would take me weeks! But this is more my style,' she adds, stroking the glossy *Vogue*, chewing her gum. 'I think she's beautiful.' She gestures to Catherine Zeta Jones, who glares at us from the cover.

'She's old-school glamorous, and there's not much of it about these days,' I say.

Arabella looks at me and smiles. 'You're right – I love glamour. But look at us, I think we both do!' She flicks her hands at her hair, and nods at me, and I smile, stupidly pleased.

'That's eight pounds forty-five then,' she says with a smile.

I pass her my card.

'You come in here quite a lot, don't you?' she continues.

111

'Yes – I work around Soho most days, so it's my local.'

'My local's the Gay Hussar,' she says, and giggles.

'A different kind of local,' I reply.

'Maybe, but sometimes I just go in there at lunch, read my *Vogue*, have a vodka, it's not that different. Other than the vodka.' She holds my books in her hands, but doesn't put them in a bag. 'I always think you look wonderful,' she says, and I feel like twenty capillaries have burst in each of my cheeks.

'Oh, thank you. I enjoy it, you know, dressing up, and I am a make-up artist so . . .' I knew that would get her. She is ignoring the line of men queuing behind me, and I hear them tut loudly when Mr Grey comes dashing over and shouts 'Who's next please?' A Financial Director throws both Isabella and I daggers, like we've just ruined his year.

'You're a make-up artist? Do you get free stuff?' Her eyes widen between hastily smudged black kohl.

'Yes,' I say, nodding my head, smiling like it's obvious, that I'm old and cynical while she's still young and innocent.

'Good stuff? Like good mascaras and glosses and things?'

'Yes, and rubbish as well of course!'

'Christ, I'd be happy with the rubbish, you know, anything. So you work around here?' She cocks her head to one side childishly.

'At the moment, yes. Down the road at one of the theatres in Covent Garden.'

'So what do you do for lunch?'

'I haven't had a lunch yet, today was my first day there.'

'But, like, what do you normally do for lunch?' she asks, playing with my books. They still aren't in a bag.

'Who's next please?' shouts Mr Grey, and I hear more tutting behind us.

'Well most of the time I'm on set. I don't really get a lunch break, and I have to be there constantly during the day in case people need touching up or whatever.'

She grins at me like I've said something naughty. I grin back, feeling a little ridiculous. It's the kind of joke that Ben would like.

'So, like, what time is an early finish for you then?' she asks, and I blink a few times. She is full of confidence; I wonder if anybody has ever turned her down; I wonder if she even knows what it feels like to be rejected, or hear the word 'no'.

Something happens. Suddenly I remember how to play this game.

'I'm not sure yet. Sorry.' I check my watch. 'I have to get going, but if I get a chance I'll pop back in later in the week,' I say, and give her a grin.

'Oh, okay,' she says. With a slice of disappointment and a shrug she thrusts my books into a Grey's plastic bag.

'Thanks, bye,' I reply, and run out without looking back, hearing the next guy in the queue practically throw himself at her counter behind me.

Walking quickly down to Leicester Square I turn left onto Long Acre. When I get to The Majestic the back door is closed, so I walk around to the front and sit down on the steps. Catching my breath I gulp twice in quick succession and practically gag. Coughing a little I pat my chest for comfort rather than necessity.

I laugh out loud. I lean back, letting my arms on the steps behind me bear my weight. The afternoon sun soaks my face for a while.

My face cools, my freckles dart back in, and I open my eyes to swear at the cloud that has stolen my sun, but it is Gavin standing in front of me, three steps down but still big enough to block out the rays.

'Have you been here all this time?' he asks, sounding only slightly more interested than the kids in yellow hats who ask, 'Do you want fries with that?'

113

'God, no. I've been all over.'

'What are you doing now?'

'I'm not sure, I've run out of things to do before Gerry's. What about you?'

'I'm ready for the pub. We're all going. You want to join us?'

'Why not!'

I push myself to my feet, shiver slightly as I feel the evening draw in, and make my way back to Soho.

Tucked into a corner of Soho Spice between Arabella's skinny nervous understudy, and giant Gavin, and chewing on a Chicken Kashmiri, I eyed Tom Harvey-Saint at the end of the table attempting to feed nan bread to a model that Gavin informed me he had seen with Tom a couple of times. Her name was Angel and her limbs were so long that her hands seemed like distant relatives of her shoulders, and her eyes glared out angrily from her skinny face. I noticed that she and Tom shared a Chicken Tikka with no rice but then pushed their chairs back simultaneously and disappeared to the toilets. Tom emerged ten minutes later, and Angel followed a couple of minutes after that, grabbing her bag and leaving without saying goodbye to anybody, including Tom, who glanced around the table and remembered that I was there, and tried to catch my eye. I kept trying not to look back but as a study in self-restraint it wasn't impressive, and became even less so the more wine that I consumed.

As Soho turned neon we stumbled south towards the Crown and Two Chairmen on Dean Street, for more wine. I chatted vaguely to Tristan's assistant who told me it was his birthday, but still didn't tell me his name. Tom Harvey-Saint disappeared, while Gavin and Arabella flirted in a corner by the cigarette machine. We left the pub as they rang the bell for last orders, and I noticed the mist again. A mist keeps falling on London, every night at 10.55 p.m. It's the Last Orders bell that seems to toll it in. It settles heavily within minutes and obscures the faces of strangers and anybody more than three feet away. It forces me to look really hard and closely at the people I am with, to make sure they are the people I should be with. Tonight I'm not so sure.

Five hours and one curry and two bottles of red wine later I sit cross-legged talking to Tristan at a table in Gerry's. It's twenty minutes until midnight, but it's still early for Gerry's.

They buzzed us in, somebody is a member, and we plummeted down the steps into the one large room. It's busy, there must be forty of us in total all squinting at the old actors' photos on the walls to see who we're standing next to tonight.

'I think my life bubble's bursting, Tristan. Can you take those bloody glasses off now please?'

'I can't, love, no. It's too smoky.' Tristan is playing an imaginary piano with his fingers. It looks like Billy Joel, and it's certainly not Chopin. His index finger bangs the air delicately while the rest tickle the space between us, racing to catch up.

'Then stop lighting those sodding cigarettes!' I lift my arm to sniff my cardigan suspiciously. 'I smell like a French shrubbery,' I whisper, to myself more than anybody else.

'Look. No. Stop it! Stop playing me up, Make-up. No tantrums. No stamping your stiletto. I'm not one of your boys. You won't wind me around your pretty little painted finger, love, you won't tie me up in knots. No batting those eyelids, no pouting, no half-smiles and dropped chins and glances up. Stop it. Jesus!' He shakes his head and his piano-playing fingers fold into fists at either side of his squeezed-shut eyes. At least I think they are squeezed shut. The muscles around his cheeks tighten, but the Jackie O's obscure my view.

'Just act natural, Make-up! And tell me: are you happy?'

'Me act natural? Me? That's rich, Elton air-piano John!'

I tut at him childishly and roll my eyes so quickly it makes me light-headed. 'Am I happy? No. Of course not. Who can manage happiness when their relationship is ending? It's not party time, it's not knock-knock jokes with every other line of conversation around at my house! It's not all whoops of excitement and belly laughs and "Ooh my thong's too tight and my boyfriend thinks I'm a size eight and I'm really a size ten and I shouldn't eat those two squares of chocolate but I'm gonna and aren't I scatty but cute and pass the Lambrini." SHIT! This is serious stuff, Tristan. I'm going to end up on my own.' My shoulders sag dramatically as if God has just poured an invisible bucket of water over my head and now I'm soaked and heavy and dripping. It's a deliberately pathetic look and I ham it up even further with a pout.

'Stop it . . .' Tristan is wagging a stiff and angry finger at me so ferociously that it makes his pink beads swing around his neck like a hula girl gone wrong. He points to my shoulders and gestures for me to sit up, so I do, and I drop the pout with a huge slug of red wine. Red. It's not Chardonnay, it's red, so red that it's staining the inside of my lips. Very slowly he gives me a grin, which gets wider by the second, until eventually I see his teeth. His mouth is huge, and so wide it should be painted on like a clown's.

'You will end up alone if you don't stop fucking moaning, love! But, still, I have to concede that you're a little dark, Make-up, and of course I like that. I like the devil in you, you're a fallen angel. You know that's what devils are – angels that fell from the sky during the battle of heaven. When the angels rebelled God punished them and sent them to the fiery furnace at the centre of the earth!' He nods his head and is terribly earnest. I pay attention. 'But riddle me this, Angel, if not now, when were you last happy?'

I don't even have to think about it, I already know. It's a

question I've asked myself a hundred times recently. I don't count sheep when I can't sleep: I drive myself crazy with nightmare posers like that. It's a peculiar masochism, and, I believe, a genuinely female form of torture.

'Five or six months after Ben and I first got together. Nearly three years ago. We were only really happy for the time it took him to leave his wife, and then maybe a couple of months after that. Then he opened the door sneakily when I wasn't looking and let her back in the room. And he seemed to forget, suddenly, what it was that he saw in me, like he'd fallen and banged his head and had selective amnesia. It made me feel like one of those supermarket-sized bars of Dairy Milk choco-late – better to dream about than actually have, because after-wards you feel a bit sick and all you're left with is guilt.'

'So . . . what's changed since then?' Tristan asks, as he watches the ice cubes rock at the bottom of his glass.

'Him.'

'Not you?' he asks, surprised.

'No.' I shake my head but the word doesn't sound right. I have trouble forming the 'o'. It's as if I cannot tell a lie, on this occasion. Because of course I can lie and I do, most of the time.

'Not you at all?' he asks. With one finger he reaches behind his ear and flicks the arm of his glasses so they spring up and down on his nose like Groucho Marx.

'Well, maybe a bit . . .'

I have changed. When Ben and I first met he thought I was exciting. I was wide-eyed and innocent and fun. I laughed all the time, and I made him run through the streets with me. And although he ran with reluctance he was still smiling while he did it. I was the confident one and he made me feel like a breath of fresh air. When I made him laugh it felt like a victory, and when he kissed my head, or ran his hand across my back, I felt like the only person that would see that side of him. I thought that I'd managed to open the door to somewhere

117

deeper, a place that he'd never let anybody in before. But then he pulled it shut again.

Now I'm this weird cake-mix of disinterest and desperation. A sprinkling of neediness coupled with long, thick lashings of 'never there'. When I do see Ben I spend my time squirming my way under his arm into a contrived cuddle, which is part of the reason that I try not to see him too much. There is only so much twisting my neck can take without snapping! The mere idea of Ben walking up to me and throwing his arms around me, bear-hugging me to near-death without some kind of coaching, is laugh-out-loud funny. It's funny awful, if such a thing exists. It's not funny ha ha. I have changed.

In the beginning I wasn't exhausted by trying to hit a nail on its head that didn't want to be hit. I wasn't desperate and crazy with the effort of trying to pinpoint what was wrong with me. When Ben and I first met I thought myself inherently loveable, and then I fell in love with him one day. Driving me to the train station, after a night spent together at the flat of a man that he worked with who was away on business, we came to a railway crossing. There were cars in front and behind us, and we were all moving at about twenty miles an hour. When it was our turn to bump over the railway crossing Ben turned to me, with his hands on the wheel and the car in motion, widened his eyes and screamed 'argh-hhhh!' for the three seconds it took us to cross. I laughed out loud and with surprise. It was the silliest thing I had ever seen him do, and suddenly I knew that I was in love. But then I learnt, as time crept on, that unfortunately I wasn't loveable, and it kicked the shit out of me.

Of course, I resolved to make myself loveable, somehow, but nothing seemed to work. So then, for my own sanity and peace of mind and pride – pride! – I resolved to pretend Ben loved me anyway, with contrived cuddles and asked-for kisses and sofa inquisitions, desperately dragging a nice word out of him that I could cling to for weeks. I have changed – I know that I have – but not because I wanted to. I read in the paper last week about a man who shot a woman dead in the street near Victoria Coach Station. They had been lovers but she ended it after a month because she didn't see a future with him. A month doesn't seem that long, I am sure she thought little of it. Unfortunately he was already so crazily in love with her that he went out and bought a 1941 German pistol, walked up to her and shot her outside Superdrug before turning the gun on himself. My first thought when I read this story in the *Standard* was: At least she knew he loved her. My second thought was terror, at my increasingly twisted psyche. My third thought was to circle the story for Ben before I left him the paper on the kitchen table that night, and to write alongside it, 'You could learn a little something.' Or maybe, 'Watch your back.' But I realise that's not funny either.

'Maybe I've changed a little. I've put on a bit of weight.'

'Have you?' Tristan chuckles. 'How much?'

'About a stone, in three years.' I take a large gulp of my wine to wash away the facts.

'Did it all go to the pillows?' He smiles warmly at my breasts in turn, as if they are two small children who have just joined us.

'No. Some of it's gone to my thighs as well.'

'They look okay from here.' Tristan isn't looking, of course. He's eyeing up the room for more fun than me, and I don't blame him. I'm boring myself.

'What do you care?' I wait for him to turn back to me with an indignant look on my face. He has the attention span of a teenager at an MTV and Xbox convention. He is staring at a crowd in the corner who are cracking open a bottle of Veuve Clicquot.

'I can still appreciate it, darling,' he says absent-mindedly, but spins back to me, shaking his head to clear it of some nasty thought or other.

'Who has told you my little secret anyway? Who's let on? I can still do it, you know, love. I may be a non-libidinist, but there are other reasons to do it. Not many good ones I grant you, and they generally aren't that convincing, but for you . . .' He lowers his glasses and flashes the reddish whites of his eyes at me. I catch my breath. For a second I think I glimpse the devil.

'I think I could be persuaded to pop a pill, Make-up, if you fancy a joy ride?'

My stare is incredulous, but he is too crazy to notice.

'No thank you, Tristan, but you're bloody Mother Teresa to offer.'

He waves his palm in front of him; don't mention it, any time. 'I just don't understand how you can be this gorgeous and this miserable!' He smiles again. He has strange yet winning ways.

'Because I'm quite obviously not gorgeous! I'm a complete construction, I'm a fabricated pretty. I'm a make-up artist for Christ's sake! I'm no natural beauty, young, fresh-faced, without lines or sagging, thin in most places but plump of breast and pout.'

'What utter shit! That sounds like a whole truckful of cobblers to me. I could pick out a thousand girls who'd eat my hand off to look like you, Make-up.'

'My name is Scarlet, Tristan! It's not a hard name to remember; can't you use it once in a while? Anyway, not in London they aren't! All the women in London are gorgeous. I am terribly, horribly average.' I stare at the bottom of my wine glass. I don't even want another one. I want to go home to somebody that loves me.

'And that's it, is it? That's the end of the wonderful world? Love, I know it's your job but you might want to think about something other than pretty, and sometime soon! It's just smoke and mirrors.' He reaches up and strokes my cheek with a surprisingly rough finger. It runs the course of my face until it settles under my chin and tilts up my head.

'I know I put a lot of emphasis on it, Tristan, but you wouldn't understand. You're not female for a start, it's not one of the essential criteria you'll be judged on. You're not subject to a bathing-suit section. But for a woman, getting older, something shifts. I know I'm still attractive but I'll never be that hot new thing any more. The problem is that I also know it kind of wouldn't matter, not half as much at least, if I had somebody who loved me: me! And not the way that I look. But I don't, and it stings like hell. It's as if it would be okay, it would be anaesthetic enough for the pain, if I had something better, something instead, but I don't. I think that's why I'm so absorbed by our problems, mine and Ben's. If he loved me it wouldn't matter so much. But he doesn't. So I don't have anything.' I shake my head and try and make him understand.

'I don't have those next thirty-something options. What next, if not with love? What next, if the next steps aren't there for me?'

'Are you sure he doesn't love you, love? You've done little but whinge at me for the whole twelve hours that I've known you, but I've already got a bit of a crush . . .' Tristan's finger is still propped under my chin, tilting my face towards his. If it were anybody else I'd show him the yellow card.

'All I have to go on is how he acts and what he occasionally says. He doesn't act like he loves me when I see him, we have no real physical contact and no affection, and he says that he can't say that he loves me, at least not yet. But . . . it . . . has . . . been . . . THREE YEARS! He should have fucking said it by now, surely!'

'Where?' Tristan looks over his shoulder, but still with his hand under my chin.

'What?' I ask.

'Shirley?' he says seriously.

'Childish, Tristan. Childish.' I tell him off.

Our faces are breathing space apart. I think that he can find sport in anything. Where other hearts might bruise, Tristan's dances.

'I'm sorry. I don't know, I'm running out of answers – could he possibly be dead inside?'

'Maybe. I just don't think he feels anything for me. I have to leave.'

'What, now? It's only just midnight, Cinderella, and I was hoping you'd lead a conga!' Tristan is so close to me that he is whispering.

'I mean I have to leave Ben.'

'You said it.' He leans in and kisses me gently on the lips. I don't kiss him back, he doesn't deserve it. There is no tongue. His Jackie O's bang against my nose.

'Now!' He pulls back, sits up straight and claps his hands, enlivened like a vampire after a sudden stabbed blood injection into a vein bursting out of a belt-squeezed arm. 'Can we please talk about something else? Please! You're killing me, Make-up, with this talk of unrequited love.'

'Yes.' I nod my head and feel the wine coursing through me. Enough sad talk, enough tears, enough melancholy, baby.

'Yes, Tristan, Lucifer, whoever you may be! Absolutely yes! I'm driving myself crazy! Let's definitely talk about something else. What do you want to talk about?' We take a simultaneous hit of our drinks as a fat man walks into the bar and shouts, 'I'm home!' Some people cheer, Tristan smiles faintly.

'Let's talk about me,' he says, searching forwards for the rim of his glass with his lips.

'Okay . . . how long have you lived in Streatham?'

'Oh, love, that's dull as shit. Something else.'

I cough with embarrassment and balk, but try again.

122

'How long have you wanted to be in theatre?' I ask, less confidently this time.

'Oh all my life, love, and I have been, kind of, and will be. No, something else, something bigger.' He nods his head but offers no clues.

'Okay, let's talk about you not wanting sex? Where does that leave you in the love stakes? Have you ever been in love?'

He smiles a long, slow smile again. I think that's better.

'Oh shit, darling, thousands of times,' he states quietly. I have to strain to hear him above the gentle Gerry's roar. 'You don't need sex for love. You need sex for a relationship, but not for love. I mean, what is love when you look at it? It's just a need to be with somebody, how they make you feel when they are with you, and how you let yourself feel when you're with them, how you reflect in their light, or their shadow. What you see in them. *"And all that's best of dark and bright, Meet in her aspect and her eyes."* Byron. He knew it. Of course he had a lot of sex as well, but he understood where it starts and where it ends. In the eyes. A back can arch,' his hands curve in front of him, 'and a smile can catch you and carry you and smash you against rocks like a cruel and powerful wave. And you can admire many things, many things,' Tristan nods his head to himself, 'a leg, an arse, a wing. Be a tit man, a bum man, a leg man, a face man, a hair man, a cock man, anything, anything. But that's all sex, it's just sex. Love? Love only comes from the eyes.'

The bar is dark now, but warm with bodies and laughter.

'Ben would much rather spend time with Iggy than with me,' I say, 'and he only kisses me with his eyes closed. I ask him to open them sometimes, but he can't. Not a passionate kiss, just a small quick peck, with his eyes open. But he can't.'

'I think he might be hiding something,' Tristan says, nodding his head, as if that's okay and not going to ruin my night and my life. 'But more importantly, who the fuck is

Iggy? Something to do with Top Cat? The small orange one with the annoying voice?'

'The cartoon?' I ask, incredulous. 'No, Tristan, Iggy is Ben's best mate. He's not a cat. He works in a warehouse in Ealing.'

'Oh. Okay. I think I'm starting to get the picture. Are you sure you're not just way too much for this poor fool, Make-up? Hmmm?' I see his eyebrows stretch up above his glasses, he is widening his eyes at me, nodding at me to agree. 'I mean, you seem like a handful in every sense.' He winks at my chest and I sigh – no more breast jokes. 'And he sounds like a simple chap, with simple friends, Make-up . . .'

'My name is Scarlet! It's easy: Scar-let. Scarlet. Try it, you might like it!'

'No, love, I can't. If I call you by your real name I make everybody else jealous. You want that, do you? You want blood on your hands?'

'But you call Gavin by his real name!' I say, tugging at his suit jacket, but he shrugs me off.

'Gavin could kill me with his thumbs. Have you seen the size of him? How big is an actual giant, I mean really?'

'He's not that big, Tristan!' I say. I was trying to be stern but now I've got the giggles. 'He's probably about six foot six. He's not clinically tall, Tristan.'

'I don't agree. I'm going to look it up. I bet you a tenner he's giant material,' he says, nodding and taking a swig of his vodka rocks, then offering me his hand to shake on the deal.

'No.' I bat his hand away. I don't know much about height, but I don't think it would go down well with Gavin if he found out we'd been betting on him being a giant, especially after the midget fiasco. 'Anyway,' I say, 'how can I be too much for Ben? I mean, how can you be too much for anybody? That's just stupid. They should just like the fact that you have all of these qualities and that you want to be with them. They should just like it, surely?'

'Where?' Tristan looks over both shoulders then back to me.

'Childish, Tristan! Stop it!'

He smiles broadly and swigs the last of his vodka and grimaces. 'Okay, my glass is more ice cube than alcohol so I know I've stayed too long with you, love. You've hogged me all night like a big greedy cow, and now you have to share me with the rest of the class. However, I will say this. Don't be naïve. You can be far too much for someone, if they feel like they don't measure up, if they can't be bothered like you can, to improve, to perfect, to challenge themselves. The reason we aren't all driven is because some of us aren't and some of us don't want to be! Some people, possibly your Ben, just want to kick back and relax and lead an average life. I personally have nearly always been too much for everybody that I've met, including my own mother. It's actually a blessing that I have no fucking libido,' he smiles at what he's said, 'otherwise I'd be as miserable as you are!'

He stands up to leave but I pull him back down by the arm of his suit. 'No, wait, just quickly. So you're saying that limited enjoyment, but with no effort, can be all that some people want? As opposed to wringing life dry of enjoyment, but with the effort that it takes to do that? I don't understand that, there's no choice there! Why would anybody settle for less?'

'Because you are you, sweet Scarlet.' I widen my eyes as he says my name, but then he puts his finger to his lips and says, 'Shush. Just once, I won't say it again. But if you were silly old Ben, there would be a choice, and it might be the one that he's making.'

'I don't want that,' I say flatly, 'I don't want to be with somebody who doesn't want to get everything they can out of life.'

'Well that's YOUR choice,' Tristan says.

I don't want him to leave, I feel like I've had an epiphany.

I scramble quickly for something to say as he looks to stand up again.

'So, Tristan, is it hard, you know, with your mother? I mean, you said, about her legs?' Inside my head somewhere I grimace. That isn't the best key-change I've ever made. Tristan, who is ready to take a swig on the ice at the bottom of his glass, stops with the rim at his lips. He tilts his black plastic Jackie O's downwards and looks up at me, so that I can see the reds of his eyes.

'Of course it's fucking hard, Make-up, she can't walk. She can't get out of her bed on her own. She can't get herself in and out of the bath.'

'Oh . . . I'm sorry, Tristan . . . I didn't mean to sound flippant or . . . Of course, I'll shut up now.'

He pushes himself to his feet. 'Perspective, Make-up. That's what you need.'

'Okay. I know. I mean, your problems are still your problems, but I know. Perspective.'

'And dedication.'

'That's what you need?' I ask.

He smiles and mouths 'cheer the fuck up' as he saunters off towards the champagne in the corner, popping his empty glass onto the bar as he goes so that he can stretch out his arms to hug and welcome all the new friends he's about to make with the orange-labelled bottle of fizz.

I glance down at my tights to check for runs, and think about getting another drink. A second later Gavin slumps down in the spot Tristan has just vacated, as well as the spot next to it that has luckily just emptied out as well. From our vantage spot we eye the room, an unhappy audience.

'You know I said she wasn't easy?' Gavin begins, staring straight ahead.

'Yep.' He is talking about Arabella, and I glance around to see if I can spot her.

126

'Case in point.' Gavin points to the end of the bar. She is leaning back against it with her elbows on either side of her super-slim torso. Her small pointed breasts jut out in her silky white top, which has been tucked tightly into her purple trousers. It's car-crash fashion, despite her beauty. I am always amazed that most actresses can't dress themselves. Stylists do a remarkable job of convincing the rest of us that these rare beauties always look amazing, but it's an utter lie. If they were left to their own devices the red carpet would resemble a catwalk of ugly chiffon chaos. Don't be deceived. But still I gasp. Arabella's top is transparent in the spotlight that has sought her out in this dim little bar, and you can clearly see the small, dark-stained circles of her nipples. She giggles with Tom Harvey-Saint, who leans in like a predator, breathing on her neck as she strokes it with thin, elegant fingers. I wait for him to bare his teeth like fangs and plunge them into her flesh. She clinks her champagne glass with his, oblivious to the danger, or loving it. He senses his audience and glances over in our direction, raising his glass to Gavin and me. I shudder.

'What the hell was that?' Gavin asks, looking from me to Tom, his voice showing traces of angry disgust.

'I don't know. He's a complete prick, it doesn't matter' I say hastily, and furious with myself for being caught looking. 'But Gavin, I think you should go and speak to Arabella, you can completely see through her top!'

'I know,' he says evenly.

'No, Gavin, I'm serious. You can see her nipples and every-thing!'

'I've already told her. She doesn't care. She says it doesn't matter, and it's dark.'

'It's not THAT dark,' I reply, pleading with him. I notice other people looking over at her, comically double-taking as they realise what's visually on offer.

'I know,' he says, 'but what more can I do?'

Gavin has bought me a drink and pushes a red wine into my hand, taking the empty glass out of it first. We lazily clink our glasses and take a desperate simultaneous gulp of our drinks.

'Do you think there are bigger questions to be asked, Gavin?' I turn to face him. He is staring down at his shirt, examining a button.

'What is infinity?' he suggests.

'Not that kind of big,' I say.

'Who's the fattest man that ever lived to fifty?' he asks.

'Not that kind of big, Gavin,' I repeat.

'Mars, Jupiter, Saturn . . . Uranus . . . which one is . . . you know . . . bigger?'

'For the love of God, Gavin, not that kind of big! I'm talking about the "but why"s, the "I don't want to do this any more"s, the "it doesn't feel like enough"s!'

'None of which sound half as much fun as my fat man conversation would be,' he says, trying not to look at the bar as I hear Arabella shriek with theatrical laughter. Her bony bare arms fly in and out of my eye-line as Tom spins her around to music that has suddenly piped up from soft speakers. Barry White croons 'Just The Way You Are' dimly out from the corners of the room, barely audible enough for us to hear it, but loud enough for Tom and Arabella to seize the chance to rub up against each other.

I sigh. Gavin sighs.

'When I was a little girl,' I say, 'there was Prince Charming. There was a book and there was Prince Charming, and he was handsome and he wanted to marry the princess. He didn't want to live with her and see, or move in, or use her, or split the rent, but not make any big decisions because he wasn't ready for that kind of commitment.'

'No! No!' Gavin violently hits his forehead with the base of his hand in mock stupidity, but it looks like it hurts and it leaves a red mark.

'What's wrong?' I ask, appalled.

'No more relationship shit, Scarlet! Don't you get tired of it? Doesn't it exhaust you?'

It does, but I can't help it. I try and make myself think of other things, but it's like an ebbing tide. Just as I manage to drift into a whole other topic, this huge wave of confusion crashes back over me, and I remember that I don't know what I'm doing with my life. I am constantly desperate to talk about it with anybody, in search of some elusive truth, but I'm not going to admit that to Gavin: he will undoubtedly leave and I can't sit here and talk to myself!

'Wait! Gavin, it's not relationship shit, it's different I promise! I'm going somewhere else completely with this! Wait! Don't go!'

He eyes me suspiciously, sitting up, ready to leave.

'Is it going to John Barnes?' he asks. 'Or Steve Ovett versus Steve Cram versus Seb Coe – who'd win now?'

'Coincidentally, yes it is,' I say, nodding my head and smiling.

'You're lying,' he replies, shaking his.

'Well you'll have to wait and see.'

'No I won't,' he says, but then, 'Jesus!'

Arabella is rubbing noses with Tom, as they eat separate ends of a Twiglet, working their way into the middle.

I grab Gavin's hands and pull him towards me so that we are facing each other. He is really heavy. I think me *and* a friend could sit in one of those palms.

'Gavin, look at me! Don't do anything, don't say anything to her, that's what she wants. Just sit here and have my conversation.'

He seems genuinely bewildered and upset by her behaviour. I'm starting to realise that Gavin is a bit squishy on the inside, like a marshmallow cake. I worry for him. That's no way to be today, that's no recipe for modern love.

'Okay, talk,' he says, 'but no crying.'

'Okay.' I swipe my hair away from my face, and compose myself. 'You tell me, Gavin: what is the point in fairytales, other than to cause inexorable harm? I think that they are the work of the devil. They are pure evil. They promise children, young girls mostly, a version of the world that doesn't exist, and they do it when you are at your most vulnerable and impressionable age.'

I stare at Gavin for a response but he just shrugs his shoulders, so I continue. 'You know when somebody tells you something when you are young that is crazy, but you always kind of believe it? For instance, my brother Richard told me when I was about seven and he was about four that babies came out of women's belly buttons, and part of me still thinks it's true.'

Gavin looks at me like I am crazy.

'I know that it's not true, Gavin, but I sort of still believe it as well. And my dad told me you should never squeeze a spot on your forehead, or anywhere above your eyebrow, because all the evil nasty yuk in it will go back into your head and you'll get brain poisoning! And you know what? I still don't touch a spot above my eyebrow, because it still scares me! My point is that I believed all that stuff, and in the same way I believed in Prince Charming. I believed in Snow White and the dwarves and the apple and the Prince, and Cinderella and her stepmother and her ugly sisters and the Prince, but now I find that it's just not true! They were all lies. Of course the stories themselves were made up, but the sentiment, the same sentiment that ran through all of them, was a big fat huge bastard lie! I know that any innocence that I do have left is just about clinging on for dear life, although it is being kicked out of me daily, and any naïvety that I had left took the last tube out of here a long time ago. But still – STILL! – I can't quite shake those stories

130

off. I know there is no such thing as Prince Charming, but part of me is still demanding to know where mine is? Has his horse got a flat hoof? Where the hell is he? And I don't expect him to be wearing velvet jodhpurs, or have that long, weird Prince hair that they always had in the books. But I was kind of hoping that I'd meet somebody nice, who'd be nice to me, and who'd love me and let me love them. That's really all I want. But . . . I'm starting to think he's not coming. Or maybe he just found some other girl, in some other forest, and decided she'd do. Everything that I've seen at the cinema, or heard sung on the radio, or read late at night, has just perpetuated a big fat lie. The same romantic myth has pervaded my life from day one, and I feel like somehow I was supposed to realise and see past it. But why wouldn't I believe it, why wouldn't it be real?'

'Oh my God.' Gavin stares at me in alarm. 'Dolly is going to tear you to pieces,' he says, but as if he is reading my pizza order back down the phone to me.

'Maybe. Do you know if she was ever in musicals, Gavin?'

'I don't. I haven't heard her sing.' He shrugs and gulps his scotch sour.

'I have always loved musicals. I used to watch them with my mum. She loved *Calamity Jane*. Have you seen it?'

Gavin shakes his head and examines his drink. I may as well be talking to myself.

'I love the fact that she wasn't the pretty one, but then all of a sudden she was! It was magical. Nobody loved her, then everybody did, and it was just make-up and a dress. A woman's touch, that's what they called it, and it's powerful stuff. I really saw the value, you know, in being beautiful, in showing the world what you've got, making the best of yourself. But now . . . now it means too much. Now, when I lose it, maybe I don't have anything. You know I shouted at some prick today for wearing a T-shirt that I hated? It said, *"Don't ask if you're ugly*". But I believe it, Gavin. I called him a prick, but I do agree, just a little. An ugly shouldn't ask him out, he won't say yes. We all know it, and she'll just get hurt because he'll laugh in her face. We can say whatever we want about personality but it only means so much. Pretty people have more choices, and more freedom to be loveable and kind and sweet because everybody loves them first. They aren't bitter because there is nothing to be bitter about – they got the aces in the deck, the genetic luck. Do you know what he called me? The prick in the T-shirt? "Just a pair of tits" – and do you know what's the most humiliating thing? Part of me believes him.'

Gavin glances up at me from his drink with surprise.

'You need to believe in yourself a bit more than that, Scarlet. You've got a great job, you're your own boss, you're a success. You're certainly more than tits. And just because you look good doesn't mean that's all you are either. Men see more than that. Granted it might take them a while, but you have to interest each other as well.'

I smile. It's the age-old male argument – you have to interest us, you have to make us laugh. They don't mean it. I have had my fair share of men talking at me and not to me, and ignoring a girl in the corner with glasses or a vast arse. They weren't so interested in what I had to say, half of them weren't even listening. I ask myself which is better: looking a certain way that results in being asked out by twenty men in one night who have no idea who you are or what you stand for and who just like the look of you, which generally means they want sex, or . . . looking another way that results in being asked out by just one guy, an average-looking guy, but a guy who has taken the time to chat to you because you weren't surrounded by good-looking losers, and who has decided that he'd like to spend more time with you to find out who you are . . . Answers on a postcard addressed to Scarlet White, The Majestic Theatre, Covent Garden.

'I think that one of the main differences between men and women is that women are ultimately looking for love, and men have to have it take them by surprise. Women are warmed up and stretched and ready on the sidelines. Men need it to fall on their heads and knock them out before they realise it.'

'That's not true, Scarlet. Men, women, blah, blah, blah. Aren't we all individuals? You can't just prescribe me with certain traits and say I fit that mould, you don't even know me.'

'This coming from the man going out with the most stunning woman in the room,' I say.

'You and I aren't going out yet, Scarlet.' He smiles to himself.

'Funny,' I say, and poke his stomach. It's surprisingly hard.

'I know. I know I'm saying one thing and doing another. But beauty only means so much, Scarlet, and I honestly believe that. Look around you: it's not the beautiful relationships that last. They might get more sex, but beautiful people are a little bit fucked up as well, because too many people want them, but for the wrong thing! It's far better to be a little bit average I think. Not stunning, but not hideous. You've got much more chance of being happy. Beauty does not breed security. Too many people covet what you've got, and you start to question whether you are good enough yourself to deserve it.' He shakes his head.

'Maybe. Oh Gavin I just want to feel like I understand something, anything, about myself. It doesn't matter what it is, just something. I don't want to be a cliché. I don't want to do things because they are a distraction, I want to do things because I mean them. I don't want to finish with Ben, miss him for a while, hate him for a while, miss him again. Then meet a new boy, get married, have a baby, distract myself. What happens if I do all of that, hit fifty, and I'm still not happy? What will I have done with my life? There just has to be an answer. Like in the musicals! At the first opportunity there was always a room full of dancers dressed as waiters or housemaids or workers in a sweet factory, and they'd be high-kicking, or doing the splits, or doing that dance where they run on the spot and kick. You know, the one that always looks vaguely Russian, and seems like a lot of work? But the implication was joy! Like in *Hello Dolly*, with Barbra Streisand – do you know *Hello Dolly*?'

'Nope.' Gavin shakes his head, bored again. I don't care, I've found my enthusiasm.

'Well, there is this scene, this song, where they all wear their "Sunday Clothes". And they all dance down the street, and they sing that whenever they feel down or blue they should put on their best dresses and suits and parade about in them and it will make them feel better. They sing about being dressed like dreams, Gavin! And they sing it! You know, part of me is always waiting for a street to burst into song. Oxford Street or Charing Cross Road could just musically explode! Or Soho Square would be perfect! And suddenly everybody could just be high-kicking on the pavement, or cartwheeling off benches.'

'There are a lot of homosexuals there, they can all dance, it could work,' Gavin says, nodding his head.

'You see! That's right! It would be glorious! And we could all sing "Put On Your Sunday Clothes"! I just think . . . I think that it might be all it takes, to make me feel better. I just need my joy now . . .' And suddenly I'm exhausted, utterly spent. This modern life. It sure is draining.

'Maybe you should have it printed onto a T-Shirt?' Gavin says, smiling.

'Not a bad idea. In large red letters. "*Where's my joy?*"'
I say, my head drooping.

'At the bottom of this glass, darling,' Tom Harvey-Saint whispers in my ear as he slides in next to me with a large glass of blood-red wine. I can smell his Cool Water aftershave and his Lynx deodorant and his Aquafresh toothpaste. I can tell you that he smoked a Camel Light earlier on this evening and has been drinking champagne and amaretto for the rest of it. Once again the hairs on his arm shriek up and static against the hairs on mine. He's way too close.

'No,' I say, flinching, and I shunt along the seat towards Gavin, but he stands up and strides over to Arabella. Two old Turkish men quickly fill the space Gavin has left, and I find myself squashed up against Tom Harvey-Saint, experiencing violent feelings towards him that I don't know if I can control. He makes me passionately angry, but I am sure this is not the kind of passion I am after. Maybe I don't get to choose which kind I get? I desperately search the room with my eyes for somebody to save me, but only Tristan's hair is visible amongst the champagne crowd in the corner, and Gavin and Arabella are already having an argument. I feel Tom's hand on the silk of my skirt, and his fingers spread like a virus to grasp the flesh of my thigh beneath it.

'No!' I say loudly, and throw his hand off my knee. 'And by the way, you're completely fucking with their relationship, but then you know that, right?'

He smiles a movie-star smile but I can see that there is nothing more behind his dilated eyes than fizz and liquor. His teeth are so impeccably white and straight that they cannot be real. 'Are you serious? It's not a relationship to fuck with. She's just trampolining on him for a while. Drink?' He pushes the red wine towards me on the table. I shake my head.

'No. Have you ever had a relationship, Tom?'

'I don't need one. I'm happy as I am.'

'What, this?' I say with a laugh, gesturing up and down his sloped and drunken form. 'Drinking and sleeping with strangers? This is your idea of happy?'

'Darling, this is a lot of people's idea of *very* happy.'

'Maybe so, but it's only temporary. It's not real, or permanent. It's gin-soaked and it will hurt like hell tomorrow. It's not an answer to anything, is it?'

'But darling, that's why people have pets. If you want to feel all warm and cute and cuddly, you get a dog, or a cat, or a baby.' He reels off the list and makes no distinction between any of them.

'A baby? Babies aren't pets!'

'Yes they are, as bloody good as. You have to feed them, clear up their shit and pay for them. That's a pet, right?'

'And they love you, and you protect them and teach them and share with them . . .' I nod my head at him like he's the class dunce, incapable of understanding.

'Oh it's a borrowed fucking innocence, Susan.'

'Scarlet,' I say.

'Can't I just call you Make-up?' he asks.

'Absolutely not,' I say.

'Okay, Scarlet, but pets certainly aren't real happiness, darling. They just put more pressure on. You think with their smiles and their wagging tails and gurgles that they are the valves that let out the pressure, but they just add to it. You need more money to buy them things, but you also need more time to spend with them so they don't grow up disturbed.'

'I assume both your parents were workaholics,' I say.

He looks angry. Something turns. 'You're very familiar with me, Scarlet, and I'm not sure that I like it. I'm Key Cast. You're Make-up. You can be quite cutting for somebody that I have barely spoken to.'

'I guess I just feel like I know you already,' I say.

'I feel like I know you too, or I'd like to know how you feel, at least.'

'I don't even know me!' I say. 'Not any more. I always thought I'd be loyal and faithful, but I'm not. I have sex with men who aren't my boyfriend: my nights are sprinkled with encounters that range from tiny chaste kisses to violent fellatio for Gods sake! And alleyway fumbles under skirts, and boobs poking out of bras, and strange, maimed sex angles . . .'

'Seriously?' He grins at me like the Cheshire cat.

'Oh Jesus, I'm not telling you to turn you on. I'm drunk. I'm saying it's a bad thing, not a roller coaster of fun. I need to stop talking now. I need to go.'

'Wait, Scarlet. Wait. What are you looking for? What's with the search?' His hand rests gently on my arm, and his whole demeanour softens as if he just thawed out of an icy shell.

'Do you really want to know?' I ask.

'Yes. Of course. What are you looking for, Scarlet?' he asks, straight-faced and serious.

'I think I just want what everybody wants, whether they articulate it or not. I just want something real. I want to experience a series of . . . joyful moments . . . that I can't corrupt with my own cynicism, or somebody else's. More than that, even. I want to share this series of joyful moments with somebody, and have them feel it too.'

'You're absolutely right, Scarlet, I've never thought of it like that, and it's perfect, it's exactly what I want. Joy. You want that, and so do I, Scarlet, so do I.'

'I have to be honest, Tom, I'm surprised you feel that way.'

'But darling, you don't even know me.' Tom's eyes widen and he smiles at me innocently. Maybe I have read him wrong. Maybe my own cynicism has morphed him into something ugly, something that he isn't.

'That's true, I barely know you,' I say. His finger brushes my thigh, but I let it pass. It's probably unintentional and I need to stop jumping to crazy conclusions. Maybe I'm the arsehole and Tom is just this sweet guy that I've completely misread, and projected all my gender anxieties onto?

We sit and smile at each other, and I reach for my red wine and take a slug.

Tom leans forward and whispers, 'Shall we take this outside?'

For God's sake. I was right the first time.

'You have got to be kidding me . . . what is wrong with you?'

'What?'

'No, I do not want to come outside with you.'

'I mean for joy, Scarlet. We could be joyful together, I know this alley. Oh come on!'

'Hell no! You think I'm going to find my joyful moment in some seedy alley? Are you crazy?'

'Okay, whatever, darling, don't have a hernia. But I think you should give it a try, it might cheer you the fuck up. And from what I've heard you're not getting it at home. We all have needs, Scarlet, don't be embarrassed. Come on, just a quick one?' he asks, shameless.

'Oh all right then.'

'Great!' He claps his hands.

'Are you kidding? I was joking! Of course not!' I say, and slap his hand off my thigh, where it has taken up position again.

'Your loss,' he replies, then gets up and walks off. I stare after him in disbelief. He's a dinosaur. I hate him. And I hate how easy it would be to say yes.

Gavin throws himself down angrily in the space that Tom leaves.

'Gavin, did you tell Arabella that . . . that I'm not "getting any" at home?' I ask, embarrassed.

138

'I might have mentioned it, why?' He knocks back half of his drink in one gulp.

'Because she bloody well told Tom and he just offered to fill in the gaps!'

'Did you say no?' he asks, eyeing up the other half of his drink.

'Of course I said no!'

'Then what's the problem?' he shrugs, and throws back his head and his glass. 'And why "of course"? He's a good-looking guy, so Arabella tells me.'

'Because he's a sleaze-hound.'

Gavin makes a sound that is half sigh, half moan, and slaps his head with one massive hand.

'Are you all right?' I am alarmed to see a red palm imprint on his cheek – he doesn't know his own strength.

'Yes. No. Yes. Tell me a joke, Scarlet. Cheer me up. She's ignoring me now because I told her she was making a spectacle of herself.'

'Because women always like that, well done,' I say. Men amaze me. They can't say their feelings are hurt or that they feel jealous or unhappy. They have to tell a woman that she is making a fool of herself. It's never about how they feel. Now isn't the time to share that with Gavin, though. So instead I say, 'Two snowmen standing in a field. One says to the other, can you smell carrots?'

Gavin nods his head and smiles. 'That's good. Again.'

'Two Goldfish in a tank. One says to the other, who's driving this thing?'

'Nice. I like it. More.'

'A tractor turns into a field. That was unexpected.' The only jokes I can remember are the ones that my nephews tell me, but at least they are quick.

'That's good, but you haven't told that one right. Plus two thirds of your jokes are about fields.'

'Yes I have told it right. And maybe I just like fields . . .'

'No you haven't, I've heard it before. It's supposed to be different.' He pokes me in the ribs and I poke him back, as Arabella swishes her coat on at the door and leaves with somebody else, exit stage left, applause, standing ovation. I don't see who is holding her hand to pull her up the stairs, but I look around and I can't see Tom. I check my watch: it's twenty to two in the morning, and the bar has emptied out, there are only ten or so people left.

'Aren't you going to go after her?' I ask, sadly.

'What's the point?'

'The point is you're her boyfriend. The point is that . . . it will make you sad if you don't.'

'She's an adult. She can do what she wants.'

'Yes, but you don't want her to. She'll think you don't care. You should tell her how you feel.'

'Maybe I don't care. Tell me more jokes, Scarlet.' He looks up at me with his huge saucer-shaped eyes, and takes my hand to hold. His hand is so big it makes mine look like a child's. He is so large and comforting, like an oversized quilt that I could throw over myself to make me feel better about everything.

'Do you live on your own, Gavin?' I ask.

'I do.' He nods his head. We stare at each other.

It would be so easy . . . but I don't want to. It will make things worse. I think this is the first time in a long while that I have located the button in my head that when pressed, even when drunk, alarms 'You don't want to do this. You think that you do, and it will feel nice tonight, but it will feel terrible tomorrow.'

'Well turn the heating up when you get in, and sleep well, lovely Gavin. I'll see you tomorrow.'

I push myself to my feet and grab my bag.

'Wait.' Gavin stands up and ducks automatically, in case

of low-flying aircraft or birds. 'Wait. Do you want me to get you a cab or something?'

Gavin hasn't found his switch.

'No, it's fine. It's a Monday, there will be loads.'

'No, let me get you a cab.'

Gavin grabs his jacket and gestures for me to climb the stairs up and out. We fire out onto Shaftesbury Avenue and a stream of black cabs with their lights on flow past us. I hail one down and mercifully he pulls up inches from my heels.

'Hey, Scarlet, wait. Where do you live?' Gavin asks, grabbing one of my hands and pulling me around.

'The opposite direction to you. Goodnight, Gavin, I'll see you tomorrow,' I say, and jump in the cab.

'Central Ealing,' I tell the driver, and wave to Gavin. The numbers on the clock immediately start to tick as we pull off. Gavin gives me a half-hearted wave back.

The cab pulls up outside my flat at 2.20 a.m.

I pay the driver and look up. The instantly recognisable blue haze of a TV in a room with the lights turned off streams out from my living-room windows. Amazingly, Ben is still up.

Climbing the stairs I can hear giggling from the living room, but it's strictly male. Ben's friend Iggy is here.

Iggy is five years older than Ben, and moronic in its purest sense. Whenever he sees me he stares as if I'm the only woman he's ever been this close too – which I probably am. He's almost primeval: short, with a lot of hair everywhere – on his face, on his arms, poking up out of his T-shirt at the front and back, and he has slightly wonky eyes that follow me around the room, and yet can never actually meet mine when I speak to him. He has a large belly and a big round woman's arse. I have never known him have a girlfriend in the three years since we were introduced, but he always

141

crosses his legs approximately two minutes after I enter any room that he is in. I don't flatter myself that this is peculiar to me. I could send my grandmother in before me and I'm sure he'd do exactly the same. He was the best man at Ben's wedding, apparently, and made an appalling speech that died like a pheasant full of shot. He is also very confrontational, and tries to contradict everything that I say, but without imagination. Often he just says, 'I don't agree.' For instance, I'll say 'It's hot today' when it's ninety degrees in the shade outside, and he'll sit there, with sweat dripping off him like a whore in church, and say, 'I don't agree.'

He works at the store with Ben. They play a lot of Championship Manager. From the giggling I can tell that they are both drunk, and I smell skunk wafting through my flat.

I hear Iggy mutter, 'Is that Scarlet?'

'Sounds like it.'

'Do you want me to, you know, clear off?'

'Don't bother, she'll go straight to bed.'

'But don't you want to, you know . . .'

Ben doesn't answer.

I consider going straight to bed like the man said, but instead walk into the living room, flipping the overhead lights on.

Both of them cover their eyes and swear like teenagers in a town precinct. 'Jesus, Scar, turn the light down,' Ben says.

I dim it slightly. Ben curses again.

'What you watching?' I ask.

'*Revenge of the Sith*,' Iggy replies. 'All right, Scarlet?'

'I'm okay, Iggy, how are you?'

'Yeah, good, thanks.' Iggy snatches at his jeans and crosses his legs.

Ben just sits there staring at the TV.

I shrug at him.

'What?' he asks like a stroppy teenager.

'But thanks for asking how I am, Iggy, it's nice to know that somebody cares.' I smile sarcastically at Ben and fold my arms.

'Jesus, Scar, you just said you were okay.'

Ben doesn't drag his eyes away from the vengeful Sith.

'Do I get a kiss hello perhaps?' I ask, raising my eyes.

'You don't even give me a chance!' he says, and sighs, making a huge deal of pushing himself up off the sofa.

Just as he makes it upright I say, 'Don't bother', and walk into the kitchen.

I hear the pair of them trying to whisper, except half of Ealing can probably hear them.

'Iggy, mate, you'd probably better go after all. She's got the arse. I'm going to bed.'

I hear them shuffling around in the living room, the TV being turned off and papers being thrown in the bin, while I pour myself a bowl of Alpen and grab the milk from the fridge. Shuffled heavy footsteps fly down the stairs and the front door slams shut.

Ben leans in the kitchen doorway with his arms crossed. 'Good night then?' he asks, rubbing one eye and yawning, texting somebody on his phone.

'Yeah, it was okay.' I nod my head and take a mouthful of muesli. 'Who are you texting?'

'Nobody' he says, and shoves his phone in his pocket. I shiver.

'What's this job?' he asks, shaking his head to wake himself up.

'A theatre, a play. Tennessee Williams. Dolly Russell, she's this old actress. She won an Oscar.'

'And who's the bloke?'

'Tennessee Williams? He wrote the play. He's dead now.'

Ben pulls an impressed face and raises his eyes. Of course I can tell that he isn't actually impressed. He would be impressed if I'd said Dolly played third Ewok on the left in *Return of the Jedi*, and Tennessee Williams wrote three episodes of *Red Dwarf*.

'I could probably get us tickets if you want to see it?' I say, taking another mouthful of cereal.

'Maybe.' He nods his head, wipes the other eye, crosses his legs. His T-shirt says '*So you wanna play?*' in lime green on black. His pyjama trousers are red and black checked, the ones that my mum bought him for Christmas from Gap last year. He is barefoot. His hair is dark and scruffy, falling over his ears. He lifts an arm and deliberately messes it up with his hand, and stretches. He lets his hands drop back to his sides. His phone beeps in his pocket.

'Yeah, or, you know, take your mum or something. Or Helen, she's more into that kind of stuff, isn't she?' His eyes are closing as he speaks. He pulls out his phone, and presses a button, and smiles.

'Who is that?' I ask.

'Jesus, it's just Iggy, okay?' he sighs, and stuffs it back in his trouser pocket.

I nod my head at him. 'Okay. You just saw him, but, if you say so. And as for the theatre, well, I could take Helen, but I thought it might be something nice for us to do, Ben. We could grab a Thai afterwards, there's a great one on Old Compton . . .'

I see him grimace at the word Thai. I've already kicked my shoes off in the hallway, but I feel the urge to go and pull one back on and boot him in the stomach with it. Instead I smile and wait for him to answer.

'Maybe. But then I'd have to come all the way up into town . . .'

'Yeah, I know it's a long way. I mean I do it nearly every day, Ben, it's such an inconvenience.' I nod my head at him and smile sarcastically again and I see him raise his eyes to heaven. He sighs.

'You know how tired I am by the time I've finished work, Scar. I just want to collapse on the sofa, eat my tea, watch some telly.'

'Yep, yep, yep, I know,' I say, nodding my head, trying not to cry. I have never cried as much as I do now, not even when I was a baby. My mum says I was never a 'crier', even when she threw me at my dad one time that he got home really late from work. She literally threw me at him down the length of the hallway. Luckily he dropped his suitcase and caught me. She apologised for that when she told me the story. But these days all it takes is one wrong word and my eyes flood like potholes in a hail storm. And I have never been this tired either.

'Well,' Ben stretches and looks guilty, 'I'm exhausted so I'm going to go to bed.' He smiles apologetically. He knows the direction I'm heading in, and tries to sidestep it, but something in me won't let him.

'I'm done here,' I say, swallowing a last mouthful of Alpen and dumping the half-full bowl on the counter, 'I'll come too.'

'Oh, okay.' Ben looks nervous. 'Well, do you want the bathroom first?' he asks.

'Why don't we leave the bathroom for a bit?' I reply, and muster up my bravest smile.

'Oh.' He drops his head with a pained expression: I am forcing him to have to explain something to me for the tenth time, like how to tune in the TV, or work the smoothie-maker. He sighs, embarrassed that I am putting him in this position.

'Do you mind if we don't, Scar? I'm knackered. I had a really hard day. Maybe in the morning . . .'

'Right. Right. It doesn't really matter if I mind, though, does it?' I feel the tears sting my eyes.

'And as we both know, we never do it in the morning, because it will make you late for work, so . . .'

'What now? Oh for God's sakes, Scar, I'm sorry but I'm tired!'

'You're not sorry, and you are permanently tired. Are you having an affair?' I ask. I haven't turned the light on in the kitchen. We are badly lit from the light in the hallway behind him.

'No,' he says, shaking his head, feigning the kind of exhaustion that suggests he's just climbed a mountain, or swum the channel.

'Do you promise me, Ben? Because that would be a shitty thing to do, you get that, right? To promise me that you aren't having an affair, and then to do it anyway. I mean, I don't know what you told Katie, you know, if she ever asked, when we were, you know . . . But that would be a rubbish thing to do, to do it again. With Katie, well, that was unfortunate circumstances, but that doesn't mean, you know, that you have to do it again . . .'

'Yes, I promise I'm not lying. And no, I'm not having an affair. Do you think it wasn't painful enough the first time? I wouldn't put myself through that again.' He smiles at me like I'm simple, but doesn't make eye contact.

'Then why do you never want to have sex with me?' I shout as my voice breaks.

'Scarlet, I am too fucking tired, all right? If you got home at a sensible hour it might make a difference. But it's nearly three o'clock in the morning! And I've been smoking, and I just don't feel like it!'

'But you never feel like it! Never! It's been months!'

'You're never here when I do feel like it!'

'What if I try, Ben, if I promise I'll try and get home

146

earlier . . . would that make a difference?' I sound like a needy schoolgirl, desperate to please her teacher. As I say the words I hate myself even more.

'Then we'll see,' he says, and nods his head. What does that mean?

I wait for him to come and give me a hug, but I could wait all night, he just stands in the doorway and looks away. So I throw the last of my pride down the sink after the last of my Alpen and walk towards him, and try and shuffle under one of his arms for a hug. He relents stiffly and rubs my back three times, up down up down up down, with all the affection of a windscreen wiper.

I look up to kiss him and he squeezes his eyes shut and pecks me squashily on the lips.

'Open your eyes,' I say.

He opens them, and pecks me on the forehead.

'I'm scared we don't try hard enough, Ben. I'm scared we're falling apart.'

'I need the loo,' he says, and goes to the bathroom.

Ben is snoring by the time I've swiped off my make-up, but I can't sleep. My eyes refuse to stay closed. I look over at him. He is firmly on his side of the bed, with his back to me. I know his back better than any other part of his body. I know every mole, every hair. I know the contours of his shoulders and the nape of his neck. I know exactly when his hair is getting too long because it sits just over the freckle at the top of his spine. But when I close my eyes I can't picture his face at all.

I get up, pull the bedroom door closed behind me and wander back into the kitchen to run myself a glass of water. It's that time of the night when all you can hear is electricity: the soundtrack of the washing machine, dishwasher and central heating hums around me. I retrieve the *Standard* from my bag and toss it onto the table. I gulp down my water.

The post lies half-opened next to the paper. I pick up the letter from the clinic, which looks well-thumbed around the edges by Ben. I watch my fingers tremble as I tear it open.

Dear Miss White,

Following your visit to this clinic on 2nd September, as agreed we are writing to inform you of the results of the tests you had taken.

You were tested for:
- *Chlamydia*
- *Gonorrhoea*
- *Trichomonas Vaginalis*
- *Candida (Thrush)*

Blood Tests
- *Syphilis*
- *HIV antibody test*

And all of these tests were negative (showed no infection).

A negative HIV result means that you have not been infected with the virus that causes AIDS. However, if you have been at risk of exposure to this virus within the last three months you will need to repeat your HIV test to be certain of your status.

You still need to consider ways to protect yourself from HIV and other sexually transmitted infections. I would like to make an appointment for you to come back to the clinic and see one of our Health Advisors or counsellors as soon as possible, to discuss the nature of your test, and the situation surrounding it. Please call this number to make an appointment at your earliest convenience.

Your negative HIV result does not automatically
mean that current or ex-partners are also negative. Only
an HIV test will determine their status.
Thank you for choosing to use our service.
Yours sincerely,
V. O'Brien
Clinic Nurse

I let the letter fall onto the kitchen table. I know why they want to talk to me.

When I first went for my tests they told me about the HIV delay and I chose to postpone, until that three-month period had passed. They made a record of it. The nurse asked why I hadn't used protection, and I said that my boyfriend had already been tested, as had I, and that I was on the pill. Then she asked why I hadn't used protection with the other man that I had just told her I'd had sex with in the previous week, and I didn't have an answer. Well, I did, but she didn't seem convinced. 'I was really trashed' didn't seem to cut it. So now they want to talk to me about the fact that I am a thirty-one-year-old woman who still thinks it's okay to have unprotected sex with strangers when drunk.

I down the last of my water, and slam the glass onto the kitchen table, trying to catch my breath.

I've been called in for slut counselling.

Scene V: Violence

Tuesday. Ben woke me up this morning, hovering over me and gently shaking my left shoulder. For a moment I wasn't sure what was happening, and I smiled with amazed surprise. Then I realised that he was fully dressed and about to go to work.

'What is it?' I asked, confused and shielding my eyes from the daylight streaming in through the shoddy bedroom curtains that my mum ran up one Sunday evening in front of *Heartbeat* after two glasses of wine and her homemade steak and ale pie, hold the steak.

'Stop leaving your make-up on the toilet cistern,' he said.

'Why?' I asked, rubbing my eyes.

'Because it's annoying. I'll see you later.' And then he left.

I stand in front of the bathroom mirror, naked but for a pair of big blue knickers with Mickey Mouse on the front and a pink lace trim, that I think are ironic, and check for lumps. I raise my arm in the air, the way that they show you at the doctor's, and work my way around my left breast. I prod and poke in a circular motion, searching for something bad lurking creepily under my skin that's desperately trying to

150

stay hidden or risk being sliced out. I am startled by my reflection as I watch myself feeling up my own boobs, like some twisted homemade porn flick: watch in awe as busty Scarlet, 34–28–34, checks for filthy cancerous lumps!

I don't look the way that I think I do. You walk about the world, thinking you look okay, functioning, getting a fair share of whistles, but standing in front of myself like this it's easy to identify exactly what I need. It's a long list: my hair coloured, my hair restyled, my eyebrows plucked – maybe threaded, maybe waxed – a facial, my first hit of Botox, a pore treatment, my teeth straightened and whitened, or maybe veneers, my one black filling replaced by a white one, a boob lift, a tummy tuck, liposuction on the top inside of my thighs, a manicure, a pedicure, a leg wax, an arm wax, a bikini wax, laser hair removal for my armpits, my eyes lasered, all-over exfoliation, a cellulite treatment for my bottom, a mud wrap, an inch-loss treatment, a colonic, a course of yoga, a personal trainer, cleanser, toner, day moisturiser, night moisturiser, eye cream, a deep cleansing mask, a blackhead mask, an anti-ageing mask, and a spray tan. In some countries they need shoes, water, lunch, and a roof.

I think it was in the 1950s that poverty got redefined; I remember reading it in the *Standard*. That's the decade when most things seemed to happen, after the war but before the hippies: sex studies conducted and social-policy initiatives implemented, while women baked and Elvis simmered on a low heat, poised to boil. They said that there was absolute poverty – the people who didn't have the shoes and the lunch and the roof, but then there was cultural poverty too: that you could be poor, or you could be really poor. Really poor were the ones without water; but you were deemed to be culturally poor, in the UK at least, if you didn't have a washing machine, or an inside toilet. And they said that these days, if you don't have a TV, not through crazy nature-loving

Guardian-reading choice, but because you can't afford one, then you are culturally poor.

I have a roof, and shoes, and lunch, and water. But I need my eyebrows threaded and my teeth whitened, and my breasts lifted. It seems to me that there's a new definition of cultural poverty in town, and this time it's serious! It's cultural poverty for girls, circa 2006. You know it's true because you feel it too. And I forgot: I need a pair of jeans that cost at least one hundred and twenty pounds, because at some point that became acceptable too. Of course, if I find a lump today that might all change, but I don't, so my list remains intact.

I slide my feet along the ground and into the kitchen for Alpen. I catch my breath when I see what Ben has done. Next to the microwave he has framed a picture from our holiday. At the beginning of the summer we went to Barcelona for five days. I lay by the pool, he did a tour of the Nou Camp, and at night we ate seafood, drank sangria, and tried to have conversation. I'd ask him questions but he'd rarely reply. He used to find my tangents fun – If you could be any *Muppet Show* character, which one would you be? If you could be any sportsman in history, who would it be? Stuff like that. But in Barcelona his answers were lazy and ill-conceived. He said he'd be Kermit, but he didn't know why, and he said he'd be John Barnes, because he just would. Every meal was over in an hour, and we were in bed by eleven. Sometimes I'd stay downstairs in the hotel bar and drink until he was asleep. Sometimes he'd drink and I'd sleep. We had sex one morning, but of course I faked it. It was utterly uncomfortable, we barely kissed and we couldn't even look each other in the eye. Ben came long before I'd even got going, so I gasped a few times and said 'great'.

It's a photo of me in an alleyway in a short white sundress and gold flip-flops. I'm looking back over my shoulder because he had just shouted 'Scar' and I'd turned around.

I grab my mobile and call him.

'It's me,' I tell him as he answers.

'Yep?' he says.

'I'm calling to say thank you for framing that photo: I've just seen it in the kitchen. That's so lovely of you!'

'My pleasure,' he says, and I can hear the smile in his voice. 'You see, I can do nice things, Scar, you just have to give me the chance.'

'I know, I know. I'm sorry. Where did you buy the frame?'

'I got it free with those new wineglasses from the supermarket, so I thought I'd stick something in it. It's all right, isn't it?'

'Oh. Couldn't you find one of us together?' I ask.

'I didn't really look, that one was at the top, but change it if you want, the photos are in the drawer.'

'Oh,' I say again. I picture air whizzing out of my ears and nose cartoon-style as I deflate.

'It is a nice photo of you though, Scar.'

'Thanks – I mean, it's lovely that you did it.'

'Well, remember this the next time you start having a go at me!' he says, then puts his hand over the receiver and adds, 'I'll be with you in one moment, sir.'

'I know. I will,' I reply, but there is a lump in my throat.

This is the extent of it. The picture on the top of the pile stuffed into a free frame and shoved by the microwave, and I'm grateful.

'I'm working, Scarlet, I have to go,' he says.

'Okay, bye,' I reply, and hang up.

I tend to remember one line from most of the arguments that Ben and I have. I never remember what I say immediately afterwards but then have dizzying scared moments of horror a couple of days later as I recall how vicious I became and what nastiness I spat at him to hurt him back. I know I've said, more than once, 'Everybody thinks you're batting out of your league, Ben, everybody thinks I'm too good for you!' He has never retaliated to that.

I know I am only goading him but I wonder if he knows it too. Still, I hate myself for saying those things. Why should he love me if I'll say things that deliberately hurt him? But then it's a self-perpetuating problem. If Ben told me that he loved me I wouldn't say those things, or try and provoke such a response. I wonder if he knows that too.

I catch a ten thirty Central Line into town, and flick through *HEAT* on the tube. Short-mega-rich is shagging tall-mega-skinny-mega-pale, even though she has only been married to tall-strangely-white-toothed Jewish comedian for three months. Brunette-tattooed-vixen is sleeping with crazy-grey-haired-Oscar-winning-method-actor, even though he has been married for five years to gorgeous-hair-girl-next-door-funny-lady. It's like I said: infidelity begets infidelity. When a star sleeps with another star, somebody else soaks it up as this week's gossip and is unfaithful with one of the bar staff in his or her local pub. We are all so scared that we are missing out, and nobody has the answer.

It's the same with soap operas. If you look at any given soap-opera square or street or farm they are all at it like rabid rampant rabbits, and it gives people ideas. A boss seduces a factory worker between seven thirty and eight on a Wednesday night on ITV, and the same thing happens the following week in Chelmsford. All it takes is the germ of the idea. Infidelity begets infidelity. If Monogamy was once our religion, we're a secular society now! It's a fact of life, and I seem to be the last one to have cottoned on. Today, everybody cheats. Should I encase my heart in bubble-wrap now, and allow nobody any closer than a cheap pop on a few of my bubbles? Or just give up completely? Meanwhile, back in Soho, I cheat constantly with a kiss or worse, but think nothing of it. I'm emotionally drained so it doesn't matter.

It's just a release, a cold comfort, nothing more, it doesn't count. Of course, if I find out that Ben is doing the same I'll cry and shake for days and throw him out on the street. What's happened to the world that I thought I'd grow up to drive a car in, get married in, buy a house and have kids in? I turned away briefly at eighteen perhaps, and when I turned back it was gone, replaced by this shambles of irony and confusion. It's certainly not where I thought I left it. There's nothing white in my world. My swans are all grey, my snow is tinged with yellow. A mist has fallen.

I turn the page in my magazine. There's a feature where they scrawl a ring around everybody's imperfections. It's called Circle of Shame or something like that, and I think it's supposed to make me feel better but it only makes me feel worse. All that is wrong with one bottle-blonde-and-tan today is her 'strangely' long third toe. That doesn't seem too bad to me. Let's see some honest-to-God crows' feet, shall we? Or some bona-fide stretch marks? Maybe, if that were the case, I'd end up feeling terrible for that poor star strung up as an example of 'real' – you see, they aren't perfect! I can't say for sure. I know that it's my fault too. If anybody is to blame it's me. I paint over the lines. I'm Make-up.

I can understand why people miss the good old days, where marriage was for life and you lived next door to the same family for fifty years, watching your kids and their kids' kids grow up. Was that all made up too? Do I only think of them as the 'good old days' because I've seen some old films of the war, where neighbours ran from house to house swapping sugar and hiding under tables when the bombs came? Our lives seem peculiarly temporary now, where once, not so long ago, they were permanent. I'd give up email for fidelity. Except if I leave Ben and have to try online dating. I'll need to do that first.

I get off the tube at Tottenham Court Road and wander

up past the cable of electrical stores that flank the road north, with their special offers on equipment that leave me cold. I am sure that most of these machines are either DVD players or digital cameras but they look crazy and alien and impossible to operate. *If I leave Ben.* I won't even think it loudly. It's only a whisper in my head.

I notice that this is mostly a male street. Tottenham Court Road is for men, who fly past me at varying speeds, which makes me think: there are so many people in the world, buzzing around me, streaming past me, hundreds and thousands and millions of men. Wouldn't it just be absolute and utter bad luck if I couldn't find one to love me? If love does really exist, after all . . .

I twitch at the clinic reception and wait for somebody to see me. I could have just phoned but I thought it might make a better impression if I presented myself in person, in a nice outfit. I want to appear willing to address my problems, have my slut counselling session, move on, and never come back.

'Hello,' says the man behind the counter. He's a flabby slim and receding, in a cheap checked supermarket shirt that is so thin I can see his nipples, and rimless glasses that contribute to the nothing of his face. At least some rims might have given him some colour. His knuckles are flaky, patches of skin, wafer-thin like ham, point in different directions from the back of his hands. I won't be shaking hello.

'Hello,' I say, and smile, with my hands clasped behind my back like an old-fashioned bobby on the beat. If I was being really authentic I'd say ' 'ello, 'ello, 'ello', bend my knees, then hit him over the head with a truncheon because he looks a bit gay.

'I received a letter that said I should make an appointment to see somebody here?' I grab it out of my bag and chuck it at him more violently than I'd intended. 'And as I was in the area I thought I may as well pop in to make the appointment. You know: show willing!'

The guy throws me a quizzical look and glances at the letter. His eyes dart up and give me the quick once-over before he finishes reading. An appointment book lies open in front of him, full of bad handwriting in red and black ink. I wonder if the colour coding is coincidence, or if it means something. Red for rude health, black for brink of death.

'Somebody could see you now actually,' he says and smiles. His front teeth are stained and pointy like chunks of Toblerone.

I feel like I've just stepped into one of those traps in the forest that Robin Hood perfected, where your foot gets caught in a rope loop and you are flipped upside down into the air. I want to cover my head with a pair of oversized boxing gloves and back out of the swing doors before anybody gets a good shot in.

'Right now?' I say.

'Yep, just for fifteen minutes or so, somebody just cancelled,' he replies, consulting his book again, throwing me his chocolate smile.

'Are you allowed to cancel?' I ask surprised.

'What?' he asks, as if I'm an idiot.

'Okay, well, the thing is, I have to be at work.' I look at my watch and grimace, without registering the time: it could be four in the morning, two in the afternoon or midnight. Both me and ham-knuckles know that I couldn't tell him the time now if he asked. I realise so suddenly that I should slap my hand to my forehead: I had only planned on making the appointment, and then missing it, crazily, and by accident. What a mistake to make, coming in person!

I'm distracted by the tall, alarmingly handsome black man strolling towards reception, and ham-knuckles calls out to him.

'Dwaja, you're free right now, aren't you?'

Dwaja gets the biggest chocolate grin of the morning. I think ham-knuckles loves him. And I don't blame him.

'I am,' he says, and gives me a warm smile. I feel the heat of it as if a tanning bed has just encased me and the neon tubes of light have sprung to life. I have to adjust my eyes. He has a beautiful broad smile that I might fall in love with, given the chance and probably a different set of circumstances. He wears a white polo shirt with a little navy horseman in the corner, and thick black-rimmed glasses. He passed six feet in his teens, and his gym membership is all paid up. The muscles in his arms twist invitingly like rope, up and under his short sleeves. The hems of the sleeves dig a little tightly into his arms, which bulge beneath the material as if inflated by a pump. I want to sit in a room and look at him for a while. I may not even care if he tells me off, although I don't know how appropriate it is to be indulging in lustful thoughts about my slut counsellor, it might all be part of the test . . .

'Let's go!' I say, smiling, tossing my hair over my shoulder like a show pony. Ham-knuckles snorts a disgusted grunt behind his counter.

'So, Scarlet?' Dwaja says as we sit opposite each other in his room and he looks over my file. I have a file now, at the sex clinic. The land is littered with all these nasty little records that are keeping track of my mistakes: first my credit history that earns me no credit, and now this.

'Yes,' I say, with a glossed smile, crossing my legs. I'm wearing a black plunging V-neck, a black pencil skirt, and grey tights with pink polka dots littered all over them that, at a glance, might lead you to think I'm ill. But my Mary-Janes are fuchsia three-inchers, and nobody with any kind of serious sickness would wear those. Illness dictates trainers or bare feet.

'You told the nurse who did your tests that you needed to wait three months, because of the HIV test validity, is that correct?'

'Unfortunately it is. But, fortunately, I tested negative, for everything, so I'm glad I waited.' Look down, glance up, smile, dismount. Judges, I'll have those scores now please!

'Okay . . .' He looks down and smiles, lost in thought. He chucks the file on the desk beside him. I notice three condoms in their sweet-wrapper packets lying casually by the phone. In any other environment it would look strange.

'So what if you're pregnant?' he asks, putting his fingers together on his chin to imply thought or concentration, and raising his eyes.

I cough up a lung. Almost.

'Why would you say that?' I ask, alarmed.

'I'm just asking if you've thought about it?' Dwaja says calmly.

'No, I'm not pregnant! Besides, I'm on the pill, I don't need to think about it. That's just upsetting,' I say, 'I would never let that happen. That would be just . . . just . . . awful!' I shake my head to chase the thought out of my mind. I don't hate babies, I love them. I just don't want one now. I'm only thirty-one. I've got at least four years yet.

'You know the pill is only effective ninety-nine per cent of the time?' he says.

'Well that sounds like pretty good odds to me. You'd take those odds on the Grand National, wouldn't you?' I nod and smile convincingly.

'And what if I told you that the odds, as a heterosexual woman, of contracting the HIV virus, are plummeting all the time. And you have NO protection against that, except blind luck, if you choose not to use disease-preventative contraception?'

'I get it,' I say.

Dwaja nods. He's made his point, albeit clumsily. He should have just chucked me a Tiny Tears wearing a jumper with 'AIDS' sewn on it. It would have been quicker.

'We're not here to tell you off,' he says, smiling.

'I know, I get it, I won't do it again,' I reply, not sure if I agree with him.

'Would you like some condoms?' he asks.

'It's okay. I'm not having sex any more,' I say, and stand up to leave.

'What, never?' he asks with a laugh.

'You haven't met my boyfriend,' I reply, grabbing my bag.

It's amazing how quickly you can go off somebody.

Heading down towards New Oxford Street, I call Ben. I need vacuous conversation, and I know that he's good for it.

'Hey,' I say.

'Hi,' he replies, sounding mildly irritated.

'What are you doing tonight?' I ask.

'Iggy is coming round.'

'Again? Sorry, are you okay to talk right now?'

'Yeah, for a minute, I'm on lunch.'

'Okay.'

We both fall silent.

'What are you having for dinner?' I ask.

'Sausages and beans.'

'I'm going to be late tonight, I think.'

'Right.'

'Sorry. I know I said last night that I'd try to be back early . . .'

'That's okay, don't worry about it. Iggy is coming round anyway.'

'Okay . . . no need to sound too relieved, Ben.'

I hear him sigh.

'Did you speak to your mother? The answerphone is full with all her messages, Ben.'

'No.'

Silence again.

'Jesus, Ben! Is this the most boring conversation we have ever had or what? Haven't you got anything to say?' I stop and stand in the middle of the pavement outside Forbidden Planet, the comic-book store. I glance in and it's packed. At the same time about thirty pale guys in long black coats stare out at me, and simultaneously look away, because a wave of embarrassment drowned them all at once.

'You called me! And I haven't done anything today, Scarlet, I only spoke to you a couple of hours ago!'

'I know, but Jesus!' I wave my arms, flailing in exasperation. 'Nothing has happened to you since then? You didn't think anything or hear a joke, or learn anything? Nothing interested you on TV? You have the TV on all morning, there are thirty of them in your shop, they've got you cornered! There wasn't anything interesting on Phillip and Fern? Or maybe a customer said something? Anything!'

'Jesus, Scarlet, don't start!'

'Or maybe you had a thought about us, or something we could do at the weekend, or next week, or next year? Or a film you want to see, or something different you might do tonight, or anything, Ben! Just give me something to work with, please?'

'I told you! I'm going to have my tea, play some Xbox with Iggy, watch some *Star Wars* and go to bed.'

'Oh my God, Ben! You do that every night! Don't you want to do something different?'

'No! I like it. That's why I do it.'

I am running out of ideas.

'Okay, just for now, just for this phone conversation then: how about my morning? Do you want to ask if anything

161

eventful has happened to me today, since last we spoke? Maybe I got mugged? Maybe I got flashed at on the tube by a guy with a six-foot-long tattooed penis and Tourette's?'

'Okay, fine! What's happened to you in the last four hours, Scarlet?' he asks sarcastically.

I open my mouth to speak and then realise that I can't actually tell him about the clinic, about the negative HIV test, about the pregnancy grilling, and how uncomfortable and lonely it all felt.

'I read *HEAT* on the tube,' I say apologetically.

'Great!' he replies sarcastically, 'I'm so glad I asked!'

That's pissed me off.

'Did you speak to Katie yet this week?' I ask.

A pregnant pause, and then, 'Not yet, no.'

'So why did you pause?' I persist, full of accusation.

'Scarlet, why are we talking about this again? I told you I'd call her for a catch-up so you should just assume that I will. I don't want to discuss it.'

'But you only spoke to her about a week ago. It was a week ago, wasn't it?'

'Maybe, but so what?'

'So . . . do you think that's healthy, Ben? Does that feel like moving on to you? Because it sure as hell doesn't feel like it to me!'

'I've told you, Scar, she will always be part of my life.'

'No, it's fine, Ben, you don't have to remind me! I remember when you told me that. I remember because I recall thinking that it's so great when you just tell me how things are going to be, and the discussion bit, the bit that other people seem to have in their relationships, gets sidestepped because you can't be arsed or just don't care enough about me to hear what I think. But I thought I might just tell you what I think about it, in case you're interested at all? I mean we both know that you're not, but let's pretend. It makes me feel horrible. It makes me feel uncomfortable. I don't know what you're talking about – are you telling her you still love her? Because I don't bloody know! You never talk to me! We don't have weekly catch-ups for Christ's sake! Do you even care in the slightest how I feel about this, Ben?'

Silence.

'Because if you don't then we don't have anything at all. You and I, we aren't a unit, are we? Look around you, things fall apart all the time, for everybody. I am trying to make us into a unit, trying to make us best friends, because you don't fuck your best friends over, and that means we won't fuck each other over, do you understand?'

Almost silence. I hear him breathing.

'Ben, have you even considered that maybe you do have to let Katie go, for the sake of us? If "us" is important to you in any way, because that has ended, Ben, and we're still going, just about . . .'

'I can't . . . I don't know . . .' I hear him exhausting himself at the end of the phone, trying to articulate something but with no idea how, and I'm glad that he finds it hard, that it drains and confuses him. If I feel this bad, it should be hard for him too.

'I can't explain it, Scar, but you have to get used to it. Jesus, I left her for you, isn't that enough?'

I sigh. 'No you didn't, Ben. Not completely.'

'Well I'm not talking about this again. I just won't tell you I'm going to call her next time.'

'Oh, because that's a healthy next step! Why don't we lie to each other more, Ben, let's really make this relationship special!'

'I'm done with this conversation,' he says.

'Do you think you're being fair?' I ask him calmly, quietly. He doesn't answer.

I say 'bye' and then hang up the phone. I refuse to have

that discussion ever again. I hear myself shrieking and I hate it. I realise that I have just said, 'I am trying to make us into best friends.' Maybe Ben has realised that we never will be.

I walk down Monmouth Street, which leads me out at the Seven Dials.

The Seven Dials of Covent Garden is the epicentre of London's magic – the fault line that runs through the heart of our town. It's a roundabout with a sundial in the middle, with seven roads that lead directly off it at even intervals, surrounded by cobbles to ward off devils, because devils wear high heels, well, their hooves are high, and it's hard to walk on cobbles in heels. I am nearly always confused by which road to take, even me, who knows where she is going some of the time. Imagine the tourists! Imagine our US allies confounded by this series of turnings, especially when you remember that across the water they don't even have round-abouts. It must be quite a puzzle! Which makes me smile. Often I find myself guessing which road to take, crossing my fingers and hurling myself forwards, hoping for the very best. It feels like a test from an old quiz show. Seven options! Seven different choices. What if I pick the wrong one? Will a trap door open above me and half a ton of green gooey gunk fall on my head?

Seven suggests itself to me as the perfect magic number, but for everybody. It could be the world's lucky number. In the same way that cats have nine lives, I wonder if I, if we all, have seven lives that we could live, seven different paths to follow, and the path we choose is dictated by some random choice that we make at some seemingly inconsequential point in our lives. Or even some deliberate turn that we take, while not fully understanding the implications at the time. And the result is the life we end up with.

Maybe when you are young, between the ages of five and six, you decide one Sunday afternoon that you prefer drawing pictures of your cat to growing cress with your daddy. Little do you know that you would have become a world famous biological scientist if you had carried on with the cress, but that option floats away that Sunday afternoon like an old balloon after the birthday party ended.

Then, when you are thirteen, you decide to go out with Barry Bloss instead of Scott Taylor, because you like Barry's hair better, and he's got a cool bike. Scott, it turns out, was a sex hound who wanted it long before Barry did: inadvertently you sidestepped the option where you were knocked up at fifteen, Mrs Taylor by seventeen, divorced with two kids by twenty-five. Then, at eighteen, Brighton and Cardiff Universities both accept you to read Business Studies BSc Hons, but you choose Brighton because it's closer to home and your dad doesn't like driving much so you've got more chance of lifts back and forth at Christmas. So you don't meet Mark, the man you would, maybe should, have married at twenty-seven, who lived in the room below the one you would have been assigned. You would have bumped into him on the stairs every day for the first two months, gate-crashed his Halloween party, and become friends. He would have kissed you in the summer rain outside the Student Union on the last night of your fresher year, but you chose Brighton instead, and although you had fun with lots of boys, none of them ever promised your idea of a life-changing love. So you leave Brighton single. Mark was one of your soul mates: but how were you to know?

Then, aged twenty-five, you drop your keys outside your front door while double-locking it one Tuesday morning because the house next door got burgled last weekend, and it takes a couple of seconds to bend down to pick the keys up and toss them carelessly into your bag. So you're half-walking, half-running to Ealing Broadway station in the way that you always do, and when you get to the main road you consider running out in front of an oncoming bus, but at the very last second you decide not to because you aren't sure how fast you can go in your new heels, which are half an inch higher than your normal stilettos. Two seconds earlier and you would have chosen to run. If you had, that bus would have hit you when your heel got caught in the manhole in the middle of the road, and you tripped and fell to your knees. The bus was moving at twenty-eight miles an hour and couldn't stop in time. So your neck doesn't break, and blood doesn't flood your mouth and your lungs as you kneel in the road in new heels, and you live, and don't die. Option four.

Option five. You're thirty-one. You live in a flat in Ealing with your boyfriend who has never told you that he loves you. After three years together, you realise you teeter precariously every day on the verge of tears, and decide to spend a day with him at the zoo. You determine that by the end of that day you will know what to do. You will either tell him that you're leaving, or remember why you love him enough to stay for as long as it takes.

I reach for my phone.

'Hey, it's me,' I say.

'Hey,' he says, waiting for me to apologise for before, because I always do.

'When is your day off this week?'

'Sunday.'

'Good, that's mine too. Will you come on a day out with me?'

'Where do you want to go?' he asks, suspicious, surprised.

'Let's go to the zoo,' I say, and hang up the phone.

I spot the *Evening Standard* seller on Long Acre and get my forty pence out of my purse as I weave my way towards him, avoiding tourists and cracked paving stones.

'Hi,' I say.

'Afternoon, dear,' he replies, folding a paper in half.

'How are you?' I ask, smiling.

'I'm well, dear,' he passes me my paper. 'You chose option five.'

He smiles. I stare.

'Was that the right one?' I ask, accepting one end of the paper, while he still holds on to the other.

'Who am I to say? I don't know anything about anything. If you forced me, well, and I had to bet, I would say I would have gone for option six myself. But what do I know?' he shrugs.

'But is that better? Can I still change it?' I ask, panic filling me like a bad transfusion.

'Of course you can, dear, you can do anything.'

He begins sorting his money into change piles: short pillars of silver, sixty pence, ready change, for the people that give him pound coins.

'How will I know if I've picked right, though?' I ask him, trying to catch his eye as he mumbles numbers at the money, performing calculations in his head, but a woman asks me to move as she offers up her forty pence. He swaps it for a paper, and asks, 'Do you want the property section?' She shakes her head, and he says, 'Excuse me, dear' to me, gesturing that I move out of the way. A young guy in a T-shirt that says '*Your mother loved it*' volunteers his money to him now.

The *Standard* seller starts to whistle.

'I wondered if you could,' I say.

He smiles and carries on. It's 'All You Need Is Love'.

As I walk back up to The Majestic I pass a series of people on the street, all of whom seem familiar. It seems to me that they are the same three people that I see everywhere. They walk in and out of my life, like extras, and

I've always seen them before. I swear I just held the door open for one of them at the clinic, and another sat next to me on the tube this morning. The same three people are playing all the bit parts in my life. Maybe God or the Devil or whoever is running this crazy show hasn't got enough people to go around any more, to flesh out all the stories being told down here.

I amble up towards the stage. Gavin is moving boxes three at a time into the wings. None of the cast is around. I can't see Tristan or hear him either. When Gavin spots me he mutters something under his breath, as he lowers a batch of boxes down and walks to the front of the stage, his giant hands on his giant hips. He is wearing a T-shirt that says '*It IS the size of the boat*' in bright pink on grey. You can't miss it. I wonder if I should buy a T-shirt that reads '*I'm good at sex*': it seems to be the fashion these days.

'You're late,' he says, as if he expected nothing less.

I check my watch: it's midday.

'I thought you said there was no late?' I reply.

'There is today. She's waiting for you downstairs, she's been here for half an hour.' He raises his eyebrows and looks at me like I've done something wrong, and I should have known better, and I am hugely irritated. I want to slap him away from me, as if he were tracing the very tip of a feather up and down my shinbones and I had my hands tied together behind my back. That kind of irritating. The kind that makes you want to scream.

'Shit. Okay. Gavin, is this bad? Are you going to call my agency? Will I get fired?'

'Don't be so bloody dramatic, Scarlet. Just go.' He turns his back on me in favour of the boxes. The air between us is electric with his animosity, which is at best inappropriate, and at worst downright rude. He didn't even proposition me

168

outright, last night; I don't know why his feelings are so bruised. But I have a more pressing concern.

I tap down the corridor to Dolly's room. My heels click like castanets on the concrete. As I try to run in a bra that was not built for exercise, my breasts bounce about like footballs that my ribs keeps 'heading' upwards to my chin. I skid around a corner at speed and find myself thrown against Tom Harvey-Saint. He doesn't miss a beat, and grabs the flesh at the top of my arms like Clark Gable grabbed Vivian Leigh in *Gone With The Wind*. I find myself inches from his face.

'No running in the halls, Scarlet, or I'll have you in for detention,' he whispers with a smirk.

'Let me go,' I manage, my heart banging so fast in my chest that I am scared he will hear it.

'If you want me to,' he says, and practically throws me away. I gasp, and run past him, screeching to a halt outside of Dolly's room. With one hand on the doorknob I freeze like a musical statue at a childhood party as somebody yanks the stylus up off a Bucks Fizz record. The 'Do NOT Disturb' sign has been removed, but the lavender parcel is still there. My heart is in my mouth. Do I knock? Do I wait to be announced, and if so, by whom? Should I just go in?

'Damn well get in here.' The old-lady mid-Atlantic voice from behind the door is louder than a whisper, softer than a shout, but it means business.

I push the door open a fraction, only enough to be able to poke my head around, and with eyes closed declare 'I'm so sorry' before Dolly can say anything. The smell of lavender invades my nostrils. It has intensified in the room tenfold since yesterday; I expect we'll be the scene of an imminent and violent wasp storm, stung to death before we've even said our hellos.

I open my eyes and smile.

Dolly sits in her velvet chair, examining the rings on her fingers. Her knees are slightly apart, and she leans back gracelessly. Her back curves with the chair for support. She wears a shin-length velvet housecoat in deep catholic purple, and a long gold chain with a black locket on the end hangs around her neck, the locket itself sitting so low that it has made a cushion of her rounded old-lady belly. She looks, if not plump, bloated. Plump is too young a word. Plump implies bounce or softness. Dolly looks brittle. Her hands rest on either side of her knees on the velvet of the chair, weighed down by the huge amethyst and amber rings that she inspects, which are apparently far more interesting than me. She wears expensive light brown trousers with crisp creases sliced down the middle that she obviously didn't press in herself, but also what appear to be dark brown men's shove-on slippers from the cheapest section of Marks & Spencer. Her hair is very short and jet-black, obviously colour-treated, and styled in spikes like black ice stalagmites on her head: like barbed wire to stop intruders. Her cheeks are heavy with gravity and coursed through with tiny fine lines. Her rounded jowls resemble weights around her neck. Her eyes are wide and violet and glassy, each one topped by a thin black pencil acute accent. In contrast to the rest of her face her forehead is completely smooth. The Botox bell peals in my head. It is striking at this distance.

The only make-up I can detect on her face is a dark bloodstain of lipstick smeared across her mouth, as if she's just sucked down a whole tin of beetroots. Her fingers dance slightly by her sides with a faint tremble. I witness a small but constant shaking in the furthest reaches of her limbs. She neither smiles nor frowns. Now she is done staring at her rings, and stares at me instead, expectantly. Her eyes are suddenly clear, if not her expectation.

170

'Hi,' I say.

Then my phone rings.

Her eyes widen as I reach inside to grab at it, apologising again, ripping it out to see the name of the caller, surprised I even have a signal in here. It carries on ringing.

'Turn the damn thing off, darling,' she says flatly, in a transatlantic drawl, and I fumble with buttons to make it stop before throwing it on the side. It knocks over one of her cards and I grimace.

'Well,' she says, addressing her rings again. 'I can be late for you.' She sighs and runs her amber ring up and down and up her finger again, sliding it over the knuckle. 'You, on the other hand, cannot be late for me. And do you know why?'

'Because you're . . .'

She interrupts me with a glare and I stop talking.

'Because I'm the one with my picture at the front of the theatre.' She smiles and blinks slowly. 'I don't care what your excuse is, or how much terrible magnetism there may be between you and Mr Harvey-Saint.'

I gasp, but if she hears it she ignores it.

'A woman should always be late for a man, I have always said that and always will, and don't say anything else to anybody because I'll denounce you for a liar. I don't disapprove of that. Men should wait. But a woman should never be late for another woman, particularly in these circumstances, but still. A woman's time is precious: she has things, so many things, to attend to, to be at her best. Don't waste her time by thinking your time is more valuable. But for now, I'm not staying. I thought that I might, but I find myself exhausted, worn out by the dreadful journey, this damned London traffic. But! But, but, but . . . I wanted to see you, of course. They told me poor Yvonne left, and of course it made me sad as I thought she was very good. Very good.

Apart from her lip-lines, which were, of course, terrible. And her eye-lines. Everything, really. Let's be honest, the poor girl is in entirely the wrong profession, she has no arm for make-up. The best have always have a certainty in their hand. But still. She's left. It's sad. And now you're here.' A smile rushes across her eyes. She doesn't seem sad. She pushes herself to her feet, but the effect isn't dramatic: she is surprisingly small, five feet two perhaps, smaller than me. She reaches forwards for a fresh batch of unopened colourful envelopes.

'Fans,' she whispers at me, widening her eyes like a flasher. 'Who would have thought I'd still have them? But here they are. Friends, really. Who write to say hello, to tell me they still think of me. It's sweet. Because of DVDs, mostly, I'm sure. They get to see me again. And yet it seems a dreadful waste of paper. I saw on the news, about the forests. I should say something really. Tell them to stop writing. But of course I love them as well. They are like love letters to me these days. I don't get many any more. In my time I've had plenty. Boxes full, houses full. But not now. And you miss what you've had, of course. A woman needs love letters. We don't ask for much. You can only dream of what you haven't had, but it's a loss if you've known it and then it slips away.'

She fusses with one of the envelopes, trying to tear it open with her old purple nails, but her hands seem weak, and they tremble in their attempts. She can't get a grip on the paper to tear it, her fingers slipping down it like it's iced. I step forward, not sure whether to offer my help or not, but she immediately tosses it onto the side.

'Bloody cards,' she says.

She rests both of her palms flat on the counter, and turns her head over her shoulder to look me up and down. Her violet eyes reveal little this time. I glance down embarrassed, as I sometimes do on the tube in the mornings if I catch

172

somebody staring at me. Who are these people who have the confidence not to look away when your gaze locks with theirs?

'I'm going to say something now, and I hope that you don't mind.' You can hear the booze in her voice. She fights hard to keep her consonants deliberate. The H in 'hope' is loud. 'You look like a girl who cries too much for my liking. You look like a girl on the brink of tears. I won't have that.' She slaps her hand down on the counter, and turns to face me.

'There will be no crying in this room unless I say so, do you understand? You can cry when somebody dies. If somebody dies. But apart from that you learn, and you straighten your back, and you smile.' She presents me with a theatrical grin. 'And put your breasts away. I don't want those damn things stuck in my face while you're putting on my mascara, you're not breast-feeding.' She glances at my chest in obvious distaste. 'I suppose you've had them done, have you? All you silly girls do these days, I see the pictures in the paper. I never needed it. Don't damn well pander to them. Men! Don't let them think you should be more than you are, just to please them! Ha! Are they so hard to please? Big titties, small titties, pointy little titties like Ava had, but God they loved her! She was ten times too much for any man! Don't throw your hoop in with those types, if all they want is titties! The point is they don't have them! Don't maim yourself for them! Tell them you want foot-longer manhoods, and ask them to chop into those! Ha! Would they be so foolish? Obviously not. But some silly girl has done it and now you all think you have to do it. Men should never be allowed to get it all their own way; it ruins them, like a bottle of good perfume exposed to sunlight, day in, day out. They go off. It's a waste. A perfectly good man can be ruined by getting everything he wants, trust me on that.'

She sighs with the exhaustion that explanation of the obvious takes out of her. 'I mean! I understand they insert some kind of water balloons in these girls' chests? Is that what you've got in there? Balloons? Ha! How ridiculous! Any real man would feel like a fool groping at a couple of water balloons and getting excited, wouldn't you think? It's degrading for all concerned. You may as well tell them to hump sofa cushions! What's wrong with a corset for evenings out? Because, darling, let's be honest, all these girls parading around with their titties out and their bellies out and their skirts! Violently exposing themselves! I've had underwear that covers more than their cocktail dresses, and do you think men didn't love me because of it? All these girls, stinking of the cheapest kind of sex, it's not doing anybody any good. Don't believe a man who says that he likes it, it makes him free like an animal, and no gentleman ever gave himself over to his animal side. A real man controls the lust in his loins, for the right time, the right place. And then – ha! Then you get the whole measure of him, and only you! Ha! That's when the fun should start, behind closed doors! That's the party! Ha!'

I open my mouth to speak but before I can she glares at my legs as if evil just walked into the room.

'Are those polka-dot stockings?' she asks, addressing my hold-ups.

'Who in Christ's name told you to wear those? The black skirt, the black v-neck, that cheap little scarf around your neck, are all acceptable – a little sombre perhaps, maybe somebody did die! Ha! But polka-dot tights? And with pink shoes? Pink shoes! My mother always said, "Only a woman with no obvious redeeming quality need ever wear whores' shoes." Apart from whores, of course, to make it obvious, and earn a living. And I have no problem with whores and don't tell anybody that I do because I'll call you a liar! If they are using the only thing God gave them, so be it. Aren't men the fools, to pay? Luckily for some of us he gave us a little more. And believe me, they'll put no price on class.'

'I like them,' I say quietly.

'Whores? Or those shoes, darling?'

'My shoes . . .' I whisper.

'Well that says a lot,' she says, with an evil smile to herself, like Elizabeth the First signing a death warrant and planning her outfit for the execution.

'So. Well. What's your name then?' Slumping back down into her seat again, she tugs off her rings, reaching for a pot of hand-cream. She scoops a dollop into her palms and it squelches through her fingers and makes a sound like squeezing rotten fruit until it bursts.

'Scarlet,' I say. She chuckles and grimaces.

'Oh dear. Oh darling. That's unfortunate! You can't win, can you? Who gave you that name? The same person that gave you those shoes, I'll bet? No, that's far too violent a name for me to deal with. Does anybody call you anything else?'

'My boyfriend calls me Scar . . .' I apologise.

'Like from an accident, like pain?' she says, and shrieks a laugh, slapping one of her thighs at the same time, leaving a creamy palm-print on her trousers that I hope will stain forever.

'I don't . . . I mean, I think it's just easy. He just abbreviates it.'

She raises her eyes to heaven. 'Is that what you think? Well, okay . . . Anybody else call you anything less damning?' she asks.

I search in my head to find something else, and not humiliate myself by making something up to please her.

'My mum used to call me Lulu.' I have almost forgotten that she did, and still does sometimes, occasionally, but not often. Only when she's had a couple of glasses of Pinot Noir and then tells me that she loves me. But she used to use it all the time, when I was very young, and we were playing in the garden or she was tickling me. Richard would glug with joy in his pram as she'd chase me round the garden, screaming, 'I'm coming to get you, Lulu!' with her tickle fingers out, and I shrieked with laughter, and she did too. Whenever I picture my mother being truly happy, she's outside. I think even the biggest room hemmed her in, if there was somebody else in it. She needs silence, preaching its virtues to me every time I speak to her, when I am confused or angry or sad. 'You need to sit alone, Scarlet. You need to listen to yourself. You'll see. Sometimes you need to think about who you are, to enable you to be who you should be.' I am generally confounded, but I nod and I smile, and sometimes I even try to sit, without the radio on or the TV, or Ben's Xbox blowing things up in the background. It's never a real silence. I can always hear the cars on the street, or a police siren screeching down the Broadway, or the bell on the door downstairs daintily tinkle with the steady stream of yummy mummies flowing in and out of Plump and Feather. My mum says there is silence where she is, and I think that's why she's there. But London is loud. It's a town-crier place. You can feel lonely in London, but you can never feel alone.

'Used to?' Dolly says.

'When I was a little girl mostly, before she left home. She doesn't use it much now.'

'Why did she leave? To join the circus?' Dolly chuckles again.

'No. I don't . . . know . . . really, she just wasn't happy, wanted different things.'

'Different to you?'

'No. Different things out of life . . . and she and my dad drifted apart.'

'You're probably overestimating how close they were to begin with. But still. I can understand that, of course. So she saddled you with Scarlet then ran off with a sailor, eh?' She smiles at me. I don't know what to say. 'Well. Good for her. At least she had the sense to change it, your name I mean, in private. Learn from your mistakes, that's what I say. So, then. I'm going to call you Lulu. I had a Great Aunt Lulu, she drank meths and married an Israeli carpenter called Joseph. Very droll.'

I don't like the way that it sounds on her beetroot-stained lips. When my mum says it, after two large wines, 'I love you, Lulu', it's like a soft gurgle, something a baby might say by mistake, without knowing what it's saying. But the way that Dolly Russell says it, quick and sharp like two gunshots? It stings, and it makes me feel ridiculous.

'Actually, I think . . . I don't think I like it,' I say. 'I think it might upset me. I don't see my mum as much as I'd like, and can't we just use something else? Or maybe Scarlet might grow on you?'

'Lulu suits you though, darling. LULU! Ha! It'll be fine. It won't hurt after the fifth or sixth time, like plucking your eyebrows or poisoned injections in your forehead. I've had some of those. And I'll tire of shouting it in this little room soon enough.'

'I really . . .'

She glares at me. I stop talking.

'Now, then. Do you have any gin?' She looks around to see if she can spot any.

'Sorry?'

'Did you bring any gin with you?' she says again, enunciating every syllable.

'Sorry, nobody told me to. And it's not even one p.m. yet . . .' I reply with a smile that I hope reflects that I mean well.

'Well.' She looks down at her hands as she keeps rubbing

them together like Fagin collecting the spoils, 'I wasn't asking for your advice, I was asking for your gin.'

'I don't have any, sorry,' I say quietly.

She shoves the rings back onto her fingers, grabs the gold arms of the chair with both hands and pushes herself to her feet.

'It wasn't to drink, Lulu. It was to clean my rings. But anyway. Be here on time tomorrow,' she says, picking up her coat.

'Sorry, but what time is that?' I ask.

She moves towards the door, and I lean against the wall to allow her enough room to get past, but she stops directly in front of me.

'What are you so sorry for? Sorry this, sorry that. Who did you kill?'

'Sorry?' I ask again.

'The apologies, and the tears! Store them both up for when somebody you care for dies, or you accidentally kill somebody, in a speedboat or with a knife or something. Don't even apologise to me, darling. The only thing worse than a girl with no respect for other women is a girl with no respect for herself. You've got nothing to be sorry for, have you? Did somebody die? And was it your fault?'

'No. I guess it's just a habit. Sor— I'll try. But there are other bad things too, that you can do. Not just killing somebody.'

Dolly smiles and it throws her off-balance, and suddenly she is leaning dangerously like the tower at Pisa. She grabs for me and I lurch out to catch her. We lace our hands together automatically, and I feel her palm and the inside of her fingers are still slippery with hand-cream. I take her weight to keep her up.

'No more apologies. Anywhere. I bet you've said enough sorries for a lifetime,' she says. Her hand is cold in mine.

Gavin knocks and opens the door. 'Your car is upstairs, Dolly,' he announces. He glances at me, but it's cold like a day-old bath.

'On time is any time before I'm here, darling,' she says to me, snatching away her hand, but Gavin has already seen me holding it. She straightens her back for the man that just entered the room. Her hand flies up to her cheek, and her fingers dance across her face nervously, obscuring her from vision.

'Gavin, help me up the stairs, will you?' she says with a roguish smile and a wink to him, reaching forwards to take one of his hands. It seems to me that she is perfectly capable of walking on her own. Maybe she just likes the lean on a man. She tucks her arm into Gavin's, who is forced to squat to half his size so that she can reach. I contemplate suggesting he give her a 'wheelbarrow' to finish her off, but think better of it. As the door swings shut behind Gavin I hear her cry 'Lulu!' one last time, and snort a laugh. She leaves without a goodbye.

I feel the tears spring to my eyes as if they have just been told 'at ease!' and they suddenly have permission to erupt now that she has left. But nobody has died. I'm not supposed to cry.

'You learn, you straighten your back, you smile,' she said. Whatever the hell that means. But I'm damned if I'm going to let her catch me crying either, she's probably hovering outside with a glass to the wall, giggling evilly with Gavin and waiting for me to break down. There is spite in her, I can tell.

I grab for my phone before I can weaken – I still have one bar of reception – and check my messages.

'You . . . have . . . ONE . . . new message. First message sent . . . today . . . at . . . twelve . . . forty . . . three: 'Scarlet, it's Helen. I'm at the hospital. Don't worry, it's not me. It's Jamie.

He . . . oh God, Scarlet, he slit his wrists. I tried to . . . well, I tried to end it and . . . Steven's not here. He left last night. Nikki with an "i" is pregnant. He didn't go out, came home early, proclaimed, "We need to talk." Then she stumbled up the driveway while I was opening a bottle of wine, banging on the door, shouting out his name. *"Baby!"* She kept shouting it, Scarlet, like he's hers . . . anyway, she's claiming she's pregnant. And, well, they left. He left. Scarlet, can you meet me at the hospital? I don't really know what I'm doing and they keep telling me to turn my phone off – something to do with equipment failing – so if I don't answer come to St George's A&E in Tooting. But I think his mum is coming, Jamie's mum's . . . Christ, Scarlet, what do I do? Bye.'

I hit a number and the phone tells me: 'Message will be saved for . . . three . . . days.'

I stare at my feet. A fist bangs on the door so strongly I think its owner would prefer to punch straight through it. Before I can say 'Come in' the door swings open and Tom Harvey-Saint fills the frame. Cue wild cheering and applause from all the teenage girls in the audience. I shiver.

'Still here then?' He smirks.

'Why wouldn't I be?' I ask.

'Cardinal sin, the Make-up being late for the talent. I thought she might fire you, and then I'd have nothing to look at. Make sure you're on time for me tomorrow. I want to try out some looks before preview, make sure you've got it nailed by Monday.'

'I'll check with Tristan,' I say, my blood running cold. I don't want to be alone with him in his dressing room with the door shut.

'You don't need to check with Tristan, I'm telling you. Be here at ten a.m.' He lingers in the doorway.

'Was there something else?' I ask.

He takes a step towards me, but then thinks better of it.

'Last night.'

'What about it?'

'When you drink, you're very rude. That's just an observation but I don't think you can deny it. I hope that our relationship isn't going to sour, Scarlet.'

'I wasn't aware that we had a relationship, Tom?'

'You see, there you go again. Would it kill you to be a little nicer? Confrontational is not a sexy attitude, Scarlet. What have I done that's so bad?'

I very nearly say, 'Apart from not remembering that we fucked in an alley?' But I don't. I don't even want him to remember the damn alley. I want to forget it completely. And he's right, as far as he's concerned I must seem pretty aggressive, unnecessarily so.

I open my mouth to apologise.

'I'm . . .' But I stop. 'Let's see how it goes,' I say, and then, 'I have to go now. I have an emergency.'

I grab my bag and stand expectantly in front of him. If he doesn't move I'll have to push past him and I don't want to get any closer, even though tomorrow we'll be face-to-face as I pad his cheeks and try to disguise the sleaze and the menace.

I am momentarily embarrassed as he stands and smirks at me, making no effort to move. I am close enough to smell his breath and I catch a wave of sickness that makes me want to wretch, so I say, 'You're being weird. I need to get past.'

He throws me a dagger of a look and walks out.

I run up the stairs as quickly as my outfit allows, and spot Gavin talking to a guy who got introduced to me at Gerry's as something to do with lighting. I beckon Gavin over, and even though he looks irritated he stops the lighting guy straight away and strides to the front of the stage. He stands above me and I feel instantly self-conscious about the ravine of cleavage he must be able to see from that height. He seems to feel it too, because he drops to his knees and says simply, 'What now?'

'Gavin, I have to go. It's an emergency. I thought I should tell somebody.'

'Tell him,' he says, gesturing to the swing doors that are flapping behind Tristan as he walks towards us in the same clothes he was wearing last night. In his hand he is carrying what looks like a swathe of Japanese material – pink and white and red, delicately dotted with tiny flowers.

'Tristan,' I raise my voice so he'll hear, 'I'm really sorry but I have to . . . what the hell happened to you?'

Tristan's lip is swollen and glistening like a doorstep slug, and he has dried blood in a patch on the side of his head. Gavin jumps down from the stage in alarm but we both leave three feet between Tristan and us in case he starts spurting blood. His Jackie O's are cracked yet still on, but he tears them off to reveal two dirty blue-black eyes, the colour of tights that you buy by mistake. The knuckles of the hand that hold his glasses are bruised and swollen like molehills.

'It's nothing, it's nothing,' he says, dismissing it with his hand.

'Who did this to you?' I ask.

'That's the way. That's what I love about women. Eh? Instantly, instantly, you've made me feel like I lost a fight to a bigger boy. So now I feel like rubbish, when of course I haven't got a clue who did it, because funnily enough they didn't shout out their names! Some kid and a couple of his mates. That's all I know. They took twenty quid and my phone, left me my wallet because it had a picture of my mum in it. And who says kids today are all bad?'

'They were robbing you!' I say.

'Yes, they were. But luckily for me, unluckily for them, I'd spent nearly everything I had at Gerry's last night. So not only did they get shit-all money, I was drunk enough not to care that much when they punched me.'

'Tristan, I'm on the way to hospital now: why don't you come with me?'

'Why? What bits of you are bruised?' He raises his eyebrows suggestively and winces with the pain.

'It's not me, it's a friend. Come with me.'

'No, love, no can do. Too much work to be done here. We open on Monday, anybody else realise that? That's come quick, hasn't it? Dolly in?' he enquires of Gavin.

'But it could get infected,' I say, reaching out to touch his fat lip but thinking better of it as something yellow oozes out.

'No, love, I just need a pack of frozen peas and some steak. Gavin, could you be a love, a great big bouncy love, and send one of your minions out to get it. I can't face the sunshine again, I might melt.'

'Dolly's gone,' Gavin says. I wait for him to say something about me being late, but he doesn't. 'I'll send somebody out,' he adds, and walks off.

'For fuck's sake! For fuck's sake!' Tristan starts spinning on the spot. I glance around for the lone gunman who must have just shot a rage arrow into his neck.

'What? What?' I ask, backing away.

'Make-up, I don't even think this play is going to open! Look around, where are my cast? Where is my set? Where are the rehearsals?'

'Aren't you supposed to organise them, though, Tristan? I mean, I don't know much about theatre, but you are the director, right?'

'Go if you're going,' he replies, and storms off backstage, turning the air blue as he does.

I hail a black cab on Long Acre and jump in but almost immediately we are stuck behind a Tesco Metro van unloading.

'We'll be a while. Sodding things,' my cabbie calls into the back.

'No problem if you turn the meter off,' I say, and he does, although I think I hear him call me a cheeky tart.

I call Helen. She answers after two rings.

'Good, your phone is on. I'm on my way . . . kind of. Where are you?'

'Outside having a cigarette. But I'm leaving in a minute. It's okay, don't come now.'

'Shut up, of course I'm coming. Shall I just come straight to your house then?'

'No, don't, Scarlet. I just need to sleep. It's fine, I'll call you later.'

'But is anybody there, Hel? Or are you going to be on your own?'

'I'll be fine,' she says.

'Okay, but that's not what I asked.'

'I have to go back in, the doctor wants to ask me a couple of things before I go,' she says, 'so I'll call you later.'

'But is he okay, Hel?'

'They don't know yet. He lost a lot of blood.'

'Oh, Helen.'

'I'll call you later, Scarlet, I have to go.'

And as if by magic the cab starts moving again.

'Change of plan,' I shout through to the cabbie.

'Where now, love?'

'The City. Monument,' I reply.

I sit at a bus stop opposite Katie's office. Suits stream past me swinging Pret a Manger bags. I just sit for a while, as the buses pull up, exhale some people, inhale some more, and pull away. Eventually I see her. She moves through the swing doors first, followed by a tall guy with blond hair and broad shoulders. He has the same build as Ben. I would bet he has skinny calves as well, and a crucifix of hair on his chest. But Ben is dark, of course. I sit at my bus stop and watch them.

They walk forwards towards the road, and stand opposite me, as if directed. She chats, he laughs, they are both animated, more so than is usual or natural, love hormones coursing through them. A bus pulls up in front of me, but I don't move, I just wait for it to pull away. Then I see that they are kissing. It's a new kiss, she seems excited. She flirts, holding on to the lapels of his jacket for a moment. She looks happy. I can't turn away.

I hear a large crack: the glass in the bus shelter shatters behind me, littering the pavement with chips and shards. People walking past gasp and jump away. I look back towards her as she pulls away from him, startled, looking over the road at the commotion. Everybody seems to stop and stare at the bus shelter, and then at me, the only person in it. A woman runs up to me and asks, 'What happened? Are you hurt?'

I shake my head. I don't even feel scratched.

'I don't know, it just smashed,' I say, bewildered. 'Was it lightning?' I ask her.

'It's not raining,' she says, patting my arm with concern.

I turn back towards the road, and Katie sees me standing here. We stare at each other. I grab my bag and run off towards the tube station, shaking the glass from it as I go.

Katie's happy, and I'm sad.

I take the overland to Woking, and my feet begin to tingle with pain as I walk the twenty-minute trek from the railway station to Helen's house. It's late afternoon. As I pass the secondary school I hear an umpire's whistle, and the girlish cries of a netball match being played. I see the caretaker mowing the grass that smells old and dry at the end of summer. It's the last time it will need to be cut this year. The

chill will set in, then lashings of rain. Football boots will
chew the field up, and spit it out as mud. I am always a little
down when the summer ends, every year it catches me by
sad surprise. I just want it to keep going. The problem is that
I want a white Christmas as well, and I don't see a way that
I can have both, and still have it be real. I have to ring the
bell four times, but eventually a soft light comes on in the
hallway, and Helen answers the door. Her eyes are red from
crying and sleeping, and there are creases in the coat that
she hasn't taken off before going to bed. I smile weakly at
her, and her face crumbles.

'Did Jamie . . . is he okay?' I ask.

'Yes, he's okay. Nobody died, thank God.' She reaches up
and puts her arms around my neck, collapsing into my
shoulder.

I let her cry, but I don't. Because nobody died.

'Hel?' I say. 'Do you believe in karma?'

I feel the sobbing gradually cease against my shoulder as
her breathing calms. We stand in silence, hugging, for what
seems like half an hour.

'Absolutely,' she says finally, lifting her head, taking a step
back to look at me. We grasp hands. The pale skin around
her eyes is streaked black with wet mascara. 'What goes
around comes around,' she says.

ACT II

Not a Rehearsal

Scene I: Hello Dolly!!

Wednesday. As I lean back against a Majestic wall a brushed velvet panel cushions me. It's hard to lean anywhere in front of the stage at The Majestic and not be cushioned by a brushed velvet panel. Brushed velvet is compulsory in the theatre in my experience, all three days of it. Brushed velvet, and unreasonable behaviour, and a sliver of dramatic madness that has infected all the principal cast and crew like they ate the same infected prawns from catering and it's caused an epidemic. The main symptom is constantly projecting their words and their actions and their expressions to the back of the hall and beyond, out onto Long Acre and east towards St Paul's and west towards Marble Arch, ensuring nobody misses a moment of their gloriously performed lives. It's exhausting, but I know a little of how they feel. I'm not as sick as the rest of them, I ate one bad prawn, maybe, the one that puts me on display. We all assume we are being watched these days.

The cast and their understudies are seated haphazardly on fold-down chairs around the stage. Those chairs took some setting up – they're the kind that will bite your fingers off if you don't give them your full attention. You can tell the

189

understudies because they all pant enthusiastically like a pack of stray puppies, poor but eager, and a little desperate for the scraps. I've only spoken to a couple of them, on Monday night at the restaurant and in Gerry's, and all they wanted to know was which other theatres I'd worked in, and who I know in casting. When I told them 'Nobody, this is my first time in theatre,' they didn't even bother to say goodbye, they just walked away. I didn't mind, it was no big loss. I heard them talking amongst themselves later, about foxes, and the 'nuance of Hellman', and I'm pretty sure they didn't mean the mayonnaise, so I'd have had nothing to contribute to that conversation anyway.

The Italian coastline has appeared overnight on Long Acre, Covent Garden. Gavin looks exhausted, as he should: it's a whole country, plus an ocean, transplanted before sunrise. But then I bet Atlas can't have been much bigger than Gavin and still have got trousers to fit, and he carried the whole world on his shoulders! Now Gavin slumps forwards in defeat. His eyes are swollen, and it looks as though somebody has squirted red ink drops into each.

The backdrop to the stage is an abstract vista. A block of black to signify rocks, I think, and a swathe of blue for the ocean. Somebody somewhere is playing with the overhead lighting. Suddenly the stage is bathed in sunset orange, then just as dramatically the bright blue-black of night-time, then the golden white of dawn. It makes me hot, then cold; I sweat then shiver in a matter of moments.

From what Tristan has been saying, and the lines they've been rehearsing, a block of pink on the canvas that at first I thought might be a large pig – A pig in a play? But what do I know about theatre? – is actually meant to represent a villa in the distance, which of course makes more sense. The stage fades and glows, the faces of the cast illuminated by fake first rays and the pretend dying light of dusk. A heavy rope swings precariously at the back of the stage, like a hastily built swing hanging from a tree branch above a lake for summer swimming. Glancing up to see what, if not a summer breeze, makes this rope swing, I spot the electrician, whose name I still haven't learnt, dangling dangerously from a horizontal ladder that runs from one side of the stage to the other, above the curtain. I catch my breath, and want to shout, 'Be careful, don't hurt yourself,' but think better of it. He is not a child: he's a grown man. Fully grown.

The cast and a couple of the crew stare in shock and awe at Tristan, who is oblivious to the shift from light to dark and the small man risking death above him as he dances about before the chorus like Barnum, his clove cigarette aglow and spitting like a Catherine wheel. He circles the group as he talks, and the creak of wooden chairs punctuates his conversation as they shift heavily in their seats to follow him with their eyes, craning their necks as all five feet five of him disappears from view. Some of them 'tut' under their breath as he flies off again in a different direction. Eyes occasionally roll. Bottoms shift uncomfortably. Somebody sighs. It's hot in here.

Dolly sits upright in the middle of them all, like a totem pole. She looks composed in a purple towelling turban, with a green and gold peacock brooch parading across its front. She glances down at her rings, sliding the amber up and down and up and over her knuckle. Tom Harvey-Saint has positioned himself back to front on his chair, with a calculated ease, his folded arms resting across its back. His pose makes me shudder, he thinks he's Marlon Brando, and maybe he is. Maybe Marlon Brando started out just like this, and a Make-up in the Fifties stood to one side and shuddered at the sight of him, and the memory of him in her. Tom is wearing a maroon Fred Perry polo shirt and an expensive-looking suit jacket with faded jeans. He looks like a mod or a football hooligan, it's a uniform of fashionable violence. He tries to catch Arabella's eye, and occasionally she lets him. She sits opposite Tom, looking beautiful but bizarre in a T-shirt that is the halfway bright blue of nothing in nature, and a long brown ruffled skirt with autumnal gypsy flowers twisting along its hem. She should thank God that she is beautiful; it is as if a three-year-old dressed her for fun. But she is, without question, stunning. Her nose is so strong, her eyes so deep and bright. Maybe some would call her handsome. She's a handsome woman, they say, about girls that ride horses, or hold it together under pressure. Politicians' wives – they are generally handsome women. The ones who stand stoically by their husbands after exposed affairs. Maybe it's an old woman's greatest compliment? You don't hear old ladies described as pretty. They were pretty, people say, or she must have been beautiful in her time. But never 'they are pretty now'. Apart from Sophia Loren. She will always, somehow, be it by the grace of God or a deal with the devil, or both when the other looked away, be beautiful. Dolly has a presence that cannot be ignored, but any audience would admit that she hasn't been beautiful for some years. When does pretty stop being pretty? Thirty? Thirty-one, probably.

Tristan is wearing the material he was clutching yesterday that I thought at the time might be a pillowcase. It is, in fact, a thigh-length Japanese kimono that sticks to his black trousers with static electricity. I can see tufts of wiry black chest hair scrambling to escape the silk as he becomes increasingly more animated, his arms thrown around without care, the movement loosening the silk knot, edging the kimono open. He has swapped his Jackie O's for a small black hat with netting at the front, the kind my Aunt Nancy would wear to a funeral, frowning at any woman there without a hat on, like the dead care what's on your head.

Tristan has been chain-smoking clove cigarettes for over

an hour, and you can hear it in his voice. I think a tiny team of nicotine goblins are at work at the back of his throat, sawing off his tonsils with sheets of goblin sandpaper.

He stops and coughs violently, composes himself, smiles to himself, and carries on.

'So, it's about love . . . and loss. In fact it should be the other way around. It's about loss . . . and love. We mustn't forget how much she's lost. The violent quiet screaming pounding at your chest, and in your head – your blood ceaselessly pumping that ache around your body – the ache that you feel when you lose the one you love. Yeah? "*The dew of the morning sank chill on my brow, it felt like the warning of what I feel now.*" Yes? Byron, anybody?'

The understudies all nod enthusiastically, but the cast don't blink. Tristan shakes his head but goes on.

'Imagine it. The masochism and the sadism rolled into one. It's you and it's your lover, you've joined forces, ganging up on your heart, to break it. You know it. It's pure pain. But there are no knives, no car crashes, no guns, no blood, no bombs, no stabbings, no dismembered limbs or open wounds or splintered bones. No obvious signs of pain. No blood! But Christ it hurts,' he whispers and shakes his head, 'because you allow it in, invite it in to hurt you, and so it hurts even more. It shouldn't but, God, it does, and it does, and it does. It hurts you more! You cry because you can't control it, there are no drugs. And there is no science. Why does it hurt so much?' he asks himself, not us, as he shakes his bewildered head.

I don't put my hand up, I don't have an answer. I'm scared of pain. Today it's the warning of pain that, like clouds hanging over the next town, looms a little way away. And I feel like I'm sitting on a tube train that has just burst out from a tunnel, from Barons Court to Hammersmith at six o'clock on a September afternoon into a squinting, eye-streaming sunset. I've been underground for a while but I can feel myself in motion again now, moving slowly towards those clouds hanging over Ealing, and my tube is on a go-slow, shunting me along, leaving my clear sky behind. It has to be done. It wouldn't do to sit on that train, in the station, forever.

'This *old dying monster*,' Tristan says, gesturing with a smile at Dolly. I wonder how she'll take that, but she doesn't blink. 'She's lost her love. "*For me there were no others!*" she says. But, not only that, not only that which would be enough to ruin us all, here, now: she's lost herself as well. This acclaimed beauty! This international screen idol and glory! Age has stripped her away, and what does she have left?' Tristan shakes his head. I have involuntarily taken a step back, anticipating an explosion from the totem pole in the middle of the room. I don't know the play – is Tristan talking about her character or Dolly herself? I think I should probably grab one of the scripts that are lying around and have a read . . .

'She has the memory of beauty. When the mirror loved her so did the world, and neither one of them cares any more. Christ! Imagine it. The world that loved you loses interest in you, and through no fault of your own, for no reason other than you've got older. Imagine it! And then you tell me, because I don't know, I haven't worked it out yet, but honestly: do we only value the things we have because inevitably we lose them? And I don't just mean beauty, that goes for the people that we love too. Can love only exist in the terrified face of ultimate loss? If we knew with some certainty, and at any time, and with any one person, that eventually that person would leave, but that love would come and find us again but bigger, brighter, stronger, would we still cry? Do we forget more easily than we'd like to believe? Was it really love at all if the feeling passes? Or simply habit? Or a phase? Is it better to have loved and lost? Really? I'm not sure, I'm not sure. "*For me there were no others,*" she says. It's acceptance. It's reasonable. It's her truth. "*I know, madame, he said, but for the others there are others.*" But whose responsibility are they? Am I only responsible for my own heart, or for the hearts of the ones I love too? Or for anybody's heart, everybody's heart! So then, where was I? We are nearly done, nearly done, I know it's hot in here. We know our lines, but we need to know *it*. We need to feel the torture, revel in the madness of a beauty turned rotten and a life passed, as she sits and waits for death. It's pervasive, that sense of loss. It hangs over the entire play, and we need it to swell up and infect our audience. Christ! It's not a happy play, I know that, but then where is the drama in happiness? The evil that men do. The evil that men do! The evil that women do too, of course. But I leave you with these final questions: Can love only exist with loss? And is true beauty only ever temporary?'

I spot Tom and Arabella trying to suppress their giggles like school kids who would rather laugh than admit they don't understand. They may as well be chewing gum and writing each other love notes. I don't understand what he is talking about either, really, but I am sure that Tristan does, and they should try to at least! They are supposed to be trained actors. I won't laugh at what somebody believes, if they believe it that much, with such passion. Passion is so rare these days. He might seem crazy, but it's still inspiring.

I see Tom mouth to Arabella, 'Who is this fucking guy?' and she bites her finger to stop from giggling. Tristan is oblivious. 'I heard he was a bloody genius?' Tom mouths, shrugging his shoulders and raising his eyes. She snorts a laugh, and quickly coughs to try to cover it up. Tristan glances over absent-mindedly but doesn't realise what they are saying, and

I am glad. I don't want him to see them laughing. They might be pretty but they are stupid, too. As is often the way.

Gavin leans on a brushed velvet panel on the opposite side of the room with his long arms crossed and a stern expression. He looks very Scottish today, although of course he still isn't. Gavin stares at Arabella as she flirts with Tom. I can sense his fury, it seems to be thudding at his temples, but the rest of his face is as emotionless as always. Gavin stares. The cast begins to chat amongst themselves, and I flap over towards him in argumentative shoes: they are having a running battle with my feet, and I am not sure who is winning. But they go with this outfit – today I am wearing cream knee-length tailored city shorts with bare brown legs and a black shirt with a big collar and short sleeves, and a loose purple and cream piano tie that I bought from my favourite second hand shop off Neal Street. My hair is pulled back, day-old dirty and loose in a knot with blonde strands making a break for it all over my head like twisted willow, and I'm wearing thick black-rimmed glasses instead of contact lenses. My lip-gloss is called 'Raspberry Split' and my toes are sometimes the only things clinging me desperately into my black 1970s open-toed wedges, the argumentative shoes, but I love this outfit. It makes me smile. No doubt Dolly will say 'Ha!' when she sees me, and hate everything about it.

I don't know how to say what I want to say to Gavin, as I watch him so painfully loving somebody who doesn't love him back, so I put my arms around his waist instead – they are a mile from meeting at the other side! – and squeeze him like an overripe orange.

I see Arabella glance over with disinterest, and then double-take. We haven't been properly introduced yet and she throws me a look so dirty it should be wrapped in black plastic and sitting on the top shelf.

'She's a silly girl,' I whisper to Gavin. 'Beautiful but silly. She doesn't know a good man when she sees one.'

He glances down at me with derision, and scoffs a laugh as if I've just spoken to him in Estonian or Cantonese and he doesn't understand a word of it. But looking up at him seconds later I see the traces of a smile at the corners of his mouth, and he doesn't pull away from my hug. I hope this means we are friends again.

I squeeze him hard around the middle like I'm trying to get the last drops of juice out of my huge orange, and let go, leaning back against the velvet again, exhausted. Squeezing a big man can be tiring! Tristan looks over at us and smiles sadly.

' "*Nor can I blame thee, though it be my lot, to strongly, wrongly, vainly, love thee still,*" ' he says to Gavin and I loudly above the throng of his school-kid cast. Gavin looks as blank as I do and I want to hug him again, for being here, which means I am not the only stupid one.

'Byron! It's Byron! Anyone? Anyone!' Tristan asks, shaking his head and rolling his eyes. Gavin and I shrug apologetically in unison.

'So!' Tristan shouts, and claps his hands. 'Let's crack on with scene one again after lunch. This is all just final timings now, we know we're there, but! And here's the thing. After lunch, I think we all need to be topless. Half-dressed. Yeah? Yeah?'

The chattering of the cast screeches to a halt, followed by the sudden and audible 'swish' of fifteen necks twisting sharply, flipping their owners' features through the air to face Tristan. This is followed by a united gasp, and then silence. Dramatic silence. Tristan smiles.

'I realised you wouldn't go for the naked thing, which is, you know, the optimum. But we need to lose our inhibitions. Don't we? Plus, you know, it's hot in here! But we need to shed a little skin, a little of this armour, this defence we build up around ourselves to protect ourselves. We must not be afraid. We need to scramble into our characters now. We can't be afraid! Because fear,' dramatic pause, slow head-turn around the room at everybody present, theatrical nodding, 'is the enemy.'

He wears a gentle smile to soften the blow, and holds his hands out at his sides, palms facing the ceiling, like Jesus at the Last Supper in every painting I've ever seen of it, except Jesus wasn't Hindi, or wearing a Romford Market kimono and an old lady's hat. Not in the pictures I've seen, at least.

'Don't be scared,' he says. 'Don't be scared to let go, or to cry! You can't be scared to take your top off! It's just a top! It's just a torso, we've all got them!' He tugs violently at the hair on his chest and I wince because it looks like it hurts. 'Don't be scared! Don't be scared to kiss a boy, or to kiss a girl, to say what you think, to love a little or live a little or do what you want to do! You mustn't be scared! As I said to Marco Rodriguez, who played a wonderful Maria in my *Sound of Music* – "You can't be scared to be a nun!" And he was, at first. But then he found her. Through bravery and honesty he found the nun inside of him. And fuck me if it wasn't the best damn rendition of "The Hills Are Alive" I've ever heard! Don't be scared, boys and girls. As long as it's legal in the Netherlands, don't be scared to try it!'

He claps his hands again and smiles. The end.

'Lulu,' Dolly screams from the centre of the stage. The heads swish inwards. It takes me a moment to remember she is talking to me, as everybody else mutters and looks around, confused.

'Hi?' I say, stepping forwards.

'Lulu?' Tom Harvey-Saint says. 'I thought her name was Scarlet?'

'I'm going to sleep for an hour now, darling. Come and

do me then. In an hour! Stop grappling with your big new beau and set your watch, Lulu, I only need an hour. Wake me with a coffee. We need to get going.'

'She left out the "Irish" in "coffee",' Gavin whispers to save us both from embarrassment, and re-crosses his arms. 'Lulu?' he asks me.

'It's a . . . well, it's a short story actually. She thinks that Scarlet is a violent whore's name. So I've had to change it, for her.' I shrug like that's reasonable.

'Whose idea was Lulu? It's the name I'd call my favourite cow if I lived on a farm,' he says, with the tone of a bank manager declining me a loan.

'My mum, who left home when I was a little girl, calls me Lulu when she tells me that she loves me,' I say, raising my eyebrows.

Gavin doesn't reply but looks as bashful as his generally expressionless face will allow. Why is a man with no expression in theatre? Or is he vital? Is Gavin, in fact, the antidote to the poison of their hamminess that would have killed me by now if it weren't for him?

'See, Gavin, it's not just me that can say hurtful and unbelievably stupid things, is it?'

'It is mostly you,' he says.

'That's fair enough. Am I your favourite cow now?'

'Shut up,' he responds blankly.

Dolly pushes herself to her feet and makes her way down the steps at the side of the stage. Gavin takes a couple of paces forward but she waves him away.

'Who is that ridiculous man?' she mutters loudly, addressing nobody. 'What was all that guffaw? All that dancing around? Olivier never danced around! Where's my script? Somebody tell him I'm not taking my damned shirt off for anybody. I haven't been nude in public for nineteen years and I'm not going to start again now!'

'Scarlet,' Tom Harvey-Saint shouts down from the stage. 'If that is in fact your real name!' His laugh is without charm, like a teenage boy spotting bare breasts on late-night TV.

'Yes?' I ask, already irritated.

'You can do me now instead.' He gestures with his head to the side of the stage, and I think I hear him whistle. Gavin and I glance at each other in alarm.

'Did he just whistle at me?' I ask Gavin.

'I wouldn't like to say.' He looks angry.

'Why would you whistle at somebody who's about to wave a mascara wand near your eyes?' I ask.

Gavin comes close to a smile.

My wedges fight my toes down the stairs backstage, but what price five foot seven? Tom is already in his room when I get there. The door is flung open dramatically, and he sits centre stage, waiting for applause. It's a shoebox, an old school cupboard with bad plumbing that gurgles loudly like an angry, stupid child. There are bare stone walls and two bright exposed bulbs dangle dustily from the ceiling. Tom has stuck a poster on the wall where a window should be, but isn't. It's a poster of himself and a thin blonde girl who I vaguely recognise. They are both staring seriously at the camera, wearing dark suits, with crossed arms and legs slightly apart, like police investigators who stand in TV posters. In real life, when police investigators talk at press conferences when a child has just been snatched or a city broker's body found, they always disappoint me. They never stand the way they are supposed to – kind of mean and firm, depressed but determined – and they are never sexual. Every police investigator on the force, on TV, is leading a troubled sex life. The real ones always look far too exhausted and ordinary to do it more than once a month with their husband or wife of fifteen years.

200

The poster shouts 'Death Watch' in large red letters, and below that, 'They've got their eyes on the murder capital of the City . . . and each other. Only on BBC1.'

The floor is bare and plastic, as is Tom's rickety chair. He has shoved about twenty cards with hearts on the front underneath the metal clips of his mirror. He is sitting, bare-chested, on the chair in the middle of the room. His stomach is ironing board flat. There isn't enough space to walk around him. I will have to be front or back. His chest is hairless like a Chippendale's, or a girl's. I am relieved that the sight of it makes me squirm. It looks cold and clammy like a slab of unidentified flesh dragged from a river. I don't want to touch it.

'Put your tits away, Tom. You can save the glamour-model look for Tristan,' I say in the doorway.

'I don't want to get make-up on my shirt. Don't go shy on me now, Lulu,' he smirks.

'It's Scarlet to you,' I say.

'Okay, Scarlet, haven't you ever seen a six-pack before?'

'Do you have to draw those lines on your stomach with shoe polish? Your sheets must be disgusting,' I say, putting my box down on the side.

'Shoe polish? I don't think so. Feel this.' He grabs my arm around the wrist and I scream as he smacks my hand against his stomach. It feels hard and cold and bumpy. I wrench my hand away and take a step back.

'What the hell do you think you are doing?' I shout, flustered, the blood rushing to my head.

'Oh calm down, Scarlet, everything's such a drama with you. Now, shall we get on?' He closes his eyes and tilts his face upwards to the ceiling. 'All we need, I think, is good foundation – I like Clinique – a little eyeliner, a bit of contour around my nose, maybe a touch of colour on my lips, but just tint, not gloss, and a hint of mascara should do it, but brown-black, not black.'

'Okay, Boy George, but I have to work in silence,' I say. He shrugs and smirks.

Five minutes later all that I can hear are our breaths, co-inciding with each other like a pulse to this little room, and the pipes as they gurgle. Tom has an incredibly handsome face. It's objective, it's a fact, no matter what the fashion or the time or the look, he will always be handsome. As I sponge on foundation I can feel his breath on my hand, and his lips part as I lean closer to him to apply eyeliner. For a moment I smell sickness again, but it passes and I ignore it. I can see why, when drunk, I found him so appealing. What is it about beauty that can override our other senses, and obscure the nastiness or the pettiness or the dullness of a character, when that character is draped in a good-looking skin? I could kiss him, still. As vile as I find him, arrogant and childish and humourless, I could still kiss him. Beauty is hypnotic – you forget, temporarily at least, the evil that can lurk beneath. I guess that's what love is for. It's the feeling deeper, the reason more. Love beats beauty like paper covers rock. We need to love people so we don't have sex with monsters.

Even when Ben and I have fought about big things, or bored each other silly, there is still something about him, about the curve of his shoulders, the space on his neck beneath his ear, that I want to sink into and kiss clean. Sometimes when we are having sex, when we were having sex, I could lose myself in his arms or his shoulders or his neck, lose myself in kissing him. His skin tastes the way it should, tastes right and clean and substantial and strong. I could lose myself in kissing Ben, even now, and yet I know he has never lost himself in kissing me. Sometimes I tried to guide him there, to lead him softly to a place where he could just honestly kiss my back, for instance, for kissing's sake, because he was allowed, because it was my back and I gave it to him to kiss and touch and stroke, because I wanted him there. But he couldn't see it aside from sex. His cock, and not love, always guided him. Maybe he has always been that way, with Katie – her name still whispered like 'cancer' in a doctor's waiting room – or me, or any of his childhood girlfriends. Maybe his sex has always been calculated, and he has never lost himself in affection. Or maybe it is just me.

'You've got a good touch,' Tom says, as I dot a slightly red tint on his lips and smudge it in with my thumb.

I don't reply.

'It's light,' he says, without a smile, without opening his eyes.

I don't know why but I have to pause to control my breathing.

'It's the lightest thing about you, Scarlet. You're so angry the rest of the time, you're positively spiky. If the rest of you were as graceful as your touch it would be quite something. I think you try too hard, Scarlet,' he says.

I feel the thought of tears behind my eyes, without the tears appearing. Nobody died.

'You're finished,' I say, and step back.

His eyes peel open slowly and he turns to study himself in the mirror to his right. He stares long and hard, as I do. His chin is a box of clean lines, his nose strong and broad. He looks like somebody traced him from a picture. He is a diagram entitled 'How a man should look'.

'It's good. We could still go a shade lighter on the eyeliner, but it's good,' he says. He turns to me and smiles. Without speaking he reaches out for my hand and turns it over, so my palm faces upwards to the ceiling. He lowers his made-up face and kisses the middle of my palm lightly, right between my heart line and my head line, and he whispers 'thank you' so I can feel his breath where his lips were. I let him. To brush him away would be an ugly insult to what he is. It would be denying his beauty, and, at this moment, I shouldn't and I can't. He looks me in the eye, and I catch my breath again.

There is a quick rap on the door and it opens, nudging me forwards, closer to Tom, who presses my open palm against his chest as I am pushed against him.

Gavin stands in the doorway and glances down at my hand, and then says, 'Dolly will be waiting,' and closes the door.

Tom drops my hand like a hot stone.

'Dolly will be waiting, Scarlet,' Tom repeats, widening his eyes, smirking again now, and it's as if that smirk is everything that he really is. Everybody has a gesture that is theirs, that typifies them or defines them. A blush, or a wave, or a laugh, or a nod, or a single raised eyebrow with a cocked head – it's your own personal stamp on the world. And everywhere you go and everything you do can be stamped 'Scarlet was here' with a blush or a wave. It's a stamp on the consciousness of others, the thing that they'll remember when you've left the room, it's leaving your mark. Tom's stamp is his smirk. It smashes away my momentary doubts and reminds me who he is, and what drives him. As long as he keeps smirking, I should be okay.

'Dolly?' I whisper.

Dolly sits back in her chair asleep. Her head has fallen to one side like a snapped twig on an old branch. She snores quietly, a soft, wet, rhythmic grunt through her nose, interposed with quick fluttery gasped breaths that rightfully belong on a hospital ward. A glass of water and a couple of pills on the counter patiently wait for her to wake. Something makes me lift the glass and sniff the water and my suspicions are confirmed. It's the alcoholic kind, otherwise known as gin. Ella Fitzgerald plays softly from the CD player in the corner, 'Someday He'll Come Along', the lullaby of an old lady. Dolly's silk scarves shimmer with dust over the lamp, and the room glows gently through purple silk. It's a heavy kind of quiet, as it always is in a room in which somebody is sleeping. 'Do NOT Disturb' signs hang invisibly in the air.

'Dolly,' I whisper again, and reach for her hand. It's cold as I squeeze it. Her eyes open slowly.

'Has it been an hour already?' she asks me groggily.

'I'm afraid so.' I place my box down on the counter. This room feels like home after the starkness of Tom's cupboard.

'No need to be afraid, that's all I need. A quick cat-nap. I'm not an invalid. Not yet at least. A light snooze, that's all that was.'

She rubs her eyes and shifts herself in her chair, and as she does I hear a short quick fart.

'Where are my pills, where are my pills?' she demands loudly with a sudden embarrassed anger, batting me backwards and out of the way. She lean forwards and grabs the glass, and glugs the gin like the water we both pretend it is. She leaves a couple of mouthfuls at the bottom of the glass. There is no spirit shiver, as in films. She is gin-ready.

'Shall I start?' I ask.

'Well why else would you be here?' she snaps.

I spritz her face with water, then toner, and wipe it gently with a muslin cloth, but very little comes with it. She isn't wearing any make-up already.

'No blues, only browns on my eyes, Lulu,' she says firmly.

'I was going to try a grey as well, to bring out the violet,' I say.

She pauses for thought. 'Okay, you can try that. We'll see, we'll see.'

We can both smell her fart, there isn't room enough in here for us not to, there is nowhere for the smell to drift to and nothing for it to hide behind. It smells musty, like damp silken wool. Dolly winces beneath my fingers.

I consider making up an excuse: that I've left something upstairs that I have to urgently run and retrieve, just to be out of this room and give her a chance to spray the smell away with lavender, but I don't. She'll live.

I squirt a perfecting serum onto my hand and dab it on with my middle finger around her eyes, to smooth out her lines. I pad the ball of my finger gently over her skin that is old and creamy and creased like the disturbed top layer of milk on the turn.

'Much better today, Lulu,' she says with her eyes closed.

'What is?' I ask, dabbing the serum around her lips as well, and on the lines that fold in her face like soft round paper creases, that run from the edge of her nostrils to the corners of her mouth.

'Your outfit,' she says, 'I like your tie.'

I study her face as I take a handful of moisturiser and press my palms together to heat it. I don't say anything.

'I'm not being wicked, Lulu, I really do like it. You have character. You look like a principal boy! Ha!'

I knew it was too good to be true. I still don't say anything.

'No, seriously, darling,' she says, as I press my warm palms onto her cheeks, then her forehead, then her nose, swapping the moisturiser from me to her. 'I think that you look fun!'

'Thanks,' I say, but just to say something. I don't mean it.

'Well, darling, if you can't take a compliment I won't give you any more. Goodness, Lulu, don't be so churlish. My mother told me when I was very young that compliments are like kisses – the best ones are unexpected. If I merely told you that, say, you look lovely, or wonderful, it would sound predictable, or worse, insincere, and it wouldn't mean anything in the giving. Like giving chocolates at Christmas or roses on Valentine's Day, it would be an empty gesture. But you do look fun, and fun is the thing you should be called! You look like a girl to be around, today.' Her words slur into each other slightly. 'You do' is 'youdo' instead.

'Okay,' I say, 'thank you.' I pat the last of the moisturiser into her skin in silence. Her breathing slows as Ella sings 'Stormy Weather' softly in the background.

'Can I turn the light up now, just a little?' I ask.

'Just a little,' she says.

I search the wall for the main light switch. It is a brand-new dimmer. It stands out on the wall like a patch of skin that was covered by a plaster during sunbathing, now ripped off to reveal the surrounding tan.

'I got Gavin to put it in,' she says, with her eyes half-open.

I turn it slowly.

'That's enough,' she says firmly, as I am barely halfway to the level of light that I need.

'Just a little more while I do the base maybe?' I ask.

'No, that's enough,' she says. 'So. Tell me, Lulu, what you did with the rest of your day yesterday? I need some entertainment, I shall fall asleep again if not. I want to know what you young girls get up to.'

'What do you want to know?' I ask, rooting around absent-mindedly in my make-up box.

'Well, for a start, did you make love?'

I am poised to trace away the thin grey bags that hang beneath her eyes with a Touche Éclat. My hand stops in midair.

'No lovemaking yesterday, no.'

'But do you make love often?'

'How often is often?' I put the tip of the brush to her skin.

'Well that depends on how old you are, darling. Once

207

every five years would be reasonably often for me these days, and about as much as my old heart could take!' She chuckles to herself. 'But you young girls are at it like the Romans,' she says, 'I read it in the papers. Everybody is having sex these days.'

'About once a month, I guess.' That's a lie, unless I am counting indiscretions. With Ben, that's a lie. It's been months.

'Oh dear. Oh dear. Oh Lulu. That is a shame,' she grimaces. 'Don't like it much? Or just not very good at it?'

I squeeze a worm of foundation onto my wrist and squash it angrily with a sponge before dabbing at her nose.

'No, it's not me. I'd like it far more often than I get it, given the option.'

'But you're a woman, darling, and women always have the option! A woman who wanted it every night of the week could get it – although God knows why she would – but if she did, she could get it. We have the option, we're further removed from the instinct, darling, and we aren't as animal as men. Why in heaven's name do you believe that you don't have the option?'

'My boyfriend . . . well . . . he doesn't like sex as much as I do.'

'Is he homosexual?' she asks frankly, as if enquiring about the price of milk. 'There were a lot of them around in my day, parading as a good catch for a girl when they were far more interested in their golfing buddies!'

'No, no. Not homosexual.' I shake my head and laugh.

'Are you sure, darling? I mean, have you actually asked him? Because a man who doesn't like sex is hiding something.'

'He's not gay,' I say, irritated, 'we just don't see each other very much, we keep really different hours.'

'How different?' she asks as I pad colour around her forehead. I've dragged back her hair with a thick black Alice band. I half-expected clumps of it to fall off in my hand when I touched it, and would not have been at all surprised if she had been completely bald like one of Roald Dahl's witches.

'Just different. He works nine to five and I don't.' I don't want to talk about this with her, she's only using me for sport, she'll just end up laughing at me anyway. And then she'll drug me like the last poor fool. I change the subject. 'So, to answer your question, what did I do yesterday afternoon? I went to see a friend,' I say.

'Where and why?' she asks.

'At her house and . . . because she is my friend.'

'And how was your friend? And does she have a name?'

'Her name is Helen and she was pretty miserable actually. Her husband's mistress is pregnant, and her seventeen-year-old lover just tried to kill himself.'

I wait for a shocked gasp that doesn't come. Instead she says, 'I see,' and her mouth curls up at the edges into a small smile. 'How suburban, and exciting!' she says wickedly.

'Exciting is not the word I'd use,' I reply, trying to dab away the red lines on her nose. The gin has had its effect. I squeeze a little green concealer onto my index finger and follow the lines of them where they crawl onto her cheeks.

'But that's why they are doing it, isn't it, Lulu, for excitement? That would seem obvious to me. What did they expect?'

'No, they . . . I don't think . . . it's complicated, and . . .' I have stopped dabbing.

'And while you are trying not to agree with me on that, darling, tell me this – what is this obsession with killing people these days? Or killing oneself? I understood it back in my day, with the homosexuals, or the bankrupt, the ones who couldn't face it. It drove them to early drink and speed, and pipes and goodness knows what else had just come in on the boat from China, but today it's so unnecessary. I mean, we used to play at it all the time in those days, of course, but we always knew what we were doing – a handful of painkillers – but never valium, we all knew that – and a slug of gin, a tearful phone call and they'd all come running. But we never did ourselves any real harm.'

'That's a pretty big thing to play at,' I say, mixing concealer with foundation on my wrist.

'Oh but darling, you had to, all the new starlets were doing it. You had to get your name in the gossip rags somehow, and it was far more acceptable than it getting out that you were having an affair with a married man, or a studio boss. No, you had to get in the mags or they wouldn't use you, you see, because you weren't known. But you couldn't get known for affairs with married men, darling, because it hurt your popularity, and then all the studio wives would tell all their studio husbands not to hire you, and then everything became far too hard. The smart girls knew that. Not that you weren't having the affairs, of course, but it wasn't news, it couldn't be, the studios were too powerful back then, much more powerful than the public, much more powerful than some ten-cent rag full of tittle-tattle. So, you see, you had to have them write about you, darling, but it had to be the right things, and the bosses would never let their affairs get out. That stopped for a while, the tittle-tattle mags. But I see it's started again, now, hasn't it? I always felt terribly sorry for those girls, the desperate girls, taking their tops off in public, sleeping with whomever, wherever, whenever, and then spilling the beans. They didn't realise, you see, that it wouldn't get them work. They never got the parts, you see. Because back then, Lulu, you needed talent as well. You couldn't get by on just your looks. Not *just* your looks. Now you can build a whole career out of it. It's plainly wrong, of course. People think that's all they have to be. No wonder everybody's got so fame-hungry, darling, when goodness knows, all you have to do these days is have a bit of surgery and hope that somebody likes the look of you. There's no more to it than that, is there? These girls. Don't they know they should have a talent as well? Their mothers should have told them that. Don't put yourself in the firing line, naked, without a talent or something to shield you. Because by Christ they'll want to shoot you down. If you're naked, well? One shot will kill you. They can see where your heart is.'

I dust a large brush in translucent powder and circle it at her temples, onto her cheeks, and then down towards her chin. She sits in silence for a while.

'I need my water,' she says eventually. I pass her the glass. She knocks it back in one gulp with closed eyes. I put it on the side and say nothing.

'Tell me more about you, Lulu. You say you have a chap and he's not queer but he doesn't like sex?'

'I do have a chap . . . well . . . kind of . . .' I flick a small flat brush into grey eyeshadow.

'Well, do you or don't you, darling, it's an easy thing to answer, surely?'

'I do. I do. But . . .'

I have a sudden urge to dump it all on this old wicked witch, everything that's been churning through my head. I'll watch her get shocked, choke on the gin she's still slugging, shut her up, stop her asking questions.

'I do, but I've cheated on him, quite a few times actually. And now the clinic that I went to, to get tested, for HIV,' I say that bit loudly for effect, 'want me to have a type of counselling. For having too much sex without protection. Slut counselling, Dolly!'

I stop and wait for her reaction. Her eyes don't even open, don't even flicker beneath her closed eyelids. I swirl my

211

Laura Mercier brush angrily into violet shadow, and blow it aggressively. But she doesn't flinch.

I brush long strokes across her eyelids.

'Well that sounds joyless, and I have no time for that at all. You should enjoy yourself! Have you thought about gin?' she asks.

'I think gin might be the problem. Or vodka, or red wine, any of them really.'

'Darling, gin is never the problem! You might be the problem if you can't take it. Besides, alcohol is no excuse for anything. Even the drunkest man wouldn't kiss another man, if he wasn't queer. You have to let yourself do things, even if you are drunk. I think maybe you just aren't happy with your chap.'

I sigh. Nothing is going to shock her. I may as well be honest. If nothing else it will be a new opinion on an old mess, even if she does just tell me to stand by my man.

'You're right. I'm not happy with my chap.'

'How long?'

'How long what?'

'How long have you been unhappy with your chap?' she asks, exasperated.

'Since a couple of months after I met him,' I say, sighing with the relief of honesty. I haven't been happy for a long time.

'And how long have you been courting?'

'Three years. Except it's more than courting. We live together.'

'Oh dear, Lulu, how did you get yourself in this mess? And if you aren't happy, darling, then call me a silly old woman, but why on earth do you stay?'

Where is 'stand by your man'? Did I miss it? I almost look behind me to see if I glimpse it shutting the door. 'Because I love him,' I say, a little confused that I should have to explain that to her. She's the old one, not me. I'm supposed to be the generation with the commitment issues.

I stop smudging white powder into the corners of her eyes. She opens them and looks at me.

'And?' she asks expectantly.

'And what if I don't love anybody else like I love him?'

She closes her eyes again. 'We both know that's not true, what a silly thing to say. Christ, Lulu, don't be a silly girl. There is nothing worse than a silly girl. Don't believe it, darling, this nonsense talk in the play: "*for me there are no others*",' she says theatrically, her voice rising and filling the room. 'But there are always others, Lulu! This idea that there is just "one" person for anybody is damned ludicrous, I don't know who came up with it. Of course you can meet somebody and they can fit perfectly and they can do it, maybe, if you like it that way, for the rest of your life. But that doesn't mean there wouldn't have been others. Of course there would! And there will be! I bet you just like the look of him, don't you? Your chap. And that makes it harder to leave.'

I smile and reach for the mascara. The air-conditioning gasps quickly.

'I do still fancy him, yes. And after three years I think that's pretty good going.'

'Well, it enables you to carry on fucking him at least.'

It's my turn to gasp.

Dolly's violet eyes flash open like a zombie just brought back to life in a music video. 'What?' she asks me dryly.

'I don't know . . . well . . . you said fuck!' Even as I say it I feel ridiculous, but it was so unexpected.

'I'm old, darling, I'm not retarded. A fuck is a fuck. I don't believe you and your chap make love because it doesn't sound like he knows how, if he can't make you happy. But you have to call a fuck a fuck. I don't believe in using the word in everyday speaking, as an adjective, it's just lazy.

But a fuck is a fuck, darling, there are no ways around that.'

'Okay, then,' I say, twisting my mascara wand slowly out of its case. 'Except none of it really matters because we don't even . . . fuck any more.' I say it, and hate it. Even though I know that Ben and I, on the rare occasions that we do still have sex, are only having sex, only fucking, it is not something that I would ever admit, to anybody. And yet I just have. Without love, it is just fucking. Suddenly it seems obvious.

'But Lulu, how old are you?' she asks.

'Thirty-one,' I say. For the first time in a long while I am not embarrassed to say it, because my audience is ancient.

'Thirty-one and you still haven't realised that a man's looks mean close to nothing, darling? Don't you know that yet? You girls, you silly girls! Looks stir you. Maybe handsome keeps you somewhere longer than you should be. Maybe it turns heads, like yours turns for Tom Harvey-Saint, hmmm? Don't look so appalled darling, I'm old, I'm not blind. That's why this "fancy" is such a good word, I do agree with it, although we didn't use it in those days, but it suits its purpose when that's all it is, just "fancy". Weren't you listening this morning, darling, during rehearsal? When my old monster says, "*My first two husbands were as ugly as apes, and the last one resembled an ostrich!*" Now there is some truth worth listening to! Dear Tennessee, he wasn't all mad. Of course he was a screaming old queer and looks did move him, as they move all men, but darling, that's for the animals.'

'I don't understand what that means, why would she call her husbands ugly?' I ask.

'It means who cares how they look, really? It's the curse of men that they care so much about looks, it's what makes them so desperately simple. But a woman should see past it. You must never, never, just love a man for his looks, darling.

214

A man will always need more to him than that. A man should be loved for his character.'

'I'm not just with him for his looks!' I lash on the mascara as angrily as I dare, but still she doesn't flinch.

'If you say so, darling. So what's he like, your chap? What's wrong with him?'

I pause. And then I think, to hell with it.

'Do you really want to know? He's not affectionate. Our sex life is practically dead. He always thinks about himself before he thinks about me. I want somebody that I can put first, because they put me first. It doesn't work if we both put him first . . . because then nobody is thinking about me . . .'

'I completely agree, anything else?' she asks.

'He won't tell me that he loves me.'

Quiet. The CD has stopped playing. Even the heater doesn't make any noise. It's as if the whole room is stunned into silence by my stupidity.

Somebody walks past outside the room, presumably towards the kitchen. Dolly doesn't say anything, and suddenly I am mad. She coaxed it out of me for fun, and now she's going to use it against me. The blood rushes to my head, and I open my mouth to shout, but as I do she says, 'Oh Lulu. Poor Lulu. You've got one of those. My second husband's brother was exactly the same. It's such bad luck. My second husband was ugly like a fly, all tongue and eyes and long skinny legs. But rich, so rich, and I was taken with him for a while. He'd do this dance to make me laugh if I felt sad. One day he danced, and then he proposed marriage. I said no, but then I was sad, so he danced again to cheer me up, and I changed my mind and said yes. He was more upset than me when I refused him, but he still danced. It was a quick wedding in a church in Boulder, Colorado. Just us and the minister. But then he took me to Denver to meet his family. And that's when I met his brother.

He was an inch shorter, an inch wider, his eyes were a shade darker, his face an angle squarer, his legs a muscle fuller. He was beautiful, with hairs on his chest that poked out of the top of his shirt and I was overcome by him for a while. But it was just looks, darling, just infatuation, you get that?'

I nod my head.

'So anyway, he was one of them. One of these boys whose daddy wasn't nice to their mummy, who didn't think he had to kiss her. He just wanted to be a man, with men, because then he didn't have to care about anything but sports. And because my second husband was a little skinny, a little goofy, a little bug-eyed, he had never been a man's man, never spent much time with his father, and he had learnt to appreciate women in spite of his father's behaviour towards his mother. His brother did not. His brother was one of the worst, one of the ones you must always look out for, Lulu, because they are the very worst kind. The most painful kind. And they will damage you. And you've got one . . .'

'Well?' I say, scared to listen but scared not to.

'He hadn't realised that girls are as important as boys, darling. Can you imagine that? He hadn't allowed himself to see any value in the feminine, as any man must who is to love wholly and properly. He just thought it silly, and emotional, and ridiculous. He didn't respect his mother, he learnt that from his father. Only a man who appreciates the warmth and the strength of being held by the woman that loves him can love you wholly in return. Otherwise, well! They will never respect your value. My mother used to say, "If a man can't kiss his mother, don't take him as a lover."'

'But why are they like that? Why don't they want to like women?' I ask, baffled.

'Oh Christ, darling, I don't know – because it's easier not to say most things than say them? And not to feel most things than feel them? Because it's effort and men are lazy, and emotions terrify them more than tidal waves? But the worst thing a man can inherit is a father who doesn't respect his mother. A man has to love his mother, and love his father, to know how to be. Otherwise it will ruin them for women. They'd have been better off with one parent gone than that. We all look up as children and learn our lives before we live them, darling. Of course that's not to say we can't learn other things along the way. Don't ever waste your time on a man who isn't even going to try and open up, darling. It's like fucking a corpse: unless you're sick, it's futile. Hell, we all grow up eventually. How old is your chap?'

'Thirty-three,' I mumble.

'Thirty-three? Thirty-three! Ha! Christ, darling, he's an adult and it's not your job to fix him. Let him rot!'

'Oh my God, I can't do that, that's just . . .' I search for the words but Dolly interrupts me.

'Lulu, do not waste your life wasting his with him. I won't allow it! What kind of silly girl sticks around for some thoughtless, careless, unfeeling toad?'

'But I love the toad!'

'Oh for goodness sake, am I ready to go? I can't bear this drivel any more! Toughen up, Lulu, for all our sakes. See him for what he is. Don't be some damned man's cushion. You've got a life to live! And at some point every woman needs a man that knows how to love and loves her back. I believe that. It might not be fashionable, but it's true. Are you going to sit around with this toad who won't love you, while all the other girls get the men that can?'

'But what if he doesn't know how to love me the way that I need him to?'

'Then you make it clear, Lulu, as I am sure you have already. And if you mean anything to him, anything at all, he will do it. Let me tell you this, and it's the easiest lesson a man can ever learn. A woman doesn't want much. They say they don't understand us, but any man who listens for one tiny minute will understand a woman. The problem isn't us, it's them. It's staring them in the face. A woman, a good woman and not a silly woman – and you have to know the difference – will hold back the broken banks of the Nile for the man that she loves. She will fight off armies for the man that she loves. She will make him feel like a hero. And all he has to do? Show her that she is adored. It's not that they don't know, darling. It's that some of them can't be bothered, the ones who would rather play with their boys than with girls. And as time rolls on, darling, and the homosexuals come further and further out of their closet and Old Compton Street breaks its banks and swallows up half of Soho, then you'll see. Those boys never wanted to play with girls anyway. A real man knows how to love a woman, darling. And a real woman wouldn't stay with a man that doesn't! Now, am I done?'

'I don't know, are you?'

'I mean my make-up, Lulu, am I done?'

'Oh, yes, yes you are.'

'Good.' Dolly pushes herself to her feet and walks heavily towards the door.

'Don't you want to see it?'

'No. Not today.'

She wrenches the door open and disappears.

I clean my brushes, and flop down in her chair exhausted.

I am nodding off when there is a small thump on wood and Gavin kicks the door open, with a hammer in one hand and a spirit level in the other, and a couple of nails between his lips.

'I'll come back later' he mumbles flatly without the nails falling out, and avoids eye contact, ducking back through the doorframe and pulling the door closed with him. I jump to my feet and run after him.

218

'No, wait, Gavin!' I yank the door back open.

'She said her mirror is crooked but I can do it later' he says spitting the nails into his hammer hand, looking down at his feet. They are huge, his trainers are like clown's shoes.

'What are you doing now Gavin? Do you fancy a walk, some fresh air maybe? I think they are going to be upstairs for a while, I'm going to take a break and some company would be nice, can you sneak out for a sandwich?' I don't find it hard to ask him to come with me, I'm not scared of his indifference, the way I would be if I were asking Tom Harvey-Saint the same question. I'm not afraid that Gavin will say something spiteful and make me feel ridiculous and rejected because he has too much . . . character for that.

'Tom not free then?' he asks deadpan.

'Gavin, you know what he's like. And that room is small and you opened the door a little hard, yes you did! And you don't know your own strength, and you sent me flying forwards and on to him. It was closer than I wanted to be, I'll tell you that. Come on, take a walk with me! If I am willing to risk Covent Garden cobbles in these heels' I gesture at my feet with my thumb, 'it's the least that you can do!'

'I have a lot to do today . . .' he says.

I sigh and put my hands on my hips. I will not knowingly enter in to the persuading business with any other men. I've had enough of that for a lifetime.

'But I do need some air' he says deadpan, 'so you can entertain me for a while Scarlet, on one condition.'

'Anything, you just name it,' I say.

'Let's not talk about Ben' he says. Gavin looks me defiantly in the eye.

'Now there's a challenge!' I say.

'What do you say, are you woman enough?' he asks, from way up Gavin high.

'I think I've still got it in me!' I say, 'I'll grab my purse.'

Gavin checks his watch as we leave through the back door, and determines that we have an hour to kill.

'Do you want to get a coffee or something?' I ask, as we stare down Long Acre.

'I thought we were going to walk. Let's see some sights, give bad directions to some tourists.' He looks about seriously to see if he can spot any Americans to confuse, and it makes me laugh.

'Well that sounds like my kind of fun!' I say.

As we walk without thought along the Strand towards Nelson's column and the newly pedestrianised Trafalgar Square, Gavin tells me about the struggles they have had with Dolly until now, and how it is only this week that she seems to have settled down, and not been so aggressive. Apparently for the last six weeks she has been leaping down everybody's throats; she threw water at her understudy Audrey, and has refused to allow anybody into her dressing room, not Tristan, not Tom. Only Gavin has been allowed in for maintenance. She has kept them all at bay until now. She spent most of her time taunting Yvonne, my predecessor, who would leave in tears nearly every night, her hands shaking a little more than yesterday, her eyes puffy and red with tears. Dolly didn't like Yvonne, Gavin thinks because she was short and fat and old – he heard her refer to her as a hobbit. Gavin escorted Dolly up and down from her car to her room every day, but that was the extent of their contact. She came up to the stage for rehearsals, but then went straight back downstairs again, ignoring anybody's efforts to speak to her.

We cut down towards Embankment and through the tube station to the river. Jogging up the steps to cross the Millenium Footbridge at Waterloo, it seems we are heading for the South Bank.

'She is certainly happier this week. You must be doing

something right.' Gavin shoves his hands in his jeans pockets as we walk.

'Oh Lord I'm sure it's not me' I say, glancing out at the river, pulling a rogue strand of hair, that has stuck to my lipgloss, back behind my ear.

'Why shouldn't it be you, you are the only thing that's different? Look, there's a police boat' he says, pointing down at a boat powering along the middle of the river sending plumes of white froth spraying behind it.

'Yes but she's a star, and I'm just Make-up. Are you sure she hasn't just changed her prescription or something? Or got a bigger hip flask?'

Gavin looks at me.

'Why wouldn't it be you? Maybe she likes having a pretty young girl to boss around, maybe you remind her of her?'

'Yeah right, with my constant tears and moaning – Gavin, she thinks I'm pathetic.'

'Scarlet you aren't pathetic. Maybe she feels a little needed. Maybe she thinks you are fun and you've just gone the wrong way, backed the wrong horse. Maybe you do remind her of herself.'

I shake my head.

'God no, Gavin. I'm just . . . not me. I'm nothing special. It must be the gin.'

'Okay' he shrugs, and gives me a doubtful look.

We don't stop half way across the bridge because that is what lovers would do. I do look down the river though, towards the city, as we walk. I can't see the view in the other direction because a railway line herded with Charing Cross trains obscures my view of parliament and The London Eye. We descend the steps to the South Bank and walk towards Festival Pier. I gulp.

I remember meeting Ben here, for our second date. We arranged to meet at the bottom of the pier at seven p.m one

Thursday night. I was early, for once in my life, and as I saw him coming I had to look at my feet, then at tourists, then at the river. He took an age to reach me, and I couldn't look at him, I was so nervous, and terrified that he would see straight through me, and realise instantly how much I felt for him, even then. I thought we were saving each other. I realise now that I believed, even then, that he was in love with me. If I had known that it was so much less, I might have run back up those steps and far away. As it was I waited for him, all that time as he got closer and I just stood there, scared by my own feelings. He didn't say anything when he reached me, he just kissed me straight away, with a forceful tongue and his eyes closed. Christ I hope he even realised it was me. Perhaps if I'd been unlucky, or lucky instead, the girl next to me would have done.

Gavin's phone rings.

'Hi, is everything okay? Did you? And how was it, what did he say? I'm sure he doesn't, you know what he's like, he just needs his space sometimes.' A quick surprised laugh. 'That's fantastic, good for you, I bet you look great. I haven't forgotten, I'll go and buy it this week and bring it with me in a couple of weeks. Okay, I'll speak to you soon. Yep, you too, and to dad. Okay bye.'

'Was that your mum?' I ask, genuinely moved.

'Yep. Sorry. She's trying to get my dad to join the lawn bowls team with her, and he's not sure. It's only because he's scared all the men there will fall in love with her.'

'And will they?'

'Probably. She's a gorgeous old girl my mum.'

'You sound close.'

He shrugs. 'She's my mum, of course.'

We follow the line of the river until we reach Waterloo Bridge and cut up to cross back again towards the bottom of Covent Garden.

'Have you been to the Tate Modern?' I ask him.

'Yep, you?'

'Not yet. I keep meaning to go, but I don't want to go on my own.'

'Won't 'he who shall not be named' go with you?' he asks smiling.

'No, he doesn't think it will interest him. I'll have to wait until they have a *Star Wars* exhibition, or *Lord of the Rings*, or something.'

'So he won't just go because you want to go then?' he says, like he understands something.

'Gavin, Ben won't do anything just because I want to do it. He actually says that to me, 'You can't tell me what to do' when I suggest things we could do at the weekends. Mostly he wants to watch the football, or go to the pub, or sometimes IKEA . . .'

'Jesus,' Gavin whistles, a little disgusted.

'We said we weren't going to talk about him,' I say, aware that even in his absence he is infiltrating my walk and ruining my mood.

'Okay, I know. I just want to say one thing. Not all men are like that, Scarlet.'

I nod. 'I know, it's just easy to forget sometimes. And you know, people change after a while.'

'No they don't. Not always. I'd go to the Tate again Scarlet, it's great.'

I nod my head in reply, and when he looks down at me I smile and shrug. I can't make that plan, not yet at least. It would be unfair.

We grab a sandwich and walk back down Long Acre.

'Good walk,' I say, 'although my feet hurt now.'

'I have to get back,' he says, and brushes my hand with his. I look away and he walks off in long strides.

The cast are mid-rehearsal as I creep in. Tristan sits in

front of the stage with his hands either side of his eyes. He is topless, his chest dark like tea and covered with black hair. Tom is topless too, hairless and bronzed and unreal. Arabella is pale, and wearing a bra and a silk vest. All of the understudies mill around, topless too, skinny and hungry. Dolly has taken off her turban. After a while she spots me sitting a couple of rows back, and raises her eyes at Tom's bare chest, grimacing, mocking him with a wicked old smile, and I stifle a laugh.

They are performing now, there is no more chatter, and it is as if two worlds exist in this one room. There is my reality, and theirs, and they are so convincing that I believe both of them at once. There is a bubble on the stage that is Italy, and Tom's name is really Chris, and Arabella's name is really Blackie, and Dolly is really somebody called Mrs Goforth.

This alternate reality is punctured occasionally when Dolly forgets a line or needs a cue. Tristan is sitting a row in front of me, directly in the centre of the stage, and every time Dolly fluffs he covers his eyes gently. Only after a few minutes have passed will he remove his hands and open his eyes again. Tom and Arabella and the rest of the cast are word-perfect. It is only Dolly who stops and starts. I can see her hands trembling from a distance.

'Bloody chair,' she says, tripping over a large old armoire, and Tristan covers his eyes again. '*I do need the company of* . . . or *I need males* . . . or . . . just give me the bloody line will you!' she demands of the wings.

I hear a whisper from stage right.

'Well you'll need to speak up, I can't damned well hear you!' she shouts. Her hands tremble a little more. She shoves them into the pockets of her trousers clumsily.

There is muttering off-stage. Tristan sits perfectly still before them, his eyes covered.

Everybody sits or stands around the stage, frozen, staring forwards. Gavin, fiddling with an exit sign above a door, stops and looks down, waiting. Tom and Arabella look around them wildly for a life jacket or a float.

'*I need the company of men . . . I need . . .*' Dolly yanks her shaking hands out of her pockets, bringing them up to her face. Her fingers shake and dance at her temples as she tries desperately to remember.

I breathe in, and hold my breath.

'Just give me the damn script,' she shouts finally, walking unevenly to the side of the stage, snatching a bundle of papers from an anonymous hand.

She reads it and composes herself. Somebody coughs nervously. Gavin still keeps looking down. Dolly tosses the play on the floor, and turns to face Arabella. Fixing her with a sad old determined glare, Dolly says,

'*I do need male company, Blackie . . . that's what I need, to be me.*'

A pin drops somewhere and everybody hears it.

Tristan peels his hands away from his eyes.

I breathe out with relief.

I am flicking through *InStyle* when Dolly comes back down to the room.

'Don't talk to me, Lulu, I'm too tired to talk.' She walks to the counter, sparks a match clumsily and lights a lavender candle. Her hands are still shaking a little. She flicks on the CD player and lowers herself heavily into her chair, which puffs out a little dust when she lands on it. She has a salty tidemark around her hairline. 'Just clean this rubbish off so that I can go home.'

I dampen a cotton-wool pad with cleanser and swipe gently at her eyes. She twitches occasionally. The flame from the candle twitches at the same time. She begins to hum along gently to Ella Fitzgerald, 'My Funny Valentine', as I circle at the hollows of her cheeks with fresh cotton wool.

Turning to open a new bottle of cleanser I see a fresh pile of envelopes have been delivered. 'You've got more love letters today,' I say. 'You certainly have a lot of admirers.'

'I'll open them tomorrow,' she responds quietly.

I toss a piece of muslin into a bowl of water to soak, and scoop some cleanser into my palms, rubbing the paraffin in circles onto her face. Her skin moves with my fingers for longer than it should, then lazes back into place as I move my hand higher.

'I'm just going to leave that on for a couple of minutes,' I say softly.

She nods.

I turn and tidy away the bottles, flinging dirty bundles of cotton wool into the waste-bin. The CD has stopped and I press play, and she starts to hum along gently to Ella Fitzgerald again, but then falls silent. I wring out the muslin, and begin wiping off the cleanser on her face.

'All that time to put it on, all this time to take it off,' she whispers.

I don't say anything.

'I met Ella, you know, Lulu. We were friends for a while. In 1950 I think it was. I was nearly twenty-one.'

'How wonderful,' I say quietly.

'Yes, it was 1950, because that was the year that I went to my first opium party in Hollywood. Everybody wore a kaftan then and not much underneath. It was way up in the hills, away from the hordes, high up above Mulholland Drive. A large flat house with a roof that hung over the walls like a wild mushroom, the poisonous kind. It was dark all the way up the hill, we had a chauffeur of course, and we climbed higher and higher, and then I spotted the house up above us, two hundred feet away. It was a haze of orange light, like somebody lit a fire in the sky. I smoked a cigarette, of course, you can hear that in my voice, that I started smoking far too young, and I watched the fire get closer, and I knew I was moving in the right direction. It was the birthday of the wife of some producer or other, some big hotshot. And it was a pretty big deal. Do you know they gasped as I walked through the door? And other people were there. Marilyn was there. Jane, too, but it was me that made them gasp, and they didn't know me then. I was still starting but it was the black hair instead of blonde, you see. It was pulled up at the sides, black curls tumbling down my back, and I wore a white kaftan with dark pink piping around the neck, and no bra. You could see the outlines of my nipples through that material, it was flimsy, I knew that when I put it on. But Charlie said "leave it" and pulled my hands away when I tried to cover myself up. I stood out. Charlie was my manager at the time but of course we were lovers as well – he took me and paraded me around like a carnival princess at some local fete. There weren't many of us English girls over there – just me, Diana, Elizabeth of course, but she was already in a different league. I had only been over there for a year, not even that. And we had just changed my name.'

She coughs slightly into a handkerchief. I press moisturiser into my palms again to heat it.

'What was it before?' I ask.

'Mary Long. Charlie said it had no magic. I always kind of liked it. It was my great aunt's name, and she had been a showgirl, and it was good enough for her. But Charlie changed it, along with everything else. Of course he was right, but still. My mother always called me Mary, or Marie sometimes, as did my sisters. But to everybody else I became Dolly. And Russell was Charlie's last name. That was before we married, but still. He said, "Take it now," so I did, and then by the time we were married I already had it, you see. There was nothing new on my wedding day, not even the ring. It was one I'd been wearing for months, that Charlie had persuaded some jeweller to give us on the cheap for some premiere or other. And Charlie slipped it off just before the ceremony, and then slipped it on again when we said, "I do." Not every wedding is the stuff of dreams, Lulu. But I was young. I didn't know better.'

'Oh,' I say, and try not to sound sad.

'I met a man at that party,' she says. 'He was Persian. Stank of cognac and money. He was a lot of fun that night, and he kept cracking jokes like Groucho Marx, but he was old enough to be my grandfather. His fingers were wrinkled like he'd left them in to soak. His teeth were the colour of my mother's eggnog at Christmas. Charlie told me to be nice to him, he was investing in pictures, and big. I slept with him, for money, I think it's fair to say. I wanted a mink and Charlie couldn't afford it. I told the Persian that I wanted a mink, and then I slept with him, and two days later it arrived at my house in a pink box with grey tissue paper and a bow the colour of blood.'

I rest my palms on her face and press the moisturiser in. I stand back and she looks shiny and old.

'I don't know where it's gone, the mink. I never took to it; I think maybe I lost it when I moved to Denver. But of course, I can't lose the memory.'

She sits in silence. Her hands tremble at her sides.

'There was one, Lulu, even that early on. It was the sex. His name was Don, like Don Juan I joked, and he was a carpenter at Universal, on the set of my first feature. Of course by then Charlie had gone back to his second wife and I was glad to be rid of him. And Universal had signed me for three pictures anyway, so I got another manager easy enough and somebody they liked as well, not a small-time chancer like Charlie. But Don opened his eyes and

228

looked at me, Lulu, while he kissed me. He kissed me while we made love. I felt it moved him to be with me. A lot of men, they can only kiss with their eyes closed, because they are scared of what they'll feel if they open them. But Don used to hug me at strange times. Huge unexpected hugs. He used to knock me off my feet with the things he'd say. Small things, stupid things, not poetry, he was just a carpenter, but just silly things. He wasn't scared either, of his emotions, of being left. He was, probably, the most marvellous man I have ever known, and yet I never married him, because I never expected it to last. He died, unexpectedly, a year after I'd last seen him. It didn't make it any less perfect. It made it perfect, in a way. He moved to New York one month for work, in the theatre can you believe? And he stayed, and it went on and on, and he never came back. There was an accident, on a set, and that was that. I certainly loved him, but then in a way I loved them all. I loved Charlie as well, he had his qualities, we had good times. Charlie and I hustled together and I wouldn't change it, Lulu. Love isn't such a crazy concept, you shouldn't put it on a pedestal, or let your chap do that either. I was happy to love them all, I saw its benefits, even though I rarely stayed for long. But I learnt early on that telling somebody that you love them makes you love them, in a way. And not telling somebody that you love them makes you not love them. And now that seems obvious, to me, and that any idiot should know it. It's a door you can open or a door you can keep closed. That's all it is. Sometimes somebody will open it for you, but sometimes it's shut so tight we have to do it ourselves, open it for them. Sometimes you have to say it to let yourself feel it.'

'We're done,' I say, wiping the leftover moisturiser into my hands and wishing I'd taped everything she'd said so I could play it back to Ben in his sleep – slip the earphones on and hope he learns it all subconsciously like a foreign language, and wakes up a new man.

She opens her eyes slowly. 'What will you do tonight, Lulu?' she asks me.

'I'm not sure. I might hang around and go for some drinks at Gerry's.'

'You should go home. You should see your chap, Lulu. Don't prolong the agony if you don't have to. Be brave. A woman needs to be brave. We have too much to lose.'

'Maybe,' I say, wishing she hadn't even suggested it. 'What will you do tonight, Dolly?' I ask, reaching down for her bag to pass it to her.

'Sleep, mostly. Of course my daughter will call – she was supposed to call last night, but she must have got caught up, or the damned stupid hotel staff mucked up the lines again and didn't put her through. I expect she'll call tonight.'

I hand her the bag, and she walks towards the door.

'Tomorrow, then,' she says, and leaves.

I turn off the lamps, pull off the scarves because I'm afraid of fire, and duck out of the back entrance without saying goodbye to anybody else. I don't want to get caught by Tom, he can take off his own damn make-up.

It's warm, early evening, five o'clock. There was a time when my five o'clocks were late. Now it seems so early, I am generally still on set, on my third glass of wine, we've only just finished lunch and we are kicking in for the main body of the shoot, hoping to get everything done by eleven. But I remember a time when it seemed like the end of the day, when kids were washing up for dinner and mums were burning fishfingers, and *Newsround* was about to come on, and then *Blue Peter*, and my dad would come in from work and wash his hands and sit at the table. It's funny how quickly I grew up, and how easily I forget. My life isn't what I thought it would be. I realise now that I thought I would be like the adults in my childhood, and that I would be the one cooking the fishfingers by now.

I check my watch and wander down to the *Evening Standard* seller.

'Hello,' I say.

'Thoreau?' he responds.

'No, I said hello,' I reply.

'I know. Thoreau,' he says again.

I sigh. 'Sorry?' I ask. I realise that I am too tired tonight to even think. It's warm and a bead of sweat trickles down the back of my neck, beneath my hair, tracing my spine like that game I used to play with my brother when we were kids: 'Does – this – make – your – blood – run – cold?' we'd ask, pressing fingers into each other's backs and then grabbing at each other's necks, squealing at the inevitable shiver.

'Thoreau,' repeats the seller.

'What about him?' I ask.

'Love your life, poor as it is,' he lisps through his remaining teeth.

'Right. Love your life, poor as it is. What does that mean, that I shouldn't change it? I should just accept it?' I ask, exhausted.

'LOVE your life, poor as it is,' he says once more, and takes my forty pence.

'Or does it mean that you should make sure you love your life, make it the best that it can be?' I ask.

'LOVE your life,' he says.

'Okay, fine,' I reply, shaking my head, grabbing my paper and walking off without a smile towards the tube.

I flap along Ealing Broadway, my tired toes fighting desperately to keep me in my shoes as I pass flower-sellers and the North Star pub, and Marks & Spencer's end-of-summer sale and a nightclub, and gaggles of giggling schoolgirls and shifty-looking texting teenagers in hooded tops who'd rather faint than look a woman in the eye. It's not quite dark, yet, but the moon is out, round and fat already. It's magnolia tonight, not neon like last night. It's always one or the other. Plain or wildly exciting. Ordinary or full-fat with possibilities.

Sometimes I feel like I have made the same mistakes as my mother and trapped myself in my own life, and they are my own teeth marks in the tape that binds my wrists and my feet. But of course she was married, and had me and my brother, and she still found a way out. My bonds are only as tight as I make them.

God is locking up Plump and Feather. She is dressed head-to-sandal in white linen, and her face is red and shiny like a washed tomato. She glances at me without recognition. I am never home this early.

'Are you a friend of Ben's?' she asks with a smile so wide she must have to practise it at yoga, as I put my key in my door.

I ignore God and shut the door behind me. She'll have to forgive me, that's what God does.

Scene II: Wife Wanted

'It's me,' I say, walking up the stairs. 'I'm . . . home.'

Ben pokes his head out from the kitchen. 'Why are you so early?' he asks, holding a saucepan. He is wearing his Everton shirt. He went to Blackpool once, on a stag do, but that's the extent of Ben's travels in the north.

'Well it's nice to see you too,' I say, determined to smile.

'It's just a surprise.' He shrugs and his eyebrows raise as he licks a spoon with his whole tongue, and it looks flat and battered like the flap of an old leather shoe.

I step forward to kiss him hello but he turns back into the kitchen.

'Hey,' I say, following him in, 'I was going to kiss you hello.'

'Oh, hello,' he replies, and pecks me on the lips. With his eyes closed.

I lean back against the kitchen counter and pull off one of my shoes, rubbing my foot with my thumb.

'I can get home early sometimes, Ben, it just always depends on the cast. But I think this theatre thing is going to be different. Dolly gets tired so I can finish sooner. It might be different once the play actually opens, but for this week at least . . . Oh my toes hurt! These shoes have been playing me up all day – I might have to get you to rub my feet later.'

'No thanks,' he replies, carefully escorting pasta tubes onto a large navy blue plate.

'Are you makin' dinner?' I ask in a silly American accent – I don't know why, maybe to seem cuter than I am.

'Yes, I am. I have. But I didn't think you'd be home.' He grinds pepper onto his plate. One plate.

'Well, I'm not crazily hungry, can't we just share yours? What are you having anyway?' I tug at his arm to get him to turn around, but he resists and shakes me off.

'Don't, Scar, I'll spill it. Tuna and pasta,' he addresses his plate, dusting on parmesan like he is sifting for gold, 'but I've only made enough for me.'

He turns around, plate in hand, and gives me an apologetic shrug. The EEC pasta mountain steams before him. I didn't realise there was a European pasta surplus until now, but there it is, on Ben's plate.

'My Goodness! Training for a marathon, Ben?'

'No . . .'

'Well, can we share? Have we got any bread? We could dip that in some oil, we'll be stuffed before you know it and . . .'

He sighs and looks at the wall, as if summoning up the energy to explain applied physics to a glamour model.

'Scarlet, I made this much because I want this much.'

I look at him and try so hard, so very hard not to let my smile slip. He looks down at his plate, back to me, at the cooker, back to me, at his plate.

'Can I have one mouthful, Ben? Just one?' I reach for a fork on the side.

'Jesus.' He whistles under his breath. 'Yes, if you want, but that's not going to be enough, is it?' He sighs and looks away again.

I'm done with smiling.

'Christ, Ben, what have I done that is so bloody bad? When did everything I do begin to irritate you so much that you can't even let me have a mouthful of fucking pasta? If it's such a huge sodding deal, don't bother! I'll starve!'

He shrugs and walks past me, plate in hand. I consider tipping it up; just for a second I entertain throwing the whole damn thing on the floor. But I don't seize my moment. I have a feeling Dolly would have let him have it. I have a feeling another man would have let me have a mouthful of his pasta.

'We do have other food,' he says, turning and standing in the doorway, his loaded fork poised before his open mouth.

'You know what Ben? I don't even care. Eat your shitty student meal, I'll have cereal, thanks.' I slam the fork down and throw open the cupboard.

'Oh here we go,' I hear him mutter as he walks off towards the living room.

'Is bloody Iggy coming around again tonight?' I ask, slamming my Alpen down on the counter so ferociously that the top bursts open and I am covered in a dusty muesli shower storm. I say 'shit' as a flake flies in my eye, and I try not to cry. I take three deep breaths. I yank open the cutlery draw as noisily as I can, grabbing a spoon, slamming it closed again.

There is practically silence from the other room. Occasionally I hear the fork clink against the plate. Once I think I hear Ben gulp.

I shake Alpen into my bowl, and then milk, and dunk in my spoon. I lean back against the counter and take a breath. I don't want an argument. Maybe I was just hungry, low blood-sugar levels or something. I take four more deep breaths, and carry my bowl into the living room.

'Is Iggy coming round?' I ask again, in more measured tones.

'No, I was just going to watch this.' He gestures at the TV with the remote control, flicking it on. He doesn't look at me, but concentrates instead on shovelling a huge mouthful of pasta into his mouth without dropping any, while simultaneously not missing any of the riveting BMW advert that is now playing.

'Okay then . . . I'll watch it with you.' I walk around our coffee table, which is loaded with PC and gaming magazines, plus a new and alarming addition that looks to be an instructional magazine that promises to teach the reader how to make his own *Lord of the Rings* figurines: part one comes with a Gandalf mould and grey paint . . .

I sit on the other side of the sofa next to Ben, trying not to think about him making pottery action figures that can fight with Iggy's pottery action figures to their broken pottery death. I repress a shudder.

'So, what shall we watch?' I ask with a smile.

'The football's on.' Still I get no eye contact.

'Oh . . . can't you tape it? And we can watch something else together? Maybe there's a film on the other side, check Teletext,' I say, reaching forwards for the remote, but he grabs it.

'But Scar, it's England . . .'

'Okay, Ben, you're being a bit weird.' I stare at the remote control but he doesn't hand it over as the adverts finish and the ITV football theme plays. I am running out of time. 'And it's not often I get home this early. I just thought we could watch something together tonight . . .'

He stares at me. Then he rolls his eyes and sighs.

'But it's England, Scar,' he says again.

'Okay, fine,' I whisper.

He turns back to the TV and puts the remote control down next to him, on the side furthest away from me. If I want it, I am going to have to fight him for it.

'FINE!' I shout, standing up. 'I'll eat my cereal in the bedroom and go to bed! Lovely spending the evening with you, Ben!' I holler, my hands shaking my bowl with rage.

He puts his plate down on his lap and throws his fork down on it. 'Jesus Christ, here we go! I had my evening all planned out, you don't tell me that you're coming home, how the hell was I supposed to know? If you had called and told me I could have made more food, and I could have told you the football would be on. You know I don't like surprises . . .'

'It's not a surprise, I live here! And it's my flat too, what if I don't want to watch the football?'

'Scar, for Christ's sake! It's one night!'

'That's right, that's exactly right! One night that I am here and everything is just too much trouble! Anything to do with me is just too much damn trouble!'

Ben sighs. I hear Gary Lineker say, '. . . and now over to our commentators.' Somebody blows a whistle. Ben picks up his plate again.

I storm out and into the bedroom with the remainder of my cereal, grabbing *InStyle* from my bag in the corridor.

Two hours later, with no sign of Ben even at half-time, I wander up the hallway. Gary Lineker is talking about the match. The room is dark and Ben is drinking a cup of tea. The only light is the blue haze from the television.

'Did we win?' I ask quietly, hanging in the doorframe.

'No. It was a draw,' he says evenly.

'Oh no, what does that mean? Are we out of something? Or does there have to be a . . . replay?' I walk around the coffee table to the sofa and sit.

'No, it's fine, it was only a friendly.' He takes a gulp of tea.

'A friendly?' I ask, incredulous.

'Yeah,' he says innocently, nodding his head.

'With who?' I ask.

'United Arab Emirates' he says.

I bite my tongue. I didn't come back in here for an argument. I might not apologise this time, for the first time ever, but I won't start another row.

'Are you excited about the zoo?' I ask, shifting in closer to him on the sofa. I rest my head on his arm but he doesn't move it to let me under.

'Excited?' he asks, sounding confused.

'Okay then, not excited, but we haven't spent a day out together for ages and . . .'

We pause, as if God hit a button.

After thirty seconds, God presses play.

'I don't know. Look, Scarlet, do you really want to go, because the weather is going to be bad and I wanted to buy a new magazine rack from IKEA, and . . .'

'I'll see if we need tickets – let's try and go early!' I say, jumping up and walking into the kitchen as fast as I can. God presses pause again, and there is a moment of heavy silence in our little flat, but then God presses play, for Ben at least, and he turns the volume up on the TV.

In the kitchen I am trembling. I hold my hands out in front of me and as I see them shake it makes me want to cry even more. When did I get so pathetic? When did I get so scared? But I am determined: there will be no tears.

'I'm going to bed,' I shout.

I hear a muffled 'Night' from the other room.

Thursday. I decide to walk to Ealing Common station this morning for a change, and because I am wearing comfortable wedges that allow me the luxury. Still high, just with a better grip and straps that hold me in. Plus, I am ludicrously early. I wonder how much I could actually achieve in a day if I were to go to bed before eleven o'clock each night, as I did last night. I was even awake before Ben left this morning, although I stayed in bed, one leg tucked over the duvet, my pillow doubled up beneath my head, and I didn't say anything when he came back in the room to swap his cufflinks over. All of Ben's cufflinks are Everton blue, I don't know what could have prompted the swap. I could hear him rooting around in his drawer, whistling quietly to himself, some Aerosmith song that I hate. Isn't whistling the sign of a carefree heart? I've never been able to whistle. I just put my lips together and blow, like they tell you to, but nothing ever comes out except air. My heart isn't quite carefree enough to allow power ballads.

I walk past the common and cross the North Circular at the traffic lights. There are a few houses dotted along the other side of the road. I think that they must all be double-glazed, being this close to the noise and the dirt and the smog that burps and wheezes out of the constant stream of traffic circling inner London twenty-four hours a day, every day. There are yellow and orange 'For Sale' signs dotted along by open, expectant garden gates. Every other household seems to want to move, and I'm not surprised.

There is one white sign that stands out. It has been carefully hammered into the lawn outside a perfectly ordinary three-bedroom ex-council-house semi. The nets look clean, the driveway is neat, the wheelie bin is tidy, and there's a row of small multi-coloured flowers running up each side of the path to the yellow front door. At first glance, with the sign hammered in the lawn, I think this house must be for sale as well. But something makes me look and read it again. It says, in big black letters on white board, 'WIFE WANTED. PLEASE KNOCK.'

I walk up the path and lift up the knocker, but decide at the last moment to ring the bell instead. I hear it buzz inside the house, and it seems like a song being sung in somebody else's head. Through the frosted glass in the door I see a man trot briskly from the kitchen at the back of the house. He answers with a smile, and a 'Can I help you?'

He is in his late forties, early fifties perhaps. He is kindly average. His hair is dark grey and thinning on top, he is nearly six foot and one of his front teeth is very slightly discoloured, but not terribly so. He wears grey trousers and a blue shirt. There are toast crumbs on his chest.

'Have you found a wife?' I ask.

'Maybe. I have a date on Saturday night.' His smile is bashful, but full of pride. 'I haven't had a date on a Saturday night for twelve years.'

'Where will you go?' I ask.

'I thought a drink in a nice pub on the Green, then maybe Thai? I have to broaden my horizons. There are a couple of them along the Broadway, my son recommended a good one, and I wouldn't expect her to drive with me anywhere, not on the first date, so that seems like a good idea. And women like Thai, don't they?'

'Yes, they do. It can be healthy, and very tasty,' I say, smiling and nodding my head.

'I thought so,' he says.

'Have you ever had a wife?' I ask.

'Oh yes.' He nods his head.

'Where is she now?'

'She died five years ago. Breast cancer.'

My eyes fill up.

'What about the internet?' I ask.

'I thought of that,' he says, smiling again, still nodding his head. 'But I thought I'd be original, try the sign first.'

I gulp and bite my lip. 'Good luck,' I say, 'I hope she likes Thai!'

'I hope she likes me!' he replies, and closes the door.

He had a nice smile. He is willing to try Thai food. He has hope.

Walking back down his path, leaving his gate slightly ajar for the postman, or other potential wives if this one doesn't work out, I remember something that my mother used to say: 'Hope, and beautiful shoes, will carry you forwards.'

I walk my route through Soho to the Majestic. I contemplate a quick detour into Grey's, but decide against it. Maybe later. I try the front entrance of the theatre and the door swings open when I push it. Stepping through those doors feels like pressing a button on a time machine. There is something maternal about the entrance, it's as if the curves of the building hug you as you enter. And there is something about this theatre that seems to muddy the time and the date as well. What's happening outside doesn't happen in here.

'Morning, Gavin!' I walk up the aisle towards him and smile.

My skirt is black cotton and sparkled netting layers that stops and flares at my knees. My shirt is light cotton and fitted, baby blue with short sleeves. It's a contacts day today, with a streak of baby-blue eye-shadow across my lids and a lash of midnight-blue mascara on both eyes. My hair is pulled back into a dirty blonde ponytail with wisps escaping around my face, pushed back behind my ears. My earrings are tiny pearl hearts. My lip-gloss is called 'Heartbreak Blue'. It's more of a shine than a colour, it's hard to describe, but then so is heartbreak.

Gavin looks up briefly and then back at the plans laid out in front of him on the front of the stage. 'You look nice,' he says, deadpan.

'Oh, do I? Thanks.'

'Making an effort for somebody special?' he asks, as the

swing doors at the back of the room flip open and Tom Harvey-Saint breezes down the aisle like a catwalk model.

'No,' I reply, trying not to look at Tom as he sings the 'La's' in 'Loving You' to attract our attention. I stare at Gavin, determined not to look around. But Tom screams a series of high-pitched notes, and my eyes dart towards him quickly.

'Really?' Gavin asks, rolling up the plans and walking away.

Tom irritates me for showing off and Gavin irritates me for seemingly deliberately catching me out. It's as if he did it on purpose, just to prove a spiteful point. Or maybe he just feels like he loses everybody to the better-looking boys. Except he has Arabella, so what's his problem anyway? Tom sniggers and exits stage left.

I run up the steps towards Tristan, who is sitting on a battered cream and green chaise longue, back and centre stage, hunched over a laptop that has wires like veins poking out of it and into the wings. His hands are locked together, his two index fingers pointing upwards and pressed together like a gun beneath his chin that is about to fire through the roof of his mouth. Every now and then he moves the gun down to the keyboard and taps something.

I stand a few feet away and wait for him to notice me. I check my watch – it's only nine forty a.m., but that's what early nights will do to you. I think Ben fell asleep on the sofa because he didn't come to bed until after three a.m. He didn't touch me, climbed in with a minimum of fuss, kept to his side and faced the wall. All the usual routine.

Tristan says nothing. I don't want to walk around behind him in case he is looking at bizarre porn, and this whole non-libidinist thing was just a crazy but clever ruse to disguise something infinitely more perverse. Although what could

242

be more perverse these days than not having any kind of libido? Sex is the fuel in our fire.

I put my box down noisily at the opposite end of the chaise longue.

Still he says nothing.

I cough.

Nothing.

'What are you doing?' I ask innocently.

'I'm worried, Make-up. I think it's all going to go tits-up. I had a dream last night that Dolly breathed fire on the curtain on opening night, and the whole place went up in flames around us. This place has burned a few times before, as I believe I told you, we wouldn't be the first. And then there was an almighty crash as the roof fell in, and it woke me up, but of course it was just Mum.'

'Oh my God, is she okay?'

'She's fine. Just fell out of bed again.'

'Oh my God! Tristan, I'm so sorry.'

'That she fell out of bed? It didn't even wake her up.'

'But do you, you know, have to put her back in bed?'

'No, Make-up, I just leave her on the boards all night and hope the mice will eat her. Of course I put her back in bed.'

He stares at his laptop.

'Where's your dad, Tristan?' I ask.

'He died. Why?'

'Is that why you still live at home? To look after your mum?'

'That and the fact she doesn't charge me rent.'

I laugh and shove his arm.

He looks at me bewildered. I think he is serious.

'So, what are you doing?' I ask.

'Right. Yes. As I said, this is all going to be a royal disaster, and my career is pretty much ruined before it's even begun, but I've had this marvellous idea – I want to remake *Death in Venice*, but with song, of course. And I'm going to use priests. There's this wonderful choir I've found, up in Pickering in Yorkshire. All of them priests. I promised them I'd get them an audience with the Pope and they were completely up for it. Plus I played the non-libidinist card – it was the perfect crowd – and I think it endeared me to them. Kindred spirits. Of course they probably just assumed I was gay, but that's fair enough, I assumed they all were too. Anyway, they've got a bus with a toilet and a hob, so I could drive us all out there, to Venice, but I'll need money for somewhere to stay when we're there. I can shoot the whole thing on mini-DV so it's not like I need a crew. Just enough money to keep us all going in a hostel. Plus, you know, they're priests so we should be okay with just the basics. If it comes to it I'll have to get some of them to turn our water into wine.'

'So what are you doing, trying to raise money? Or are you playing poker on one of those sites?' I am still hesitant to look over his shoulder.

'No. I've been banned from the good ones for over a year. Bastards. Now they'll only let me play for Maltesers. Sometimes M&Ms . . .'

'So what are you doing?' I ask.

'eBay,' he says, nodding his head seriously.

'Selling?'

'Oh yes,' he says, dramatically nodding his head again, his tongue poking the inside of his cheek and forming a lump like a tumour that just swelled up in front of me. I wonder if cancer can catch that quickly?

'What?'

'What what, Make-up?'

'What are you selling?' I am intrigued.

'Oh I'd rather not say.' He studies the screen intently, then makes a tutting noise. He lowers his finger-gun and presses a key, then replaces the gun beneath his chin, poised to shoot.

'I could just lean around you and look at the screen, Tristan. What are you selling?'

'I'm not telling, Make-up, go and play with Gavin.'

'Why aren't you telling?'

'It's personal.'

'Is it sperm?' I ask.

He widens his eyes and looks directly at me.

'Shit,' he says, rolling his eyes.

'Did I guess right?'

'No, but I wish I'd thought of that earlier.'

'So not sperm, but it's personal? Oh just tell me, you big baby! Don't be afraid, Tristan, you mustn't be afraid, Tristan – remember, fear is the enemy, Tristan.'

'Okay, you attentive witch.' He glares at me, opens his mouth, then pauses. I nod my head at him to go on.

'My soul,' he says.

'What about your soul?'

'That's it.'

'That's what?'

'What I'm selling. On eBay.'

'No you are not.'

'Yes I am.'

'No you are not.'

'Yes. I am.'

'No, seriously, Tristan, what are you selling? Tickets to this at a discount? Or a director's tour or something?'

'Both of those are good ideas, and I wish I'd thought of those earlier as well. But no. I'm selling my soul.'

'Have you had any offers?'

'A few. There's a bidding war.'

'Cool. What's it up to?'

He clicks a button. 'One hundred and twenty-two quid.'

'Oh.' I am embarrassed. 'How much longer?' I ask, forgetting to disguise my grimace.

He double-takes at me with reproach. 'Twenty-three hours,' he says, nodding his head seriously.

'Oh. Well. I reckon you'll get at least three hundred quid for it, Tristan.'

'Hmmm. Yes. Probably. I'll be honest, Make-up, I was hoping for a little more.'

'Well you would.'

'That won't feed me and twenty priests for a month at Venice prices.' He hunches back over the laptop.

'What do you think you'll have to do, you know, when somebody buys it?' I ask, a little scared for him.

'I'm not sure, Make-up, to be honest. I don't think I really thought it through. I guess I should just cross my fingers and hope they aren't into heavy metal.'

'Okay then, I'm gonna go,' I say, brushing off my skirt.

'Love and death, Make-up. The two most important things in the world and don't let anybody tell you different.'

'Okay, I won't,' I say.

'Seriously. Anybody that trivialises love is a demon, a monster. They think they know something they don't. It's important. It's like . . . it's like fuel. When it stops, you die. It's the point of us, the centre of us, it's what we need. Love and death, Make-up.'

'Roger that. What's with the pep talk?'

'*Death in Venice*, it's got me thinking.'

I turn to walk away, but stop and ask, 'Tristan, what will your mother do if you go to Venice with the priests?'

'Oh I'll probably take her with me. She could do with a holiday.'

'On a bus, all the way to Italy?'

'She's sitting down already, Make-up, she'll be the last one shouting to stretch her legs.'

'But what if she doesn't want to go?'

'Who's pushing the chair?'

'Oh . . . I just . . . I don't know, I thought . . .'

'Make-up, do you think anybody that doesn't look like you doesn't function? Is everyone bar the pretty people locked up in your world? Is there a secret law that says all uglies must be shut-ins?'

'I . . . ' I don't know what to say. I didn't think I came across as that shallow, but perhaps I do. I do believe that pretty is important. The world is always nicer to me when my make-up is on and my hair is freshly washed. I thought it was a universal truth. I thought it was the same for everybody.

Tristan smiles and glances down at the laptop. Clapping his hands he jumps to his feet and shouts, 'Fantastic.'

'What?'

'One hundred and thirty quid! Come on, you bugger, come on!'

'You're through the channel tunnel at least. It could always be *Death in Calais* instead, your hero could get squashed under a crate of cheap Stella or something.'

He chuckles and points a finger at me and says 'Good one' but doesn't look up.

'I'm going to go down and prepare for Dolly then, sort out my shadows, clean my brushes, that kind of thing. Don't let it be said that I am not terribly professional,' I announce, glancing towards Gavin who is pulling at wires on the opposite side of the stage. I thought I felt him watching me but if he was he's looked away again now.

Two hours later the door bursts open and I jump behind my *Hello!* magazine.

'Get up get up get up,' Dolly demands sternly.

'Me?'

'Of course you, who the hell else? Is there anybody else in this glove-compartment of a room? Maybe a dwarf or an anorexic or a small child? Of course you! Are you drunk?'

Dolly throws down her bag and spins quickly on the spot, grabbing hold of the arm of her chair for support. She wags a finger at me and I feel like I've been dropped into a pantomime.

'You went out last night, didn't you?' she says, narrowing her eyes.

'No, I took your advice and went home,' I reply, and what rubbish advice too! Except of course I don't say that.

She turns to face the counter, and places her palms flat in front of her, hunched over like a politician with the world on his shoulders and at his feet, deep in contemplation, wracked with emotion and guilt. I back away towards the door.

'Pardon?' I say, when I hear her muttering something just under her breath like Hail Marys after confession.

'Don't lie to me, don't you lie to me, Lulu!'

Dolly looks up at me and her face is red and pumped full of blood. She looks like death might be standing beside her, ready to catch her when she falls.

'You stand here and you stink of booze and cigarettes. You reek of booze when you know I can't drink!'

'What?' I am incredulous. The stench of booze only hit me when she walked in. It smells like she's had a gin bath.

'Don't lie to me!' She slams her fist down on the counter. Except it sounds like 'don'tslietome' instead. 'You stand there with your plastic titties out again when I told you to put them away! Put them away!' she shrieks and dramatically covers her eyes with one hand.

Dolly and I stand still, frozen by her performance, as we try to determine in our own heads if she really just said what she said, and if so, did she even mean it?

There is sudden knock, to the theme of *Hello Dolly*. I take a step back against the door, and pull it slowly open with my hand behind my back. My spine is the only thing on view to whoever just knocked, but I am scared that if I turn and face them, Dolly will stick a knife in my back.

Somebody prods me in the arm like a finger punch and I turn around to see who it is. Tristan fires me a broad smile. He is wearing his hat again.

Dolly barks 'Come in' as sweetly as a bark can be, but Tristan isn't quick enough to get into the room before I have whispered to her, 'You're a nutcase.' Who cares, if she is going to have me fired anyway?

She raises her eyebrows at me, and half smiles like it's a game.

'Dolly!' Tristan says, lifting the veil on his old-lady black funeral hat. 'I just wanted to, you know, wanted to check in on you, make sure everything is okay. Super. Wonderfully okay.'

Dolly beckons him in with her hand and closes bashful eyes. He smiles and shunts into the room like a naughty schoolboy, and stands in front of her expectantly and in awe. She lowers her head and opens her eyes, looking up at him. It's a practised routine, the angle of her chin is perfect, pointing down towards her chest but not leaning, not creating double or treble chins, or any unsightly rolls of face fat. The look almost floors Tristan, the non-libidinist, and he reaches out to grab on to something and finds me, using my arm as support as if I were a piece of old furniture. Dolly smiles at him wickedly.

'All is well in here, my darling, although Lulu has been at the booze and we were just having a laugh about it, because as you know I am teetotal, have been for three years since the doctor warned me off it. It will age you, Lulu,' she says, throwing me a quick glance like a knife through the air. 'It will make those tremendous breasts of yours sag and deflate like punctured footballs. I think it's already started . . .'

I feel my shoulders rolling in, my chest becoming concave.

Tristan loves it. His eyes are wet with excited tears, and he keeps licking and smacking his lips, as if ready to lunge in and kiss the breath out of her. He seems utterly aroused by this daft and evil old lady. It occurs to me like lightning that it isn't how she looks that turns him on, it's who she is.

'Well, good, good.' He nods his head and holds her eye contact. 'As long as you are happy,' he says. They fix each other with a stare.

A laugh bursts out of me like a projectile sickness that I can't control. These two are pretending to make eyes at each other but all to see who can control whom. I have never seen anything like it.

They don't even look at me when I laugh, it is as if I have disappeared.

'Don't mind Lulu, she's not the brightest penny in the jar,' Dolly says, as I stand three feet away from her.

Tristan giggles.

I look from one to the other, incredulous. I am standing right here!

'After lunch I thought we would pick up from Arabella's "*everything signifies something*"' Tristan says.

'How appropriate,' she replies, nodding, smiling.

'I think you are doing just wonderfully, Dolly – just wonderful things up there. You bring that old stage to life.' Tristan presses his hands together in prayer and rests his fingertips on his lips. He closes his eyes and I wait for him to genuflect. Dolly lowers her eyes again and passes him her hand, like royalty, but Tristan has his eyes closed. I watch as Dolly comically holds out her arm, waiting for Tristan to open his eyes and take it. She refuses to look at me, all three feet away in this tiny dark lavender room filled with flowers and cards and make-up and half-light, dim like it's three in the morning and the rest of the world is asleep but us. I want to laugh again, but I find I can control it this time. Dolly coughs sharply and Tristan opens his eyes, looks down at her hand and smiles to himself. He slowly reaches forwards, her hand hanging foolishly in the air waiting for him to support it. I think he is doing it to humiliate her, and I see the anger flash behind her eyes and her shoulders stiffen with shots of rage.

Tristan, finally, takes her hand.

'That role is a tired old rag transformed into a wedding dress when you throw it on, Dolly.' The rage dispels in her shoulders and she giggles like a barmaid who needs the tips, rather than responding with her usual gunshot 'ha!'

'Well, I should get back upstairs. How long do you think you'll be, my star?' Tristan fawns. I think I'll need to mop the floor for grease when he's left.

'I can only be as quick as Lulu is,' she says, shrugging.

'So not that quick,' Tristan responds, and they both raise their eyes and share a stifled giggle like naughty lovers rubbing naked feet under a restaurant table.

'I am right here!' I say loudly.

But they ignore me.

'*Adieu!*' Tristan kisses Dolly's hand, but turns and shows her his back as he leaves and closes the door behind him.

Dolly shakes her old head. 'Ha!' she says, 'Ha!'

'Sit down and I'll get started if you're in a rush,' I say angrily.

'Rush? For what? For that fool! Lulu, are you out of your mind? There is no rush, let's take our time, have some girl talk!'

'I think you should get upstairs,' I insist, tight-lipped, and shove past her to get to the cleanser.

251

'Lulu, whatever is wrong with you, dear? You're behaving strangely, and I have to say, you are being very rude.'

'Me, rude? Me!' I can't turn around and look at her in case I explode.

'Yes, darling, you,' she says, and I hear her lower herself heavily into her chair with the creaking of furniture and bones.

I can't say anything. She could easily have me fired and now the madness has passed I remember that I can't be seen to anger talent – my agency wouldn't let me near a star again.

She sighs and I squeeze cream onto my hands.

'Oh, men. I do love them. Idiots to the last, of course. Fools. But the queers are always far more loveable. It's the passion, it's such an attractive quality to a woman. It's like they've lost their fear.' She rests her head back and closes her eyes and I streak her face with cleanser.

'Tristan isn't gay, he's a . . . he isn't gay,' I say.

'Ha! Of course he's gay, I've met few gayer! Whatever line he has spun you, don't believe it. Believe what you feel, what you instinctively feel, Lulu – if you think a man is gay they generally are.'

'But he said . . .'

'Men say a lot of things, Lulu, you should believe about a quarter of it. The other three-quarters are rubbish. Half is trying to get you into bed, and the last quarter is fear. Men are scared of lots of things and they haven't found a decent way of hiding it yet, darling. Bravado, machismo, whatever you want to call it, it's all just fear. But not the queers. They've faced their fears, darling, and come out the other side. It's why they are so attractive to a woman.'

'Do you actually loathe men, Dolly?' I ask.

'No, Lulu, far, far from it. I love men, wretched as they are, ruinous as they can be for most girls, terrible and mixed up and confused and scared, and petrified of anybody needing them and terrified of not being needed! But I, personally, have never had any interest in fear. I was never scared. I showed no interest in them, which is what got them every time. Of course, then, when they were desperate and needy, it repelled me even more. But it taught me an easy lesson, Lulu: If a man gets what he wants too easily he thinks he should have tried for something better, that he has set his sights too low. A lot of them will walk away from women that love them purely because they do love them, and these stupid boys get confused and think that they can obviously do better. But I was rude to them, and stubborn in my disinterest, and it made them think I was better than they were, and of course there was no better or worse, it's like peaches and bananas. Yes I was violently rude a lot of the time, and frank and honest and vile, and they often loved me for it. I approve of a necessary violence, you see, emotive violence, and physical violence as well if needs must. Sometimes it is your only source of protection, Lulu.'

Dolly opens one eye comically to look at me, and then closes it again. I circle highlighter at her temples.

'So you are basically saying that you hurt men? Is that right? You used them?' I don't feel like softening any blows today.

'Often I did, I suppose, I did use them, but not once they loved me, that is plainly wrong.'

'But you used them before that? And that's not wrong?'

'Yes, darling, but I couldn't help that. They kept hurling themselves at me like lemmings off a cliff, I couldn't get out of the way quick enough some days! Ha!' She slaps her thigh and kicks off her shoes like a girl.

I shake my head. 'You see I just don't think it's necessary to hurt people like that. You can take responsibility for your actions. You can be honest enough to walk away before it hurts them too much. It's just . . . wrong to do anything else.'

253

Dolly grabs my hands as I move towards her with lip plump, and claps them together, sandwiched between hers. I can feel her age in the cold wrinkles in her palms pressing on my skin. She smells of mothballs and lavender and soap and alcohol.

'But Lulu, you say it like it's deliberate! Do you know how very few people are malicious and cold and mean?' She shakes my hands to make me understand. 'People don't want to hurt other people, they just can't help it. We are animals, darling, life is going to be painful. I never really meant to hurt anybody, but I did. Christ, I did, over and over.' She throws my hands away and shrugs. 'And I got hurt too, Lulu, oh yes. It didn't kill me! And who says it's so bad, just because it makes you cry? Who says crying is so bad, when something really hurts? Good heavens, Lulu, what do you think love is? It's just habit, darling, it's just habit. Finding somebody who makes you laugh, and doesn't kiss like a circus ape, and weaving them into your life like yarn. What did you think it was going to be, darling? Obsession? Obsession isn't healthy. Or trying to please somebody who can't be pleased, like your chap by the sounds of it. And trying to make somebody care about you who doesn't want to, like your chap. But Lulu, that's not your fault, darling! You just don't fit him. Not loving somebody is just not accepting part of their character, and he doesn't want to accept part of yours. Love isn't the unexplainable at all. It's easily explained! Declaring to somebody, 'I don't love you', or 'I don't love you any more', like some kind of metaphysical argument that needs no definition. Well, Christ, darling! That's not an answer to anything. What is it that you think love is?'

I stand and think and search for an answer. It's not even liking somebody a lot, but then it kind of is. I think about the people that I can say that I love. I love my daddy because he is my daddy, in spite of his distance, perhaps sometimes because of it? Knowing that he loves me anyway but doesn't find it easy to express makes me want to protect him from anybody that would try to force it out of him. I love Richard because he's my brother and because he is so easy to love, and he is obviously so in love with Hannah, and his boys, and his life. Richard met Hannah at sixth-form college, they were childhood sweethearts and their love happened the way that it does in romantic films. They fell for each other before they learnt about cynicism. They sat next to each other in A-level maths. They became friends. They sat in Richard's Ford Fiesta outside Hannah's house in the evening and talked. They only ever really stood out to each other, but they are a team. Richard is the only real-life example that I have, that I cling to desperately, to prove to me that romantic love actually can happen, and be real.

I love my mum so much, because she's my mum, and because she didn't really leave. She took me with her, every night at ten p.m., and every weekend, when she could have just walked away and enjoyed herself and kicked up her heels and travelled the world. I always knew, maybe more so because she didn't live with me, that she loved me. She didn't have to call me every night, but she did. She didn't have to get tears in her eyes every Sunday night when my dad came to pick me and Richard up, but she did. But I don't really know what it is about their characters that means I love them or not, because just knowing that they love me isn't enough to love somebody back. I don't know how to choose to love somebody or not. I love Helen because she is my best friend and she has a good heart, and she makes me laugh, and she has always been there, always. I just love the people I am supposed to. Maybe they don't do everything I'd like them to, and maybe I don't either, for them. And maybe me and my daddy wouldn't even be friends in another life, maybe we'd drive each other crazy. But I love him because he's mine.

Dolly looks at me expectantly. She is waiting for an answer. What is it that I think love is?

'I don't know. I don't.' I shake my head and feel like a fool. 'And I don't know what to say when Ben won't say that he loves me, or can't say he loves me at least.' I feel my shoulders slump, the fight draining from me.

'Oh no, darling, you got it right the first time. It's not "can't" say it, darling, it's "won't". Know that, if nothing else. It seems to me, Lulu, that you are infinitely loveable. It seems to me that you are welling over with love for this chap. I don't think there is anything about you that he can't love, Lulu. You're not a wet fish of a girl, you're not a silly girl, as silly as you might occasionally seem. It seems to me, Lulu, that you have a bit of a fire to you, a lot of life. It's not "can't", darling, it's "won't".'

'Okay, won't. But what difference does it make, it's the same result. Maybe he just doesn't take me seriously enough to even try to love me, or think that he might. There is something about me, or him, or who he was, or who he is, that stops him seeing us as a real thing, with possibilities and a future. I don't know if he's serious about me, can you believe that? After three years, Dolly! But we live together, how can he not be serious?'

I am standing, tired and helpless, in front of her. She reaches behind her and yanks out a cushion, and throws it on the floor.

'Take those stupid shoes off and sit down, darling,' she says. 'You need the rest.'

I do as she says. I cross my legs like a little girl in assembly and stare up at her.

'Oh Lulu. Men can do many things and not be serious about the girl they are dating. They can even marry a girl, standing next to her at the altar with a rose in their lapel and a top hat under their arm, and not be serious about a girl. They think it's fine as long as they are getting what they want.'

'Which is?' I ask, desperate to know.

'Often no more than somebody to fuck when they feel like fucking, darling. That is brutal, I know, but I believe it. Don't forget that they are closer to animals than we are. Maybe that's what your chap was doing with you, except now of course he doesn't even feel like fucking, ha! That's it. No more emotional investment than that. They'll keep you at arm's length and treat your courtship like something that is second, third, fourth, fifth on their list of priorities. Their friends will come before you, and their work, and their sports, so many things. Because they just aren't taking you seriously. I've seen it happen to girls a hundred times, the girls like you, who loved somebody willingly and openly and tragically, really, darling. And of course it's fine, darling, to not love somebody, to place them low on your list, if you both feel the same. If it suits both parties I mean. But you take your chap quite seriously, Lulu.' She smiles at me sadly.

'I do. I do.'

'And he knows it I'm sure. And maybe he even hates himself a little too, for the way that he is treating you, darling, but that's not good enough, because it's his choice. If he spots for even one second that you might be in love with him, then a man who respects women would do the honourable thing. Step up to the plate and take it seriously, or walk away. Do you want to know what I think, in all my years, is the worst thing in the world, Lulu?'

I nod my head.

'To knowingly use a person that loves you. For whatever reason. For nothing more than amusement, or weekend sport. That is the difference! Right there, on the table, bang!' She slaps the counter suddenly with a wide open palm, and it makes a noise that stings the air, and I jump.

257

'That is a man who doesn't care that he hurts you. We all hurt people unintentionally, Lulu, and it is forgivable. But to see it, know it, do it anyway? That's the worst a man can do. Yes, the worst thing a man can do is treat a woman like weekend sport. Because he knows how much it hurts you, deeply. Especially you, Lulu, look at you, you're like a pretty puppy.' She takes my hand. 'A woman will throw everything she has into making a man love her when he has no intention of doing anything of the sort. He doesn't even care, really, if she comes or goes. He just uses her for exercise, and he thinks, Why not? She is here, there is no gun to her head.'

'But Dolly, I don't understand – you say that people loved you, and you hurt them . . .'

'But I always knew, darling, when a man had fallen for me and I didn't feel the same. I always respected them enough to be honest. Anything less, in matters of the heart, is for the animals. A man who doesn't respect a woman who loves him lacks the essence of a man. He isn't a man. He's a boy who never grew up. He shouldn't be fucking he should be painting pictures, running in the school yard in shorts, modelling characters out of plasticine to fight with. And no more than that.'

I take a sharp involuntary gasp, and picture a vial of free grey paint stuck to a magazine.

'Now, I should get on. You've kept me gassing and I shall get in trouble, Lulu.' She gestures with her hands that I should get up.

I push myself to my feet and lift each leg, examining the soles of my feet that have already turned grey around the edges from the dirt on the floor.

Dolly looks at herself in the mirror today, tilting back her head. When she raises her hand to pull back the skin beneath her chin I see that she is suddenly trembling again.

'You know I've always felt the envy around me, Lulu.

258

Some days you enjoy it, some days you want to run from it screaming. But what I wonder, often, now that it is gone, is how my life might have played out differently, if I hadn't looked the way that I did. If I had been just a little bit less beautiful – it's not as if it had anything to do with me, it was all luck, decided in the womb – but if I'd looked like my sisters perhaps. Where would I be now?'

'Where are your sisters now?' I ask.

'Oh all dead Lulu' she says quietly. 'We always kept in touch with letters and cards, and they all stayed close to my mother's house except me, but once mother died, we lost our focus, really. She was our scaffold. She was the thing we built our dreams on. We had a glorious time when we were young, she saw to that, I'll tell you about it when we have the time. But you know, when she died, I didn't know anything about it for three weeks. I didn't get to go to the funeral. My sisters couldn't track me down you see, I was off filming somewhere, cavorting with some leading man whose name escapes me now, and of course they couldn't wait, so . . .' she shakes her head slowly, and stares at herself in the mirror.

'Why are you doing this play Dolly?' I ask. I want to protect her, what if they savage her? What if the critics rip her apart? Or worse, what if she collapses under the pressure and runs away?

'It seems like a lot of effort, you seem a little tired, and . . . have you got enough money? Did you need to say that you'd do it?'

I look in the mirror next to her and she stares, not at me, but at my reflection. Standing next to each other I wonder if anybody could think us related: she could be my grand-mother, perhaps, or my crazy great aunt. We have the same nose at least. The same-shaped eyes. Of course hers are violet whereas mine are plain old Everton blue.

'I have more than enough money, Lulu. I am staying at

the Dorchester, I have a suite. I have my house in Santa Monica, and the villa in Stintino, both of them empty without me but I was always very wise with my money, because a woman should be with her own money. She should spend other people's freely, but be careful with her own. But I divorced four times of course, yes, four. And I had the luck to marry some very rich men. Very rich men, Lulu. Of course not Charlie, he was a church mouse, but the rest were all independently wealthy. But it's not the money that attracted me to them. Nothing should ever be about the money, if you can help it at all. It's the passion. You can't hide from it. Of course it's an effort, at my old age, but I have never been one for fear. Sometimes a girl has to be brave, Lulu.'

Dolly brushes herself down and inspects herself one last time in the mirror. She tugs back the skin at the side of her eyes, and I get a glimpse of a smoother, younger version.

'Thirty-five was my prime, Lulu. They say it's your early twenties, but they are wrong. It has to be on the inside, and on the outside, to really knock their socks off. You have to wear it well. When I was thirty-five, Lulu, well. There wasn't a head I couldn't turn. I knocked everybody's socks off then.'

As she walks towards the door I see her hands shaking at her sides and I want to grab her from behind and hug her and stop her going up there, to the stage, to be laughed at by Tom and Arabella, and manipulated by Tristan.

'Did your daughter call?' I ask as she opens the door.

'No . . . she didn't. But it's the damned hotel, Lulu, I am sure of that. She is obviously trying and they just damn well muck it up. I shall speak to the manager this evening, if I am not too tired, and give him a piece of my mind.'

'Do you miss her?' I ask.

'Who, Chloe? Oh, yes, I suppose I do. The older I get of course, and isn't it always the way. We don't talk that much to be honest, Lulu, she doesn't have much to say to me. I

260

was never really anybody's mother, never wanted to be, until now . . . It made me feel old. I just thought that I should have a child to try it, I suppose, like taking a drag on a joint that's being passed around, you don't want to miss out on something that everybody else is trying. But Chloe was living with her father and his new wife by the time that she was six, and I'd been on the valium for three years by then, so I don't remember most of that. No, I was never much interested in mothering, but now I see that it must be quite something. To pass on the few lessons that life might have taught you . . .'

She is almost out of the door when she asks, 'Do you speak to your mother much, Lulu?'

'As often as I can.'

'And do you love her?'

'Oh, very much. Very much. I can't really breathe if I think about her . . . not being around, when I need her. I can't even think about it. She has always been there for me. Even when she left, she was still there.'

Dolly swallows loudly.

'You should tell her that, Lulu. Pass me that water.'

I hand her the glass. It is water, because it is mine. I think I see surprise when it touches her lips and it isn't the gin that she was expecting. She is used to her water with a little more kick these days.

But still, she takes a swig, then says, 'Lulu, will you pop to the bathroom and get me a tissue, my nose is cold.' She reaches up and grabs it for effect.

'Of course,' I say, even though she is halfway out of the door, and I have to push past her to get into the corridor.

I come back from the toilet and the door has been closed. Pushing it back open I catch Dolly chucking a bottle of gin hurriedly into her bag. Her cheeks flush, and her hands seem to shake even more.

'It's so damned warm in here, isn't it? Are they trying to kill me? I have to stand on that stage and project with a throat red-raw from air-conditioning, for that ridiculous little man with his strange notions of nudity.'

'Actually, you are getting a little hot on your upper lip.' I reach for the powder.

'For Christ's sake, Lulu, just damned well leave me alone! Stop playing with me, can't you see I'm old now, and ugly, and you smell like a brothel and you whine like a toddler – and you're just making it worse!'

I take a step back, but she won't meet my eye, and I run out of the room.

Coming out of the toilet that smells of fresh vomit, and with swollen eyes and mascara stained cheeks, I bump straight into Arabella in the hall.

'Sorry,' I say, and hate myself. Apologies and tears, I am pathetic after all.

'So you're the Make-up for Dolly?' she asks. Her voice is cool and wealthy. She reeks of blue blood and horses and tea parties and pheasant shoots and all-girls' schools and privilege. She wears her stupid mismatching clothes because she is too rich and too well-bred to care. I look like a tramp next to her, all mascara and fashion, trying too hard to please. Arabella has always pleased everybody immediately, or dismissed those she hasn't with an arched eyebrow and a sneer. She looks at me now, like she could afford twenty of me.

'Yes, I'm Make-up,' I say.

'Well I'm going to stick with Greta, I think it's only right. She's a lovely old girl, and I think it's terrible that they'd even dream of replacing her.'

'Fine with me,' I say, sniffing.

'Plus, you know, I don't like my make-up too heavy.'

'Oh fine,' I say, and push past her, but she grabs my arm and spins me around.

'Look, we both know how it is,' she states in a measured tone.

'What on earth?' I glance down at her fingers digging into my arm.

'With Gavin,' she says, coolly.

'With Gavin what?'

'Oh come on. Look at you. Look at me. We both know that Gavin's not really . . . permanent. If you want him, well, you can have him.' She lets go of my arm and crosses both of hers. She eyes me up and down like the head prefect of an all-girl school, assessing a first year with the wrong shoes.

'What do you mean, look at you, look at me?' I shake my head in disbelief, I have never known anything like it.

'Look, it's Scarlet, isn't it? We both get what we want. I mean men. I'm sure we go about it in different ways, but it's not like we have to take whatever's left over . . . I have my charms and you have yours. And Gavin is sweet, you know that, so if you want him, take him, I'm practically done with him anyway.'

I can't believe what she is saying. I feel like an arctic wind just blew down the corridor and my features have frozen in disbelief.

'I think, Arabella, that Gavin has feelings for you, and I don't know what you are talking about with regard to me wanting him or not wanting him or whatever, and no, I don't always get what I want, and this whole conversation is strange, and . . .'

'No, he doesn't have feelings for me,' Arabella interrupts, 'significant or otherwise. We both know that's not true, Scarlet, let's not lie, between girls. Gavin barely knows me. He knows what I look like, yes, but that's about it. He doesn't know what I think about, I don't know, religion, or politics, or Ethiopia.'

'What do you think about Ethiopia?' I ask.

'Oh I don't know, it was just an example. That they're hungry, there's a famine, etcetera, etcetera. You know what I'm driving at. He doesn't care what I think any more than I care what he thinks.'

'I don't know why you're saying this to me but I think you've got the wrong girl and . . .' I start to walk away again.

'Don't play dumb, Scarlet,' she says to my back, and I stop walking. 'We're both grown, adult women. We can tell it how it is.'

'And, just for clarity, tell me, how is it?' I don't turn around to face her, speaking over my shoulder instead.

'If you want him, have him. I'm done. That's all I'm saying. I thought you'd appreciate my candour.'

She brushes past me, and I smell her flowery old-fashioned perfume as I stare after her. I remember to remember that it's not just men who break hearts.

Gavin jogs heavily down the stairs at the end of the corridor holding a tin of paint. He is walking towards Arabella and I see him smile. She stops him and turns them both, like a pro, so that her audience, me, can see their profile as she kisses him hard on the mouth, and proclaims loudly, so the whole corridor, me, can hear, 'Let's have dinner later, Gavin darling.'

She saunters off up the stairs and Gavin watches her go, before turning around and walking back towards me with a half-smile.

'Hi,' I say.

His smile fades. 'If you're looking for Tom I just saw him upstairs,' he announces, walking past me, ducking his head instinctively so he doesn't hit a low pipe.

'Will you stop that Gavin, please?'

He stops a few feet in front of me. His back blocks out the light from the bulb hanging ten feet away. He's like a walking eclipse.

'You were the one holding his hand,' he says, swinging the tin of paint in his own hand.

'Gavin, he was sleazing all over me, that's all. I thought that we had cleared that up? And I would have thought that you, of all people, could grasp the kind of man he is. It was a complete misunderstanding. Please don't keep going on about it. He was just singing really loudly, before, I was bound to look up.'

Gavin practically melts in front of me, and I feel a shudder down my spine, as though my feet are suddenly wet with the water of his feelings, and I should be raising my skirts and tiptoeing away. Ben always fights back, always accuses me of something, he never wants to believe me, but Gavin does. He turns around and I shudder again as a wave of unspoken feelings emits from Gavin to me. I realise that he hasn't just been trying to make me feel better. He likes me more than he has been letting on.

'Okay, I'm sorry, Scarlet, but Jesus, it's this place! These people – they make you act weird. I'm really sorry.'

'Honestly, Gavin, don't think about it, don't even worry about it, it's fine.' All of a sudden I want to run away. But I want to protect him too.

He smiles a big faux Scottish smile. 'So are you going out to dinner with Arabella tonight?' I ask. I can't help myself.

He looks bashful for a moment, perhaps even guilty, but then he looks like a man again.

'It sounds like it, and I always have to pay. I don't mind but she orders champagne, and, you know, she earns ten times more than me.'

'You'll never get a beautiful girl to buy you dinner,' I say.

He shrugs and smiles. 'Well, I have to go and paint Tom's

door dramatic red,' he tells me evenly, the same old Gavin tone. He starts to walk off down the corridor.

'Don't go, Gavin!' I shout.

He turns towards me and looks confused. 'I'll only be ten minutes, it's just one door.'

'I mean tonight, with Arabella, don't go.'

'Why not?' He tries hard to look me in the eye, but then he looks away at the last second.

'Because. Because! Because she can't just click her fingers and have you jump. You're bigger than that. No pun intended. But it shouldn't matter how beautiful she is.'

Gavin smiles.

'What?' I say.

'But it does. Look at her,' he replies, like I should be impressed with him or something because of it, and it makes me mad.

'Oh for Christ's sake, Gavin, grow up! See past it. You're not an animal! And it's not impressive if she's a horrible person, no matter how nice she is to look at!' My cheeks are burning red with my outburst.

Gavin looks away, embarrassed, and so am I. I have gone too far.

'I'm sorry,' I say.

'Do you want to have dinner with me instead?' he asks quietly.

'Me?' I say feeling like I just threw myself down a hole.

'You,' he replies.

'Oh. No. I can't.'

Gavin bristles and goes red. 'Right. Fine. I have to go.'

He turns and walks away.

'No, seriously, Gavin, I have other plans and . . .' I call after him. His stride is so long he is almost gone, but I can still see that the tops of his ears have turned red.

'See you later!' I shout after him, but he just keeps walking.

I slump back into Dolly's room without knocking, but Dolly isn't around. I am glad, I don't want to apologise to her when it was her doing the shouting, but that is what I'll be forced to do when she turns up, because she's old, she's talent, and she's got an ego the size of Russia. I spot a piece of paper stuck in the centre of the mirror and I lean in to read it, my eyes reflected above it:

Lulu,
I get weary, sometimes, with the world, and with myself. You'll see, one day, and then maybe you'll remember and understand this stupid old woman, and forgive me. The world isn't always warm, you see, like this dreadful room with its dreadful pipes, when we are in it.
I've gone to find you biscuits.
Dolly x

I tear the note off and put it in my purse.

The door opens and she is carrying a pack of digestives.

'I had to steal them from the understudies, and they probably won't eat for weeks now. Ha! But I think we need some sugar.'

'Shouldn't you be upstairs?' I ask.

'Yes, I should, and I'm going, but I wanted to give you these first, Lulu. Take them.' She thrusts them at me clumsily

I lean forwards to give her a hug, but she turns and walks away, shutting the door behind her.

Scene III: The Truth Game

I have barely finished flicking through *Elle* for the second time when the door flies opens and Dolly stumbles back in.

'That was quick,' I tell her.

'I'm spent, Lulu. I'm exhausted, and that fool is driving me doolally, doolally I tell you! Take it all off again, Lulu, I'm going back to the hotel.'

'Fair enough,' I say, as she slumps down into her chair and drops her rings on the counter, scooping up a dollop of hand-cream. 'Shall I put a CD on? Have you got any others, or do you want Ella again?' I ask.

'Ella will be fine. Good music can stand repeat plays. It occurred to me, Lulu, when I was upstairs just now, that I meant to ask you: When you went home did you talk to your chap? Last night, when I sent you home to confront him? Did you actually confront him?'

'There was no confrontation. Well, not that kind at least. Although there was a pasta . . . incident. But there was foot-ball on.'

'So you didn't even try, darling?' she asks sadly.

'No, well, barely. But he wanted to watch the football, there was nothing I could do.'

'But you must try, Lulu. We must always try, in everything. And you say he wanted to watch football? Well he couldn't have watched it if you'd, say, thrown a plate through the television. This is what I mean, Lulu, we must try, and try, and try harder! If something is to be wonderful we must all try harder to make it wonderful. I hear this damn foolish notion these days that if something doesn't come utterly naturally, then it is too much work. Love shouldn't be that hard, they say. What rubbish! What could be harder than love, day in, day out, when there is a choice there? But what can be more rewarding? You should try tonight instead, perhaps, Lulu?'

I sigh. 'We'll see.'

'But you must.'

'Why? What is it that's so important to you?' I ask, already exhausted at the prospect of trying to pin Ben down, again, to a conversation he doesn't want to have and a truth he doesn't think he owes me.

'Well, now. It *is* important to me, Lulu. Because I don't want you to be a silly girl who lets this fool get away with it. And because, in a way, you remind me of me. I like your glamour, Lulu. And I like your spirit. And I won't let some damned man spoil those for you.'

'Thank you,' I tell her, and pull her hair back from her face, wiping her clean. The CD plays quietly in the corner.

'Dear Ella, she smoked about one hundred cigarettes a day, you know.'

'It's amazing she didn't cough up ash,' I say.

'Well, darling, so did Nat King Cole, that's where his voice came from. Cigarettes aren't all bad, especially if you don't want to live to a hundred. Do you smoke, Lulu?'

'Sometimes. Not often. Mostly if I'm drunk.'

'I think you might like it, as a habit. It gives you a bit of time to yourself, during the day, these five-minute pockets

of time just for you, dotted into your life at regular intervals, and it might calm you down a little, Lulu, stop you
getting so flustered all the damn time.'

'Do you still smoke?' I ask, dabbing at the black mascara
on her eyes.

'Oh no, Lulu, not now, but I used to, all the time. Oh I
smoked in public, Lulu, when it wasn't fashionable for a
woman to do so. But it empowered me, in a way. I think
perhaps a little too much. This was in the Fifties, and the
Sixties, when my hair was still dark, and so long I could
wrap it around my throat like a scarf to protect me from
the wind. It was down to my waist, almost black, and it
always smelt, faintly, of those menthol cigarettes, and
lavender. We all smelt of Lavender, my sisters and I. I told
you I would tell you about them, didn't I? Well when I was
young, before Charlie took me to Los Angeles, we lived in
Broadstairs, darling, by the sea. And my mother's house
always smelled of lavender, you see, there were bushes all
around the house like a sweet-smelling insulation, keeping
out the bad smells, Lulu, and the bad people as well. The
wasps warned them off, they would sting the bad ones away.
I stayed out of the sun, I was pale, with this long, dark hair.
I had four sisters, Lulu, four. Imagine that! The fights were
glorious in our little house, we all shared a room, and Eileen,
my oldest sister, she would boss us about and the screams
could be heard down the beach and beyond, across the water
maybe! But I was the youngest, Lulu, the baby, and so everybody spoiled me and nobody wanted to upset me too much.
We all looked the same of course, me and Eileen, and Lucy
and Margaret and Anne. We all had our long, dark hair and
our violet eyes. My mother used to say we were one egg split
into five.'

'But they weren't all as beautiful as you?' I ask.

'Well, yes and no, Lulu. Striking, yes. But everybody

always used to say there was something about me. I was the grand one, the dramatic one, sweeping into rooms. I knew the effect that I had. You must feel it too, Lulu. When you walk into a room, and you see one hundred sets of eyes flick towards you all at once like the breeze blew them your way. It's a warm breeze, that's for certain. But it's still just a breeze. For a while I thought those eyes meant that I deserved the world, and should have it – *But look how much everybody wants me*, I thought. *I am a goddess, and a goddess should get what she wants.* But age teaches you that it is just not true. You get what you deserve, and beauty only deserves those glances. Anything more you have to fight for like the rest of them. But my mother always called me urgent, you see, and the boys always called me luminous. I suppose I practised it as well. I developed this lonely quality to my voice. A kind of arrogance, I suppose, because of being so spoiled, and being the baby. My mother always said that I was flushed with life and that is what really gave me my beauty, so even though as sisters we all looked almost the same, I had a look that was only mine as well. She said that I always appeared excited and a little out of breath. I had the look of a girl who had run all the way down the beach, desperate to find somebody, to tell them good news. That's how she described me.'

'It sounds like you were very close.' I rest the hot muslin on her face and it makes her jump a little, but she doesn't say anything, and instead takes deep breaths.

'Oh, yes, we were very close. We were like a fairytale really. We lived in Broadstairs all that time, in the lavender house, and my mother, Winifred –but her friends called her Fred – was a tiny woman, with glasses that sat on the end of her nose as if poised to fall off. My sisters were all just older versions of me in temperament, and we were all just younger versions of our mother, truth be told. And she wanted us to

271

do everything, try everything. We'd read poetry to each other and sing songs and dance. Men would come and call and we'd each go off for walks along the beach. Anne was the worst, sometimes two walks a day, with two different men! And sometimes we'd come back with sand in our hair, and sometimes not. And some of our neighbours would tut at us in town, but my mother would fix them with a stern stare and say seriously, "I have been a slut myself, so why not my girls?" She rolled her own cigarettes. Maybe one of these days I'll show you. And when Charlie said he'd take me to LA, well she damn near put me on the plane herself. And there were no tears. Because nobody died, you see, Lulu. That was her motto, you know. "A woman should display strength and grace," she said. "A woman shouldn't topple in the wind."'

'What about your father, where was he?'

'Oh, he left one day, and nobody really seemed to notice. It was better that way. I think the noise disturbed him, you see.'

'And you slept with boys on the beach and your mum encouraged it? How old were you?' I ask, surprised.

'Oh, in my teens, I suppose. Eighteen, maybe. But it wasn't sordid, Lulu, it was joyful. Life-loving. We had so much fun in those dunes, it was the start of life. Some people thought that life could escape you, in a little village like that, but you can bring life to you anywhere you go, it will come and find you if you want it to. The problem was that the boys didn't always see it that way, as fun and life-loving and joyful, and they always proposed, to all of us. Of course, Anne fell pregnant, so she accepted quite early, but not the rest of us. And of course in those days most girls longed to marry, the boys couldn't understand it, but we were never the sort, we were having too much fun with our mother in Lavender House. And it was always a mistake to ask us. Of course I did end

272

up marrying, four times, but still. It was always a mistake to ask. I can't count how many proposals I've had, more than there are Chinamen. And I always thought, why have you proposed, you see? Just to keep me, just to trap me? Let's just take what we can give each other and move on. You don't have to give it a name, or make it permanent. It won't be. You can't be happy all of the time, you can't live like that forever. And I'd mourn them, these men who weren't always ready to move on, but my heart was still in the grave of one love affair when I'd start making eyes at another man. It nearly killed me, but I couldn't help it, Lulu! It was all because I was beautiful. Oh Lulu, I was spreading havoc before I knew any better.' She smiles sadly and it slips from her face as she falls asleep. I take off the last of her make-up, but she jolts upright about five minutes later as I whisper around the room tidying up. Pushing herself to her feet, she shuffles her M&S slippers towards the door.

'My car will be upstairs. I'll see you tomorrow, Lulu. Friday. For fish!'

I check my watch. It's an hour before I am due to meet Helen for dinner. I look in the mirror. I look okay. I swipe 'Heartbreak Blue' across my lips and head for Charing Cross Road.

I spot her stickering books on a table. She looks even more unkempt than usual. Her blonde hair has formed a thicket on her crown, it looks like it hasn't been combed or washed in days. Her cardigan has a hole which she pokes her thumb through. Her dress is pink with black and yellow flowers, buttoned up at the front. The top button is straining to burst. Her cowboy boots are scuffed and dirty and brown. The black around her eyes is the same as usual, with lashings of mascara. She has a layer of puppy fat that keeps her warm. A streak of cheap glitter is splashed across her lips.

Her cheeks are more flushed than usual, she has gone crazy with cream blusher and she has a round pink circle, like an apple, on either cheek. I grab a book off the nearest counter – it's Steinbeck, *The Winter of our Discontent* – and head over.

'Oh, hi,' I say, as if I am utterly surprised to see her, here, where she works every day.

She looks up, and a smiles breaks across her face like a warm wave.

'Hi! How are you?' she asks, her eyes wide. She reaches out a hand to touch my arm but stops herself.

'I'm good, I'm well, how are you?'

'I'm good. Really good. I mean, I'm bored, of course,' she gestures at the books on the table, 'but I'm so glad you came in. Can I tell you something stupid? I've been waiting for you for days!' She rolls her eyes dramatically and laughs.

'Really?' I ask, taken aback.

She points at her cheeks.

'I don't know what I am supposed to be looking at,' I say, confused.

'My blusher!' she says triumphantly.

'Right?' I am confused.

'I, like, completely copied you. I know that makes me, like, a complete rip-off, of you, but I just thought it looked so nice, and then I saw it in *Vogue* as well, and I thought I should, like, try it, but I wanted you to see it. So . . .'

'So?' I say.

'So what do you think?'

'Of your blusher?' I ask.

'Yeah! Does it look all right?'

'I think . . .' She looks like a Russian doll. I lean forwards and rest my thumbs underneath her cheekbones. 'I think you need to blend it a little more,' I say, and smudge it in. Her cheeks feel plump under my thumbs like stress balls that bounce back into place as soon as you've squeezed them.

She stares at me, her pupils dilating. I don't know what I am doing. 'Do you think you could, like, show me? Properly?'

'What, how to blend blusher? I suppose, I don't see why not.' I hold her gaze for as long as I can before looking away.

'How about tonight?' She claps her hands and squeals like a child.

'Oh no, I can't tonight, I have plans.'

'How about Saturday?' she suggests, without a breath, without a doubt or an insecurity.

'Okay, I could do Saturday.'

'Great! Fab! I know this great bar, it's all dark and mysterious and you can smoke one of those hubble bubble pipes. It'll be, like, a complete laugh. What do you think?'

'Okay, it sounds like fun. Shall I meet you here?'

'Yeah, I'm working till eight on Saturday – boring! – so if you want to swing by here, we could get a cab. It's near Marble Arch.'

'Okay. I'll bring some samples.'

'Great, why not?' she says, and smiles a huge smile again. I smile back as honestly as I can.

'Well, I'll see you then, then. My name is Scarlet, by the way. Oh, can I pay you for this?' I offer her the Steinbeck.

When she takes it from me she touches my hand. 'Don't be rubbish, Scarlet, I'll get it for you, I get a staff discount. It'll cost me, like, two pounds or something. I'll give it to you on Saturday, then you can't stand me up!'

'That's sweet of you, thanks.' Her enthusiasm is unnerving.

'It's like, no problem. I never use my discount anyway, unless it's, like, Christmas or whatever. And then everybody complains, "Not books again, Isabella!" Like it's the only thing I ever buy them! The thing is, it kind of is the only thing I ever buy them!' She laughs at herself.

'Okay, well, I'll see you on Saturday then, but I have to go now,' I say.

'Great, see you then, Scarlet.' She smiles, and I walk away before I can change my mind.

Helen and I are eating dinner at Café Em on Frith Street. Two men sitting on the table next to us keep looking over and smiling. They look Greek. They aren't talking to each other, just scanning the room for women. Helen is less tired today. Her brown hair is clean and pulled over one shoulder. She looks like a grown-up with her glasses and her dark matt lipstick, and her suit.

As soon as I sat down I wanted to tell her about Isabella, ask her what the hell I was doing, but I didn't, I can't. I don't know what I'll say.

Helen takes a mouthful of red pepper and rice and a swig of red wine, gulps, and carries on talking.

'So, I saw this couple on the tube on the way up here, and they were wearing matching clothes. I swear, Scarlet, they were completely matching. Jeans the exact same colour, jumpers exactly the same! With this weird teardrop in the middle, and a puddle at the bottom. They were seriously ugly. The jumpers I mean. And even the same kind of trainers, white, plain lace-ups. And I had to ask them – are you married? And they loved it. The woman laughed and the man said, "Yes. This is our fifteenth year!" So I said, "Do you always dress the same?" and I think they could tell that I thought it was a bit weird. But they didn't seem to care, and he said, "We've done it every day since the day we married. It's us, it's our team colours. It's us against everything." Then I had to get off at Leicester Square. But Scar, even their smiles matched! After fifteen years!'

Helen shakes her head and her smile fades to sadness. She takes another gulp of wine.

'That's so funny,' I say. 'On the tube this morning I was sitting next to this girl; she looked like us, I mean, our age and stuff, but I looked down and she was reading the Bible, Hel! And my immediate reaction was to switch seats! That's how freaky I find reading the Bible in public. That is weird. I would have found it far more acceptable if she was reading, say, porn, or a pamphlet on how to spot a terrorist bomber, or anything. But the Bible made me want to switch seats. And I just thought "Freak!" That's nice, isn't it, I'm a nice person.' I take a mouthful of falafel.

Helen starts to laugh, but it fades quickly. 'He says I've ruined him,' she whispers.

'Who?'

'Jamie. He says he loves me and I was just mucking about and now I've ruined him and he'll do it to somebody else and then they'll hurt like I should. And the whole time he's wearing those awful bandages around his wrists, and wincing. Christ, Scarlet, let's not talk about whether we are nice or not . . .'

'Well,' I say, 'they are some mighty big words for a seventeen-year-old. You've ruined him?' I ask, pretending to look impressed.

'He reads,' Helen says darkly.

'Yes, *Harry Potter*,' I reply.

'Not just that, Scarlet, other stuff as well. He reads poetry. He keeps quoting it at me.' She grimaces.

'Any Byron?' I ask.

'Christ, Scarlet, I don't know! I don't know anything about poetry. But he keeps coming out with it!'

'That's unlucky. What are the chances of that?'

'I know. He's the only seventeen-year-old in the country who has heard of Yeats.'

'Christ!' I say, mortified. 'Which one was he again?'

'I don't know, but he keeps quoting some poem called "When You Are Old"' she says, '"*But one man loved the pilgrim soul in you*" – he says it over and over. It freaks me out if I'm honest, Scar.'

'But what does it mean?' I ask.

She shrugs and we take a mouthful of wine, and gesture to the waiter for another bottle, as the Greeks try to catch our attention and we ignore them.

'But it explains the gesture, Hel. He's romanticised you and him. He thinks he's a poet. You can't feel guilty about that.'

'Yes I can, I absolutely can! We weren't equal, Scarlet. It's not like if you meet somebody our age, and you do whatever you do – at least you know that you've both been around the block, and you just know what's going on. We know that. But Jamie didn't. He thought I, you know . . .' She pauses, and takes a breath. 'He thought that I loved him.'

I push my plate away. I've lost my appetite.

'Maybe you do love him, Hel, a little bit. Love isn't such a crazy concept. Maybe you just think that you shouldn't because he's young enough to be your son.' I smile at her.

'Thanks,' she says, and laughs.

'It's my pleasure. But maybe you do, a bit?' I persist.

'Maybe I do.' Helen nods her head.

One of the Greeks says, 'Excuse me' and we both say 'No' at the same time. The Greeks say something rude and turn away to find new girls to harass.

'But what of Steven? And Nikki with an "i"?' I ask.

'Turns out she's not pregnant after all, and what a surprise,' Helen says, pushing her plate away as well.

'Is he coming back?'

'He might be . . .' Helen looks like I've just discovered her guilty secret.

'Will you take him, Hel?' I ask, reaching for the dessert menu.

'I'm not sure . . . I feel like I shouldn't . . . but I feel like I might . . . Will you hate me, Scarlet, if I do?'

'Don't be ridiculous. You should do whatever you want to do. The only thing that worries me is, do you love him, Hel? Is it large and dramatic love?'

Helen laughs. 'Scarlet, that's not for me, that's for you.'

I grab her hand across the table, and she looks alarmed. 'No, no! Hel, it should be for everybody!'

'Not everybody can stand the pace and the drama, Scarlet. And the tears, and the rows, and all of it. I think I'd just like an easy life.' She pats my hand simply.

'God, do you want Ben? He wants one of those too.' I sit back in my chair and study the desserts rather than think about it.

'You haven't failed, you know, Scarlet, it's nobody's fault.'

'Ice cream and coffee,' I say to the waiter, smiling and passing him the menu, before throwing my napkin down on the table in exasperation. 'But I love him, Hel. And he doesn't love me. What do you do about that?'

'Do you love him, though, Scarlet? Is it urgent and dramatic and passionate?'

'You know, I think it is. I didn't think it would be, but I think it is. Except now I just feel so rejected, all the time, that it's hard to be anything but bitter.'

'But are you sure there isn't just a bit of you hell-bent on hearing him say it? And once he does say it, once he says, "I love you, Scarlet", you'll leave instead? Are you sure it's not just you that is urgent and passionate and the other one, so it just feels like you feel that way about him?'

'It doesn't matter because he'll never say it, not now. Our window has passed. And the problem is I can't stop myself asking the same question over and over in my mind: Why doesn't he love me? What have I done that is so wrong that he doesn't love me? Is it that I squeeze a spot sometimes? Or that I like to talk dirty sometimes, dirtier than him? Or is it that I need too much attention, or I'm too demanding? Or is it that I spend too much money? I just don't know! Or because I've put on weight, because, you know, I've put on a stone, Hel . . .'

'Stop that!' Helen says, appalled.

'But Hel, it's true. Does he think I'm greedy? I don't know what it is and it's driving me crazy! But I also know that I don't just get on with the business of loving him and maybe that's what love should be like. I should just keep loving him in spite of his feelings for me. And, you know, Ben is Ben. He doesn't do feelings, or emotions, or honesty really.'

'Love him anyway? You sound like one of those women who write to death-row inmates and then marry them in jail. And as for Ben not feeling or emoting or being honest, well – that's a life sentence, Scarlet. Even Steven can tell me that he loves me.'

'And probably Nikki with an "i" as well,' I chip in, and then regret it.

'Maybe,' Helen agrees, nodding honestly, 'but that doesn't mean he doesn't love me. And at least he's got the guts to say it.'

'I know, I know.'

'So what you have to ask yourself is, are you ready for prison, Scarlet, and a lifetime of Ben? You didn't do anything wrong, you know . . . you're not guilty.'

'Oh Helen.' I take a mouthful of ice cream and shudder, and wait for it to slip its way down my throat. 'I did, though, didn't I? I took him.' I take another mouthful of ice cream and shiver again.

'No you didn't!' Helen says sternly, and puts down her spoon for effect. 'No you didn't! He makes you feel like that

280

and I hate it! He left. He's the one who should feel guilty, not you!'

'Oh Helen, it's not just him, it's me as well. I do it to myself.' My ice cream is all gone, and I reach across to grab a spoonful of Helen's, and she pushes it towards me.

'Well it's not true, whoever is thinking it. He's a grown-up, and he left. That's that. And it was three years ago! Jesus, these things happen, you weren't the first person to have an affair and you won't be the last! For Christ's sake, my husband is shagging somebody else, and even I know it's got nothing to do with her, really. If we were happy, it wouldn't have happened!'

'We're going to the zoo,' I say, and I have to put my glass down on the table quickly as my hands start to shake again.

'Good place. Like in that song. "Tell Me on a Sunday".'

'I might not do it, Hel,' I say, flooded with an absolute sadness that I have never felt before.

'You might not. You might not. You might, though,' she nods her head.

'I don't want to be on my own, Helen. I like being in a relationship. I like the closeness. I like having somebody care where I am if I don't come home.'

'But you won't be on your own, Scarlet, not for long. Go and find somebody a little more "you".'

'But . . .'

'But what?'

'But what if I'm not pretty enough any more? To get some-body else?' I feel guilty and stupid just saying it, but I really feel it.

'You're just using that as an excuse,' she says evenly, pouring out the last of our wine.

'Am I? There are a lot of younger, prettier girls out there now, believe me, I've seen them, Helen! And blokes don't want the thirtysomethings who want babies. They just want fun and no responsibilities and to not have anybody hoist any decisions on them and . . .'

'Okay, Scarlet, you've been reading the wrong magazines. If you think your face is all you have then you deserve what you get.'

'Oh don't be naïve, Helen, we're talking about men! I'm not the prettiest girl around any more!'

'Well, you know what, some of us weren't the prettiest girl around to start with and we still did all right!' She is angry with me. 'Don't you be naïve, Scar. Love isn't pretty. If there's anything I know, it's that.'

Standing outside the restaurant on Frith Street, Helen hails a black cab.

'Are you going home?' she asks.

I stare down towards Old Compton Street, and think about heading to Gerry's.

'Can I come and stay at yours, Hel? I can't face him tonight,' I ask instead.

'Of course,' she replies, and we travel home in silence. Helen gives me a hug around Vauxhall.

Friday. I call Ben at 9.52 a.m. as I walk back along Ealing Broadway to the flat.

'It's me,' I say. I don't know why I always say that, I assume he has my number in his phone by now.

'Hi,' he replies.

'I didn't come home, I thought you might be worried . . .'

'Right.'

'But obviously not.'

I hear him sigh at the other end of the line. 'Jesus, Scarlet, will you give me a chance? I was going to call you later.'

'Later? What, like, lunchtime later? Or next-week later? I could have been dead in a gutter for twelve hours "later".'

'You never give me a chance, Scarlet.'

'I give you every reasonable chance, Ben, unless you are clinically slow. It's like the time the bombs went off on the tube, do you remember that, Ben? And I had to phone you to tell you I was okay about three hours later. There were no missed calls on my phone. You were just watching the whole thing on a hundred TVs at work, it's not like you missed it. At least have the guts to admit you just don't fucking care, Ben!'

He sighs again.

I hang up the phone.

My head is foggy from last night's red wine.

I walk down and along Aldwych today, from Holborn Station. I think I have wandered into the middle of a fireworks display. Cabs streak past and beep their horns and suits laugh at each other loudly and my ears are ringing with the shriek of rockets falling around my head, but nothing seems to explode. I'm just nervous and poised and waiting for the big bang.

A plane passes above our heads, low and heavy and loud in the sky, and I look up. It's a two-man plane, and I am surprised because I didn't think that they were allowed over central London, because of bombs and terrorists and things. I've never seen one this close before.

It has a banner blazing behind it. 'Look Up', it says.

Every time that my phone buzzes in my pocket I pray that it's Ben, but I also pray that it isn't. He could make it better, if he wanted to, but he doesn't seem to have it in him. He's no grand-gesture kind of guy, and it's getting to that stage. Soon, 'I'm sorry, Scarlet, I love you' won't even be enough. I'm already too damaged for that. No, it won't be enough. When was the first time that you glimpsed the edge of the world, and thought that you might fall off?

I think I hear kids in a playground somewhere, in central

London, at the back of Covent Garden, and I stop and stand still and listen. I can definitely hear a playground and children screaming and running. I can hear laughter, and even though I know that they are learning to be awful to each other, there is still joy. I hear the delight and the squabbles and the cheers and the arguments, skipping ropes cutting through the air, and hopscotch on concrete, and footballs being booted carelessly from one end of the court to the other. Even though I know that some of them will learn to hate each other this morning, it is still wonderful. They don't hate each other yet.

I wander up a Majestic aisle and hear somebody say, '*I've got to stay slightly drunk to bear the pain.*' I assume it must be Dolly in a rare moment of candour, but looking up I see it is Audrey Winston, Dolly's understudy and also the actress playing 'the Witch of Capri', or something like that – Tristan told me, but I've forgotten already.

'Again, but with a laugh, Audrey, please. You need to make light of it more. It's not riddled with meaning, she's removing the meaning. Again, please, love.'

Audrey says it again, to Gavin, who is standing in the middle of the stage looking ridiculous in Dolly's purple turban.

'What's going on?' I mouth at him, tapping the face of my watch. It isn't eleven thirty yet, and generally they wait for Dolly to rehearse Dolly's scenes.

'Tristan's having a panic,' he mouths back, but then looks away.

Tristan has covered his eyes again at the front of the stage.

Gavin reads lines back at Audrey, who hams it up for all she is worth.

'*Sally was trying to prove she was a generation younger than she was and thought she could get away with it,*' she says, smiling at Tristan theatrically. He gets up and walks

284

out. Gavin walks off backstage. Audrey stands in the middle of the stage and looks around for somebody to impress, but nobody comes. She sits down quietly on the chaise longue.

I follow Gavin and call after him, but he is moving too quickly. I call out his name again, but by the time I reach the bottom of the stairs he has disappeared completely.

Tom comes round the corner to a round of applause and screaming girls in his head. He is wearing a crisp light-blue shirt with a stiff collar and the top two buttons undone, and well-cut dark jeans. He has a jumper tied around his waist. He looks like he's walked off a runway.

'Have you upset simple Gavin?' Tom asks, sidling up towards me.

'No. Maybe. I don't bloody know, and he's not simple,' I reply, trying not to be affected by the light sting of his after-shave on my senses. It smells like Penhaligons, dignified and manly.

'Nice outfit,' he says, raising his eyes and giving a little whistle. I am wearing a navy blue polo shirt, a white pleated knee-length tennis skirt, and navy Mary Janes with white heels. I've got a string of long pink pearls beneath my collar, and my hair hangs heavily down my back, tousled and finger-dried. I'm wearing my heartbreak lip-gloss again; it just seems to go with everything these days.

'Do you know when Dolly is coming in?' I enquire. I have a pang as if I haven't seen her for a while. How much gin will she have knocked back today?

'She's not due in until two apparently, she's had to see a doctor this morning.'

'Oh my God, why?' I ask, a sick feeling flooding my stomach.

'Oh, nothing apparently, she just moaned a lot in the night and now she wants some valium or something. So . . . we find ourselves with some time on our hands.'

'Speak for yourself,' I say.

'Why, what have you got to do?'

I stand and think. 'No, you're right, nothing really.'

'Good, let me buy you lunch then.' Tom stands above me and gives me a cheeky smile. His eyes are deep and dark, and they sparkle with a dirty evil. I think he has a fan club. I think there might be whole websites devoted to him. And in spite of myself I can understand it.

'I just ate,' I reply.

'Then you'll eat again,' he says, and grabs my hand, pulling me behind him and then pushing me up the stairs in front of him. I can smell his aftershave and it's making me giddy.

Walking down and towards the Covent Garden piazza, I can't help but feel like I've been dipped in gold or draped in diamonds. It is one thing to get stared at by builders and cabbies and couriers, but quite another to walk somewhere with Tom Harvey-Saint. His blue shirt cuts crisply through the murky browns and drab reds of the tourists. It is still warm, for September, and we turn right at the piazza and head towards the sandwich shops behind the Strand.

Teenage girls look at him, women stop and stare. Well-dressed men, i.e. gay men, follow him with their eyes and smile. We don't talk, but he places his hand on my back and guides me through the crowds of tourists milling around on the cobbles, staring at jugglers and mime artists and comedians.

'Street performers, how depressing,' he whispers to me. 'They always try too hard. And I bet they don't pay their taxes.'

I am silently appalled, and yet utterly overwhelmed by the attention we receive as we walk through the square. There are wolf whistles, which I ignore, of course, because I don't know if they are for Tom, or me, or both of us. One thing is for certain: I have never felt quite so admired as I do right now, and I think I suddenly understand a little something about Tom. If I am confused by the way the world treats 'pretty', what must it be like to be him? He is crass, and rude, and arrogant. But everybody loves him on sight. I wonder who he would be if he didn't look the way that he does. I wonder what parts of his personality got subdued, overlooked, because he didn't need to do much more than shave in the mornings to have the world love him.

We grab crayfish and rocket sandwiches and two bottles of water from Pret a Manger, and a chocolate brownie to share, and Tom pays for them all without a word.

'There is a square up here, behind this church, that I go to sometimes,' he tells me.

'Behind a church?' I ask, arching an eyebrow with surprise.

'Sometimes I even confess my sins – if you're a good girl I might just let a few slip today.' I look at him for a beat too long, and then turn away. I hear him chuckle.

'I don't mind sitting on the grass if you'll sit on this,' he says, offering me the duck-egg blue jumper hanging loosely around his waist. He smiles. I am amazed how easily he affects me. My willingness to cut beauty a break and forgive all previous offences is disturbing.

I cross my legs in front of me at the ankles, eat my sandwich and sip at my water. Tom inspects the grass quickly for mud, and then lies down in a model pose, propped up on one elbow, feeding himself his sandwich greedily with the other hand. He closes his eyes and faces the sun, and we sit in a warm silence. The square is half-full, and anybody who isn't reading or talking seems to be staring at us. And I thought I got my fair share of stares on my own.

'The sun feels good, doesn't it,' he says with his eyes closed, face angled towards the sun.

'Yep,' I reply as nonchalantly as I can.

'Imagine you're on a beach, Scarlet, in some little bikini, or maybe even topless – do you go topless, Scarlet?'

'Sometimes,' I say, taking a large bite of my sandwich as an excuse not to talk.

'I love the way women's breasts shine in the sun, their nipples dark brown from the heat, there is something so natural about it.' I can feel him looking at me and I refuse to look back.

'You look at women's boobs on the beach, now there's a surprise,' I say sarcastically, trying to draw that line of conversation to a close.

Tom coughs, and pushes himself to his feet. 'I'll be back in a minute, nature calls' he says, and darts off towards the street. I sit back in the sun and concentrate on forgetting everything, relieved that I put factor twenty moisturizer on my face this morning so I can sit here exposed but guilt free.

After five minutes Tom lands back down beside me and takes a slug of water.

'Everything okay?' I ask him.

'Why shouldn't it be?' he asks smugly.

'I don't know, because you are you,' I say, still facing the sun with my eyes closed.

Tom props himself up on his elbow. 'Scarlet, I'm going to say something and I don't want you to jump down my throat.'

'What?' I ask, ready to jump down his throat.

'You seem sad. You look sad. I mean, you look great, but also sad. And nothing is more attractive on a woman, on anybody in fact, than a smile.' To prove it he smiles at me from beneath his dark fringe. I look away.

'So are you?'

'Am I what? Sad? A bit, yes.'

'Because you're not having any sex?' he asks earnestly.

'Oh my God, what is wrong with you? You seem all normal and almost nice and then you say the weirdest, strangest things!'

'What? What did I say? I'd be sad if I wasn't having any sex, that's fair!'

'Okay, it's partially the sex, but it's bigger than that. I think I'm just confronting some stuff that I have ignored for too long. And yes, it's making me a little sad. My life isn't what I thought it would be.'

'What did you think it would be?' he asks, addressing his bottle of water.

'Undoubtedly happy,' I reply.

'Let's play the truth game,' he says, wiping his hands on a Pret napkin.

'Oh my God, are we kids?' I ask.

'No. But it's a good game. You can either ask me something, and I have to tell the truth, or I can tell you something about you that I think is the truth.'

'Fine. Whatever. Ask me something,' I say, looking around the square for something else to do.

'Do you really go topless?'

'Yes, sometimes. Only in private. Not on the beach.'

'Why not on the beach?'

'I don't know.'

'Do your nipples go dark brown when you do?'

'Yes. My turn. Have you ever told a woman that you love her?'

'Yes.'

'That wasn't your mother, or your grandmother, or some other old relative?'

'Yes.'

'Did you mean it?'

'As much as I can, yes. Right, my turn.'

'Fine, tell me something then. This is getting boring,' I say, hot and bothered and flustered and pissed off and ready to leave.

'Okay, you think too much. About love and all that shit.'

'Nice,' I say, refusing to really listen.

'And you over analyse everything, and when you do that you kill it,' he continues matter-of-factly, like I should know this already.

'Okay, but has it ever occurred to you that if you aren't happy you should find out the reason why? Hmmm?' I ask him, like he's the class dunce.

'Maybe it's the constant questioning, Scarlet – the "Oh my God, am I happy? Am I unhappy? Does he love me, doesn't he love me?" that actively makes you unhappy, have you thought about that?'

'I don't think that's true.' I don't want to hear any more. Why is everybody so determined to tell me how I should behave?

'You should just stop thinking so much. Just live it.' Tom sits back, satisfied with himself.

'Women think, Tom. That's what we do.'

'And that's why men leave you. Or don't love you. Most men just want a simple life.'

'Then pick a simple woman,' I say, jumping to my feet and walking off.

I hear him call my name once, but that's it.

The first months that Ben and I were together were wonderful, when he opened up to me, and seemed happy to see me, and *wanted* to see me, in fact. I thought I'd found something. But then the door started to close. Initially his feelings were a wave pouring out and over me, it was like some kind of relief for him to talk. It was never dramatic or overly analytical, but it was open and it was honest. I believe there are things that he told me that he has never told anybody. He told me how he felt when his mother left and how it felt when she came back. He told me how he coped with being lonely by making lonely the best way to be. But then, a few months after he'd left Katie – her name still whispered like the word 'bomb' on a jumbo jet – he just stopped talking. Something happened, I don't know what, but Ben just closed off. We carried on, but every day with him got harder, like I was pushing a ball of hay up a hill and it was gathering straw and dirt and grass and getting heavier and heavier. I feel like Ben let me walk a few steps ahead of him and then watched as I turned one way, and he decided to turn the other. One night, he breathed something in, and it was something bad, and that night he decided not to love me. Maybe it's that simple.

I walk briskly up Long Acre towards the theatre, noticing that I only get half of the attention that I received when Tom was by my side. I reach into my bag for my purse.

'*Standard*?' my old guy says, still in his overcoat, in spite of the heat.

'So what have you got for me this afternoon?' I ask, smiling.

'Paper, dear?' he asks, volunteering a folded *Standard*.

'Yes, of course, but what else?' I ask, confused.

'It's forty pence, dear,' he says.

I feel rejected.

'Yes, I know that it's forty pence, but what else? I mean, you usually say something or . . . you say something to me, don't you? I'm not going mad, I haven't dreamt it. You say stuff, like you said "Thoreau" the other day, and I had to look him up on the computer, and he was a writer, an American writer, and you said that to me.' I am almost desperate for him to agree. I am not going mad, but he looks at me like I'm an idiot.

'Okay,' I say, passing him my forty pence, 'I must have been mistaken.'

He hands me the paper, folded in half. 'Sometimes things are that simple,' he replies.

I look up at him with a smile. 'I knew you couldn't stop yourself! Ha!' I say, and walk off, aware that I sound like somebody.

Sometimes things should just be simple.

I grab my phone and call Ben.

'What?' he asks, instead of hello.

'I am officially calling you to tell you that I am coming home early, tonight, on a Friday night, in case you are cooking food, or there is football on.' I smile. That was easy.

'Oh, I'm going to the pub for a few after work, but I shouldn't be too late,' he says, sounding a little bewildered.

'Okay, well, that's cool, I'll see you later on.'

'Okay, bye,' he replies, confused.

'I'm spending the evening with Ben tonight,' I tell Dolly as I strip off her make-up. It is six o'clock and she has been tired all afternoon. She was up in the middle of the night with pains, she said, and the doctor had to prescribe her codeine. It has made her woozy.

'Good,' she says, her eyes closing in the chair. 'Try tonight, Lulu.'

'I will, I will,' I say.

I even stop and buy vegetables on the way home, and chicken. I am going to eat a proper meal, the type that my mother might cook, and have one glass of wine, just one, and be civilised and grown-up and responsible. And maybe Ben will cry off from the pub early, because he knows I am at home, so I'll cook a little extra, and then we can watch sitcoms and laugh, and maybe talk a little as well.

By nine o'clock Ben hasn't come home, so I turn on the radio while I make dinner. Ben has it tuned to the same station wherever he goes. In the car, in the house, at work. The same songs, dad rock, everywhere, and all the time. I retune it quickly – it's my house too – and find a golden-oldie station. Buddy Holly sings 'Love is Strange'. I chop mushrooms and hum along. There are violins. Love and violins are synonymous, aren't they? Except my violins are playing sad songs. I need joyful violins, like Buddy Holly's.

Two hours later I am crying, but it's not my fault, they aren't real tears. I have been watching a makeover marathon on cable TV. Selma, forty-two and twenty-three stone, lost her husband in a mudslide when they were on honeymoon in Venezuela. She broke both her legs at the same time, and because she is so heavy she has been having trouble recovering, and then she lost her job. After that she was evicted and now she is living back at her mother's, except her mother is really ill, too, and probably won't make it to Christmas. But Selma decides to leave for two months anyway, even though her mother might die while she's gone, because it will be worth it, she says. So when they come to pick her up in a limousine bigger than the trailer she and her dying mother live in, it's like she might be saying goodbye to her mum for good, and they both cry, a lot.

The following week they staple Selma's stomach so she can only eat soup, and give her liposuction, veneers, hair extensions, a tummy tuck, a nose job, a breast reduction, and false nails. And she isn't allowed to look in the mirror for those entire two months, and they don't let her call home either, so she doesn't know if her mum is dead or not, but apparently that all just adds to the suspense . . .

So two months later they do the 'reveal'. She looks beautiful. They've sucked about three stone off her, and she's lost another two herself. Her mother, who is still alive, barely recognises her. They hug and cry, but Selma can't hug her too tight because she has still got bandages on under her cocktail dress. But she is beautiful. Selma can't stop looking at herself in the mirror. Her mum cries so much when she sees her, and I wonder if it's because she's nearly dead, or because her daughter is suddenly beautiful.

This is the third episode I have watched. They all just seem to get more tragic. But look how they look! Look how they have been transformed for this one moment.

I mute the TV and lay my head back on the sofa and wonder why it means so much to look in the mirror and see something wonderful when you've never seen it before? Is it because we think it will make people love us a bit more than they already do? Is it because it makes us feel that we inch a little closer to love? Or that maybe we've just found a shortcut?

I turn off the TV at one a.m., turn off the lamp in the living room so it's dark, and stare out of the window. It's noisy, the late bars are just chucking people out to the clubs. It's a clear night, and I am distracted by what seems like a shooting star. I think it must be a CIA plane, or a satellite crashing to earth. But then I see another one, and another. People on the street below start to look up as well, as the stars shoot across the sky. There is a shooting-star storm outside my window. If Ben were here he would say it's like the *Day of the Triffids*, and we should cover our eyes. But Ben isn't here. At two a.m. I crawl into bed on my own.

Scene IV: The Heart Must Pause to Breathe

Saturday. I squeeze my eyes open just enough to register the numbers on our Mickey Mouse alarm clock. If you actually set the alarm it sings 'It's a Small World After All' in a squeal so high-pitched it affects fishing channels and diverts whales up the Thames towards Richmond. So obviously we don't set it. I forgot and set it once a little while ago and it caused mayhem! Ben uses the alarm on his mobile phone to wake him up every morning. I hate the noise that it makes, like a pulse that grows steadily louder and more menacing, thudding through me until it makes the walls and my bones shake. Although it doesn't wake me it consistently penetrates and ruins my dreams. That tinny beeping pulse tolls in at seven a.m. every morning, and it always means that Ben is leaving. Ben never ignores his alarm. I am more likely to encounter Lord Lucan hiding under our duvet with one finger to his lips 'shushing' me not to reveal his whereabouts than I am to find Ben snoozing his phone to spend more time with me between the sheets.

Mickey Mouse says it's six twenty-three a.m. I roll over

heavily in bed, expecting to see the moles on Ben's back, but he isn't there. He hasn't come home.

Despite my nagging anxiety, I drift off again, my body automatically shutting down at the ungodly hour. I wake up again a couple of hours later. Forcing my eyes open I register through a sleep blur that Mickey says eight thirty-two, as suggested by the light streaming in through the curtains. I hear somebody crashing up the stairs, and I know that it was the front door slamming that woke me. The bedroom door creaks quietly open, and seconds later so does Ben's cupboard. I hear him swear softly under his breath, 'bollocks', followed by the sounds of him frantically kicking off his trousers and scrambling into a new pair, and throwing on a clean shirt. He tiptoes out of the room and closes the door behind him. I hear him bash about in the kitchen, say 'bollocks' twice more, and still I don't get up.

I check my phone at nine a.m. while munching on a bowl of Alpen, leaning on the kitchen counter in a vest and knickers. There is a text from Ben, sent fifteen minutes ago, which reads: 'I STAYED AT IGGY'S'

It's to the point at least.

I consider a thousand quick replies, but then simply text back: 'DON'T FORGET THE ZOO TOMORROW'

Ten minutes later, as I am about to step into the shower, my phone buzzes. Ben's text reads: 'ARE WE STILL GOING? WHY?'

I take a long and deliberate shower and scrub at my scalp, opening up the follicles so that the fury can get out and not cause my head to explode. I sometimes think that showers should be fattening, high-calorie indulgences. The water pushing you away and soaking you and warming you is just too good a feeling to be fat free.

Dripping on the bathroom mat, I reply: 'WHY NOT'

No question mark, I don't want a reply.

I moisturise my body with cocoa butter and spray perfume in all the right places. I take my time on my hair – first blow-drying, then straightening, then curling the ends. I apply my make-up base, ready to be added to later for full effect. It feels important that I look my best today. I need to compete.

I wear a flimsy pink silk shirt-dress with floppy collars and cuffs, a men's black cummerbund, and high black rattan court shoes with toe cleavage. I have painted my toenails baby pink, and I pull my hair back into a loose ponytail, posting two pearl drops through the holes in my ears. At the last second I disregard 'Heartbreak Blue' gloss for 'Grapefruit' Juicy Tube. Today is not a day for heartbreak.

Riding the tube with the Saturday shoppers and tourists up into town I think about Ben's text messages. You can be a 'why' person or a 'why not' person. You can seize things, do things, or not. You can look for the positives or the negatives. If Ben asked me, today, 'Why do you love me?' I think I would be inclined to say 'Why not?' just to prove a point. It doesn't have to be explained to me, or justified, or dragged out of me begrudgingly. Why not?

I take the tube all the way to Covent Garden station and walk the short distance back down Long Acre to the theatre, glancing in shoe shops and clothes shops as I go. For the first time in what seems like an age I don't feel emotionally exhausted. I see a young girl walking towards me and before I can stop myself I wince and whisper 'Oh no . . .' She is breaking one of the new and as yet undeclared public decency laws. They haven't been advertised on the tube next to the poetry, or leafleted on lampposts, or inserted into *HEAT* alongside adverts for women's car insurance, but we all know these laws. This late-teenage girl with a sour face has a tight ponytail, gel-scraped back from her head aside from two long, stiff poker-straight sections of hair that hang either side of her centre parting like switchblade curtains that cut each of her cheeks in half. She is striding towards me with, and here is the illegal bit, an entire rubber ring of stomach flesh naked and spilling over the top and out of her jeans, squeezed out further still by the tight cropped top that has been forced over her chest. The protruding rolls at her stomach are translucent, veined and fatty like sausage meat that's just been piped into its skin casing.

I see a couple of women on the other side of the road glance over and double-take in shocked horror as they pass her. I can only imagine how many insults she will have to endure today, as they are clumsily hurled at her out of white van windows, and from scaffolding platforms, and outside McDonald's and Burger King and KFC. Just for wearing clothes that don't fit, on a frame that bulges, she will shock mostly everyone that she passes. Perhaps she won't care about any of those remarks; not knowing their perpetrators will enable her, perhaps, to dismiss them as soon as she hears them, like water trickling out of her ears. Somebody might say that she looks disgusting; another will ask her, rudely, to put her fat away where they don't have to look at it; someone else still might heckle her as ugly without even noticing her face. Every put-down that she will undergo will be generated by the way that she looks. Strangers will think they can comment on her, to her, in the street. We are all that shallow now. I didn't mean to hurt her feelings but perhaps she just saw me wince? We all sit in judgement, like some undisclosed beauty council in constant session, passing out rulings and sentences: *Imperfections should be hidden at all times! Not hideously exposed like a museum of the grotesque!* I don't even know how not to judge this girl any more, and how not to be that shallow? I don't know to stop myself being repelled by the bad judgement she made this morning while getting dressed, very possibly in the dark . . .

Tristan is dancing backwards and forwards at the front of the stage as if he's rehearsing a samba but he's lost his partner. Ordering the young crew around to move props and stage minutiae that nobody will notice but him, he manages to chain-smoke his clove cigarettes and eat a hamburger while constantly ashing the carpet beneath his feet. Gavin stares at each flicked amber with alarm, terrified that it may be the spark that brings the house down.

'Is Dolly in yet?' Towering above him in three and a half inch heels I tap Tristan on the shoulder. He spins on one foot and stares at me in disbelief, as if I just popped out both of my eyes and gave them to him as an early birthday present.

'Are you taking the piss?' he screams, an octave higher than I have ever heard him before.

'No,' I say, alarmed, taking a hasty step backwards. Gavin, who is unscrewing a vent at the side of the stage, looks over towards us with blank concern, if there is such a thing.

'Is she fuck, Make-up! We only open on Monday, it's the last day of rehearsals, it's a quarter to twelve, and she hasn't turned up yet!'

Gavin stands up straight, his screwdriver in hand, and takes a couple of steps towards us.

'Okay, calm down, Tristan,' I say, 'I didn't mean to upset you. Have another cigarette.' I gesture at the pack in one hand and the smouldering cigarette butt in the other.

He takes a long and agitated drag on the butt, smoking the filter, but breathes it out slowly. 'I'm sorry,' he says to me.

'It's okay,' I console him, patting his arm. 'It's completely understandable. On a separate note, Tristan, your black eyes still haven't gone down: do you want me to put some make-up on them on Monday night? If you tell me now I can make sure I bring the right concealer?' I lean forwards to touch one of the bruises that circle his eyes like coffee rings on a wooden table, but he ducks out of the way.

'I couldn't care less about them, Make-up,' he says, flicking his cigarette nervously. 'Some of us couldn't give a shit what we look like. Some of us have careers that are about to . . .' he snaps open his Zippo lighter, and takes a drag on a fresh cigarette, '. . . go up in smoke.' He exhales from the side of his mouth and a stream of smoke slithers like a ghoul up into the Gods.

'All right, Tristan, I was only trying to help.' I glance around and realise that everybody is looking at us, and I feel foolish and shallow and of no consequence. I turn on my heel and head towards the door at the side of the stage.

'Look!' Tristan shouts after me. 'Look, don't take offence, Make-up, you know me by now. You have to understand the pressure I'm under. You know that I like you, but your crazy old lady is pushing me to the edge! And I am not used to kowtowing to crazy old ladies! Apart from my mother, and you can always go upstairs if she gets too much, and turn off the Stannah stairlift.'

I suppress a smile. 'You can be mean,' I say to him sternly.

'Not mean, Make-up, Byron-esque.'

'And what does that entail?' I ask. 'Being rude and snapping at the crew and making people feel trivial?'

'No! God no! Well, maybe a bit. But I'm anti-establishment, love. I'm a loner. I don't care about black eyes! In fact I like black eyes, if it's going to shock a few people, make them think how I got them. I'm like George Gordon himself.'

'Who?' I ask, looking around for some new member of the cast I haven't noticed.

'George Gordon,' he says, nodding.

'I thought we were talking about Byron?' I reply, confused.

'We are,' he nods enthusiastically.

'So who is George?' I ask, starting to feel silly.

'That's his real name,' Tristan says, trying to suppress a smile.

'Not Byron?' I say, feeling ridiculous.

'No. Well, he was Lord Byron.'

'I don't understand.'

Tristan can't fight his smile any more, and it spreads all over his face like a plague. He isn't wearing his hat or his beads or his glasses today. He looks positively normal in a grey roll-neck sweater and a black suit, except for his high hair and black eyes.

'Let's be honest, you're Make-up. You don't have to understand.'

'Okay, that's rude,' I say, and turn to leave again.

'I didn't mean it! I didn't mean it! Come on, I'm sorry, accept my apology,' he wheedles, running around in front of me. 'I'm just nervous, Make-up! What if it all goes wrong? We preview on Monday! Monday!' Tristan screws his hands into fists and holds them at the side of his face, squeezing his eyes shut. 'What am I doing, what am I doing, edelweiss, edelweiss, edelweiss,' he mutters to himself.

Gavin takes another giant step towards us.

'You'll be fine, Tristan, you're too passionate to fail. It will all be wonderful. You'll see.'

'But why?' he asks, his eyes snapping open, red from smoking or tears.

'Why not?' I reply, and shrug and smile.

Tristan nods and points at me as if I'm on to something. Gavin seems sufficiently relieved to kneel down and continue unscrewing the vent.

'And you know, if it starts to feel like too much, just stop and think, What would Byron do?' I say.

301

'Oh, love, he'd be off shagging the principal boy, and girl, in a cupboard.'

'Well then, there's your answer,' I say, but I can't help a quick grimace. The runners look on nervously.

'You got it!' Tristan replies, biting his lower lip and firing a finger gun at me. 'Pow,' he says.

'Right, can I go now, or do you still need me?' I ask, my hand resting on the door, poised to leave.

'Do you want something that's just for you, Make-up?' he asks with a wink, that obviously sends a shot of pain through his face because it is quickly followed by a stream of expletives.

'I'm not sure . . .' I say. It makes me nervous. The kids on the stage have stopped moving lamps and vases and rugs, and they are all staring down at him expectantly. I realise like a sandbag falling on my head from a great height that they worship him. For all of Dolly's derision, and Tom and Arabella's disdain, these kids think he's a genius, and I should let him show it, revel in the opportunity. It is not often that you meet men of passion these days, especially one that claims to have no libido.

Tristan composes himself with a cough and looks up, fixing me with his big brown vein-infested crazy eyes:

> For the sword outwears the sheath,
> And the soul outwears the breast,
> And the heart must pause to breathe,
> And love itself have rest.

He winks.

I don't know what to say, so instead I say, 'Tristan and Byron sitting in a tree,' childishly, and I hear a runner tut at me like I've just sworn in front of the Pope.

'Yes, it's true,' Tristan says, nodding, laughing.

'"*The heart must pause to breathe.*" I like that,' I say. 'What does it mean?'

'I don't know for sure, Make-up, but at a guess I'd say that sometimes even love has to stop and catch its breath.'

'Even love?' I say.

'Even love,' he replies.

'You see, now, that is beautiful,' I say.

'To love!' Tristan shouts, then spins on his heel and lights another cigarette.

An hour later Dolly is sitting comfortably in her chair, practising her lines.

'*Blackie! Blackie, don't leave me alone!*' she says. She keeps looking down at the play, and then off into the distance, and then at me when she delivers her line.

'*Blackie! Blackie, don't leave me alone!*' she says again, as I dab highlighter on what I can find of her cheekbones.

'Is Arabella playing Blackie?' I ask as casually as I can.

'Yes, she is,' Dolly answers absent-mindedly, looking back down at her script, muttering.

'What do you think of her?' I ask.

'What do you mean, Lulu?' – except it's 'Whatsdoyou-meanslooloo?' She's had two gins already this morning to my knowledge.

'I mean, she is obviously very beautiful, of course, but in a horsy kind of way . . .' I wait for her to tell me if she likes her or not, but instead she says, 'My mother always used to say to me, Lulu, "Pretty is the wallpaper, but wallpaper won't hold up the wall." Now, did you have it out with your chap, finally, Lulu?'

'No, I wanted to, but he didn't come home.'

'Oh, do you think he stayed with somebody else?' she asks, but with little obvious concern.

'He might have done.' I pause, a brown eyeliner hanging

303

in the air between her face and my fingers. I feel sick. 'I don't think he would lie to me,' I tell her, but more to control my own nausea.

'But have you asked him, Lulu, outright?'

'No.'

'Then he hasn't had to lie. Ha!'

'Don't laugh at that, Dolly, please,' I say, and she purses her lips but stops talking.

We are silent for a moment.

'Well, you should know by now, anyway, Lulu, if he is an honest chap or not. Because you can't tell the truth to a liar, it doesn't work. The truth bounces off a liar like a tiny rubber ball on a tennis court, quick and uncontrollable. The only way to communicate with a liar is to lie a little too.'

'I don't understand,' I say.

She sighs. 'Honestly, Lulu. I mean, is it easy to be honest with him, or does the honesty slip off him, and you find yourself telling half-truths as well?'

'I do keep trying to be honest, but you're right. It just doesn't work. It doesn't come out. And more than that, I can't be honest half of the time, because I'm trying to cover up all the little lies in my head: that this is enough, or that we are enough, or even that he is when he acts like he does. I don't want the world, Dolly, but I want more than this. How do I say that and still keep him? How do I tell him that and not have him leave me? How do I do any of this and not have it hurt us?'

'I don't know, darling, but I have to go upstairs now or that strange little man will have a hernia. I'll have a think. Ask somebody else as well. Another man, perhaps?' She shuffles out of the room.

I grab my phone and make my way upstairs. Wandering down the road, staring into LK Bennett and Reiss, I call my dad.

It rings three times before he answers in his telephone voice. 'Hello?'

'Hi Dad, it's Scarlet,' I say.

'Scarlet, how are you?' He always sounds genuinely pleased to hear from me.

'I'm okay, Dad, how are you?'

'I'm fine. Fine!'

'What have you been doing?' I ask.

'Oh, you know, just pottering around. Fixing the car. Playing some darts with the lads down the pub. Watching some football. I see Everton lost, I bet Ben's not happy! How about you?'

'Just work really. I might go down to Sussex and see Mum soon.'

'Right, right.' My dad has never once said a bad word about my mother, not to me anyway. I think that he might still love her, even after all this time. He loves her enough not to attack her, at least, for leaving him, when women didn't really leave, with two kids to look after. My parents shared us soon enough, but Dad had the hard shift, during the weeks, because Mum couldn't get a place that close to our school. So Mum got us larking about at weekends, and Dad got us moaning about having to go to bed early every night, and doing our homework on the kitchen table when he was trying to serve up fishfingers.

'How are you, though, Dad?' I ask again.

'Yeah, I'm all right, Scarlet, I just said I was all right.'

'And how's the house?'

'Yeah, it's all right. Richard came down, brought Hannah and the boys last weekend, which was lovely, because they've got so big! But how are you, Scarlet?'

'I'm fine, Daddy, fine. Lots on, but I'm okay.'

'Right, right. And how's Ben?'

'He's okay. Well, not really. I don't think he loves me, Daddy,' I say.

'Right. Right. You should speak to your mother about that sort of thing.'

'Can't I speak to you about it?' I ask.

'You know I'm no good at that stuff, Scarlet. I'm a man.'

'Do you love me, Daddy?' I ask, feeling sorry for myself.

'Of course I do! You're my daughter!'

'But that doesn't mean you have to love me . . .'

'Of course I do! Of course I do! Will I see you soon? It would be lovely to see you,' he says, moving on quickly.

'Yes, soon, I promise. I'm crazy busy but maybe in a couple of weeks, or you could come up to town and we could have lunch or dinner or something?' I say, and hear him freeze up on the other end of the phone line. He doesn't like London, it's 'too crowded, too busy, too dangerous'. Of course it's not, but he thinks it is.

'It's fine, Daddy, or I'll come home.'

'Right, yeah, that's probably best,' he says.

'I'll speak to you soon, Dad, take care, lots of love.'

'Lots of love, Scarlet, see you soon,' and he hangs up.

I wander back up towards the stage to watch the last of the rehearsals. Dolly is nowhere to be seen, but everybody else is milling around nervously, glancing anxiously at Tristan as he wrings and shakes his hands like some kind of 1950s dance he's learnt in order to win a jive competition.

'There you are!' I look behind me, because it seems as though he is talking to me, but there is nobody there. It is me. What have I done now?

'Go and get her! Go and get her!' he pleads, grabbing me by the shoulders and shaking me so my head rattles about on top of my neck.

'Okay,' I say, 'but where is she?'

306

Tristan lets go and points dramatically at the side of the stage with one hand, covering his eyes with the other. 'She's on the sodding phone! In the middle of our final dress rehearsal!' he says, and a bead of sweat shoots down the side of his face. 'Please, Make-up, for the love of God, for the love of God! Somebody give me strength!'

'Okay, I'll go and get her,' I tell him, as if talking a potential jumper back in off a ledge. I walk up the stairs at the side of the stage, slowly, glancing back over my shoulder at my audience of cast and crew, forty fingers crossed for me. I scan for Gavin and spot him at the side of my stage, and feel a little safer than I did a moment ago.

Leaning around the curtain nervously, I peek at what is lurking in the wings.

Dolly is indeed on her mobile phone to her daughter. Her voice sounds cold and hard, and sad. 'I know you're very busy, Chloe. Oh it's just some heap, some stupid British theatre, some stupid play, but that's not the point . . . Of course, of course! And I know he's busy, and they've rented the cabin now, of course! And she's in school . . . of course you can't take her out, I didn't ask you to, did I? . . . I just though that if you did come over I could take you down to the Lavender House, where my mother used to live, because you've never been, and . . . I'm not getting defensive, you are the one who always does this, Chloe, and . . . I'm not telling you what to do . . . I know I wasn't there for much of it and . . . no, I don't expect you to drop anything, it's just that of course when you get to my age you think that it might be your last . . . I'm not being dramatic! I'm not trying to make you feel guilty. Well, I can't help that . . . but if . . . If you feel guilty just damn well feel guilty then!' She throws the phone down the stairs and wipes an eye quickly.

'Hi,' I say nervously, five feet away.

'He wants me out there, doesn't he?'

I nod.

'It's fine, Lulu, I'm going. Will you get my phone?'

I nod again.

'Never have children, Lulu,' she says, wiping her other eye. 'They'll kick the shit out of you.'

An hour later, Tristan calls a break for tea. Everybody hovers on one side of the stage, laughing and chatting through their lines nervously, apart from Dolly, who sits in the seats opposite on her own with a cup of tea. I look over and see that nobody, not even Tristan, has gone to talk to her. She glances at the young cast members, and then sips her tea again. I look over and smile until she sees me, and she beckons me over.

'Come and sit with me, Lulu, you're the only one I can bear.'

I slump down next to her.

'Now Lulu, you are flushed, and you are wearing a very saucy dress, ha! What's going on?' She eyes me mischievously.

I haven't told anybody. 'I have . . . well, I think I have a date tonight,' I say, playing with my ponytail nervously.

'With your chap?' she asks, blowing on her tea.

'No,' I say, reaching for my powder as I see the sweat prickle through on her forehead, but she bats me away.

'Leave it, Lulu. So, not with your chap. With another chap then, eh?' she asks.

'Not exactly, no,' I reply, and look at my nails.

'Then who with?' she asks, staring at me.

'With . . . another girl,' I confess, and then cover my face with my hands, waiting for the shock and outrage, that, as usual, doesn't come. I look through my fingers at her and she is blowing on her tea again.

'Well, does she have a name?' she asks. She reaches down for her bag at her feet, but it's clumsy and she almost spills her tea, the cup teetering precariously in the saucer.

'Let me do it,' I insist, reaching for her bag. I pull out her hipflask by my feet, take her cup off her and throw a shot of gin into her tea, handing her back her cup, screwing the lid back on the hipflask and chucking it back in her bag.

'You know it's just medicinal, Lulu,' she says quietly.

'You don't judge me, I won't judge you,' I reply.

'So what's this girl's name?' she asks again, taking another sip of tea, but with a slightly more contented smile.

'Isabella.'

'And what are you looking for with this girl, Lulu?'

'I don't know.' I shake my head. 'I don't know what I'm doing, really. It's like I'm free-falling or something.'

'Well, how do you feel about seeing her?' she asks seriously.

'I don't know – scared? A bit sick? Nervous?'

'But are you excited, Lulu?' she asks, eyeing me intently above her cup.

'I don't know! I don't know if that's the word. I feel like it's some kind of an experiment. I feel like . . .'

'Like you are being unfaithful to your chap?' she says matter-of-factly, and it hadn't even occurred to me until now.

'No, actually, not at all. I don't know, it doesn't seem the same as that.'

'Oh but darling, it is. Imagine how you would feel if he was out on a date tonight, but with another chap?'

I burst with laughter. And then stop quickly. 'That would be awful!' I say, shocked. 'So you think I shouldn't go?' I ask.

'No, you utterly must go, Lulu! Of course you must! I did it, absolutely! I loved a woman once. It wasn't the answer, not for me, but Christ I had the guts to find out. She was famous too. She was older, far more beautiful than I was. Perhaps the most beautiful woman I have ever known. It was just before I won my Oscar. I was in love with her on Oscar night, you know, but of course I had to take my third husband, Bob. What a ridiculous name, Bob. I should have known. Of course he was a darling man, died horribly from pancreatic cancer, left me a fortune, but it wasn't why I married him. He was desperately good at poker, darling, and I found it amazingly attractive.'

'Isn't that strange! Ben is a fantastic surfer, amazing. It's bizarre how attractive I find that.'

'Anyway, Lulu, I was in love with Penelope on the night I won my Oscar, but she was there with her husband and I was there with my Bob. From the start it was a little ridiculous. We were both highly strung and erratic. Her hair was bright auburn, and she had freckles to match. We argued terribly, of course, both shockingly jealous. It quite quickly descended into disaster, and in the end we had to call a halt to it or kill each other. But my God she was beautiful. A man will never have the beauty of a woman. As chiselled, as handsome, it's not the same. And they don't need to be adored for it. It's a strange man that does, and beware. We all have our roles. A man who wants to be loved more than he will love is rotten and spoiled, probably by his mother, or some other fool who told him he was the world. And he walked all over her and he'll walk all over you. Whenever you meet a man, if you think it's serious, you should always observe, early on, the way that he treats his mother, but then I've told you that already. Because inevitably that is how you'll be treated, Lulu. Everything he feels about women can be heard in their conversations and the affection he has for her. If he can't tolerate her for more than ten minutes then beware! It will happen to you. I would be interested to hear how our Mr Harvey-Saint talks to his mother . . . '

Ben sees his mum on Boxing Day, and sometimes on her birthday. The answerphone, if I ever check it, is filled with messages from her that he hasn't returned. She worries about him, about me – he even told me she thinks I'm 'reckless', and her worry drives him crazy with irritation. He told me once that when she left him as a little boy she surrendered the right to worry about him, and he is still punishing her for it today. He won't let himself be cared about, by anybody. Would it be easy to say it's in case he finds that he cares as well, and then they leave again? I don't want to think that because then he'd be little more than a cliché, a rudimentary counselling problem that a junior could tackle in six weeks of non-intensive therapy. There has to be more to it than that.

Dolly swills the last of her tea around in her cup.

'You know, you've done a fair amount in your life, haven't you?' I say.

'Yes, I have, Lulu, and it was deliberate and thank God. I only ever think about life, and living, Lulu: about how much love I've squeezed into it so far, and how much more I can squeeze in yet. Don't limit yourself by thinking about the end. It's like the man says, dear Tennessee: "*Death is one moment and life is so many of them.*" What a shame to waste them. Of course, sometimes I'd stop myself and think, What in hell are you doing, Mary? Just going from one goddamn frantic distraction to another, till finally one too many goddamn frantic distractions leads to disaster, and then the end, blackout? But then I decided the best thing was not to think about it, or plan too hard, or worry too much. Life is the thing, Lulu.'

Tristan claps his hands twice in quick succession, like a toy monkey mechanically smashing symbols together. 'Can we go again in two, loves?' he says on the stage, biting his lower lip.

'The circus calls, Lulu,' Dolly remarks, and downs the last of her tea.

*   *   *

311

Tom knocks on Dolly's door just as I am about to take my first swipe at her mascara with a cotton-wool ball dripping in cleanser.

'Come in,' she barks, and pushes my hand away.

He pokes his head and shoulders around the door, and the room becomes a different place, filled with teenage girlish screams and boy-band mania.

'I just wanted to say that it's an honour, Dolly. I haven't really had the chance, as yet, but I wanted to make sure I told you, before Monday.' He flashes her his best movie-star smile, and her hand shoots up to her neck, her fingers dancing around the folds of her skin.

She turns to me. 'Lulu, will you run and get Tom and I some more biscuits?' she says.

I push past Tom, who barely acknowledges me, and he shoves the door closed behind me. I childishly kick it ajar again with my foot. He doesn't get to shut me out.

I snatch the driest, mealiest biscuits from the cupboard, which are so stale they are soggy. Muttering under my breath as I walk back up the corridor I slow down as I hear Dolly talking. It isn't my intention to eavesdrop, but I find myself tiptoeing closer to the door, which is still slightly ajar.

'You are a very handsome young man, Mr Harvey-Saint,' she says, in an unfamiliar tone. She sounds like a seventy-year-old schoolgirl.

'I've been very lucky,' he replies, a world away from modesty, and it makes me want to gag.

'We both have, darling. Let me show you some pictures of me, Tom, as a girl. We could have been quite a couple, you and I,' she tells him.

'Well!' I hear Tom laugh nervously. 'You are still a very beautiful woman, Dolly.'

A feeling of dread catches in my throat. The room is suddenly quiet, and I am poised with my hand on the doorknob, almost

312

certain that I should go in, when the sound of a teacup smashes suddenly on the floor.

'Jesus!' I hear Tom swear, 'I'm sorry, I'm sorry! Let me clear that up – I just, I wasn't expecting, I mean, I didn't mean for that . . .' I hear Tom blurting out his lines urgently.

'Just get out . . . get out,' she says quietly.

'I'm sorry, I didn't think of you and I like that . . .' Tom blusters.

'Get out!' Dolly screams.

I take a step backwards out in the hall, as the door flies open and Tom rushes out. He looks at me, appalled, and shoots off along the corridor at speed.

It's awful and embarrassing and I don't know what to do. I am frozen in the hallway as I hear Dolly quietly sobbing. I take a step forwards, with my hand on the doorknob as I hear her say, 'Pull yourself together, you old fool.' She coughs a couple of times, in quick succession, and I decide to go in.

I talk straight away. 'I found some biscuits, Dolly, but I passed Tom in the hall and he said he was late for the dresser so he had to run.'

'Yes, he had to run off,' she replies, shielding her eyes.

'Oh my goodness, I've got cleanser in your eyes and they've gone red. Let's get that mascara off now, shall we?' I say, practically shutting her eyes for her.

As I wipe the cotton wool across her eyes, she reaches up and squeezes my hand.

'So I'll let you know all about my date when I see you on Monday shall I?' I say. 'You never know, I might have an epiphany? It might be my route to happiness.'

'Well, darling,' she replies, composing herself, letting go of my hand, 'as long as you know that the most life has to offer is a series of joyful moments. That's it. You can't be permanently happy. Where was I when somebody was promising day-in, day-out happiness? Happiness isn't a constant, if you are lucky you glimpse it. Who told you girls you can have it all? Nobody ever got it all, not the men, not the women, not anybody. Not even the Caesars in their vast Roman palaces. Not even Cleopatra on the Nile. Nobody was ever always happy, except the idiots in the nuthouse. But if you glimpse it, just for a series of moments, then what more can you ask?'

'I suppose. But some days it does feels like, if I could just get it right, the balance, then maybe I could have a little of everything, if I could just focus a little harder . . .'

'Lulu, haven't you heard a word I've said? What more can I tell you than it's just about you! About doing something that makes you proud of yourself. About acting a certain way. About being honest. Not regretting whole years, whole segments of your life. About loving somebody as much as you can, as hard as you can, but then having the courage to move on when the time is right. People outgrow each other all the time, like sunflowers. Some people need more light than others. But know yourself, Lulu! That's all you can do.'

I carry Dolly's bag upstairs for her and pass it to Gavin as Tristan clinks a glass to make a speech.

'Loves,' he says, looking around the room. 'Get some rest tomorrow. Watch *Antiques Roadshow*, and I'll see you all on Monday.' He turns his back on them. It was his big moment and it's the least I have ever heard him say.

Dolly leans on bent-over Gavin, who carries her bag out to the car. Tristan wanders around on the stage, picking up the occasional prop and placing it lightly down again. He turns and faces the front of stage, as everybody disperses. He notices I am still there and smiles as he walks over.

'What are you doing tomorrow, Make-up?' he asks from the front of the stage, flicking imaginary specks off of his jacket, and addressing me in the first row of the stalls.

'I'm going to the zoo, with Ben,' I say, crossing my arms.

'Right.' He nods his head. 'Silence and tears,' he adds finally.

'Let me guess . . . Byron?' I ask.

'You got it,' he says.

'We'll see,' I reply. He flashes me a smile and walks off to the wings.

I spot Gavin loitering by the steps at the side of the stage.

'Hi Gavin, how are you?' I ask. It feels like ages since I have spoken to him properly.

He doesn't answer my question, but says instead, 'You're going to the zoo with your bloke tomorrow, then?'

'Yes, I am,' I say, nodding and smiling.

'London Zoo? Sounds ominous.' He shoves his hands into his jeans pockets and lowers his chin to his chest.

'Maybe . . .' I reply. 'I don't know yet. How was your dinner with Arabella?' I ask.

'Didn't happen. Decided not to go. Decided not to do that anymore.' Gavin stares at his feet.

'Oh,' I say.

'Well . . . be brave,' he says, and looks me in the eye for a moment, before wrenching his hands out of his pockets, turning and jogging up the steps by the stage three at a time.

'Why does everybody keep saying that to me?' I ask as he heads backstage.

He turns to face me. 'Because we can see you've got it in you.' Gavin exits stage left.

What do they know? I've got to get through tonight first.

Scene V: Rapunzel

I am no good at kissing strangers. I think too much about what they are thinking, care too much about what I'm doing, worry too much about my intentions. Kissing Ben, the first time, and even now, is a different experience to anybody I've ever kissed before. It was like we knew each other straight away. We didn't even have the same kissing technique: he was firmer, more of a pusher; I was slower and definitely softer. But it was like we knew each other anyway. With others, with strangers, I'm no good at kissing. I'm not reckless with abandon, wild and free and crazy. Unless I'm drunk. Then it's easy, but I don't remember it the next day. I just remember that it was easy.

Isabella breaks the ice by giving me my Steinbeck that she got on discount and refuses to take the money for now. She hails a black cab on Charing Cross Road and ushers me into it before her, gesturing with her handful of chipped nail varnish, as if we are on an old-fashioned date and I am the woman. She is all wide eyes and smiles, and control as well. In the cab she tells me, unprompted, that she is twenty-three.

I smile. 'You're a baby,' I say.

'How old are you?' she asks.

'Thirty-one,' I tell her with a shamed laugh, like nobody was ever this old before. Not giant tortoises, not Moses or any of his wives up on Sinai, nobody. I'm the human miracle, I'm ancient.

She raises her eyes and clicks her gum in her mouth. 'I thought you were, like, twenty-eight maybe. But Jennifer Aniston is thirty-seven,' she says with a smile. I think that is supposed to make everything better, heal the world. Jennifer Aniston is thirty-seven and looking good, and we can all sleep safe in our beds tonight.

'Well, I feel old,' I say, but it's a lie. I'm scared I look old, that's all. I still feel stupid and ridiculous and young.

'Hell, who gives a fuck about age. I don't. I don't care if somebody is fifteen or fifty, or, like, eighty. If I like them, I like them.' She thrusts her splayed fingers into her hair and shakes them. It is a little messier than it was a moment ago, and she seems satisfied.

'Okay, but be careful how much you like the fifteen-year-olds because they aren't even legal . . .' I reply.

'Yeah, but, you know, I knew what I was doing at fifteen, and I bet you did too. Fifteen-year-olds know, I don't care what anybody says. I knew. I had my first bra when I was, like, eleven. And did you know, in the Netherlands, or some-where like that, the sex age is, like, twelve or something? It's got nothing to do with the government or whatever. You're just ready when you're ready.'

'Well if it's legal in the Netherlands,' I say.

She is chewing pink gum with her mouth open, and a speck has stuck itself to the gloss on her lips. 'Besides, nobody even cares about, like, age any more, or any of it. I'm having surgery. I'm having Botox, everything. I'm already saving for it. I'll have my boobs done. I've saved three hundred pounds already. I had six hundred but then I went to Ibiza last summer. It was wicked, though, I'd definitely go again. You should go, you'd love it!'

I don't know how she knows that I haven't, or assumes I haven't at least. But it's true.

'I just have to, you know, save some more. But it's so hard!' She hits her forehead with her palm and screams like a little girl, and rubs it and laughs.

'Fuck,' she says, smiling, shaking her head. I don't know what that means.

'You'll care about getting older when you get older,' I say, 'whether you've saved for surgery or not.'

'I don't think so.' She shakes her head, but seriously now. I stare out at Oxford Street as we inch along, a bus to our right, a bus to our left, flanked by monster department stores and mobile-phone shops and stalls selling three brightly coloured pashminas for five pounds. It's like the red sea parting for our cab, with buses banked on both sides, and yet streams of people are still queuing at bus stops, cold and sad. A sea of disaffected faces staring in. Isabella keeps looking at me out of the corner of her eye, squinting, really.

'What?' I ask.

'I was just looking at your mascara: sorry! Was that annoying? Sorry! I just, I don't know how you get it to go, like, like that.' She flicks her fingers upwards by her eyelashes.

'I think it's just my eyelashes. They just go that way. But you could use curlers, if yours are too straight . . .'

'No, they're cool. Or maybe I will. It's cool.'

She touches my hand. She has this youth glossed over her, a sheen, like our lip-gloss – hers cheap, mine expensive. I don't know what I am doing. I am bored but I'm nervous. I think about Ben, at home maybe, thinking about the zoo maybe, worrying about me maybe, wondering where I am maybe. Or not. I am on a date with somebody else. Except it really doesn't feel that way. It doesn't feel like cheating, like it would if I were sitting here with Gavin, or Tom. I could call Ben right now and tell him I am in a cab with this girl and he wouldn't bat an eyelid.

Except maybe she doesn't think this is a date. Maybe we are just here to talk make-up and so I can give her free eyeliner. As if reading my mind, she says, 'I'm so glad you came. I thought you would, but I wasn't sure. But I thought you would.' She smiles at me and winks.

I smile back, but terrified.

She leans forwards, her breasts, her hair, her chipped nail varnish, her smudged eyeliner, her gloss with the chewing gum stuck to it, to kiss me.

I jump backwards in my seat so sharply that I smash my head on the window. I scream, 'Shit!'

'What the hell?' the cabbie asks, yanking open his dividing window.

'It's nothing, I just banged my head!' I say, rubbing it like crazy to dull the pain.

'You sure you're all right, love, there wasn't a bump in the road or anything,' he says.

Maybe not in yours, mate. Maybe not in yours.

'Are you okay?' Isabella asks, half worried, half smiling. She covers her mouth to pretend she isn't giggling.

'Yes. I'm sorry, that was stupid. I just . . . I just . . .'

'Okay, okay. Composure. Be calm, breathe.' She shakes my hand to loosen me up.

'I'm calm, I'm calm,' I say, rubbing my head.

'Okay, then, can I ask you something, like, personal?'

'Okay . . .' I say.

'Haven't you ever kissed a woman before?'

Immediately I think: shouldn't that be 'Have you ever kissed a woman before?' Because 'haven't' implies that everybody is doing it . . .

'No, sorry, I haven't.'

She stares at me, eyes white and wide in disbelief.

'What?' I ask.

'No. It's fine, you are a bit older, I guess.'

'What does that mean? Older than what?' I ask, incredulous.

'Nothing, I just . . . So you've only ever kissed, like, boys? Like, men?'

'Yes, why is that so hard to comprehend?'

'It's not. It is just . . . it's just a bit strange. I can't think of any of my friends, you know, who have only been with blokes . . . oh, hang on, maybe Charlotte. No, she was seeing Daisy for a while. Hang on . . . ' She sits and thinks.

'But I'm straight,' I say, as if that's explanation enough.

'Okay,' she replies, grimacing.

'Okay,' I say, ignoring it, nodding my head so that it's straight too.

'So why are you here with me? Oh my God!' She covers her mouth with her hand and her chipped nail-polished childish fingers. 'Did you think we were just, like, becoming friends?'

'No, I don't know what I thought. I just thought . . . that I wanted to come. And that you . . . you remind me of me a bit.'

'Oh my God! Well, at the very least you'll have snogged a woman by the end of tonight! I feel like a teacher!' she says, sitting up and doing a prim impersonation of Miss Jean Brodie, straightening her collar, brushing down her jeans. I noticed outside Grey's, when she sauntered out and said 'hello', that she is wearing baggy jeans that are so loose they are bunched around her crotch, giving the impression of a full set of working testes. And she has gone mad with the blusher again; she is disfigured by violent streaks of red scarred across both cheeks. It makes her look a little ridiculous, like a gargoyle, but she is still young enough to carry it off.

'Okay . . . maybe . . .' I say.

The cab turns left along Regent Street, and then right, travelling along the back of Selfridges. I wish we were going there instead, I feel lost. We pull up outside a Turkish restaurant, 'Levant'.

'I'll get this,' I say, and she jumps out with a grateful smile.

When I say thank you for my receipt, the cabbie gives me a wink and says, 'No, thank you!'

I turn to go in but Isabella grabs me by my hands, jumping up and down like she's just eaten too many blue Smarties.

'No, wait, wait, wait. One second. So, just so I'm clear, you've got a boyfriend then, right?'

'Yes,' I say, shrugging.

'Okay,' she replies, nodding wisely. 'Well, this should be interesting!' Sticking her fingers in her hair and messing it up again, she turns to go in.

'Okay, you hold on for one minute. So haven't you got a boyfriend?' I ask, confused. I just assumed that she would have.

'Not really. I was seeing this guy, Rupert, but he was, like, really possessive. He didn't want me seeing anybody else, or, you know, even kissing anybody else, and I'm just too young, you know, for that kind of commitment. And then he said we could still go out anyway, but then I said no. Because he would always be trying to control me, you know?'

'But you go out, I mean you date, boys and girls? I mean, men and women?'

'Yeah, of course.'

'So you're bisexual?' I ask.

She rolls her eyes dramatically and sighs. 'Oh God, I don't know. Who cares? I mean, who's asking, really? I'm like, whoever I like, then I like. Those kinds of boxes? They are, like, for other people. I don't think people do that any more . . .' she explains sagely.

321

'I am old!' I say. 'But let's go in anyway, before it's past my bedtime.'

'We're going to have so much fun!' Isabella says, clapping her hands and jumping up in the air.

I wince as her breasts jump as well, seemingly independent of the rest of her, bouncing violently towards her chin. I think she might knock herself out. We must be the same cup size and I would never jump like that, I'd be scared that I'd give myself two black eyes, or there would be an earthquake in China. But she doesn't care. She isn't a younger me at all. She is a thousand times less scared. I don't know if it's money, or breeding, or just the generation that separates us. It seems a lot happened in those years. Now it would appear that there are no boxes any more, and everybody is kissing everybody, and there is no such thing as straight or gay or bisexual, for girls at least. In London at least.

We sit on low sofas at our table in the bar, surrounded by cushions, sipping on house wine, and picking at vine leaves and rice things, and meatballs, and we find easy small-talk in *Vogue* and *InStyle*.

I am almost immediately hazy with the smoke, as pink clouds form and float behind my eyes – everything becomes a little woolly and confused, and I have to fight to focus. Purple and bruised sunken sofas, crumpled cushions covered in sequins. Swathes of muslin swing from the ceilings, and a belly-dancing woman, loaded with gold coins hanging from her clothing, flexes her breasts. She is actually flexing her breasts.

'So what's your boyfriend like?' Isabella asks, pouring us more red wine.

'He doesn't love me,' I say, almost casually now, I am so used to saying it.

'Shit. Men. You know, I am just, like, learning now, that they are, like, completely rubbish. They only love the ones that are mean to them, it's true! I bet you're just too nice. It's like Rupert only really liked me when I said I didn't want to see him any more. He, like, completely freaked out, and was all, like, "But I really like you, and we have great sex and we have this connection, blah blah blah." But it's all horseshit. My friend Jemmy – Jemima, but we all call her Jemmy – she is so utterly, like, foul to boys, and they all just queue up for her. And she isn't even that pretty although her arse is amazing. But she just acts like she isn't even interested and all these boys just, like, swarm over her, like she's honey or something. Are you gonna dump him?'

'Ben?' I ask, and two grains of sticky rice fall out of my mouth onto the table. 'Well, it's a bit more complicated than just "dumping" him.'

'Why?' Her eyes swell whenever she asks a question.

'It just is. You'll see, when you've lived with somebody, and your lives become . . . entwined. Somebody owns the computer, and the car, and, you know, the sofa . . .'

'Oh, like, just stuff?'

'Yes, but it's more than that . . .'

'Yeah, because that's just stuff. Like, it's not a life. It's just things.'

'Well it's more than that – you're used to having them around and – you'll understand soon enough.'

Isabella looks like she doesn't believe me.

'Okay, but when my mum and dad split up it was just because he said "Araminta, I've been seeing somebody else and I don't love you any more", and she said, "Okay, have you thought about this?", and he said, "Absolutely", and so she said, "Leave tonight", and he did. And they had, like, the house in Fulham, and the house in the Cotswolds, and the chalet in Courchevel, and Poppy – that's our mare – and, like, two cars and, you know, the business. And me and Jez and Minty and Georgie as well. But my mum still told him to leave because he didn't love her.'

'Okay. Well, that was very brave of her, but also, and no disrespect to your parents of course, but if you are that wealthy then you have a safety net and you don't have to worry about bills and things like that, and it's easier.'

'I don't think so. I mean my mum hadn't worked since she was a model, since she was eighteen, and she didn't even have, like, typing skills or anything. She couldn't even use Excel. And the business had taken some hits, and we certainly weren't loaded.'

'You have a mare,' I say, 'you're loaded.'

'Not any more. Mum had to sell her to pay for Minty's nose job.'

Isabella takes a slug of wine to numb the pain of her lost mare or her sister's plastic surgery, I am not sure which.

'So where is he tonight? Your boyfriend?' she asks me, forking up another meatball and forcing the whole thing into her mouth at once.

'I don't know.' I shake my head.

'God, you guys sound close.'

'I know it sounds bad . . . but . . .' I shrug and smile.

'Do you love him?'

'Yes, unfortunately.' I take a hit of red wine.

'You see, now that's the complicated part,' she says, chewing on meat, sucking the tomato sauce off her grubby fingers. 'But I don't think I could love somebody who didn't love me back.'

'Oh my God, of course you could. Of course you could!' I say.

'No, I mean, I couldn't stay with them. It would be too depressing. And it would make me all, like, needy, and wanting to talk to them about it all the time, you know? You know when women get like, all, why doesn't he love

324

me, blah, blah, cry, cry? How fucking depressing! I would hate that. Like, you know, a victim?'

I don't say anything, because I am nearly choking on the vine leaf in my mouth.

'You know what? Us being here, it, like, completely makes sense. I've seen you every time you've come in, I think. And I couldn't believe it when you said we should go out, because you are so glamorous. You are so beautiful.' She touches my face with a tomato-stained finger.

I wince.

'Don't you like me doing that?'

'I'm just not used to it,' I say, shrugging stiffly.

'You mean from girls?' she asks, doing it again. I force myself to keep my eyes open and not pull backwards.

'No, I mean, at all.'

'Doesn't your boyfriend tell you you're beautiful?'

'No. Although he did describe me as his Jag XK8 once.'

'Like, a car?'

'Not like a car. It is a car.'

'Why did he call you a car?'

'He was being nice. It's his favourite car. It's his dream car. He was being lovely.'

'Like, when rappers say that girls remind them of Jeeps, like that?'

'I don't know, Isabella, but I think he was being nice.'

'Why couldn't he just tell you you're beautiful?'

'You know what, he really was being nice. I can't attack him for that.'

'Okay, but I think you are expecting way too little. If that was the nicest thing that my boyfriend said to me, well. He wouldn't be my boyfriend.' She leans back and rubs her belly, bloating out her cheeks, without vanity.

'You're not scared, are you, Isabella. Of anything. Of being alone?' I say, staring at her. She's like a well of honesty.

'No. I like being on my own sometimes. Like, sometimes I just have to be, for a while, to even think.'

'But I mean of being alone permanently. Not getting married, not having kids.'

'No, I'm not scared of that. Why should I be?' she says, shaking her head.

'I'm just trying to remember how I was, eight years ago. No, I still think I wanted babies and marriage.'

'But why? Why them and not other stuff?' she asks, considering the rice and meat remnants on the plates in front of us, deciding whether any of it is worth eating. She prods things with her fork.

'Because that's what I want. What I thought most women wanted. Or I thought I wanted . . . Or . . .'

'Oh, okay, is that why you're with your bloke, when he calls you a car, because you're scared of being on your own?'

'He was being nice. The car thing, he really was being nice.'

'Well I think he should be able to say more than that. He's not, like, eighty. Is he?'

'No, he's not eighty.' I shake my head and sigh. Why does everybody keep asking me if he is ancient?

'You should definitely dump him. And you shouldn't worry, Scarlet, about being on your own, if you don't want to be. Look at you. You're beautiful.'

'I don't feel beautiful. I feel false, and made up, and unreal, and a fraud.'

'Well . . .' She moves a strand of hair away from my face, tucking it behind my ear. 'I think you are glorious,' she says.

'And I think you're lovely,' I say back, and smile.

She leans forwards to kiss me.

I throw myself backwards so violently that I fall into the lap of a guy on the next sofa. My head lands in his groin, and I find myself staring up at his chin. I am flailing in a

326

strange position, my stomach muscles too weak to hoist me back up. The guy inhales on his strawberry pipe deeply, exhales through his nose, and says, 'Either that's a woman in my lap or I can't take my hubbly bubbly!'

His table collapse into hysterics, and Isabella is in front of me, taking my hands, lifting me upright.

'I'm so sorry,' I say, to the guy and the table.

'It was my fault, sorry boys,' Isabella adds, winking at them all at once.

'Don't apologise, ladies, join us!' the pipe-smoker says. He pants at us excitedly like a golden retriever.

'A bit later, yeah?' she says, winking again.

I shrug and mouth 'sorry' one last time.

Isabella waits for me to sit back down. She looks sulky and pissed off.

'What?' I ask.

'Scarlet, you're going to have to, like, relax a bit.' She won't look me in the eye.

'I am relaxed, I just feel – it just feels weird for me!'

She turns to face me, and we are dangerously close. I have no personal space left. 'Well then maybe you don't want to do it!' she says, edging closer still.

'No, I do, I do, I do! Especially if everybody else is doing it! I need to make sure I'm not making some massive mistake. I just need to not be scared. Please bear with me,' I say, squeezing her hand.

'Okay then,' she replies, smiling at me, inching closer.

I feel myself go rigid, like somebody just sprayed me with dry ice. 'Okay, we're going to need more drinks, and some of that strawberry stuff,' I say, pointing at the hubbly bubbly pots. 'Waiter!'

An hour later and somehow Isabella and I have managed to assimilate with the table of guys sitting next to us. The red wine flows, and I feel myself getting higher and more drunk. The pipe gets passed around and everybody tries to blow puffs of smoke out of their nostrils. I keep saying to whoever will listen, 'I can't chase the pink dragon any more.'

The guy whose lap I fell into is called Howard. 'Are you twins?' he asks, studying me and then Isabella intently.

'Thank you, but I am about fifty years older than she is.'

'No you aren't, you aren't! You simply can't be! You're my age, surely. How old are you?'

'I'm thirty-one,' I say.

'Fucking hell!' Howard spits out the mouthful of wine he just took. 'I thought you were the same age as me! And how old are you?' he asks, leaning across me to address Isabella. 'No, don't tell me, you're fifty!'

'I'm twenty-three,' she says.

'Same age as me!' Howard replies, banging the table with the palm of his hand, then leaning back against the sofa. 'You look damn fine for a woman your age,' he says to me.

I smile at him. These boys are babies. Isabella is a baby.

'I'm going to leave now,' I whisper to her, grabbing my bag and standing up.

She looks alarmed and stands up as well. 'Don't go,' she says, but I am already edging myself out from behind the table.

I run quickly up the steps and open the door, breathing in the cool air. My head is full of pink clouds.

'Don't go,' she says again, following me and taking my hand, pulling me back against the wall. She turns me around, pressing me into the darkness, and kisses me. This time I kiss her back. It's soft, and strange. She smells nice. She feels small, and round, and fleshy. It feels equal, but not lustful. It feels like friendship, in a way. She almost feels familiar.

Her tongue moves in and out of my mouth slowly, and I do it back. I think of Ben quickly, and bet he wishes that he were here. But I don't want to tear her clothes off, or feel any particular part of her body. I put my hands on her back, but when she squeezes one of my breasts with her chipped nail-varnish fingers I'm not intrigued, and I don't grab the opportunity to do it back. Maybe I should, but I feel like I know how it will feel already.

As she kisses my neck and squeezes me, I realise that I am up against a wall, again, somewhere in W1 with somebody that isn't my boyfriend. This is no different to kissing Tom Harvey-Saint, up against a wall, somewhere in W1. I just keep cheating, and it makes me hate myself. I don't feel any better or different about doing it just because it's a girl. Kissing a man is just like kissing a woman, if you know you shouldn't be doing it. I feel suddenly, horribly ugly. Ben doesn't deserve this, and neither do I. Maybe I should have done this ten years ago, ticked it off my list then, or done more. Maybe I should have had the courage to be Isabella. But not now.

I push her away gently.

'Blimey. Do you want to come back to mine?' she asks, tracing her fingers in circles on my thigh.

I shake my head and screw up my nose, smiling. 'No, I don't think so,' I say.

'Too much too soon?' she asks with a laugh.

'No, just not right really,' I reply.

'But you haven't even got to the good bit yet!' She gives me a dirty smile and grabs at the fleshy part of my thigh.

I reach down and pull her hand out from underneath my dress. 'I love somebody else, though,' I say.

'Yeah, but this could just be, like, sex,' she insists, her smile fading a little.

'But I need to sort that out. And I need to sort my head out too. This is cheating, and I don't want to do that any more.'

'Even if he doesn't love you?' she asks, and I wonder if it is meant to sting.

'Even if. It's not just about him.'

'Okay, but we should still go out again,' she says.

'I don't know, Isabella. What with your gloss and my gloss, I don't think it is ever going to work. We'd be a sticky mess. But I do think that you are wonderful. Wonderful. But then you know that already.'

'Thanks.' She glances at the door of the restaurant. 'Are you gonna go now, then? Because if you don't want to come back to mine, I think I'm going to hang out with those guys – that Howard guy is a riot! He keeps body-popping, did you see him? And he says he dates women, for, like, a living! How does that work?' She smiles a huge and childish smile.

'I'm sure there is a very reasonable explanation. Are you going to be okay, I don't like leaving you here on your own.'

'I've been in much worse places than this. Can you still get me free make-up?'

'I'll drop some of the good gloss into Grey's,' I say.

She leans forwards and pecks me on the lips. 'I couldn't believe it when you said you'd come out with me, Scarlet. You're how I want to be, when I'm older.'

I say 'Thanks' and she smiles and sashays back into the bar.

Standing on a cold, bright London street, I feel strangely sober. Tonight, perhaps for the first time, I realise that one good thing about older is wiser. I don't need to make Isabella another one of my mistakes.

I flag down a black cab.

ACT III

The Show Must Go On!

Scene I: Zoo

Ben and I stand a couple of feet away from each other appraising a series of green wooden signs:

> *Meet the Monkeys – Walk Through: 2 p.m.*
> *Peckish Penguins!: 11 p.m. and 3 p.m.*
> *Lively Spiders!: 1 p.m.*
> *Discover Reptiles: 11.15 a.m.*

Ben has his hands stuffed into the pockets of his jeans. He got hot on the tube and peeled off his sweatshirt and tied it around his waist, to reveal a T-shirt that reads, 'No I *don't want F*cking Fries with that!*' in yellow, on red. It has an asterisk where the 'U' in fucking should be. It seems to me that if you are going to wear that kind of T-shirt you shouldn't be afraid to spell 'fucking' correctly . . .

'Where do you want to go?' he asks, eyeing up the map on the pamphlet in his hand. He looks uncomfortable. I look up. The sky is overcast and it is threatening to rain and I have worn open-toed brown sandals to London Zoo. Both of my big toes are grubby already. I am wearing wide-legged jeans that are rolled up around my ankles, and a yellow T-shirt and a black V-neck jumper over it. My hair is pulled back in a low, loose ponytail and I'm wearing diamond specks in my ears, and a pink clear bangle around my wrist.

'I'm not sure really,' I say, reading the signs again for inspiration. Where would be a good place to talk and relax? I ask myself. 'Not the reptiles,' I tell him.

'We could just wander,' he says, aimlessly.

'Why don't we follow the arrow?' I suggest, pointing at the green line of paint on the concrete below us.

Ben reads his map aloud: 'Follow the green arrow and it will lead you all around the zoo, showing you the direction you are supposed to be moving in.'

'Where's that been hiding my whole life?' I say to myself.

'Tell me about it – we could have done with it at the tube station!' Ben adds. I made us walk five hundred yards in the wrong direction from Baker Street before conceding that we were heading the wrong way.

'Then that's sorted.' I ignore him. 'Let's go this way.'

The zoo is one giant packed lunch. Kids scream and roll towards and around my feet like footballs that I try to dodge and not fall over. We walk through a tunnel with replica caveman prints on the walls but none of the children are paying much attention, preferring instead to see who can shout the loudest and make the biggest echo.

We come out of the other side and see more signs. 'When do you ever get anywhere?' Ben asks, irritated.

And I think, look who's talking, but of course I don't say it.

'Shall we do the woodland walk? Or the giraffes?' he asks, following both arrows with his eyes but seeing nothing of any interest, just more bends in the pathways.

'Oh, let's just go where we go. Let's go and see the giraffes. I've never seen one before,' I say.

We walk up an incline, Ben holding his map, and me with my arms crossed against the cold, and in doing so we avoid holding hands like every other couple visiting London Zoo today. As we reach the door to the giraffe house the smell hits me like an evil wall of damp, warped straw-stench!

'Mother of God!' I exclaim, thrusting my hand under my nose to smell my moisturiser instead.

'They are animals, Scarlet,' Ben says, and strides in, so I hold my breath and follow. I catch up with him while he is reading a sign about somebody called Sir Harry Johnston who discovered the horse/zebra creature standing behind bars in front of us, when Sir Johnston helped save some kidnapped Pygmies.

Ben carries on reading the sign and I look at the horse/zebra, who is picking at hay. I can't get over the cages, how small they seem for fully grown animals that are supposed to run and graze and splash about in watering holes.

'They look so hemmed in,' I say quietly.

'It's a zoo, Scarlet, what did you expect? They don't know any better.'

'They just look really claustrophobic. Can you imagine feeling that trapped and isolated?' I ask, and then wish I hadn't when Ben turns and gives me a strange look, as if I had said something completely different.

'Is that how you feel, Ben?' I ask, suddenly brave enough for me and the poor horse/zebra.

'What?' he asks, irritated.

'Do I cage you in?' I persist, standing in front of him, looking up at him, waiting for him to look back.

He sighs.

'Do I?' I ask.

'Oh God, Scarlet, I don't know, maybe?' he replies.

A row of children dash through the door, piling into us with a scream, and shouting 'Hello!' at the poor horse/zebra, who turns away from the din. 'Turn around,' they scream at it, banging on the railings, but it refuses and I am glad.

Ben walks off and I follow.

There are two giraffes standing further down in their own enclosure. They are huge, much bigger than I was expecting. I watch them as they move around their space together, leaning on each other's neck with obvious affection, and stroking each other. When they do this there is an audible 'ah' from the crowd, and people whip our their mobile phones, holding them aloft, snapping away. Then everyone looks back down for five minutes as they send their various text messages, and the giraffes turn away, ignored.

'They are definitely a couple,' I say, 'they are obviously in love.'

Ben has found another sign to read, and shouts over his shoulder at me, 'Only if they're lesbians. They are two girls: Crackers and Dawn. Been together years, they are both twenty-seven, retired, and they've had nine kids between them.'

'Goodness,' I exclaim, looking back at them. They certainly seem close.

'It's still love,' I tell him as he sits down on a bench and leans back against the wall. I sit next to him and watch Dawn and Crackers stroking each other's neck with the brush of hair on their backs.

'It's like you and Helen,' Ben says with a sneer.

'Or you and Iggy, and the good-looking one is Iggy,' I say. We smirk at each other.

Ben reaches behind him and pulls a leaflet off the wall and casts his eye over it. 'Do you want this? It's about adopting an animal. It would be sweet for your nephews, maybe?' He offers it to me as we stand up.

'Yes, actually. Thank you.'

He shrugs and smiles.

As we wander back along the path, following the green

arrow, I feel my nerve slipping away. There is noise all around us but we are in silence as it starts to spit rain.

'Insect house?' he asks, looking for cover.

'I suppose!' I say, and we run in as the rain turns dramatically to hail and a thousand others follow us inside.

We inch through the noise and cramped space, past windows that apparently hold different types of beetle. German tourists depressed by the hailstones have their faces pressed up against the glass walls on the inside, steaming it up as they look out at the puddles forming on the paving stones.

'What if it wipes away the green arrow?' I ask, mildly alarmed.

'I think they've probably thought of that, Scarlet, I imagine it's waterproof.'

'Of course,' I say. I only ever seem to say the really stupid things when Ben is around. I wonder if I do it subconsciously – I KNOW they wouldn't have painted the arrow on the ground in, say, watercolour, but something makes me blurt out the beginnings of a strange scenario in my head, where the arrow suddenly disappears and the hoards emerge from the insect house and a riot breaks out at London Zoo because nobody knows where they are supposed to go next. I never share the full fanciful story with Ben, just the starting point that, on its own, makes me simply sound like an idiot. At the same time it makes him sound like the adult, the grown-up, the protector. I wonder if I do it because I love him, and I want him to feel important.

Ben and I are squashed violently together by a crowd surge in front of a pane of glass that shields a whole room of twigs and branches, big enough for a man to stand in because there is one, in what looks like a beekeeper's outfit. A cricket makes its way up the glass in front of my nose.

The man is holding something behind his back. He looks

337

over at us all in front of him, and then pulls the sign out and holds it in front of his chest.

In black writing on a yellow board it reads, 'I love you. Will you marry me?!'

The crowd gasps. I stare at it numbly, and then look up at Ben, confused.

But he is just staring straight ahead at the man with the sign, aghast.

I feel all the faces around us turn west, and I turn with them.

Next to me is a young guy, and he's down on one knee. A brunette with steamed-up glasses is looking from him to the insect house, and back to him, pointing, her mouth fallen open and tears streaming down her cheeks. The girl nods and says in a voice thick with laughter and tears, 'I will, I will, I will!'

The young guy jumps up and pushes a ring onto her finger, and they kiss passionately, right next to us.

There is a huge cheer from the assembled crowd, from everybody but Ben and I.

The hailstones stop suddenly, and sunshine bursts through the glass walls from outside, momentarily blinding the German schoolchildren with their noses pressed up against it.

'Reptile house?' Ben says to me.

I follow him out.

The air is cool and warm, and my grubby toes get soaked by rain puddles. We reach the reptile house and I spot a big picture of a snake, and shiver.

'Ben, I don't want to go in there, you know I'm scared of snakes. How about the tigers instead?'

'But this will be the best bit!' he says.

'You can go in it later, and I'll sit outside,' I suggest.

He turns to face it longingly, and then looks back at me.

'Can we please just go and see the tigers?' I ask, feeling my courage return. I need to start the conversation now, or perhaps never.

Ben nods and follows me down the path, and I feel myself start to shake.

'They keep yawning,' Ben says, as we stare at two tigers ambling about behind the glass looking like they've been given tranquiliser shots.

'They look really bored.' He consults his array of pamphlets hoping that one of them will be able to tell him why the tigers are so lethargic.

'Poor things, I hope they were born in captivity, and this is all they have ever known,' I say.

'Why?' Ben asks, not looking up.

'So they don't know what they are missing out on,' I answer, but think again. I bet they still know that something isn't right even if they were born in a glass box, and even if this is the only experience of life they've ever known. They must have a sneaking suspicion, at least, that there is something else out there.

Ben and I stand and watch them in silence.

I could just say it – 'We should break up' – but I can't get the words out.

A couple our age with a baby move and stand next to us. The dad is holding the little girl, who is wearing an all-in-one snowsuit and looks about eighteen months old.

'How does a tiger go?' the daddy asks her.

'Grrrr,' she says. The mum looks on, holding the pram upright, loaded down as it is with bags of baby wipes and juice cartons.

'But how does a crocodile go?' the daddy asks her.

'Snap!' she screams, clapping her hands together.

'And what does the crocodile eat for lunch, Megan?' he asks her, widening his eyes.

'Megan!' She screams and laughs.

Ben and I are both laughing as well, and the dad gives us a smile. It makes me feel self-conscious and I look at Ben. We catch each other's eye and the laughing stops. Ben ambles away.

'The penguin pool was designed by the Russian émigré Berthold Lubetkin in 1934. He also designed Highpoint apartment building in Highgate, one of the highest points in greater London,' Ben says. 'Its brand of modernism was unusually elegant and playful at the time, and is a reminder of how innovative the style must have looked when it first appeared.'

We sit opposite the penguin house on a bench. The penguins all follow each other around the pool, sliding up and down interlocking ramps.

'You see, I want that,' I say to Ben.

'A penguin?' he asks, confused.

'No. Megan. "*What does a crocodile eat?*" At least, I want that to be an option,' I say, but staring straight ahead because I can't look at him. My hands shake and my mouth dries up. Ben leans forwards and rests his elbows on his knees, holding his head in his hands.

After half a minute's silence, he says, 'What do you want me to say, Scarlet?'

'What you feel,' I reply.

'I don't know . . . I just . . . I don't know.' He shakes his head.

I gulp, and he hears it and looks up.

'Do you love me?' I ask.

He stares at me sadly. 'No.'

'Why are you ignoring that?'

'I don't know . . .'

'Why did you move in with me?'

340

'Because . . . you asked, and I thought you'd get angry if I didn't.' He talks to his open palms in front of him.

'Oh for God's sake, Ben! Is that all I deserve? Are we that far from honesty? Don't you know what I went through just to be with you? Don't you know how hard it was for me, watching you miss her?' I lower my voice as an elderly couple walk past and give me a disapproving look.

Ben doesn't respond.

'So you definitely don't love me,' I continue masochistically.

'Yes, I mean no, I mean: I can't say that about you, Scarlet.'

'Do you even know what love is? I mean, if you loved Katie, why did you leave her?'

'I don't know.'

I stare at one crazy penguin, out on its own, sliding up and down a ramp on its belly, squawking penguin giggles.

'Then what else can I do?' I ask him.

I see him nod his head slowly.

A bullet of fear fires in my stomach. Jumping up violently I exclaim, 'Are you hungry? Let's get pie and mash, you love that kind of food, come on, there's a pie shop over there.'

I trip towards it, turning around to make sure he follows me, and he pushes himself slowly to his feet and walks heavily my way. I order us two chicken and mushroom pies and mash, and he pays. I say thank you. We sit back down now, opposite pelicans. I glance down at my pie and wonder if I'll even be able to stomach a mouthful. Ben's is already half gone. Temporary distraction passed, I feel terrible again.

'Do you think you've been fair?' I ask him.

'Maybe not,' he says, shaking his head.

'Maybe? Maybe?' An angry heat shoots up my windpipe like a volcano rushing to explode, but he looks away, and for some reason, I don't know why, I bite my tongue. I'm not going to get any answers. He has never offered them

before, and he won't volunteer them today. He doesn't seem
to think the last three years of my life deserves explanation,
and it doesn't matter how hard I press him, those answers
won't come.

'So, this is it then?' he asks me quietly. 'No screaming
argument in the street? No smashed plates?' He smiles
ruefully.

'Ben, this isn't a soap opera, this is real.' My hands are
shaking and I throw my plate full of pie down on the bench.
'I'm going to go,' I say.

'Back to the flat?' he asks.

'Yes. Will you be able to stay at Iggy's tonight?' I ask.

'Of course. I'll come and get a bag later.'

'Okay. Then we'll sort out stuff from there. I'll find somewhere else. It's your flat really, not mine.'

He nods his head.

'Okay, then.' I turn away as my lips crumble and I hold
my breath to stop myself crying, and swipe at my eyes. 'You
don't have anything else to say, do you?' I ask as brightly as
I can, giving him one final chance.

He shakes his head and looks away.

'Okay,' I say. 'Bye.'

I feel myself walking away. My feet are shaking in my
sandals, and my hands are trembling and the tears are
streaming down my cheeks. I see a wooden sign that says
exit and I follow the green arrow on the pavement through
a dark, thin deserted tunnel and out the other side, but everything looks unfamiliar, and not at all like it did when we
came in. I look down at my feet and I can't see the arrow
on the floor any more. I am on my own. I glance behind me
and I can just make out Ben, still sitting on the bench in the
distance, his head back and angled towards the sun. I think
about going back. But then I spot a small green exit sign,
practically camouflaged, and a grey turnstile tucked away in

the corner. As there is nobody around I muck about with it for a minute feeling useless and trying to get it to open, the tears still streaking down my face, until I eventually push the right way, and finally, finally, I burst out onto the main road. I see a lit cab and hail it straight away, and say, 'Ealing please.'

I am curled up on the sofa in my dressing gown, with wet hair and no make-up, and with the TV on although I'm not watching it, when I hear the key in the door.

'Hey,' Ben says in the living-room doorway.

I turn to face him but don't say anything. He shudders at the redness of my eyes.

'I'll just get some stuff, throw it in a bag, and go to Iggy's.'

I hear him grabbing things in the bedroom and I pad through behind him, and lean in the doorway with my arms folded.

'Can't you stay for tonight?' I ask quietly.

'No,' he says, sitting on the side of the bed.

'Why not?' I ask.

'Because I know how this goes, Scar. I've been here before. You'll hate me being here tomorrow morning.'

And I think, no, you haven't been here before. Not with me.

Scene II: Like Steak

Monday. The flat feels peculiarly empty as I move down the hallway and into the kitchen, and yet it is always this quiet, this still, when I get up in the mornings. Ben has generally left for work, but he has never left for good before.

I pour too much Alpen clumsily into a bowl, and push it around with a spoon until it is sludge. I force myself to swallow two mouthfuls before I start to retch. I sit it on the table and pad through to the bathroom calmly, throw up the toilet seat and stick my fingers down my throat. Nothing comes. I tickle my tonsils cruelly, and one mouthful of Muesli quickly chases the other up my throat and into the toilet bowl. I gag three more times, and my stomach manages to coax up the glass of water I had twenty minutes ago. The tears stream down my cheeks silently at the heaving, painful exhaustion. I brush the hair away from my face and splash cold water on my cheeks, surveying the damage in the mirror above the sink. I feel like calling Ben, but of course I can't, despite the fact that even an argument would feel good at this moment, and its familiarity would be comforting. Arguing with Ben would mean I am still half of something. Standing in my quiet flat on cold bathroom tiles in bare feet, shivering in my knickers and vest, I feel stark and exposed and horribly lonely.

I manage to make myself up as usual, I am a professional after all. I collapse into unprompted tears four times in the hour it takes me to get ready. I take the decision, mascara wand in hand, to be realistic about the prospect of streaming eyes throughout the day, and apply one slight streak of black to each set of lashes.

I call Helen on the way to the station.

'Hello,' I say.

'Hey,' Helen replies.

'How is Jamie?' I ask, before she can say anything else.

'Yeah, he's okay. I saw him. He called me and asked me to go around to his mother's house: Christ, Scarlet, when she opened the door I knew she would have punched me if she could have gotten away with it. And he's got Everton posters up on his wall! Doesn't Ben support Everton?'

'Yep,' is all I say. I can't bring myself to admit anything about the zoo to Helen yet. The words aren't even stuck in my throat, I haven't even assembled them into a sentence in my head that I could say out loud and which wouldn't crumble halfway through the telling.

'So I sat on his Everton duvet on his single bed and he showed me his scars – the cuts weren't too deep although he'll need some physiotherapy, because he severed the nerve that runs to one of his fingers or something. But that's NHS, so that's okay. And he wants to start up again, Scar . . . He told me that he loves me and he thinks that I need him, and he doesn't expect anything from me and that we should just have sex and see . . .' Helen's voice trails off.

'What about Nikki with an "i"? And Steven?' I ask.

'I think she's off the scene. He told me she was and I think I believe him. I saw Steven last night, he came around for dinner. We've just got such a history, Scar, I don't think I'm

345

ready to give that up yet, and then of course he ended up staying, and even though we didn't do anything, really, he was still there, this morning, for coffee and toast . . . I don't think I am ready to not have him there for toast, Scar, I don't think I choose that.'

At least Ben and I never got up at the same time. The only ritual we will miss is the *Evening Standard* on the kitchen table. He'll just have to buy it himself instead. Our breaking up will at the very least cost Ben forty pence a day.

'Okay, but Helen, you sound a little confused, and fair enough, but think before you do anything else, with either of them, because you can't do both, not now, after what's happened. You know that, right?'

'Maybe . . .' she says.

'No, you can't! Somebody has to ring the bell and say that you have all lost! Helen, you can't just drift with this stuff, it's too important. You owe it to all of you, even cheating Steven, to make up your mind. Look how easily people get hurt! Look how much it hurts them! Jamie tried to kill himself, for Christ's sake!'

'But that was just poetry, you said that,' Helen argues, sounding a lot like a smoker who is about to watch her last pack of cigarettes get thrown in the shredder.

'Yes, but he still did it. It's bad luck, you got a beautiful seventeen-year-old poet more interested in sonnets than shoplifting, but that is still your bad luck, and how he feels is still, partially at least, your responsibility, if you are going to carry on doing what you are doing, Helen. You can't just say "Not my problem", can you? Everybody's heart is our responsibility, the minute we say hello to them! It's not just about how you feel, Helen. And it's not just about how pretty he is, and how flattering that is! You need to leave Jamie alone. He's just a kid, and he's too young to be learning half of what he'll learn if you do it to him again. He's told you as much himself!'

'I know! But Christ, Scarlet. He is so pretty!'

'Pretty isn't enough,' I say.

'Are you okay?' Helen asks after ten seconds of silence. 'You sound tired, and a bit weird, a bit spaced out or something.'

'I'm okay, I'm . . . I'm okay.' And still, I can't say it. 'I'll call you later, Hel,' I finish, hanging up the phone.

I check my watch as the tube rushes into Tottenham Court Road station, which was my intended stop, but it's barely nine fifteen. I don't stand up and relinquish my seat to the hovering hordes. The doors zip open and closed like a transparent sandwich bag, locking me in, so I stay where I am and ride the train a few more stops to the city.

The glass has already been replaced in the bus stop, and scrawled on as well, in fresh black ink. Cassie and Kylie were here, apparently, and Cassie loves Johnny, and Kylie loves Christian, and they both hate somebody called Julie 'the pig' Sergeant.

I sit outside Katie's office again, but I'm too late to see workers filing one after the other through swing doors that revolve importantly and at speed. City people start work at strange and ungodly hours. They can probably watch breakfast TV at their desks. Some of them even finish work in the afternoon, at four or five o'clock. They must all have hobbies, or go to the gym a lot. Otherwise what would you do with that amount of time?

I'm not even thinking about Katie, particularly, as I sit here at the bus stop. I am profoundly aware of a sense of my own relief. Two large sacks of guilt have been lifted from each of my shoulders, as if Ben had slipped rocks into my jacket where shoulder pads should be, and they've just disintegrated into dust. He can go back to her now if he wants to, and nobody will hate him for it – not his friends, not his mother, not me. My stomach lurches, and I feel sick, but I'm not in the way any more. Maybe they were meant to be together and I just ruined everything, like a fly, in high heels, in their ointment? If I wasn't so numb I might shake so violently I'd sprain joints.

Instead of focusing on the traffic as it coughs and wheezes past me, I picture Ben. He is bound to be at work. He won't have taken the day off, calling in with a sad tremble in his voice, professing 'personal problems'. I wonder where he is, exactly, now, at this very second? At the till perhaps, or in the warehouse, or standing in front of a Widescreen TV laughing at *Dude, Where's My Car?* . . . again. I can't phone and find out. It makes me feel like I've been demoted, from top security clearance to 'need to know' information only. Maybe Ben is already thinking about somebody else. Even the idea that he might be picturing somebody other than me, with a knot of excitement in his belly, is like an ulcer in mine. It feels like a bloated sulphur sickness that reeks and swells and rushes foul air up my windpipe and threatens uncontrollable meltdown. I can't even let myself think about it, for one second more, and instead I find myself dreaming him dead. It surprises me that it's less painful to think of him that way than to think of him falling in love with somebody else. But that is what I will have to do for now, for today at least, and cross my fingers that by some nasty twist of fate a truck doesn't veer off the Broadway and smash up Dixons and everybody in it, making me feel like I jinxed him. You have to stay alive today, Ben, while I think of you dead. It's one last favour, please. I think maybe that's how I can be so sure that whatever love I had has turned bad. Some people say if you love somebody you just want them to be happy, with or without you, but I don't feel like that about Ben. I can only think of him loving me today, or his version of loving me at least; the kind where he didn't quite say it and didn't quite do it. Anything else burns – and yet, as much as I know that it will hurt when tomorrow or next week or next year I decide I am ready to confront the possibility that he will have told somebody else that he does, perhaps, love them, I still know that nothing will ever hurt me like the denial I have been drowning in this last while. As painful as facing up to future possibilities might be, I am still over the worst of it. And I hope that in time I will be able to deal with all of the rage that is building up inside me for him, swelling like blood behind a clot. I hope that it will disperse itself eventually, naturally, without any need for anaesthetic or surgery. I hope I hope I hope. That's got to be a good sign . . .

I sit outside Katie's office for an hour, looking up at the building's windows and wondering which one is hers. I can see small figures moving about behind them, but I couldn't tell you if one of them was my own mother, the distance is too great. I wonder if Katie was the first person Ben called, to tell her we were finally through. I haven't learnt this much about anything since I crammed for my exams. Feelings should be policed. I'll never be naïve again. Like your virginity, once it's gone, it's gone. The major difference, of course, between then and now, is that I aced my GCSEs.

A sheet of the *Standard* crunches along the pavement and sticks itself to my leg as I try to kick it off. The wind is wrapping it around my calf and I shake myself wildly rather than just lean down and rip it away. I can tell by the layout that it is the review section. Tonight is the first night of previews for the play. It doesn't feel like anything to do with me now. The cast and crew seem to have melted away in the last twelve hours, unimportant and unrelated to my life and what's happening in it, and yet without them I know I wouldn't be sitting here, feeling lost. These ridiculous theatre people, all bursting with emotion and strange passion, demanding I confront my fears and my failings and my dead-on-arrival relationship. Maybe if I had taken the Andrex job I had been offered last week instead – two days on a set in St Albans with a mum and a little boy and seven puppies – I'd be going home to Ben again tonight? In fact I think that I know I would. But this was my fifth choice, my fifth road and choice and path out of lucky seven, and this time I took it. I don't know what made me so brave yesterday. I don't know if I'll be that brave again, if choices six and seven present themselves so obviously.

It's grey today, and cold. I shiver in the bus stop as an old lady with black and grey steel-wool hair and skin the colour and consistency of the best dark chocolate sits down heavily next to me and gets out a clump of orange knitting.

The needles begin to click quickly and don't pause for respite. She isn't even watching her fingers. She stares across the road, just as I do. Perhaps her ex-boyfriend's ex-wife works in that building too, and she has been sitting here for forty years, wondering when the right time would be to go and apologise to somebody who demands no apology? Perhaps she is knitting a huge banner, in orange, that she will drape across the main road when she is finished so that everybody knows that she is sorry too. I am struck with an electric shock of clarity at the absurdity of my situation, like sparks flying from her knitting needles and burying themselves arrow-like into my goose-pimpled skin.

I sit up straight, roll back my shoulders, and address the building in front of me.

'I'm sorry,' I say.

The needles pause. 'It's no problem,' the old lady says. And then begins clicking again.

I walk back to the station.

I barely recognise the theatre as I walk up the aisle at ten fifteen. There are no discarded Starbucks cups or holders or brown bags or muffin wrappers or juice bottles. The stage has been swept, and polished as well I think. The aisles are clean. The rocks and the villa and the swathe of the ocean are lit by a bright white and pink glow. I spot Gavin and the electrician at the side of the stage sorting through wires. One of the runners polishes a mirror like it's a Gestapo death-squad demand – any streaks and you die! – while another remakes the large bed that sits on the left-hand side of the stage, plumping up feather cushions to bursting point.

Tristan is talking earnestly at his assistant while listing things on his fingers, as the boy makes notes on an A4 pad. Tristan isn't wearing his funeral hat today, or his Jackie Onassis sunglasses, or his pink beads, or his Romford Market kimono. He is wearing a white shirt, a black tie, and a dark grey suit. He looks like Sammy Davis Junior's cousin, just flown in from Mumbai.

Everybody looks like they mean business today.

I slip up the stairs at the side of the stage and go quietly down the corridor to Dolly's room, and nobody notices. I feel partially invisible, as if some of me has been scrubbed out, albeit temporarily, although the exact length of time is yet to be determined.

Dolly hasn't arrived yet, as I expected. My stomach grumbles loudly in the quiet of her room. I place my box on the table and walk to the kitchen to make a slice of toast, determined to keep it down.

Passing the toilet I hear somebody being violently sick on the other side of the door. It sounds loud and serious and uncontrollable. If I hadn't already thrown up the food in my stomach this morning the noise itself would make me sick again too. I knock on the door timidly.

'Are you okay?' I ask, but whoever it is retches again in reply. 'Okay, well, I'll be in the kitchen if you need anything,' I tell them, and run away.

I find bread for toast, but can't stomach it, so I pour myself a cup of hot water and head back. The door to the bathroom flies open as I am about to pass, flooding the corridor with the stench of fresh vomit. It reminds me that I have smelt it here a few times already. I have to throw my hand violently over my mouth and nose and breathe in the moisturiser on my hands deeply to stop my eyes from watering.

Tom Harvey-Saint adjusts his shirt and walks out of the bathroom. Cue gasps from his horrified teenage fan club. His eyes are red and swollen, and he looks pale like runny egg-white.

'Tom, are you okay?' I ask, alarmed.

'Of course I'm okay. It's just some bad prawns,' he says, straightening his cuffs and tucking his shirt in to the tops of his trousers, over the flat board of his stomach.

'Okay,' I say, and a penny drops as he walks off. It's not just the girls who are on show these days . . .

A waft of lavender swarms over me as I reach the dressing-room door, and I know that Dolly has arrived.

She is already sitting in her chair, shaking quietly. A pile of cards lay unopened in her lap, and two fresh bunches of orange and pink roses have appeared in vases on the counter.

Her eyes look red and puffy as well. A single card sits in front of the flowers. It has a glossy photo of two young children on the front, a boy and a girl, and their mother in the middle, trying to keep them all together for a hug while the kids squirm and laugh for the camera. The woman looks like Dolly.

'My daughter, Lulu,' she says, nodding at the card.

I pick it up and study the photo. She is haughty, and beautiful. I place it back down on the counter.

'No, read it, Lulu. You can read it.'

'Okay,' I say, and pick it up again, flicking it open.

It says,

Good Luck, Mum. Sorry we can't be there.
Chloe, Dan, Danny and Charlotte x

'Well that's nice,' I say, placing it back down on the side.

'I thought they might still come,' she replies, and coughs.

There is a rap on the door, and she whispers, 'Come in.'

One of Gavin's runners pokes his head around the door-frame. 'Sorry, more flowers,' he says, carrying two more vases full of black roses.

'Never apologise for roses, just put them over there.' Dolly gestures to the corner.

The boy backs out and closes the door behind him.

'When do you want to start today?' I ask her. 'I mean, I don't even know how this works – if the performance starts at seven thirty, do you need time on your own beforehand?'

She looks up at me sadly. 'Of course, none of them think I'll go on, Lulu.'

'Oh.' I place the blusher brush that I have been playing with back down on the side. 'Do you think you will?' I ask.

'I will. Of course I will! I have never been afraid of anything. I'm not going to start now.'

'It's probably okay, though, if you are a bit afraid, Dolly,' I say, and shrug.

She shakes her head, biting trembling lips closed. 'Why are you so sad?' she asks, glancing up and noticing the tears in my eyes.

'Ben moved out last night. I ended it, yesterday. In front of a paddling pool of penguins at London Zoo. Well, that's not strictly true. I didn't end it. I asked him if he loved me and he just said "No". So, what else could I do?'

I shrug and try not to cry.

'Nothing else, Lulu. You could do nothing else. And how do you feel now?'

'Terrified,' I say with a laugh, tears streaming down my

face. She reaches out and takes one of my hands. We are both shaking.

'The terror will pass, Lulu. But the strength remains.'

I nod my head. 'But I feel like I failed,' I say, my lip crumbling.

'Do you love him?' she asks sternly, her eyes red too.

'Yes,' I reply, pressing my lips together to control myself.

'Well then, you didn't fail. Do you hear me, Lulu? You must never see loving somebody as a failure. Not loving somebody: now that's entirely different. Now put Ella on and let's make me look beautiful! Ha!'

Ella sings 'Someone to Watch Over Me' while I dust her with make-up and blot both her eyes and mine every now and then. I chuck twelve tissues away in total.

'Well, I have a cast talk to attend,' Dolly says, pushing herself to her feet. 'You stay here, Lulu, you don't need to go outside today. It's cold!'

Twenty minutes later I take my third gulp from Dolly's hipflask and shudder violently. I look at my phone. I shouldn't call him. Everybody always says, 'Don't call them, let them miss you, leave them alone to realise their mistake,' blah, blah, blah. But they don't know me, and they don't know Ben. And they don't know Dutch courage until they've tasted whatever it is in Dolly's hipflask.

I hit Ben's number in my phone.

'What if I took it all back?' I say, as soon as he answers.

Silence, and then, 'We can't, Scarlet, can we? It's done now.'

I think he sounds relieved. Then he says, 'Don't be sad, Scar, we had a great three years.'

If he were here I'd slap him. It occurs to me like a bucket of water thrown in my face that he may be oblivious to the pain that he has caused. He just doesn't feel it, and it enables him to say things like that. I want to scream, 'But I feel ruined! Like a goddamn overcooked steak!' And I want to say, 'No, we didn't have three great years. I am exhausted! And I'm damaged! And it was a waste of my time!'

But I don't say it, and I don't even know why. Maybe because I feel like I'm a little drunk, and maybe because I don't want to hurt him, even now, when I really think that he deserves to know. He'll be happy soon enough, whether I tell him or not: he left us a long time ago.

'I'm scared,' is what I say instead.

'I'm sorry,' he answers, but he doesn't sound it.

'God, Ben,' I whisper, I can't shout any more, 'you just sound so . . . so ambivalent about the whole thing . . .'

He raises his voice. 'I'm not ambivalent, Scarlet, but we've broken up.'

'Don't say it like that, it was only last night! Don't say it like it's been months and it's a done deal!' I say, raising mine too.

'But it is a done deal,' he replies, exasperated again.

Silence.

'You took the first get-out I ever gave you, didn't you? But you never did it yourself . . .' And now it's Ben's turn to fall silent on the other end of the phone.

I sit in his silence for twenty seconds before he says, 'Well . . .'

Maybe it's the last thing I'll ever hear him say.

'Fine. It's done,' I snap, and hang up.

Scene III: The Half

'It's the half, Dolly, what do you want to do?'

Dolly stares at herself in the mirror without acknowledging Tristan, who jumps once on the spot in the doorway and squeezes his eyes shut. I lean against the back wall and watch the scene nervously. Tristan is standing in front of Gavin, who fills the doorway completely. Like Little and Large, Gavin towers head and shoulders above Tristan, even when Tristan jumps. Gavin looks down at Tristan's crown, once, alarmed.

'She is driving me crazy, crazy! Edelweiss, edelweiss, edelweiss . . .' Tristan whispers, tapping his cheeks with his fingers.

Dolly's eyes, reflected in the mirror, cannon across the room to address him, as she growls, 'Get out! Get out! Get them out, Lulu, will you?' Dolly spins around and shouts at me, wringing her hands. 'It's the half, don't you people know anything about actors, anything! I need my space. I need time alone! Get out!' She turns to face the wall and covers her eyes.

Tristan and Gavin look at me for direction.

I shrug and shoo them back through the door and into the corridor.

'I'll be outside if you need me, okay,' I say, pulling the door closed quietly behind me.

'Not you, Lulu!' Dolly says, and spins around. 'You can stay.'

'Are you sure? Don't you need to be alone?' I ask, confused.

'Just stay here. Please?' she replies.

I take a step back into the room, and turn around to push the door closed on Tristan, who looks wounded: his mouth falls open like his jaw has just lost the springs that held it together.

I mouth 'sorry', and close the door in his face, wincing when he fails to move even an inch backwards and the wood softly shunts his nose.

Dolly is sitting in her chair, facing the mirror again. She stares at herself in distaste. 'Look at me,' she whispers. 'Look at me. Who wants to see me now? Look at the state of me. I'm a sight, a wreck, aren't I? I'm the bloody Blackpool Tower. Nobody is bothered about me. It's Tom they've come to see, or Arabella. Nobody is here for me anyway. What does it matter?'

'Gavin thinks you're the reason they've sold the theatre out,' I say, looking down at my feet innocently.

'What does he know?' she whispers.

'I don't know, but he's worked here for a few years, and they don't normally sell out, he says, but now they have, and anyway, that's just what he said.' I shrug and smile like it's unimportant.

Dolly gives me a weary look in the mirror, and then addresses her reflection again. 'Getting old is terrible, Lulu. Terrible. Don't do it.'

'Do I have a choice? Besides, I think you look fine.'

'Ha! What woman wants to be described as looking fine? That's the kind of foolish thing a man would say!'

'Okay, I think you look wonderful, but I didn't think you'd

357

believe me if I said that because it is too obvious a compliment tonight, so I just shot for something you might believe. Is that good enough for you?' I study a vase of orange roses on the side as if I'm interested, delicately playing with their petals, lifting each of them up one by one and letting them fall again. I feel like I'm the one acting.

'Do you? Do you think I look wonderful?' she asks, straight-faced, stark with desperation.

'I honestly do. I'm not so sure about me, but I know that you look wonderful, Dolly.' I take a step forward and cross my finger over my heart as a promise.

'Oh isn't it funny, Lulu, right now, this very second, this moment, faced with the prospect of stepping out onto that stage, I'd trade the whole world to look like you again.'

I fold my arms and shake my head, leaning back against the wall. 'No you wouldn't, Dolly, not really.'

'Oh you don't know, Lulu, you'll see. In time, you'll see.'

'You've had a lifetime of looking beautiful, of looking like you. Most people only get a series of moments. How's that for lucky?' I ask.

'Moments,' she smiles, with familiarity. 'That was my line,' she says.

'Yes, it was.'

She smiles again, but when she turns back in her chair to face the mirror her smile slips like it's too big for her face, and falls off her.

'I can't, Lulu, I just can't. I have to go home.' She pushes herself to her feet, and her hands have begun to shake again, but violently now.

I am desperate, and running out of options.

'I wish you wouldn't, Dolly. People have paid, and they are excited at the prospect of seeing you, and . . . you know that you can do it! That is what is so annoying, what are you so scared for, suddenly?'

358

She slumps back down in the chair and holds her hands up in front of her and watches them tremble. 'I just . . . Lulu, I don't know how I'll get through it tonight.'

'Have you taken anything?' I ask quickly.

She looks at my reflection in the mirror.

'Where is your bag?' I demand.

She keeps looking at me sadly.

'Would you like some water?' I say, leading her to the answer by the hand.

'Oh, Lulu, you know I . . .' She shakes her head, but her eyes plead with mine.

'Look. I'm not saying it's an answer forever, or for the whole damn run, or even for tomorrow. But get up there! Get through it tonight – you do want to do it, don't you?'

'Very much,' she replies, nodding.

'Well then. You know that if you want something you just want it, and you shouldn't be ashamed to admit it or make it happen. So,' I reach into her bag, retrieve her hipflask, and snatch the glass up from the counter. I pour a long measure in and pass her the glass.

She takes it without question, and gulps it down.

'Okay,' she says. 'Okay. Give me fifteen minutes on my own, Lulu.'

I leave her staring at her reflection in the mirror, pulling the skin back at the sides of her eyes, giving herself temporary and painless surgery.

I pull the door closed behind me and Gavin and Tristan jump on me.

'Well?' says Gavin.

'Well?' says Tristan.

'Well?' I reply, enjoying the moment. 'I think she's going on. I think. But she'll need you in the wings, Tristan. You can't let a kid do it, it has to be you. You have to look after her up there, you can't leave her vulnerable or open to ridicule.'

Tristan is nodding his head enthusiastically. 'You're right, Make-up, you're right, aha, yes, whatever it takes. If she goes on . . .'

The three of us stand in silence for a while. Gavin leans against a wall. I sense him staring at me, and glance up quickly to catch him, but his eyes dart away. Tristan looks from me to Gavin to me again, and shakes his head slowly, smiling. I inspect my shoes. Tristan jumps on the spot. Gavin shoves his hands into his pockets. I inspect my tights for ladders. Tristan coughs once, nervously. I inspect my nails for chips.

The door opens and Dolly steps into the corridor.

'Dolly! I thought I might prompt tonight,' Tristan says loudly and firmly.

'Fine,' she replies, and holds her head high. She is wearing an old white lace gown as Gavin takes her hand and leads her upstairs to the wings.

I stand stage-side. You can hear the audience barely feet away, behind the curtain, perilously close and loud like a wall of water, building into a mighty terrible wave about to crash down upon the stage. Dolly's hands shake a little by her side. I retrieved her glass from the room and now I hold it for her. Everybody buzzes about, and then an expectant silence falls in front of the curtain, and Dolly looks at me nervously.

'Do you need another slug?' I ask.

She takes a sip.

Gavin gives me a look like I'm crazy but I brush it off.

I don't think I can watch.

I spy Tom on the other side of the stage and he looks green like mushy peas. Arabella stands feet away from Dolly and I, giving the impression of a woman completely composed. Dolly eyes her jealously. Arabella has a bonus confidence, certain as she is that whatever happens tonight she looks wonderful.

Tristan stands beside me, script in hand, wide-eyed and still. 'Dolly, I'm here for every line. If you need me. On this side.' He licks the ball of his index finger and runs it down the page.

The lights dip.

A voice on the PA system says, 'Due to the nature of the play, there will be no interval.'

The curtain is dragged up.

I walk down the stairs backstage, and away.

I hear it first. A swell of approval that might bring the house down. A stamping, thudding roar of applause threatening to burst the roof off the theatre and into the London night.

I leave the room and walk quickly upstairs. I have to stop myself from running, but I want to see it.

I spot Tristan first, holding himself up at the side of the stage, looking on as his cast take their bow. He looks appalling: devastated, exhausted, frazzled, sweat-drenched.

The cast file off into the wings. Dolly is on the opposite side of the stage. She reaches out and grabs Gavin's hand to support herself. The cheers from the audience get louder. Dolly straightens her back and walks back out on stage, alone.

The volume threatens to shake the foundations. The slow hand-clap like cannons being fired over and over, the screeched whistles, the throaty cheers. Dolly stands in front of them all, smiling easily. She gives the audience her own small round of applause. Tom brings on a vast bunch of wild flowers, and Dolly accepts them graciously, with a kiss to both his cheeks. She nods her head slightly at the audience, and smiles warmly. The claps and cheers continue. Then Dolly shrugs. Did they expect anything less? The delight explodes from the stalls.

Dolly retreats stiffly to my side of the wings, where Tristan stands, beaten, the script in tatters at his feet. She snatches his hand and wrings it hard. Tristan has tears in his bloodshot eyes as he looks up at her, but she says nothing. She spies me in the corner, and says simply, 'Come on, Lulu,' and walks past me, back down the stairs towards her room.

'Every third line,' she says.

'Pardon?'

She slumps in her chair. 'He gave me every third line, Lulu, that strange little man. Didn't miss it, didn't rush it. Didn't crowd me, knew my signs. He was wonderful.'

'Well, I've heard wonderful things,' I say, soaking a cotton-wool ball in cleanser, before Dolly interrupts. 'Don't take it off tonight, Lulu. I want to leave it on for tonight.'

'For the party? But I can do it again, now, quickly, if you want me to, and a little less heavy around the eyes?'

'No, no. Call Tristan in here, will you, Lulu. I'm sure he's lurking somewhere close.'

Confused, I open the door to the rabble in the corridor, and Tristan practically falls through the doorway with his red glassy eyes, a shirt soaked in sweat, and hair so drenched in fear that it has frizzed into a giant fuzzy Shredded Wheat atop his head.

'What in hell's the matter with you? Ha! You look like you've fought an army!' Dolly says when she sees him, chuckling. Her hands have stopped shaking.

Gavin pokes his head around the door too. 'There is a queue of people out here, Dolly – Jerry Hall, Prunella Scales . . . Tony Bennett . . .'

'How kind, how kind,' she says, 'but Gavin, send them to the party, tell them I'll be along in a little while and that they should drink, and I'll see them there. But be sure and tell them that I love them, and thank them, Gavin, very much.'

Gavin shuts the door.

'He's a lovely man' she says. I smile and nod my head.

'He has character.' She winks at me, and then turns to face Tristan, who smacks his lips together and smiles.

'I'm not coming to the party, Tristan,' Dolly says. 'And I'm not coming back tomorrow. I'm going to leave for New York in the morning. I've done what I could but I've had a call from the States and I have to go to my daughter.'

'Why, what's happened?' Tristan asks urgently.

'It's personal,' she says, 'and besides, the smell of the grease-paint . . . the roar of the crowd – there will be another time for me.'

Tristan slumps to the floor, devastated.

Dolly ignores the dramatic gesture and carries on. 'Audrey can fill in for me for the short term. She'll be terrible, of course, but you'll get another star, perhaps, soon enough. I do wish that I could stay, but I simply can't. I have to go and see my daughter. I've had an urgent call . . .' She is no less convincing this time than the last.

Tristan looks up like a child sat on an assembly-hall floor. 'One week,' he says to her. 'Just give me one week, we'll be one of those amazing sought-after hot tickets, and we'll pack them out for a week, and then we'll say it was our choice to fold.'

Dolly shakes her head and smiles.

'I am very sorry. It's impossible. I can't. And besides, we all know it's a ridiculous play. A vanity play – it was for him and it is for me. Enough is enough.'

There is a heavy knock on the door.

'Come in,' Dolly barks.

'Your car is here, shall I tell him to drive around for a bit?' Gavin asks.

'No, I'll only be a few minutes, tell him to wait.'

Gavin nods and closes the door, and Dolly looks expectantly

at Tristan, who takes the hint and pushes himself to his feet. There is a ring of dust on the seat of his trousers.

'Is it worth me saying you have a contract?' he asks quietly.

'That was never signed,' she replies with a soft smile.

'Right. Right. Well, thank you for tonight at least,' Tristan says sadly, his hands in his pockets, his chin down. He glances up at her and there is still a twinkle in his eye.

'No. Thank you,' she answers him, and Tristan turns and walks out.

Dolly looks at me. 'Lulu, will you ask Gavin, after I've left, to pack up my things and have them sent on via the Dorchester? They are very good, they'll sort it out for me. Do you want some of these flowers?' she asks me, gesturing lazily around the room. 'Take the pink ones, Lulu.'

'Okay, I will.'

She grabs her bag up off the floor.

'Bring me the black roses, just that bunch, Lulu, will you? And walk me up?'

I grab the bunch that her daughter sent her, and wrap a plastic bag around the bottom.

'Perfect,' she says, walking ahead of me.

'Have you got everything?' I ask as she leaves.

'I think so,' she replies, walking out without looking back.

Everybody has gone to the party, and the backstage area is finally quiet. The back door is deserted. Gavin helps Dolly into her car, guiding her head into the back seat gently as if she were a genteel criminal being ushered into a squad car.

'Where do you want the flowers?' I ask, standing at the car door.

'I'll just take them here on my lap, Lulu, no fuss,' she says.

I hand them in to her and she puts them down on the seat, and grabs my hand.

'Lulu,' she says quietly, and squeezes my hand in between both of hers.

I crouch down at the door.

'I think that we pooled our strength, didn't we?'

'We did!' I reply, hardly able to look her in the eye, trying to fight the tears off.

'Toughen up, Lulu,' she says, her voice breaking. Dolly pulls the back of my hand up to her mouth and gives it an old, squashed kiss. Her lipstick stains my skin and I feel the tears tumble out of my eyes.

'I will, I promise,' I say. She lets go of my hand as I stand up.

'The Dorchester, one last time!' she says to the driver, with a wink. I close the door and her car pulls away.

Back in the dressing room I grab my bag, and wrap newspaper around the wet stems of the pink roses, and head upstairs again without lingering. I find Tristan sitting with his legs stretched out at the front of the stage, resting on the palms of his hands behind him.

'Hey,' he says, as I walk to the centre of the stage, and lean.

'Hey,' I reply. 'Don't you want to go to the party? Don't you want to read your reviews?' I ask.

'Oh, they'll be average, Make-up, the critics hate this play anyway. And what does it matter? Dolly's gone. We're a one-night stand. A quick cheap thrill, gone tomorrow. The show will close when people realise she's not coming back.' Tristan looks up and around him, leaning his neck back, and shouts, 'This bloody theatre! Damn you, damn you!'

I don't know what to say and we stand in silence as I search for a silver lining. After two long minutes of sighs, I find one, of sorts.

'But now you can do *Death in Venice*! With the priests! You won't have sold your soul for nothing, Tristan.'

'That's true,' he says, sitting up and brightening slightly.

'As long as, you know, the priests will get on a bus with a man with no soul.'

'Oh why not, love, they've all sold theirs to the same guy,' he replies.

'Don't say that on the bus,' I tell him, alarmed. 'Anyway. How do you think it went? The applause was wonderful, wasn't it?'

'Yes, it was. She was wonderful. The bastard is she only had the one performance in her.' Tristan sighs again, and examines his fingernails.

'Tristan, I can't come back tomorrow either. I have to leave too,' I tell him apologetically.

He looks up and smiles. 'An urgent call from New York for you too, Make-up?'

'Not quite. Rottingdean.'

He looks perplexed.

'It's near Brighton. On the coast. I have to go and see my mum.'

'Oh, is she okay?' he asks, pushing himself to his feet, wiping down his trousers.

'Yeah, she's fine. It's not her, really, it's me.'

'Oh.' Tristan stops dusting himself down and looks up at me. 'Are you okay?'

'I'm . . . okay, yes. It's nothing fatal. It hurts at the moment, but I'll be fine.'

Tristan smiles and winks at me.

I smile and wink back.

'Oh for fuck's sake!' he says, shaking his head. 'Ha!' he shouts, and walks off backstage.

Gavin coughs. I turn and see him standing by one of the stalls' entrances.

'Gavin, you are always standing behind me, coughing,' I say.

366

'Why are you going?' he asks, walking forwards slowly.

'I just have to get out of London for a while, Gavin. Everybody should, sometimes. I have to clear my head. I think I've got a bit cloudy and I need some seaside air to wash those clouds away.'

Gavin stops a couple of steps away from me.

'I'll miss you,' he says.

'Will you?'

'Very much,' he replies, and I am amazed.

'What?' he asks, at the incredulous look on my face.

'Nothing, really, it's just that it's funny. I've only known you, what, a week? And nobody has ever told me they'll miss me before. I mean, apart from my mum, and she has to.'

'Not even Ben?' he asks, baffled.

'Oh my God, especially not him! Sometimes I'd even ask him, "Did you miss me?" This was before we were living together, and he'd gone camping or walking with Iggy for a week, and he'd just say "No". I think he thought I should admire his honesty . . .'

'It explains a lot,' Gavin says, placing a huge palm facing downwards on the stage as we stand in front of it, studying his fingers. He seems nervous.

'Maybe it does. How many signs can a girl ignore? But not any more . . .' I try to laugh, but it won't quite come out.

'How was the zoo?' he asks.

'Conclusive. Sad. But overdue.' I say.

'So . . . can I call you?' Gavin says, and stops looking at his fingers, looking at me instead. I knew that the question was coming, in the way that you always know. Sometimes you can just see people's hearts through their jumpers.

'I don't know, Gavin . . .' I reply, looking him in the eye.

'Well, I've got your number so maybe I'll just call you anyway,' he shrugs.

'Okay, well, that's another approach,' I say, and give him the biggest smile that I can muster. 'Dolly asked if you'd get somebody to pack her stuff up and send it to the Dorchester to forward on?' I continue, picking up my flowers wrapped in newspaper.

He nods.

'Bye, Gavin,' I say, grabbing my bag, walking back down the aisle on my own, and away.

The *Evening Standard* seller is clapping his hands against the cold, outside Covent Garden tube station.

I check my watch. It is eleven fifteen. 'Shouldn't you be closed?' I ask, confused.

'I've got one paper left,' he whistles.

'Well I'll take it!' I say.

'Forty pence please, my lovely,' he replies.

I root around in the bottom of my bag for change.

'Have you found it?' he lisps. I look up and notice that another two teeth have disappeared, and now only two remain like an odd couple at the front of his mouth.

'I'm just looking now,' I say, concentrating on what my hand can feel in my bag.

'But it looks like you've found it: what you lost,' he persists.

I stare at him, and feel two twenty-pence pieces fall into my hand in my bag.

'Maybe I have,' I tell him.

'It took a while,' he comments, and offers me the paper, folded in half.

'Bye,' I say, accepting my *Standard* and walking away backwards.

'Goodnight, my lovely,' he replies, and I turn away before the rest of his teeth fall out.

Scene IV: Refuge

Tuesday. I take a train to the seaside. I manage to sleep a little during the hour that it takes us to fly, metal sparking on metal, to Brighton. Last night's sleep was fitful at best. I dozed in twenty-minute bursts, woken suddenly, consistently, violently, by night falls, or jumps, or spasms. I'd lurch forwards and wake myself up, over and over again. It's not as if I miss the hugs, they weren't there to miss. I miss his back, a little. I feel like I've misplaced something.

I am obviously overtired. When we speed past a cemetery I am overwhelmed by the peculiarity of keeping our dead in boxes in holes in the ground. When will there be more bodies in the ground than people walking on it? When will the dead bodies reach critical mass? Does the day draw near? Meanwhile we lose somebody and we store their bones and skin in a box and bury it somewhere to rot, and sometimes we go and see the space where they rot, and talk to it. Our dead are gone: if we want to we can talk to them anywhere, and just pretend we are on hands-free to Heaven. There are no polystyrene cups with string attached: one cup resting at one end on their grave plots, the string shooting high up into the sky to heaven, and our dead friend or lover or relative cross-legged on a cloud with the other foam cup pressed to their ear, chatting away on the other end. Sometimes you lose people, and it's better to let go. Retain a symbol, perhaps, of what they meant to you, but don't keep turning back. You have to look forwards. It's the only way to have a future, in anything!

I scan the train carriage and wonder if anybody else has been dumped in the last few days. Dumped. It's such an absurd and terrible phrase. It makes me sound like trash. I know that there was more to it than that. I am sure Ben thinks we both did the dumping, by mutual consent, and consoles himself with the fact that it was us both somehow, like he gave me a choice that was more than 'hurt or stop hurting'. Maybe that's what men do, when they can't face the fact that they are hurting somebody? Women acknowledge, through their own tears, that people get hurt. Ben, with his lack of tears, pretends that they don't. Perhaps he was only able to continue behaving in the way that he did by not admitting that he was hurting me. It's as old as the hills. There is a Japanese girl with huge headphones two seats in front of me, facing forwards. I wonder if she has just been dumped. She doesn't look particularly melancholy, she looks like a student. I am pretty sure she is fine, but then I can think what I like about her really. You can violate anybody's character with your own thoughts, if you want to. It's strange and reassuring. Maybe she did get dumped this morning, because she is needy and desperate and clawing and whining, all of the time. Maybe she was that way after a month! At least it took me six months to get to the needy, desperate, whiny stage with Ben. Then I simply managed to drag that out into two and a half years. You've got to admire my stamina in a way. I should consider marathons. They say it's a wonderful day. It's the atmosphere that helps people finish, they say. It's bizarre when you think of it. Loads of people just running through town. Just running. And loads of other people standing around cheering and waving and clapping, while the other people run. I think a lot of people must simply go for the cheers. Who cheers you on normally, in everyday life? 'Go on, Scarlet, dig deep! You can do it! Another ambivalent phone call! Another thoughtless gesture! You can stand it, go on! Another argument where you apologise for just being you, for even feeling something! Go on, girl! Another random cheating embrace that makes you hate yourself even more, desperate for affection! – go on, go on, go on!' Where have my bloody cheers been?

There is a man, thirty-five maybe, except I always get ages wrong. He gave my red swollen eyes a suspicious look when he sat down opposite me at the little train table. They are the glory seats, the train tables. If you can get one whole one to yourself then you win! But he didn't look away. He gave me a smile. Maybe he thinks I am going to a funeral or to see a dying aunt, travelling sadly out of town. In my head I can make him anything. In my head he can be the type of man who cares about people, and isn't self-absorbed and self-obsessed. He has an iPod nano, and he is listening to something melodic, leaving it alone, not fast-forwarding through every track to get to the next one, in case it's better. He looks relaxed. Ben used to make play lists for his iPod, loads of them. He liked his dad rock. I would go so far as to say he almost loved it. Note the almost, let's not get carried away.

I said to him once, 'Do you know why I think you love your music so much, Ben?'

And he said, 'No, surprise me!' just like that, sarcastic straight away.

So I said, 'Because it's the closest you get to emotion. You think it's "genius" that somebody had a feeling and wrote it down, because you could never do the same. And you sing their feelings with emotion, but you do know that they actually felt them, right? If you think about that, Ben, all these people writing down their emotions, does it put you off the songs a bit? Like mould gathering around the top of them? Because, you know, being you, you'd think that it would . . .'

'Another fascinating dissection of my character, Scarlet, thank you,' he'd said, sighing and weary and bored and not really listening. He should have listened sometimes.

'You know what's really sad? You couldn't write a line of one of those songs,' I'd say, under my breath and behind his back when he'd walk off into the kitchen, singing. 'The closest you get to expressing your feelings is singing what Jon Bon Jovi feels. Now that, Ben, is sad.'

It occurs to me that I will need to stop having these thoughts soon. When should I leave him alone? Stop picking apart his character to find the bit that explains my rejection? Maybe this is me sitting at the grave of our relationship with the foam cup to my ear and the string in the air, a ladder to the sky, hoping he'll pick up. Maybe I need to look forwards. Out of the window I glimpse the sea.

My mum lives in Rottingdean village, in a house by the lake. There is a path that separates her garden from the rushes. People have been warning her about damp in her foundations since she moved in, fifteen years ago, but the walls haven't fallen down yet. It is an old house, though, with dark wood beams and low ceilings. Gavin would have to come in on his knees or risk a crick in his neck.

I get a taxi to Rottingdean from Brighton station, and somehow my mum does what she always does, and is standing at the front door of her house as my taxi pulls up. Her grey hair is still long and pinned on her head, her glasses have slipped halfway down her nose, and she's wearing an old jumper that she gardens in, and wellies.

'Hello darling!' she shouts, grinning and waving, as I pull up.

'Have you been standing there all morning, Mum?' I ask over my shoulder as I pay the cabbie.

'No, darling, I just this second opened the door. You know I can be a little bit psychic, Scarlet. I thought you might get that train as well.'

I lug my bag along the short path, and drop it down at her feet. She opens her arms out wide and hugs me, hard and tight, like she's counting my bones. I start to cry and she doesn't say anything. She doesn't know yet, I haven't told her, but it doesn't matter. You are allowed to cry when your mum hugs you. That's allowed. Eventually she whispers in my ear, 'Silly stuff? Or is something wrong?'

'A bit of both,' I say.

'Tea?' she asks.

'Yes please,' I say, between sobs.

She holds me at arm's length. 'You look skinny, Scarlet, have you been eating?'

'Mum, I don't look skinny, I look huge.'

'No you don't. Don't argue with me,' she says, picking up my bag and carrying it into the hall. The stable door is open and I can smell the flowers in her back garden, and the damp smell of shovelled earth.

'Garden looks fabulous, Mum,' I say, leaning on the table in the kitchen, staring out of the window.

'Oh, do you think so? Thank you. Have you seen my peonies? Over in the corner?'

I stare out, trying to spot some colour because I don't know what I am looking for. I say, 'It looks lovely.'

I rest heavily on the table, my chin on my forearms, while she mucks about at the stove with the old kettle, tossing in tea bags like they are going out of fashion.

'I like your skirt!' she comments, as the kettle starts to whistle. It's yellow silk.

'How is the shop?' I ask. My mum manages a shop in the

village, in the mornings, that sells scarves and plants and picture frames and candles. She has been there for ten years, and it's what keeps her in bread and bulbs.

'Fine, darling, the same as always.' She turns and smiles at me. 'How is the big city?' she asks, widening her eyes, rubbing dirt off her forehead with the back of her hand.

'Oh it's . . . it's been a bit much, recently. You know I love it but sometimes you have to get away. You can never clear your head in town. You can walk, in Hyde Park, or Green Park, and think you've cleared it, but then you remember everything the minute you get back on the tube.'

'Well, you know what I think, Scarlet, too many distractions. I love London, but not to live, not to be. It's for fun.'

'Maybe. How are the ducks?' I ask, as I hear them throwing themselves into the lake at the front of the house and arguing in noisy squawks.

'Oh they're okay, darling. One of them got run over a couple of weeks ago, but the rest seem all right about it. Tim had a good cry, of course.'

Tim is the man who lives next door. He's never married. Mum goes to the cinema with him. Whenever anybody asks me if there is anything going on between them I say that, 'He's never married', loaded with meaning.

'How about you? Didn't you cry?' Mum is quite attached to the ducks. She has given them all names. One is François, one is Dave, and one is called Derek and she thinks he's bisexual. It's bizarre.

'Darling, I'm not going to cry about a duck.'

'Even if it died?' I ask, standing up straight.

'Even if he died!'

'But that's when you're allowed, when somebody dies,' I say.

She looks at me over her glasses with concern. Her jumper is coursed with runs and she is wearing an oversized orange vest underneath that pokes its noisy colour through. 'Besides, it was John, and he was the oldest by far. And one of his feet had been mangled and his eyes were red, and he wasn't long for this world so it was probably for the best. I think it might have been premeditated actually. He was generally near the front of the line, but that day he hung back, and then just stopped in front of a four-by-four, and of course it was one of the old girls and she didn't brake in time.'

'You think John the duck committed suicide?' I ask, accepting a cup of steaming tea and trying not to smile.

'Yes I do, actually, so don't laugh.' She looks at me sternly. 'Well, what do you want to do?' she asks. 'You look tired. Do you want a nap?'

'I think so.'

She passes me a pink wafer biscuit. 'Eat this and drink your tea. I'm going to finish turning over that earth, so go to bed, and we can have dinner later.'

And I do.

I stay in bed all afternoon. I fall asleep straight away, but then wake often, my brain working overtime, trying to answer a thousand questions in my head that can't be answered, to explain behaviour that refuses to be explained.

When I get up it's late, almost seven, and mum is cooking us dinner. A heavy dusk has settled around the house, and with it a silence punctuated by an occasional car, or François or Dave or Derek bombing in or out of the pond. My mother has no concept of fats or carbs, she cooks her roast potatoes in thick, greasy slices of lard, and eats the skin of chicken and turkey, and pork crackling. Her pasta is always soft, as are her carrots. Her meat is always on the rare side. She cooks things how she cooks them, and hates recipes.

We chat about my brother over dinner, and how busy we've all been, the family excuses that we have all made that have kept us away from each other for too long. She tells me that the library in the village has been threatened with closure, and they've been having meetings about it but she always falls asleep halfway through. My mum tells me that seven families of immigrants have moved into the empty houses at the other end of town, and how some people have been terrible about it, but she saw some of the children by the lake throwing bread to the ducks and they seemed nice enough so she took them biscuits.

'Not much English, of course, but then who are we to judge? I can't speak Romanian.'

'Neither can I,' I say. 'I'm not even sure where it is.'

'Exactly, Scarlet,' she says with a smile, as if I am actually very, very clever.

By nine p.m. I am tucked up in an armchair in the dark little house, a cup of strong coffee sitting on the floorboards next to me, watching *Morse* repeats on the TV and the light fade to black through the curtains and over the lake. With the back door open and the sound of silence outside, it feels like midnight.

'Shall we walk by the sea tomorrow?' Mum asks me. 'Come and meet me at the shop at lunchtime, you can post some letters for me in the morning, Scarlet, then we can go for a nice long walk so we deserve fish and chips.'

By ten p.m. my eyes are closing again. Mum has poured herself two large glasses of white wine and now she is sipping a brandy. Her socks are old, her feet propped in front of her on her wooden coffee table. One of her big toes is making a break for it through a threadbare patch, the fibres worn gently down day-in, day-out by her old wet wellies, which have been kicked off by the back door.

'I'm going to go to bed, Mum,' I say, and sleep-stumble over to kiss her goodnight.

She grabs both of my arms and gives me a hug. 'I love you, Lulu,' she says, with a hint of a slur.

'I know you do. I love you too.'

In the doorway I turn around, and ask, 'Mum? Why do you call me Lulu sometimes? Instead of Scarlet?'

She gurgles a cough and smiles, and pulls off her glasses clumsily so one of the arms bangs her nose.

'It's what my grandfather called my grandmother when I was a child, and he whispered to her that he loved her as she stood at the sink or the stove or sat in her chair. And it always sounded so sincere, coming from him. It sounded like love should.'

I walk up the stairs and bat away a tear. I knew Ben was wrong. I knew I was loveable really.

I sleep in late and have a long, hot shower, throw on some jeans and a T-shirt. I toss my head upside-down and blow-dry my hair without spray or mousse or serum. I apply a minimum of make-up – I'm not quite ready for the fresh-faced look yet. I still feel numb, but even today it's better. It feels like months already since I last spoke to Ben. In my heart, I know, I am forced to admit that he is probably fine. No doubt he is watching *Dude, Where's My Car?* . . . again. I'm not holding out hope for some strange and atypical romantic gesture. I don't expect him to land on the doorstep bedraggled, with red eyes and a bunch of flowers and a thousand gushing apologies, reeling from some strange epiphany, realising the error of his ways and what I've meant to him all along, finally acknowledging how much there is about me to miss. That simply won't happen. That *is* for romantic comedies. Ours is not that kind of story. Ben won't come after me, on a horse, in a car, or on a train. I know that much.

I see Mum now, walking along the beach towards me, trundling clumsily and without grace, grey hairs flying, huge sunglasses on to fend off the wind that makes both our eyes stream.

We walk for a while. Mum folds her arms and looks out

to sea, and I kick through shingles and throw stones sometimes.

Without Ben, the knowledge of Ben, the idea of being in a relationship, I feel like I am on my own. But of course I'm not. I stand and stare at an old fishing boat bobbing about two hundred feet out. It looks empty. I wait for the wind to feel colder but it doesn't. I wait for my eyes to water more than they normally would in this crazy wind, but it's the same. I feel a shiver in my back, but it's not fear. I remember how good it was with Ben, when it was good. I remember back to a time, very early on, maybe even before he left, when we did laugh and muck about, and there was genuine affection. Then I think, *Imagine that, but fifty times better. Imagine that plus somebody actually loving me back.* I can't help it and the feeling surprises me. It's exciting.

We turn around and walk back towards the village rather than head into Brighton, and the pebbles crunch beneath our feet. The wind gusts suddenly and whips our faces and our eyes both stream with windy tears.

I am wearing one of my mum's big old jumpers, a scarf and gloves.

The waves crash about angrily. There is an old man further up the beach with a metal detector, scanning for treasure in two-pence pieces. A young couple walk their baby in a pram and he pushes. Some kids in hooded tops skim stones at the water and occasionally at each other.

'What are you scared of, Scarlet?' my mum asks, as we climb over a wooden beach-break.

'Rats. Alligators. Heights, sometimes. Flying, sometimes. Snakes. Getting old. Not having a baby. Not finding somebody who wants to marry me, or that I want to marry. All the usual stuff, I guess. Missing out . . .'

My mum stares at me and I know she is thinking about Ben, but she doesn't ask me the question. Instead she says,

'Well, yes, a lot of people have babies and get married. But what about the other stuff? What if you miss out on something else, something just as wonderful? Maybe you'll miss the right man, Scarlet, because you're so scared of being left on the shelf that you shack up with Mr Wrong! Or maybe you miss out on the opportunity of a lifetime, of living in a place you never would have known, or meeting important people, having important experiences, because you were hemmed into some semi somewhere just because it's where you thought that you should be? Just because that's where everybody else seems to think they should be! But do they look so gloriously happy to you, Scarlet? Like they didn't miss out on something? Because most of them look miserable as hell to me! Maybe there are things, other things, that aren't worth missing, just because you think you need a baby and a man? I thought that things had changed, Scarlet, for young girls today, but maybe they will always be the same . . .'

'Maybe I'd have missed meeting a crazy old drunken lady with too much to say,' I put in.

'Yes, or that . . .' my mum replies, bewildered.

Tired thigh muscles slow us up as we trudge up a hill of shingles towards the road.

'Scarlet, I am determined that you won't spend your life sitting at home changing the nappies of a baby conceived with a man you don't even like much any more! Or that you didn't much like in the first place! You are my daughter, Scarlet, and you are wonderful and stunning and strong. Don't apologise for it!'

'Oh, I'm not any of those things, Mum, I'm certainly not strong' I say.

'Yes you are. You are. And if no man fits the bill then so be it, and that's just their bad luck I'm afraid!'

'Okay, but then I don't get to have somebody that loves me, or a baby, do I?' As I say it I finally realise that it's true.

379

Maybe I really don't get to have a baby and a marriage. Maybe it just isn't meant for me.

'Please don't take this the wrong way, darling, but babies can be overrated. Some children grow up to be distant drug addicts. No, don't look appalled, just listen to me, Scarlet. There is a lot of luck involved these days, in getting a nice child. Some kids drive their parents crazy, I've seen the programs on TV. They have to send them off to special camps, special wilderness camps in the desert, just to get them to stop spitting and swearing! And a lot of people just have kids because they are scared of being on their own, and so they end up with children like that! I bet they are wishing for some of that quiet alone time now! If you can get past that fear, darling, of being on your own, then you are halfway there. It really isn't bad, you know.'

I stare at her, shocked, but she just nods her head wisely.

'You didn't hate Dad, did you?' I ask.

'Oh no, Scarlet, you know your father, he isn't hateful. He's just distant. He was disinterested in me, we just weren't right. I couldn't think when I was around him. I just felt trapped. And of course I got lucky and had you and your brother, and I think I managed as best as I could not to harm you too much in the leaving process. And of course I worry that I hurt your father, that saddens me still, even today. But I made a mistake. He wanted that life, and I wanted a different one. And I know it might seem strange to you, with me living here, in this poky little house. But it's my house, darling, and my thoughts, and my washing, and my dreams, and my films. Of course I am a little sad, that I never met a man that I could share those things with in the way that I would have liked to have shared them. Sometimes I think maybe I missed that man, when I was with your father, at home, cooking dinners? I don't regret it, darling, because of you. But my life is still my life, and yours is yours. I love you but I'm not going to live my life for you. You are a very important part of it, of course, but it's still my life. And I could meet somebody yet, down the road, tomorrow. I haven't given up! But you can't just live for other people, for your children. You have to have something for yourself as well, Scarlet, for you. You have to be happy, to be able to make them happy, I think. Dreams are dreams, and you won't know until you get there if the perfect kid, the perfect family, was as much of a lie as Prince bloody Charming. Prince Thoughtful with a Nice Smile, darling, that's what love will be. Don't be scared, Scarlet, please.'

Facing away from the wind our eyes stop streaming. The fish and chip shop has recently been renamed 'Things Can Only Get Batter!' There is a huge queue that snakes out of the shop and around the corner like a long and slippery jellied eel.

'Let's go tomorrow instead, it will still be there then,' Mum says, frowning at the queue. 'I've got toast and Marmite and cheese, that will do, won't it?'

I nod and smile.

I stayed because I was scared. I jumped, at the zoo, because I wasn't.

I'm thirty-one. I'm only thirty-one! Everybody else can pretend it's ancient, but it's not. It's nothing. I'm a baby. I'm not ninety, I haven't lived yet! The papers can sell their scare stories to somebody else, I've got a long way ahead of me yet. And I've learnt some stuff too. Love is just making somebody else happy, being made happy in return. You can do that with laughter lines. I'm going to love somebody again. What else could be more important than being happy, if you are lucky enough to have the choice? I'm not going to be mean with my feelings, or scared to give them. I'm going to give them as honestly and freely as I can.

As we get back to the house I hear my mobile ringing. I feel a nervous sickness, and look at the screen; it's Gavin.

'So . . . I called,' he says sternly.

'So you did. That was quick,' I reply.

'Was it too soon?' he asks, but answers himself. 'But I just thought, to hell with it – if you want to call somebody, you should call. You could have met a man on the train. I didn't want to take that chance.'

'I could have, I guess. But I didn't.'

'Was it too quick?' he asks, hesitation creeping in.

'No, Gavin. It's nice that you called. It's nice when somebody actually wants to speak to you. But . . . I'm not going to say yes.' I take a deep breath.

'I'm going to try and be really honest with you, Gavin, and even if it's disappointing I hope that you'll like me for it. I think that you are lovely, and strong, and funny, and dry. Christ, I think you'd protect me, you really would. But I don't think we'd be lovely, as a couple, definitely not right now. I barely know you and I don't know if you're right for me, and I don't know if I'm right for you. But even if we both feel like exploring it for a while, now is not the right time. My feelings are all bruised, and I need to take a while to get better. Please don't think me awful for saying this, and tell me that I am wrong if I am, but a couple of things that you did, and that you said, well, they made me think that you have feelings for me, strongish feelings, already.'

I pause.

'Go on,' he says.

'I haven't been in a place to feel those things for you, Gavin, and I am certainly not in a place, right now, to feel them for you either. I'm not saying never, I don't know how I'll feel in a few days or weeks or months, but it wouldn't be fair to you, right now, for me to say, "Let's have dinner." We'd be starting at such different places, and I'd be leading you on, and using you. And believe me when I say I'd quite like to use you, for a while, it would be the easiest thing in the world, because you are bloody lovely! But I wouldn't feel comfortable doing that. I wouldn't respect myself for doing that. I'll just have to take my chances, Gavin, and when I come back up and out of this, and when my head is sorted out, I may well come and see if you are still free. But I'm not going to use you, Gavin. That wouldn't feel very nice, for either of us, and somebody told me that it's the worst thing that you can do to a person, and now I know that I believe them.'

'Okay . . . fair enough. But what if I said I don't mind if you just want to use my body for a while? Just for science or something?'

I laugh. 'We're too far gone for that already, Gavin. I like you too much to use you for weekend recreation.'

'What about mid-week recreation?'

'That too. I'm sorry if that wasn't the answer you wanted, but I promise you I haven't lied.'

'It's fair enough, Scarlet. Well then. Maybe I'll see you around?'

'I hope so.'

'As long as it's not on the cover of *Hello!* with Tom Harvey-Saint,' he adds.

'Not in a million years,' I assure him.

'Bye, Scarlet. Get well soon . . .'

'Bye.'

I'm hopeful. The world still wants me, even if Ben doesn't. And it still hurts now, of course, and maybe it will pass in weeks or months. But it will pass in time. And then, when my head is clear, and the opportunity presents itself again, to be really loved. Well, then I'll feel fantastic.

Scene V: Things Can Only Get Batter?

Wednesday? Thursday? A day in the middle of the week, I know that. I'm not sure which. I've lost track . . .

I'm hanging out at the beach with my mum. I could live here for a while, but I'd have no money. There isn't much call for a Make-up around here, unless I want to do weddings or portraits, and if I'm honest I'm not ready yet. I love London. I will go back up to town. But Ben can have custody of Ealing, he works there, it's only fair. It was always more his than mine. My mum says, 'Call your brother, you could rent his flat in West Hampstead for a while.'

I call Richard and he says, 'Of course, but it will take me a couple of months to get the tenants out, so you can stay with us until then.' Maybe I will, go and spend time with my nephews and their dirty eight-year-old jokes. I forget that Richard got married when he was twenty! Twenty! It seemed like madness to me at the time, but he and Hannah are still happy, and the boys are happy. They got it right. It happens!

I sent Ben a text a couple of days ago, saying I'd come and get my stuff next Friday afternoon, but I'd be at my mum's until then, so he should move back into the flat. I asked him not to reply. I can't be sitting about waiting for something that's never going to come, or, if it does, will just disappoint me again. If I'm going to move forwards I can't keep one eye on my mobile phone, waiting for a text from the past.

But last night I got a drunken text message from him anyway. It said: 'HOPE U R GOOD. I HAVE GOOD NEWS. TEXT ME BACK IF YOU WANT THE DETAILS.'

I showed my mum and she said, 'If it was really good news, Scarlet, and he wasn't playing games, he'd just tell you, darling. He'll regret sending that in the morning. Don't text him back. I'm angry with that boy. He doesn't get to play games with my daughter any more.' She moved to snatch my phone from my hands, but I darted out of the way.

'It's fine, Mum. I agree,' I said, and reached instead for a pen.

So I took his number out of my phone. I wrote it down in my mum's address book first, in case I ever need it, but I don't need it in my phone now. Ben might not agree, but sometimes to have a future you have to let some people go.

I haven't heard from him since then. Of course, a little part of me is still desperate to hear from him, but also, now, desperate not to. The thing that I realise already is that all that Ben and I will be, even in a few months' time, is 'I don't love you.' Nothing else will remain. He will just be the person who didn't love me. Unfortunately I know that it will be bigger than all the other things, the fun things, the good things. And I need some happier thoughts than that, to still believe in what I might have to offer somebody, what somebody might offer me. I need to feel better about myself than that. So I am desperate, really, never to hear from him again.

I do think I expect a lot, maybe everything, maybe the world. I think I deserve it, just for being me, here, now, living in London, in heels. Just for living. But you can't expect to be happy, I see that now. It's not a thing you write on a 'to do' list along with a list of names, ticking them off until you find it, and you can't force it or make it happen. I'll be lucky if I find it. I'll try to remember that if I do. But my eyes should be open and ready to see it, and not tired from fighting all night, or bleary with frustrated tears. I'll be ready if it shows itself, happiness, I'll be warmed up and stretched on the sidelines, determined to throw myself in, as fearless as I can be, pretending the hurt didn't happen. And I'll be me, and living my life, the life that I choose and I want, and that I have a passion for. A bigger passion. It's easier than you think. I am so very lucky to have the choices that I have. I have to remember that too.

My mum is shouting at the ducks on the lake.

'Dave, you are violent! You are a violent duck.'

Pulling on her back-up wellies I poke my head around the door to see what Dave is doing.

'Come on, Scarlet, for goodness' sake!' she says, giving me as stern a look as Dave just got. 'If we don't get down there soon the queue will be out of the door again.'

'I'm coming, I'm coming! Mum, have you seen my lip-gloss?' I shout, rummaging through the pockets of all her jackets that I've been borrowing over the last week or so when I walk down to the sea in the mornings, fresh-faced but for moisturiser, to let the salt exfoliate my skin and the wind redden my cheeks.

'Scarlet, you can't wear lip-gloss on the beach, your hair gets stuck to your face. Besides, we are going to be eating fish and chips.'

I run into the kitchen to get my gloves. My lip-gloss is sitting on the side, next to my mobile phone. I pick them both up guiltily.

I stop and stare at them in my hands.

I throw my Juicy Tube on the kitchen table. And then my phone too.

'Two plaice and chips,' Mum says as I lean on the hot glass protecting lines of fish and sausages, in 'Things Can Only Get Batter!' 'Lots of salt, lots of vinegar,' Mum tells Al, the old Greek guy who runs the place.

'Is this your sister?' he asks, winking at her.

'It's my daughter, Al, and isn't she beautiful,' she says, smiling at me.

'She is. Just like her mother,' he says, and my God do we smile, all of us, it's helpless, it just spills out.

Happiness isn't a white dress. That's just a day. Happiness isn't the word 'marriage'. I am talking about passion, but not the kind that needs to scale mountains or scuba-dive. Just living, cooking, working, sleeping, kissing. All the day-to-day stuff. Unless it's right you have to be brave.

I remember something that Dolly said to me. 'You girls these days, you have so much more choice. Why don't you use it?'

Mum and I sit on a bench. The sun has come out but it's still cold by the sea. I peel off my gloves to eat my chips.

'Blow on them, darling,' my mum says.

'Are you happy, Mum?' I ask, blowing on my chip.

'Yes, I am.'

'Good. You know you watch all your films, Mum, have you heard of Dolly Russell?'

'Of course. She won an Oscar. Very beautiful. She must be dead by now.'

'No, not dead. Still alive and kicking. I was doing her make-up before I came to see you.'

'Oh, that's lovely, darling! What was she like?'

I think for a minute, contemplating a chip.

'Crazy,' I say, nodding my head, 'but wonderful.'

'But do I make you happy, Mum?' I ask, as we walk back up to the house, stuffed full of grease and comfort.

'Yes, but that was for me. I got lucky. You have more choices. I wouldn't trade you, Scarlet, but I am me and you are you. Stay here.'

Mum goes into the newsagent's to buy a paper.

We sit by the lake, watching the ducks, the wind flipping our hair. I found a grey hair this morning, sitting right in the middle of my crown. I managed not to pull it out. That's a big deal, for me.

It's threatening to rain, but we'll wait until the last minute to go in.

'What do you want to do this evening?' I ask.

'I have some films,' Mum says. 'We could watch *Some Like It Hot*, have some cake and some tea and get the fire going.'

'That sounds perfect,' I reply.

'Oh, look, there's a thing about your Dolly Russell in the paper,' Mum says, slapping it crisply, then pushing the glasses up on her nose to read it properly. 'Oh dear. Oh Scarlet, she was nearly kicked off a BA flight for throwing a drink over an air stewardess who asked her if she needed help going to the ladies.'

'Ha!' I say, without thinking.

Mum looks at me with reproach, and then back at the paper.

'She's gone to New York on a family matter it says here. Oh, that's nice, she's got a daughter there apparently.'

Mum folds the paper and looks up at the sky. 'It will rain,' she says, 'but God knows the garden needs it.'

* * *

'So, what about your Ben, then? Is that it?' my mum asks, as we sit on the sofa, sipping tea, the remote control in her hand, her finger poised above 'play'.

'He's not my Ben any more,' I say.

I read something important somewhere, and it said 'Don't waste time'.

COSMOPOLITAN

3 issues of Cosmopolitan for just 99p*

Subscribe and enjoy:

- Your first 3 issues for 99p **saving 89% off the cover price**
- **Still save 39%** after your first 3 issues
- Our **exclusive subscriber VIP club** where you can benefit from discounts and exclusive offers
- **Free home delivery** of your favourite magazine

Subscribe now:

www.qualitymagazines.co.uk/cosmo/MA14